Lookin' For
LUV

Lookin' For Luv

Carl Weber

KENSINGTON BOOKS
http://www.kensingtonbooks.com

KENSINGTON BOOKS are published by

Kensington Publishing Corp.
850 Third Avenue
New York, NY 10022

Kensington and the K logo Reg. U.S. Pat. & TM Off.

ISBN 1-57566-695-2

First Printing: September, 2000
10   9   8

Printed in the United States of America

This book is dedicated to
Martha Weber
Who is as much the author as I am.
Thank you so much for all the work you've done on the book.
Words could never describe how much I honestly love and appreciate you.
But I guess a new house will so lets get back to work.

Acknowledgments

First off let me thank God, for answering my prayers and fulfilling my dream of becoming an author. When times were hard and others didn't think it possible, He alone gave me the strength to continue, and for that I give Him praise.

I can't thank my friends and family enough for hanging in there with me during the process of writing and getting this book published. It took quite a while but it finally happened.

To Bettie: they say a mother's love is unconditional. I know yours is. I love you.

To my grandmother, Sarah Weber: thanks for everything Nana, I love you.

To my grandmother Emma Barron: just 'cause you're in Texas doesn't mean I forgot you. I love you Emma.

To Harold: thanks for keeping the stores and me together. Since my Pops passed away you've been as much a father to me as anyone. I love you for that.

To Bob and Dot: most people are lucky to have one set of parents. I've been lucky enough to have two. Thanks. I love you.

Special thanks to my sister Maria, my sister Teresa, brother Kevin, Alisha Cross, Ann Murphy, Crystal Burson, Kim, Sharnise Wingate, Brenda Cheese, and Valerie Skinner. You read the book during its infancy and helped mold it into what it is today.

To my partners in crime: Jeff, Walter, Albert, Bryant, Stan, Chip, and Mr. T. Thanks for always being there when I needed you. Oh, by the way, I've taken a bit of each one of you for the characters in my next book, *Married Men*.

To my brothers Terrance and Barron: thanks for being you.

Thanks to my fellow authors who came by the stores and encouraged me to write: Grace Edwards, Shandra Hill, Van Whitfield, Kim Roby, Donna Deberry and Virginia Grant, Denise Davis-Pack and Michael Baisden.

Special thanks to Donna Hill and Robert Flemming. I couldn't have done it without you guys.

A special high five to Anita Diggs for introducing me to my agent, Marie Brown.

To Marie Brown: thanks for being patient and putting up with my constant phone calls. You were right, of course, the publishing industry moves at its own pace. Well, you've done your part. Now it's time to show you what I can do.

To Kristy Noble-Mills: thanks for a great cover.

Big thanks to that sexy voice over at Kensington, Jessica McLean, for introducing me to my editor, Karen Thomas.

To my girl Karen Thomas: I don't think I could have ever asked for a better editor. Both professionally and personally thanks for everything. You're a true friend. Now take some time off and relax, you deserve it.

Special thanks to my brother Jeff for the poem.

Last but not least I'd like to thank all of my customers at the African-American Bookstore. This is the book you've all asked for. It's hot, funny, and has mad drama. I hope you enjoy it.

Lookin' For LUV

1

KEVIN

It was almost midnight when Kevin heard the phone ring. *Who the hell's calling at this time of night?* he wondered. He finished his push-ups. Lifting his dark six-foot frame from the ground, he grabbed a small towel from the back of a chair and wiped the sweat off his face. Sweat glistened against his smooth dark-chocolate skin and trickled down the muscles along his broad shoulders.

"Hello?" his deep voice grumbled into the receiver.

"Kevin, is that you, baby? Lord, don't tell me I done made a long distance call all the way to New York City and it's a wrong number," the voice had a strong but friendly southern accent. Kevin smiled.

"It's me, Mama," he answered happily.

Kevin and his mother were very close, even more so since his father died five years earlier. His mother lived in Hopewell, Virginia, where he had spent his entire childhood. She lived with his two sisters, Whitney and Phyllis. He liked to speak to his mother at least once a week to be sure she was doing all right.

"Is everything all right down there, Mama?"

"Everything's just fine here, baby. But what about you? I expected to get that answerin' machine of yours on account of it's Friday night. What's wrong, boy, you sick?" she prodded as only a mother could.

"Oh, I'm fine, Mama. I was just doin' some push-ups, that's all. I was just about ready to take a shower before you called."

"Push-ups!" She laughed. "Now, Kevin, why you gonna go an' lie to ya mama like that? I know you like the preacher knows Scripture. You got one of them New York City girls over there, don't you?" She barely paused to take a breath. "Lawd have mercy, boy, I hope you usin' them condoms I sent you. As much as I want some more grand-chillin', I want you married first, son. You hear me, Kevin? God knows them fast New York City girls gonna try an' trap a good-looking boy like you."

Holding the receiver away from his ear as his mother's voice increased in volume, Kevin sighed heavily before interrupting. "Mama. Mama, stop," he pleaded as she finally paused for a breath. "I don't have a girl over here. Things are a lot different up here. Oh, and, Mama, how many times I gotta tell you? I don't live in New York City. I live in Queens. And in Queens I'm just another guy."

Mama exhaled loudly. Her voice was calm but full of intensity. "Just you wait one damn minute, Mr. Kevin Raymond Brown. I didn't go through seventy-two hours of labor to have just another guy. You been special since the day you was born, son. Your problem is that you think havin' a bunch of gold-diggin' tramps chase after you makes you special. Well, I got news for you—it doesn't." She paused, but not long enough for Kevin to respond. "What you really need is to find yourself a nice church-goin' girl and settle down. But don't you worry, son, Mama's gonna get the whole church to pray on it."

Kevin cringed as he heard his mother mention her church. Mama had always been a strongly religious person, and while Kevin respected her for her faith, he didn't necessarily want all the good people of Hopewell Baptist Church knowing about his dating problems.

"Mama, do you really think gettin' the church to pray for me is somethin' you wanna do?" Kevin asked, imagining his mother standing in front of the whole congregation saying "Would you please bow your heads and pray for my poor, lonely son to meet a real churchgoin' girl?"

He could practically hear the chorus of amens that would follow her request and was sure Old Miss Williams would offer to send her homely daughter up to New York. The thought made Kevin's temples throb, so he quickly changed the subject

"Mama, why you callin' me at this time of night anyway? You know I call you every Sunday when the rates are lowest."

There was a pause before she answered, still lost in her thoughts of matchmaking. "Lord have mercy, why did I call you? Oh, yeah, the coach from that Italian basketball team called here today. He wanted me to give him your phone number. But I told him I'd have to call you and see."

Kevin released a long, sad sigh at the mention of basketball. Since moving to New York, he had done everything in his power to forget the sport entirely. Basketball had been the center of Kevin's universe from the time he was old enough to tie his first pair of high-tops. He spent four years at Virginia State University, where he was captain of the team and the top scorer, leading his team to a NCAA Division II Championship. Becoming a professional basketball player had been his only goal after graduation, and he seemed well on his way to achieving that dream when the Charlotte Hornets offered him a chance to try out as a walk-on.

Kevin spent a month in Charlotte trying out, and his performance was strong. After practice one day he had a particularly encouraging conversation with a Hornets coach, who told Kevin he was a shoe-in to make the team. Still a little immature, and feeling triumphant from the good news, he skipped curfew and spent the night partying at a University of North Carolina frat house. During the party he hooked up with a particularly wild group of his frat brothers, who convinced him to go into a private room to share a joint with them. Normally Kevin treated his body like a temple, staying away from drugs of any kind. But this night was different. He felt like his life had just begun, and in his jubilance he threw all caution to the wind and got high.

That joint turned out to be the destruction of Kevin's dream. Three days later he discovered that before he could officially be signed to a contract, he had to take a drug test. He seriously considered packing his bags right then and there but decided he couldn't give up that easily. In a panic he resorted to drinking gallons of goldenseal tea, which was rumored to mask marijuana in a drug test, and spent many hours praying for a miracle. When the test results showed evidence of drug use, Kevin was denied a contract and returned home to Hopewell empty-handed.

Back in his hometown he tried to hold his head high and find a new direction for his life as a physical education teacher. He began teaching "phys ed" in the small rural school, but the town's residents had viewed Kevin as their own hero, and now looked on him with pity. When a local radio station called to ask him for an interview about his fall from grace, it was the final blow. Kevin quickly decided to move as far away from Hopewell as possible. With the encouragement of his church pastor he completed the necessary paperwork to have his credentials transferred to New York and took the first job he was offered. He packed his bags, drove his Toyota Celica to Queens, and vowed to forget he had ever wanted to play basketball.

Now Mama's phone call was threatening to stir up painful memories for him.

"Aw'ight, Mama, you can give him my number," he told her sadly. "That way I can tell 'em that I'm not interested."

"If that's what you want, baby." She wished her son would reconsider and decided to try one more time to change his mind. "Son, all your daddy's life he wanted to be a train engineer, and he knew those trains good too. But them white folks wouldn't even let him try on account 'a he was colored. So he ended up becoming a repairman just to be close to those trains, hoping one day he'd get his chance. Well, when that chance never came, he died more of a broken heart than he did from the alcohol. If you really love basketball like I believe you do, I think you should go to Europe and show the NBA they made a big mistake. Baby, this is your chance."

"I 'preciate what you're tryin' ta say, Mama, but this is my life, and I have to live it." There was true love and affection in his voice. "Basketball's just not an option for me anymore."

"Aw'ight baby, if that's how you feel, Mama's gonna leave it alone. Now let me get off this here phone. I love you, baby."

"I love you too, Mama. I'll call you Sunday."

Kevin hung up and picked up his to-do list. He scribbled down *Send Mama some flowers*. Then, trying to relieve the stress that his basketball memories had stirred up, he went back to his push-ups, working his powerful dark arms until they began to ache. Satisfied with his workout, he peeled off his tank top, wrapped his towel around his neck, and sauntered into the bathroom. The towel dropped to the floor and Kevin slid his tight Calvin Klein underwear down his muscular legs. The cold air hit his naked body and he shivered.

"Damn, it's late," he said aloud as he took off his watch. Frustrated, he turned the water on and stepped into the warm spray. The soothing warmth soon turned scalding hot. "God damn you, Monty," he cursed, glaring at the ceiling and wishing his landlord would separate the plumbing. "Every time your fat ass flushes, my cold water shuts off. It's almost like you know when I get into the shower so you run to the john to flush." Disgusted, Kevin shut off the shower and stepped out. He shivered as the cold air hit him, wondering if Monty realized it was fall, time to turn on the heat. Grabbing a plush towel, he paused. His eyes closed and his shoulders hunched. As was happening more often lately, the pressure of being an unsuccessful black man fell upon him.

Look at my life, he thought, staring at the dingy walls. *Barely a year ago I was bragging about this great NBA career I was going to have. Now I'm blacklisted from the league and I'm too embarrassed to show up at homecoming.*

Wrapping the towel around his hips, Kevin walked into his bedroom and searched for a pair of boxer shorts to put on. His bedroom was small. Assorted boxes of clothes filled much of the space, holding most of his extensive designer wardrobe. Although living from paycheck to paycheck, Kevin took enormous pride in his appearance. He chose to spend his money on clothes rather than a dresser to keep them in. Digging through a box, he finally found a pair of silk boxers.

Kevin sat and watched the Playboy Channel for about fifteen minutes. He was not really interested in naked women playing volleyball, so he checked his *TV Guide* to see what was playing on BET. He grinned when he saw they were running *School Daze.* A good Spike Lee movie could always take his mind off his problems, even if only for a while. Scanning the channels, he arrived at BET just as his favorite Chris Rock 1-800-COLLECT commercial was ending.

The commercial faded and a gorgeous woman appeared on the screen. Kevin thought it was Melanie Mann, an ex-girlfriend from Virginia State. He had many fond memories of their dates. Grabbing the remote, he turned up the volume to find out why his ex was on the screen. As he heard the woman's voice, he realized it was not her, though she looked like she could have been her twin sister.

"Hi. Are you lonely?" the woman asked, flashing a brilliant white smile. "Are your weekends filled with too much TV and takeout?"

"Yeah," Kevin answered the television pitifully.

"Well, I was that way too." She put her arms around a Denzel Washington look-alike. "That is, until I met Derrick."

Kevin laughed out loud as he opened a bag of chips.

"All I had to do was call 1-900-BLACK-LUV, and before I knew it I had a date for each night of the week. I finally settled on Derrick, and in three months we're getting married!" The two actors kissed.

"Yeah, right!" Kevin groaned as the words 1-900-BLACK-LUV flashed underneath the kissing couple. *Like either one of them has ever had trouble finding a date.*

When the commercial ended, *School Daze* came back on and Spike Lee's character was begging every woman he met for sex.

That's one desperate brother, Kevin thought, watching another woman turn Spike down. *Jeez, the stupid thing is I'm starting to feel a little desperate myself. Maybe not for sex so much, but for a quality relationship. Damn. It would be nice just to hold a good woman.*

He looked at the phone a long while and finally grumbled, "What the hell. It can't hurt if I call." Reluctantly he walked over to the phone and dialed 1-900-BLACK-LUV. *Lord, what am I doing to myself?* he thought. He almost hung up as he heard the connection on the line.

"Hello, you've reached 1-900-BLACK-LUV, the ultimate African American date line. If you are a woman, press one; if you're a man, press two; if you're calling to receive your mail, press three." Kevin began to pace across the living room floor but hesitated before responding to the prompt.

He pushed two and heard, "Hi, brother. Your mailbox number is twenty-nine twenty-nine. Please write this down so you will be able to retrieve any and all messages in your mailbox. Now you have the option of listening to other callers' personal ads or leaving one of your own. If you would like to listen, please press one. If you would like to record your message, please press two and start talking after you hear the tone." Thinking that he'd seem less desperate if the women came to him, he chose to leave his own personal ad. He pressed two and waited for the tone.

"Hi," he said in the sexiest voice he could manage. "I'm Kevin and I'm a twenty-three-year-old phys ed teacher from Queens. I'm six feet one inches tall, dark-skinned, with a very athletic body. I've been in New York only a few months, and I'm really a country boy at heart. I like reggae music and all sports. I'm not interested in playing games. I want someone who'll keep it simple and down-to-earth, so if this sounds like you, please leave me a message at box twenty-nine twenty-nine. Thanks."

Listening to his message play back, he decided it was adequate. At least it was honest. He wasn't about to start lying just to get a date on some phone service. He saved the message and hung up, still not sure about what he had just done. The whole idea of leaving a message on a 1-900 number left him a little queasy. No longer in the mood to watch television, he turned off the set and headed into his bedroom. As he drifted off to sleep, he wondered what types of women might answer his ad, and if he could admit to his friends at work how desperate he had become.

* * *

The Alternative High School for Boys in Queens, formerly known as Jackson High School, was considered one of the worst high schools in the New York City public school system. Jackson High, once a pillar of the Queens community, was closed down by the city in the late eighties due to gang violence and poor test scores. During the late nineties, as overcrowding became an enormous problem for the city schools, Jackson High was reopened with a new name and an entirely different population. The Alternative High School for Boys in Queens, as it was now called, serviced two thousand adolescent boys whose behavior had gotten them suspended or expelled from schools throughout the city. The student population was tough, and the teachers worked under a great deal of pressure. Many faculty members left before they even finished a year, and those who stayed on had to find coping mechanisms to keep them from losing it.

Kevin had been in a state of shock during his first few weeks as a teacher at the school. He had not been prepared for just how difficult these students would be, and many nights he went home to search the classified ads for a new job. One particularly bad day he had started searching the ads in the faculty room during his lunch hour. An English teacher who had become well liked among the students spotted Kevin's distress and explained to him that the best way to deal with difficult students was to get to know them. He offered Kevin a position with the after-school program so that the boys would have an opportunity to interact with Kevin on a social level. The man's name was Antoine Smith, and Kevin accepted his offer like a drowning man accepts a life preserver.

The two men spent countless hours after school each day counseling and advising young minority boys on how to survive the rat race of inner-city life. What began as a mentoring situation developed into a steadfast friendship for Kevin and Antoine.

During their afternoons at the school the men got to know many of the building's security guards. One guard, Tyrone Jefferson, entertained them with his quick wit and generous laugh. He would stop by briefly at first, but as the men became more familiar with one another, they each looked forward to their afternoon meetings, and a true bond developed between the three.

During one conversation Antoine mentioned that he was eager to lose some weight and asked his friends if they would join a local

gym with him. Tyrone immediately nixed the idea because he could-
n't handle the membership fees. Then Kevin suggested they use the
school facilities during their lunch hour as an alternative. Their
lunchtime workouts quickly became a daily bonding session for the
men.

On the Monday afternoon after Kevin phoned the date line, he was
finishing up another workout with his friends. Tyrone, a tall, skinny,
dark-skinned man, struggled under the barbells as he lay on the bench
press.

"Come on, Ty!" Kevin yelled as Tyrone finally pushed the heavy
barbell up. Grabbing the weights from him, Kevin placed it effortlessly
on its holder. He smiled as he grabbed his friend's hand. "Not bad for
a street punk." He laughed at Tyrone.

"What? What? You must be crazy. That's two hundred and ten
fucking pounds. Forty pounds more than I weigh." Tyrone grinned,
proud of his new personal best. He stepped aside to let Kevin do a set
on the weights.

"Ay, I wasn't tryin' to put you down, brotha." Kevin slipped onto
the bench and did twenty reps with barely an effort. "Truth is, I'm surprised your skinny ass didn't break a damn bone with all that weight
over your head."

"You see, Antoine, that's why I don't wanna work out with y'all no
more." Tyrone pointed his finger for emphasis. "Between you quoting
everyone from Martin Luther King to Farrakhan an' Kevin's country
ass cracking on a brotha's physical appearance, I'd be better off joining
a damn gym."

Antoine, a stout, light-skinned man, removed his glasses as he gestured for Kevin to move off the bench. The most serious of the three,
he wasn't sure if Tyrone was truly offended by Kevin's joke, but he
tried to diffuse the situation. "First of all, Tyrone . . ." he said, lying
down on the bench and struggling through twenty quick reps, "this
lunchtime-workout thing was your idea. If I remember correctly, you
didn't have the money to join a gym. Second of all, you're the last person who should take offense to jokes about physical appearance. All
day long I'm the object of your fat jokes."

"Well, you do look like an expectant cow," Tyrone joked, patting
Antoine on the belly. Neither of his friends responded, so he shook his
head at their blank stares. "Damn, I guess you guys can't take a joke.
Fuck it, I've got to get back to my post before Pretty Boy chews me a

new butthole anyway." He turned toward the locker room but paused when Kevin finally spoke.

"Yo, Ty, hold up a minute. I found somethin' you might be interested in." Tyrone was unsure if this was the beginning of another joke, but he was curious, and returned to the weight bench.

Kevin turned to face both men, feeling strangely nervous; he wanted his friends' opinions of the 900 date line he had called. But knew he might be inviting a string of jokes at his own expense.

"I was watchin' TV the other night and I saw this commercial. I figured since you're both single, this might come in handy." Handing them both a three-by-five index card, Kevin smiled sheepishly, trying to read his friends' expressions.

"What the fuck? Very fuckin' funny, Kev." Tyrone threw the card to the floor. "You need this a hell of a lot more than me."

"Kevin, please tell me you're not serious about this 900 stuff. Are you?" Antoine asked as he stared at the card. "Y'know, I thought we were friends."

"I am your friend, Antoine. And I'm serious about this too. Think about it. When was the last time you went out on a date?" he asked rather pitifully.

"Speak for yourself," Tyrone quipped. He considered himself a player.

Kevin ignored him and continued. "Look, y'all, we get in here at seven o'clock in the morning and teach until three. Then you have computer club, Antoine, and I have JV basketball practice. By the time we get outta here, it's six o'clock. And, Ty, you stay here longer than both of us."

"What you tryin' to say, Kev, I don't have no women?" Tyrone asked with attitude.

"If you do, I ain't ever seen or heard of 'em!"

Placing his hand on Kevin's shoulder, Antoine tried to sound as compassionate as possible. Maybe his new friend from the South was more naive than he thought.

"I know you're just trying to help, but 900 numbers are kind of taboo in New York. Sorry, Kevin, single or not, I still have my pride. I'd hate to think I'm so desperate that I had to call 1-900-BLACK-LUV to get a date."

"Yeah, thanks but no thanks!" Tyrone laughed, trying to back up what Antoine had just said.

The laughter was interrupted by the deep voice of the principal, Dr. Johnson. None of them was thrilled to see him. The man was on a twenty-four-hour power trip, and his favorite pastime was belittling his staff.

"Shit," Tyrone mumbled as he made eye contact with the tall, green-eyed man.

"How you doin' today, Dr. Johnson? What brings you back here to the weight room? Gonna pump some iron?" He doubted it, since the principal was dressed in his usual attire, a well-tailored designer suit.

"Actually, you're what brings me back here, Mr. Jefferson. It's fifteen minutes past one." He flashed his gold Rolex to Tyrone. "You're supposed to be at the front desk at one o'clock so someone else can enjoy lunch today. I suggest that you get back to work while you still have a job." Tyrone retreated into the shower room, and the principal turned to the other two men.

"Don't you two have classes to teach?" he asked in his typically condescending way.

"No, Maurice." Antoine faced the principal defiantly and crossed his arms over his chest. He was the union president and not easily intimidated. "Matter of fact, we just finished lunch, and this is our preparation period, which by contract we can use however we choose."

"Well, I suggest you use your prep time more wisely in the future." The principal scowled as he watched the two men follow their friend into the shower room.

As he turned to leave, Maurice noticed the piece of paper Tyrone had thrown on the floor.

Damn fools can't even clean up after themselves, he thought.

Even if his school was plagued by some of the city's lowest test scores, Maurice insisted that it be kept spotless. This scrap on the locker room floor offended his fastidious nature. He bent over and grudgingly picked up the paper.

"1-900-BLACK-LUV!" he read, and turned abruptly toward the shower room. Using school property for their own personal use he could tolerate, but leaving phone-sex numbers that students might find was definitely intolerable. He was about to walk into the locker room and reprimand the men but stopped suddenly. Something about the number seemed strangely familiar to him.

He couldn't place it. Maybe it was something he had read in one of his girlie magazines, or his buddy David had mentioned it, but he had definitely heard of 1-900-BLACK-LUV before. Then it hit him. The number wasn't a sex line. It was the new black dating service advertised on TV.

Hmmm, looks like the three stooges are having a hard time getting some. He laughed, but then had a sobering thought as he realized his own situation was not so different. As he left the locker room, he placed the number in his breast pocket with a smile, thinking it might come in handy sometime.

2

ANTOINE

Antoine paid the cabdriver and stepped out into the warm breeze. He carried both a knapsack and briefcase. The briefcase was filled with paperwork from school. The knapsack carried his personal books, which he spent most of his free time reading. Antoine loved the English language. Unlike most of the men from his neighborhood, he very rarely cursed or used slang. His behavior set him apart. In fact, he was something of a folk hero in his area, always helping the elderly and mentoring the youth. The teenagers had respectfully dubbed him Little Al, after the Reverend Al Sharpton, because Antoine was always around to offer support when someone was in trouble.

"What a beautiful night," he hummed as he strolled down Jamaica Avenue. Smiling at a group of ladies walking by, he sucked in his belly in a self-conscious gesture. He knew women thought he was cute. That had never been his problem. Ever since he could remember, women had commented on how cute his features and baby fat were. But now that he was thirty-five, the problem was that his baby fat had turned into a less attractive spare tire around his waist. For several weeks now he had been making a concerted effort to get rid of the jiggle around his middle.

He was pleased with himself for asking the cabdriver to let him off a mile from his home in Hollis, Queens. A few weeks earlier Kevin had advised him to change his late-night eating habits and be sure to walk at least twenty minutes every day. For three weeks Antoine had religiously followed Kevin's workout plan and diet. He had avoided a scale during this time, but now he was curious to see if his hard work had really paid off. The walk home was particularly brisk this evening because he was eager to weigh himself. He made it back to his apartment in just over ten minutes, winded but proud of his new speed. Catching his breath, he paused to wipe the sweat from his brow.

"Yoo-hoo! Antoine!" A voice came from the direction of the beauty shop, which occupied the storefront below the apartments.

Shoot! I was hoping she wouldn't see me, he thought, giving a weak wave in the direction of the voice. He headed for the stairs, hoping his hello would be sufficient. Tonight was not the night he felt like dealing with his landlord.

"Oh, look! His sexy ass is wearin' shorts," his landlord announced as she stood in the entrance to her beauty shop. Keisha was a short, pretty woman with huge breasts and a large behind. She had a real thing for Antoine.

"I don't know what the hell you see in him, Keisha," a woman from inside the beauty shop shouted. "He's not all that with his pudgy ass. Besides, he thinks he's white."

"He don't think he's white!" Keisha stepped back in the shop.

"Oh, yeah? How come every time he opens his mouth he sounds like a white boy? All proper an' shit." Everyone in the beauty shop fell out laughing. "That motherfucka acts just like Carlton on *Fresh Prince.*"

Keisha turned her head, glaring at the laughing women in her shop. Then she pointed her finger at the woman with all the mouth. "You know, y'all some ignorant heifers. You got the nerve to call him a white boy 'cause he speaks proper. For your information, he's an English teacher. He's supposed to speak with proper diction. An' you of all people need to shet-the-fuck-up, Brenda. With those barefoot-and-pregnant high-school dropouts you got at home. Hooked on Phonics couldn't help them ignorant wenches." The room became quiet, and everyone hoped Brenda's comeback would be a good one.

"I'll have you know my oldest, LaShandra, just passed her GED," Brenda said proudly.

"Well, damn. It's about time! What is she, twenty-three?" The beauty shop erupted with laughter.

"You know what, Keisha? I'm not even gonna trip in here. But don't talk about my kids no mo'. Besides, don't nobody want Antoine's fat ass but you anyway."

"I know you ain't talkin' 'bout fat. When was the last time you missed a meal, Ms. Size Eighteen?" The whole room fell out laughing as Keisha stepped out to look at Antoine again. "I don't care what y'all

say. That man is fine. I love me a man with some meat on his bones."
Keisha ignored the laughter of the women in her shop as she approached Antoine near the stoop.

"Hi, Antoine," she purred, puckering her lips as if waiting for a kiss.

"I said hello," he reminded her. Now he didn't bother to suck in his stomach.

"I heard you, Antoine. I just wanted to see you in those shorts. You don't wear shorts very often, do you?"

"No, I don't. But with this weather we've had this week and the long walk home, I thought it appropriate to change into my workout clothes."

"Workout clothes, huh?" She smiled, thinking, *I'd like to work you out one time.*

"Yeah, I'm trying to lose some weight," he answered bashfully.

"I can tell. It looks good. But don't lose too much. A woman needs a man she can hold on to." She smiled again.

She was about to ask Antoine out for a drink later that evening but was interrupted by a young lady.

"What, Terri?" she snapped.

"Mrs. Martin is finished under the dryer and she won't let nobody but you touch her," the young lady said. Her eyes were on Antoine, and she smiled flirtatiously.

Keisha stepped closer to Antoine. "Well, I have to go. But when are we gonna go have that drink you promised me?" She smiled. "I'm free tonight if you're not too busy."

"Sorry, Keisha, I'm pretty busy tonight," he lied, holding up his briefcase. "But soon, real soon."

Keisha was encouraged when he said soon. "What about tomorrow? The day after? This weekend?" she called after him as he disappeared into his apartment without an answer. She shrugged, thinking he must not have heard her. He did.

In his apartment Antoine put away his briefcase and knapsack and headed for the hall closet. Moving a few things around, he pulled out a scale. He closed his eyes and stepped on it. The memory of Keisha's compliment about his weight loss made him smile.

Maybe all this hard work is starting to pay off, he thought, opening his eyes to read the number on the scale. *One hundred and seventy-six pounds. Eleven pounds in three weeks and I'm definitely starting to get some muscle tone. Fourteen more pounds and I'll be looking like my younger self!*

He began to flex his muscles like a bodybuilder, until he realized his blinds were wide open for the whole neighborhood to see. If there was one thing he couldn't stand, it was appearing undignified. He hastily placed the scale back in the closet and closed the blinds.

The weight loss made him more determined to continue, and Antoine decided to skip dinner. Instead, he sat down at his computer to enter his students' grades. He was distracted by Keisha's loud, unmistakable voice outside his window. Removing his glasses, he began to think about the full-figured woman.

There was no doubt in his mind that she liked him. From the first day she had rented him the apartment, she was always very attentive to his requests. When he went down to her apartment on the first floor to give her his rent check, she always invited him in for coffee or dinner. Antoine quickly realized she was not so accommodating to her other tenants.

At first he was flattered. Keisha's shapely, full figure was enticing. He had joked many times with his friends, "There ain't nothing like a big-boned woman!" As a beauty shop owner, her hair and makeup were always impeccable, accentuating her smooth caramel skin and light brown eyes.

After several months of flirting, Antoine had even made plans to take her out on a date. He still wished she were a little more refined, but he had been dateless for a while, so he decided to give it a try. But the date never came to pass. The day they had planned to go out, Antoine was awakened by Keisha's screams. Running to his window, he saw Keisha beating the hell out of one of her customers with a hair dryer.

When he arrived on the sidewalk, Keisha turned her anger and the bloody hair dryer on him. Fifteen stitches and a concussion later, he had not even received an apology. He never again considered taking her out, deciding her abrasive personality was more than he could handle. She, of course, had not given up her pursuit.

Reaching up to close the window, Antoine put Keisha out of his mind so he could concentrate. He worked diligently for the next few hours. He considered relaxing in front of the television for a while but didn't think he could bear to listen to any more news about the president's infidelities. Instead, he decided to edit the poetry he had written.

Teaching English at the high school was a challenge, but it left him little room to be creative, especially when he was constantly worrying about keeping his classes under control. In his spare time he exercised his artistic mind by writing poetry.

As he read his poems he made some minor changes. He felt pride in what he had accomplished and wished he could share it with someone. For a brief moment he considered going down to Keisha's apartment. But as soon as he opened the door, the loud thumping of rap music bombarded him. The music was coming from Keisha's apartment. Antoine shook his head and closed the door, returning to his chair. He thought about calling one of his friends to read his poetry to, but when he remembered it was after eleven, he knew there was really no one he could bother at such an hour.

He felt desperate. After several minutes of internal dialogue about the pros and cons, he sighed heavily and went to his briefcase, searching for the index card Kevin had given him earlier in the day.

I wonder what Kevin would think if he knew I was about to call this 900 line, Antoine thought as he dialed 1-900-BLACK-LUV. He listened to the instructions, then pushed the appropriate buttons to allow him to leave a message. Clearing his throat, he spoke slowly and seriously.

"Hello, my name is Antoine and I'm a writer. I'm not looking to meet anyone. What I would like is a little feedback on a poem I wrote." He proceeded to read expressively:

LOVERS ON A BLANKET

Let us sit hand in hand,
On my blanket in the sand.
Watching the sea gulls high,
As they soar, as they fly.

Let us share a warm embrace,
As the sun shows its face.

Two lovers, side by side,
From each other they need not hide.
I am in love with you and you with me.
Deep inside, emotions are set free.

I love you like no other,
Someday soon you will discover.

Two lovers, hand in hand,
Sitting on a blanket in the sand.

Antoine paused and completed his message. "Thank you so much for listening to my poem, and I hope to answer all responses as soon as possible."

He hung up the phone and went to bed, wondering what kind of women called these lines. Would he get some serious responses, or had he just made a huge, embarrassing mistake?

B

MAURICE

Sylvia had prepared all day to make love to Maurice. She started by going to the hairdresser and nail salon early that morning. Then she rushed home to cook his favorite meal, stuffed young duckling. As she stood in her bedroom, unzipping her dress, she hoped Maurice would appreciate her effort to please him. She had been waiting almost three weeks for his schedule to allow them some time for intimacy, and she was horny as hell. She threw her dress on the chair near her makeup table.

It was funny how things had worked out. When they were first married, he couldn't keep his hands off her. He would always remind her that he was in his sexual prime and her wifely duty was to satisfy his needs. Sylvia laughed as she remembered how pathetically he used to plead, promising that he would be there to take care of her when she reached her sexual prime. Now the tables had turned, and it was rare when he showed even the slightest interest.

Boy was I stupid! Sylvia moaned. *I'm damn near forty and I'm still waiting for that son of a bitch to take care of my needs.*

But Sylvia didn't want to spoil her planned night of intimacy, so she put aside her memories of Maurice's false promises. When she heard him walk in the front door, she made her final preparations. Taking off her shoes, panty hose, and jewelry, she checked herself in the full-length mirror, pleased with what she saw.

Tall and slender, she had gained only ten pounds since her daughter's birth twenty years before. Most of that weight was in what men call "the right places." For a thirty-eight-year-old mother, she still had a body that would make any woman proud. An expensive designer wardrobe paid for with part of her million-dollar inheritance accentuated her curves. She admired her olive complexion and big brown eyes in the mirror as she picked up a comb and stroked it through her long black hair. Placing the comb on her dresser, she removed her bra and panties. Her plan was to greet Maurice naked to start the evening off right. As far as she was concerned, dinner could wait.

In his personal bathroom Maurice sat on the toilet, reading the latest issue of *Blacktail* magazine.

You'll do just fine, he thought, admiring the breasts of a beautiful young model. *The things I could do with a hot little number like you.* He flipped the page to see another of the young woman's erotic poses.

Softly tapping a fist against his forehead, Maurice stared at the young woman on the page. *The last thing I want to do tonight is fuck Sylvia's old ass.* It made him ill that he had to resort to magazine photos to get aroused for the event. Disgusted, he threw the magazine on top of a small pile of others.

For Dr. Maurice Johnson, making love to his wife was more of a chore than a treat, and his marriage was more of a business arrangement than a love affair. He had married Sylvia because of her father's money and struggled to keep up the facade of a healthy, loving marriage long after his newlywed passion had died. All the while he carried on a string of affairs with the college freshmen he taught as an adjunct professor. However unfulfilling his marriage was, he never doubted his wife's unconditional love and saw no reason to change their situation. She seemed satisfied as long as he performed his duties in the bedroom once or twice a month, and he was able to satisfy himself with other women whenever he desired. Sylvia never seemed to question his actions or his whereabouts in their twenty years together.

As he entered their bedroom to give Sylvia her monthly pleasure, Maurice forced a weak smile.

Sylvia noticed that her husband did not look too enthusiastic. She knew he was not going to make things easy, but she was not going to back down this time.

"You are going to make love to me like you promised, aren't you, Maurice?" she asked in a sweet voice.

Maurice didn't answer right away. He actually considered faking a bout of diarrhea. She would probably buy it, considering how much time he had spent in the bathroom. Putting on a fake frown, he almost gave her the lie but reconsidered. He wanted to get it over with rather than postpone it. This way she'd be in a decent mood when he asked her to help him get some stock tips from her friend Bernard.

"Sure I'm gonna make love to you, sweetheart." He pasted a fake smile on his face.

Watching his clothes hit the floor, Sylvia threw the comforter back, exposing her naked body. Gazing at her husband, she admired his tall, athletic body. He was still the finest man she had ever seen. She scanned up to his sexy blue-green eyes set in a face that looked much younger than his forty-two years. His striking good looks always made Sylvia forgive and forget his many indiscretions throughout the years. Every time she was suspicious, he could just look at her with those beautiful eyes, and she would forget she was even angry. In spite of the distance that had grown between them, she had loved him since the day he took her virginity.

Maurice slowly crawled onto the bed and moved on top of Sylvia. He kissed her neck softly, and she moaned with pleasure in response. He could still give her goose bumps with just one touch.

While his wife thought about the pleasure she was about to receive, he was busy worrying that he couldn't complete the act while looking at her. Closing his eyes, Maurice began to fantasize about the young woman in the magazine. Taking hold of his limp penis, he slowly tugged on it until it was erect enough to enter his wife.

"Maurice, honey, can I be on top? It always feels better that way," she asked timidly.

"Come on, Sylvia," he groaned. "You know this is my favorite position."

"Okay, honey. But I was thinking you might want me to go down on you first. I wanna make sure you're satisfied in every way." Sylvia knew from past experience that she had to work hard to please her husband if she wanted to get any real affection in return.

Maurice was tempted. It wasn't often that his wife offered him oral sex. He could just sit back and let her do all the work. Then he realized her intention was probably to ask him for the same pleasure in return. The thought of that made his stomach turn.

"This will do just fine, Sylvia," he answered, trying again to form a picture of the young woman in the magazine in his mind.

"All right, honey, just put it inside of me."

She sighed, realizing that foreplay was not on the agenda. Gasping as he slowly pushed himself into her, Sylvia wrapped her arms around him and moaned.

"Oh, Maurice, that's it, baby. That's the spot."

When Maurice and Sylvia had first met, she was a virgin, and very timid during lovemaking. Even when she was very excited, she barely made a sound. Maurice had ignored this behavior for a while, even though he found it a turnoff. Finally, he confronted her on it, demanding that she act more aroused and become more vocal. Sylvia tried unsuccessfully to change, but it was uncomfortable for her to scream without feeling embarrassed or whorish. Over the years she realized her husband was asking much less often for sex and figured it was because of her reticence. She loved him and was so desperate for his affection that she eventually learned to loosen up during sex. Unfortunately her changes did not increase their lovemaking, but on the rare occasions that they did have sex, Sylvia screamed and moaned like a pro.

Sylvia's screams excited Maurice, and he began to pump faster. Really enjoying it now, she kicked her legs high in the air. "Oh, don't stop now! Please don't stop now!" she shouted, concentrating as the intense pleasure increased and she felt herself nearing orgasm.

Maurice had become engulfed in his fantasy, and a few thrusts later he gasped as he climaxed inside of her.

No! she thought. *Not again! Please God, not again! I was almost there. Damn you, Maurice, all I ever asked for is one pitiful orgasm.*

Rolling off Sylvia, Maurice seemed oblivious of her disappointment.

"Are you happy, baby?"

"Yes," Sylvia answered weakly as she envisioned her hands strangling the life out of his body.

Looking up at him with desperation, she remembered her girlfriend Vivian's advice: Always ask for more. They last longer the second time around.

"Ahhh, Maurice, do you think we could do it one more time?" She was humble, almost pleading.

"Hey, I know I'm good." He smiled, shaking his head confidently as he wagged his finger at her. "But let's not get greedy."

He slipped into his robe. "I'm going downstairs. I'm going to eat in my study and finish up some work." He didn't make eye contact once.

Sylvia threw a pillow at the door as he closed it behind him.

"You arrogant motherfucker!" she cursed him. Sadly she walked to her closet and searched until she found a thin, rectangular box. "You won't let me down, will you?" she sighed, letting a six-inch vibrator slide out of the box.

*   *   *

Downstairs in his study Maurice took two Tums to settle his stomach and pulled the trash can closer to his desk in case he had to throw up. Every time he had sex with his wife lately, he felt as if someone had turned his stomach inside out. The only positive thought he could muster was the relief that now he would be off the hook for another few weeks.

Sitting back in his chair, he could feel some relief as the antacid began to work. The past two weeks had been difficult for him. His high school was ranked among the lowest in New York State in all subjects but English, and that was in jeopardy because a publishing company was trying to lure his finest teacher with a book deal.

He knew he had to find a way to convince the teacher Antoine Smith to stay. If those test scores plummeted, Maurice could quite possibly be out of another job. He slammed his hand on the table as his memory wandered back to the adjunct professorship he had been forced to give up.

As a professor at York College, he had taught basic algebra in their night school program. Many of his students were young girls just barely out of high school, who were taking the night courses to qualify for college admission. In many cases the girls were eager to do well, since their future success was at stake, and Maurice took full advantage of their eager young minds. For two years he had enjoyed the pleasures of over a dozen fine young bodies in exchange for good grades in his class. It was a sexual playground for him. One girl, though, was not quite as naive as the others and reported Maurice to the college administration when he abandoned her in another state after they had made love. Immediately many of the other girls came forward to report similar experiences, and Maurice was forced to leave his position.

Recalling the incident caused Maurice's anger to flare. He could remember verbatim the letter he had received from the dean. It had left him no choice but resignation.

Dear Maurice,

In light of the sex-for-grades incident you were involved in this past semester, I highly recommend that you resign as associate professor. As I promised, I have been in contact with several of the young ladies involved and they plan to go to the press if you are kept on. Please, as your friend and colleague, I ask you

to spare yourself, your family, and the college the embarrass-
ment. Resign before this becomes ugly. An incident like this
could very easily ruin your life.

Your friend,
Thomas

As much as the letter had pained him, he had to admit his friend
had really saved his neck.

God, if I had to do it all over again, I would never have left that
tramp in Vermont. Maybe if I'd given the bitch a ride home, she
wouldn't have cried foul.

He had convinced himself that these silly girls asked to be used, and
he was sorry only that he was caught. For a while he had behaved sim-
ply out of fear of being caught again. But the incident was almost six
months in the past, and he was getting restless for a new thrill. Making
love to his wife that night had just pushed him over the edge.

He reached into his briefcase and pulled out the index card he had
found in the locker room earlier in the day. Smiling, he dialed 1-900-
BLACK-LUV and left his message.

4

KEVIN AND ALICIA

Kevin returned home from work at seven o'clock. Famished, he grabbed a quart of orange juice and the turkey sandwich that he had forgotten to take for lunch. Sitting in his beat-up recliner, he ate and daydreamed about being a star in the NBA. Shortly he was fast asleep and his daydreams became real dreams.

At nine o'clock a fire engine drove by and woke him. He rubbed the sleep from his eyes and grabbed the remote. He flicked on BET and caught the end of the 1-900-BLACK-LUV commercial they seemed to be playing all the time now. Seeing it reminded him of his own message recorded a few days earlier. His curiosity was aroused, and he dialed the line to see if he had received any responses.

He nervously waited for the recording. "If you're calling to retrieve your mail, press three." As he felt the sweat build on his forehead, he pressed three. "Please enter your mailbox number." Kevin punched in 2929 and waited. "You have five messages. If you would like to listen to your messages, please press one." Taking a deep breath, Kevin pressed one.

"Hi, Kevin, my name's Paula, and I'm a twenty-six-year-old full-figured woman from Queens." The voice was sultry and immediately captured Kevin's attention. "I'm light-skinned and love both reggae and sports. I'm also an exceptional soul food cook." This brought a broad smile to Kevin's face as he looked down at the half-eaten turkey sandwich on the floor. "I have a real attraction for dark men. The blacker the better. So please give me a call. My beeper number is 555-1231. Sorry I can't give you my home number, but my husband would kill us both."

Kevin threw the pen he had grabbed to copy down her number and pounded his fist into the arm of the recliner. *Damn. She had my taste buds going. I could taste her fried chicken and macaroni and cheese. Shit. Why you gotta be married?*

"If you would like to save this message, press one; if you would like to delete this message, press two." Kevin pressed two angrily. "Next message."

"Hey, baby, I'm Desire. I listened to your message and it really turned me on. How about the two of us getting together for a hot, steamy love session? Just in case you're wondering, my breasts are a perfect thirty-six C and my ass is shaped like a ripe peach waiting to be eaten." Kevin gulped hard when he heard her last comment. Snatching another pen from the table, he eagerly waited for her to get to her phone number. "Kevin, I really need a man like you to put out the fire building inside me. Please give me a call at 555-3—" Kevin waited for the last three digits of her phone number, but they never came. Her voice faded away as if she had placed her hand over the receiver, teasing him.

"Oh, noooo. God, please don't do this to me." He swore, hitting three to replay her message, again with the same results. Kevin's thoughts were lustful now, and his main purpose had become finding a sex partner. Anxiously he listened for the next message, hoping it would be someone as tempting as Desire, who actually left her number.

"Hello, Kevin, my name is Sister Mary Pat, from the Gotta-be-Saved storefront church in Jamaica, Queens." The pleasant voice sounded as if it belonged to an old woman. "I've been saved by our Lord, Jesus Christ. Have you? You seem like a nice young man from your message. But nice is not good enough. You need to find Jesus and forget about the lustful thoughts these women can bring about in you. Why don't you come down to our church and be baptized? Both the Lord and I will be here waiting."

Kevin looked upward, astounded, as if God had known exactly what he was thinking after he'd heard Desire's message.

Sister, if I wanna find Jesus on the phone, I'll call my Mama's prayer line. He shook his head. *How do people like her get on these lines, anyway? They need to do somethin' about that....* He pressed two and hoped for a better message.

"Ay, baby, what's up?" a seductive voice purred. "My name is Champagne, and I'm nineteen. I'm an exotic dancer, and I'm looking for a man who won't stress me about my job or the hours I keep. At the same time, I want someone to treat me with the respect I deserve. I heard your ad, which said that you have a good job and a nice body.

Those are definite pluses, 'cause a high-maintenance woman needs a man who can take care of all her needs."

"Stupid gold-diggin' bitch," Kevin growled. He pushed two before the message was even over. Disgusted, he was about to hang up, when he heard a very sexy but nervous voice.

"Hello, Alicia, my name's Kevin. I mean Kevin, my name's Alicia. Sorry about that. I guess I'm a little nervous. I was listening to your ad and something in it made me leave a message. You know the part where you say you're not interested in playing games and want someone to keep it simple and down-to-earth? Well, I think that's me. I'm not promising I'll go out with you, but I'd love to talk. Give me a call. 555-6443."

Thoughts raced through Kevin's mind as he scribbled down the number. She sounded so sincere and straightforward that he was instantly attracted. He was getting tired of the many fast-talking, dishonest people he had met since moving north. Alicia's message had made her sound ideal, and now he was eager to meet her. He grabbed the phone to dial, but then had a quick flash of reality.

Damn, what if she's real ugly? Or what if she's real fine and thinks I'm ugly? What if . . . Kevin stared at the phone. *What if I don't call and she's the girl of my dreams?* Picking up the phone, he dialed the number.

"Hello, may I speak to Alicia please?"

"This is she," a sweet, almost poetic female voice answered.

"Hi, Alicia, this is Kevin."

"Kevin?" she sounded confused.

"From 1-900-BLACK-LUV."

"Oh, I'm sorry. How are you?" Her voice tensed.

"A little nervous, to be honest."

"I know the feeling. I can't stop my foot from shaking."

Kevin smiled when he heard that. He liked that she was being honest. No games.

The line was quiet as both of them tried to think of something to say.

"I don't know about you, but I've never been on a blind date. I have no idea what I'm supposed to say or do," Kevin finally admitted.

"Neither do I." She laughed.

"Look. Why don't we make up our own rules as we go along?" he suggested.

"Sure," she answered, "maybe that way we can get to know each other first."

"Okay, rule number one. You have go to dinner with me Friday night. No commitment, no expectations. Just two friends trying to enjoy each other's company."

"I like the idea of no expectations, Kevin, but is this a date, or what?"

"Why don't we decide that at the end of the night?"

"Okay," Alicia answered. "Rule number two. I get to pick the restaurant."

"Aw'ight, but just remember, I'm a teacher, not a banker." Both of them laughed.

"Call me later in the week, Kevin, and we'll make the plans."

"No problem, Alicia. Good night."

"Good night."

Kevin hung up the phone with a huge grin on his face. This girl definitely had promise.

Kevin and Tyrone walked into Mama Dee's soul food restaurant at 8:30 Friday night, both dressed to impress. Searching the bar for a woman in a red dress, both men smiled when they realized that Alicia was not there yet. It had been four days since Kevin's phone call with her, and he was extremely nervous about their first date. He checked his watch and realized he was a half hour early, not fifteen minutes, as he had planned. Placing his arm around Tyrone's shoulder, he steered him to the bar.

"Yo, Ty, I 'preciate you comin' out here with me tonight, bro." He ordered two beers as he patted Tyrone's shoulder.

"No problem, Kev. I still can't believe you're goin' through with this shit."

"That's the same thing Antoine said."

"Don't worry, Kev. Even if she's a dawg, an' I got twenty says she is, I'm here for ya." Tyrone laughed as he downed his beer and motioned to the bartender for a refill.

"I bet you do, Ty. But this sistah Alicia seemed aw'ight on the phone. I'm just gonna play it cool and keep it real. Besides, I'm lookin' forward to having dinner with a nice female."

"I hear that, Kev. But what you gonna do if she's a female gorilla?" Kevin laughed at his friend's joke, but inside he prayed that the joke wouldn't be on him.

Kevin couldn't help but notice that Tyrone had already downed his second beer. "Tyrone, man, aren't you drinking those a bit fast?"

"Come on, Kev, this is pisswater beer. It ain't like it's Old E or somethin'." As he said it, the bartender had already placed a third in front of him. Tyrone turned toward the door and almost choked on his drink. "Damn! Didn't you say she'd be wearing a red dress?"

"Yeah."

"Well, brotha, I think she's here, and she ain't no dawg either. Homegirl is fine as frog hair." He gestured toward the entrance.

Trying to look casual, Kevin glanced at the woman. "Whaa! She is fine, isn't she? Damn, look at those legs."

"Yeah, an' baby got back too. Damn, Kev, you done fucked around and hit Lotto."

All Kevin could do was smile.

"Tell you what. Why don't you go home and I'll be Kevin?" Tyrone laughed, half serious.

Kevin took a second look at the woman's pretty face, the color of cocoa, which complemented the near-perfect picture.

"Not in this lifetime, bro. Besides, she's expecting Superman, not Clark Kent. Now, if you'll excuse me, I've got business to take care of." He straightened his collar and stood up.

"Yo, Kev, I'm gonna chill here for a while just in case. You never know. She could be a chickenhead in disguise."

"Aw'ight, this should cover the tab until I'm ready to leave." Kevin reached into his pocket and pulled out a twenty-dollar bill. He handed the money to Tyrone and winked.

"Yo, thanks, man." Tyrone took the twenty. "And good luck."

Kevin approached the woman, who was talking with a waitress. He cleared his throat as he approached them. "Excuse me."

The waitress turned to face Kevin. Giving him a quick head-to-toe look, she smiled at him approvingly. "Yes, can I help you?"

"I wanted to ask the young lady if her name was Alicia." Kevin smiled as he noticed she was even more attractive up close.

"Yes, I'm Alicia. Are you Kevin?" She tried to appear calm, but she was busy praying that this fine man was her date for the evening.

"Yes, I'm Kevin." He extended his hand. "It's a real pleasure to meet you, Alicia."

"No, the pleasure's all mine." She blushed. "I hope you don't mind me saying this, but I really wasn't expecting someone so handsome." The waitress chimed in with an "mmm-hmm."

Now it was Kevin's turn to blush, and it wasn't easy for him to stop.

"We'll take that table now," Alicia told the waitress as she and Kevin finally took their eyes off each other.

As the waitress led them to a table in the back, Alicia let Kevin lead. *Damn, he's got a nice butt.* She thought as she smiled to herself.

They were seated at a small round table in the corner, and Kevin ordered a beer. Alicia ordered a glass of white wine, and they sat and smiled at each other until Alicia finally broke their contented silence.

"Did you have a hard time finding this place?"

"No, your directions were great. How'd you find this place anyway? My mother would love it."

"It is nice, isn't it? I work across the street as a legal secretary, so sometimes I come here for lunch. I wanted our first date to be in a familiar surrounding."

"Hmm, that makes sense." He nodded. "Is that also why you didn't want me to pick you up at home?"

"Sort of, but the main reason is I didn't think it was proper for you to meet my son until I get to know you. He's a very bright and impressionable kid, and I don't think I should bring every Tom, Dick, and Harry home to meet him. No offense."

"None taken. I'm a teacher, remember. I always want what's best for the kids."

He meant that, but he couldn't help thinking about himself too. He wondered if he could handle a relationship with a single mother. And he already knew he would have some explaining to do to Mama, who had her own opinions about unwed mothers. She would say he deserved to have his own children, not some other man's.

"You're really sweet, Kevin. Why don't you tell me a little about yourself?" Alicia gently touched his hand.

This is the part of a date I always hate. He smiled nervously but thought this woman was definitely worth the effort, so he began. "Hmmm. Let's see. My full name is Kevin Brown, and I'm the oldest of three. I'm from Hopewell, Virginia. I graduated from Virginia State University." He paused for a second and looked in her eyes. "I feel like I'm at a job interview. Why don't you just ask me some questions? I'm sure there's something you wanna know." He hoped she didn't sense his discomfort.

"Okay, Kevin. I really didn't mean to stress you." She smiled. "Why don't I start?"

Nodding, Kevin sat back in his chair and relaxed as Alicia began to speak.

"As you already know, I have a little boy. His name is Michael, and he's seven years old. And yes, I had him when I was seventeen." She looked a little worried as she revealed the news.

"That's none of my business," he answered honestly, not trying to judge her.

"It could be your business if you plan on seeing me again. So I just wanted you to know that I'm no tramp. I was with Michael's father for eight years and would still be with him now if he didn't beat me so bad."

"He beat you?" Kevin tried not to sound too shocked.

Alicia knew she was revealing a lot of information for a first date, but she had decided that if she met a man who couldn't handle her past, she wanted to know right away. She wasn't about to waste time. She looked Kevin directly in the eye. "Yes, Trevor used to beat me."

"You did call the police and have him arrested, didn't you? Any man low enough to hit a woman needs to be in jail."

"No, I didn't call right away. Not until he put me in the hospital and the police visited my bedside. I know you probably think I'm a fool, Kevin, but the story is more complicated than you think."

Kevin folded his hands and sat back in his chair, wondering what excuse she would come up with for the lowlife. He waited silently for her to continue her story.

"You see, my problems started long before Trevor. They started with my father, Kevin. As long as I can remember, my father has been an alcoholic, and when Dad drinks, he becomes violent. Unfortunately for Mom, over the years he started drinking every day. So when I started dating Trevor"—she took a deep breath—"he was doing the same thing I saw growing up. For me it was normal for a man to hit a woman. I thought he honestly loved me. Then, as the years went by and the beatings got worse, I tried to leave. That's when he put me in the hospital."

A tear slid down Alicia's cheek, and Kevin leaned forward to touch her hand gently as she continued.

"Thank God for my social worker at the hospital. She got Michael and me into a shelter, then an apartment of our own."

"So what happened to that guy Trevor?" Kevin asked with sympathy. He wished he knew so that he could beat the hell out of him. He had no patience for men like that.

"I heard he was living in Brooklyn, but I haven't seen him because of a restraining order." She wiped away a few tears as she regained her composure and realized she had just poured her heart out to a man she hardly knew. She hadn't expected to cry in front of him.

"I'm sorry, Kevin. I hope this isn't freaking you out. Sometimes I get a little emotional. I just felt comfortable with you, but now I'm afraid I went too far."

Before Kevin could even respond, the waitress approached the table. She eyed him with suspicion as Alicia quickly wiped away her tears.

"Is everything all right?" the waitress snapped as she placed their drinks on the table.

Kevin sneered at the nosy woman as Alicia nodded and gave a weak smile.

"Would you like to order?" she asked.

Realizing that they hadn't even looked at the menu, Alicia and Kevin quickly scanned the choices. Alicia ordered a fish dinner with french fries and corn bread. Kevin, unable to make up his mind between pork chops or chicken, finally decided on the combination dinner with collard greens and macaroni and cheese. The waitress left, and Kevin gave Alicia an understanding smile before speaking.

"I know how it is to have an alcoholic father. My dad died of cirrhosis of the liver five years ago."

"Oh, my God, Kevin, I'm so sorry," she mumbled, her eyes full of tears once again.

"Hey! Hey! Don't cry again. It's aw'ight. My dad was never there for me. I played basketball all my life and he never came to one damn game. I don't want you to feel sorry for me. I just want you to know I understand and I want to be your friend."

This man is too good to be true. Alicia reached across the table and gently held Kevin's hand. She picked up her glass with her free hand and looked into his eyes.

"Here's to friendship and possibly more."

"And possibly more!" Kevin repeated as he raised his own glass.

They laughed and joked like old friends for hours, never realizing that the entire restaurant staff was waiting for them to leave. Suddenly the waitress was at their table.

"Look. You two seem to be getting along real good. Why don't y'all go down to the Kew Motor Inn and get a room so the rest of us can go home?"

Embarrassed, Alicia surveyed the room, only to find the whole staff staring at them. Kevin quickly paid the bill and made sure the waitress saw him leave a twenty-dollar tip. "Sorry about the inconvenience." He grabbed Alicia's hand softly as he led the way out the door.

They walked to Alicia's car holding each other closely. He had his arm around her shoulders, and she was pressed against him with her arms wrapped around his waist. At her car Alicia stepped back and looked into Kevin's eyes.

"Tonight was really special, Kevin. I have a good feeling about you."

He smiled at her and hugged her against his chest. Looking up to the sky, he silently prayed, *Thank you, God, for answering my mama's prayers.*

She nuzzled her chin against his chest, thinking about how many times she had almost canceled their date. Now she was grateful she hadn't missed out on this wonderful man.

He bent to kiss her but was startled by Tyrone, who stumbled toward them.

"Yo, ma'fucker 'member me? I'm the fool who been sittin' on your car for three damn hours!" he slurred.

"Kevin, who is this drunk fool?" Alicia whispered nervously.

"Well, I hate to admit it, but this fool is a friend of mine. I brought him along in case our date didn't go well. I guess when we were busy getting along so well, he was busy drinking half the bar." Alicia exploded in laughter as she let go of him.

"Shit!" he said. "I really messed up, didn't I? I am so sorry. I had no idea you were gonna be such a beautiful woman and that we'd have so much in common. I'd heard so many horror stories about date lines."

Still laughing, she grabbed him in another hug.

"Remember the bitch of a waitress we had?"

"Yeah."

"Well, she's my best friend." Kevin laughed with her as she told him, "You're not the only one who had some backup."

"I'm glad you two find somethin' funny, but I'm tryin' ta get my black ass home," Tyrone blurted out, falling on the grass.

"Look, Kevin, it's getting late, and your friend's waiting," Alicia said, stifling her laughter. She kissed him on the cheek. "Give me a call tomorrow. Please."

Kevin watched as Alicia got into her car and pulled away. Agitated by the way his date had ended, Kevin seriously contemplated kicking Tyrone in the ribs.

"Dammit, Tyrone, you have the worst fucking timing!"

"Wait a damn minute. You're the one who gave me the money to stick around at the bar." Tyrone belched.

"Yeah, I did do that, didn't I?" Kevin helped his friend up from the ground. "I'll tell you what though. She's the most attractive woman I've ever met. And not just physically attractive. She's got a beautiful spirit. Ty, man, I honestly think I just met the mother of my children."

"Well, whoop-de-damn-do," Tyrone answered, vomiting all over Kevin's shoes.

5

TYRONE

Tyrone Jefferson always considered himself a product of the streets. Growing up in the crime-plagued Marcy projects of Brooklyn, he became a member of the notorious street gang, the Bloods, for protection. At seventeen, like many young men in his neighborhood, Tyrone was a father forced to sell drugs to support his daughter. Two years later, trying to escape the responsibility of a second child by another woman, he joined the navy, looking for a new start. Unfortunately his past caught up with him with horrible results.

After navy boot camp he was informed by his commanding officers that both of his children's mothers had placed claims against his earnings and that each would receive a large portion of his income. Swearing that "neither one of those bitches" would get his money, he went AWOL, hiding from the navy in South Jamaica, New York, until his arrest for possession of crack cocaine two years later. He was given probation because of the small amount of crack but was turned over to the navy to face desertion charges. Having no further use for a crack-addicted sailor, the navy found him guilty of desertion and sentenced him to a year in Fort Leavenworth prison.

After serving his sentence Tyrone was given one hundred and fifty dollars by the government, along with a bus ticket back to New York. He swore that he was going to beat his drug addiction and become a better person and entered the Apple drug program in East Hampton, New York. There, along with his drug-treatment program, he took fatherhood and self-improvement classes. Slowly his self-esteem started to improve.

Tyrone was always leaving graffiti on the desktops while in the program. Rather than punishing him for it, a counselor who noticed the graffiti gave him a set of pens and a sketchpad, which he used to hone his artistic talents. Soon he became known around the program as the "black Rembrandt" and was never seen without his drawing supplies in hand. What began as graffiti scribbled on a desktop developed into beautiful, bold art that represented his people, their beauty, and their struggles.

His newfound love for art gave him a purpose and the strength to stay in the program. Within a year he was addiction free and was released from the program. He decided against taking the counseling position Apple offered him and instead took a job as a security guard at a Park Avenue art gallery. The job was his for two years, until he was caught having sex with the owner's nineteen-year-old daughter. Still, he was determined to keep his life on the right track, so he applied for a job as a school security guard and was assigned to the Alternative High School for Boys.

The day after his fiasco at Mama Dee's, Tyrone was still a little hung over. He was looking at a picture of his two daughters as tears rolled down his face.

"Daddy's working fifty hours a week, living in this shithole of an apartment, and all I can afford to send your mothers is a hundred fucking dollars a week. I'm one sorry-ass excuse for a man," he told the picture as he stuffed the child support checks into two separate envelopes. Picking his shirt up from the floor, he wiped his tears from his eyes. He hated these moments of weakness.

Aw'ight, Tyrone, get yourself together. What you really need is some booty.

Striding across the room, Tyrone sat on the edge of his Murphy bed and took his phone book off the nightstand. He flipped through several pages, and each time he paused at a number he would recall the woman written there. Most of the entries in the book were so old, he couldn't even be sure the women were still living at the same addresses. Finally he found a number for Shelly, a woman in Brooklyn whom he had been seeing casually a while back.

Smiling as he dialed her number, he thought about the cocoa-brown beauty. Shelly was fine in every sense of the word. Tall and slender with just enough breasts and hips to make a man take a second look. He especially liked the gap between her bowed legs. Remembering how her sexual appetite well surpassed his, he eagerly dialed her number.

"Hello," a groggy, yet seductive voice answered after four rings. "What's up, baby?"

"Tyrone, is that you?" She was suddenly sounding less tired.

"Yeah, baby, it's me." He couldn't remember why he hadn't spoken to this fine sister in so long. "I haven't seen you in a while, so I thought I'd come by and let you cook me dinner."

"That sounds good. Why don't I make some fish and corn bread?"

"Yeah, that'll work. Oh, can you make some candied yams and greens?" His stomach began to growl.

"Sure, baby, I'll make you some greens and yams." She paused, and her voice became low and sultry. "What about me, don't you want to eat me for dessert? A little whipped cream and a cherry, and I make a hell of a sundae."

"You damn skippy, I want you for dessert. What would a good meal be without dessert?" The image of Shelly covered in whipped cream awakened his manhood.

"Mmm, I can't wait," she purred. Then her voice was all business again. "Oh, damn, Tyrone, can you pick something up for me on the way over?"

"Sure, baby, what do you need?" he asked eagerly as he stood up and grabbed his coat from the back of the chair.

"What I need is the goddamn two hundred dollars you owe me!! Gimme my money, motherfucka!!" She screamed into the phone. "Did you actually think that you're so good in bed that I wouldn't want my money? You must be crazy, nigga! I want my goddamn money! Where the hell is my money?"

By then Tyrone had slumped down on the bed, any sign of arousal long gone. "Calm down for a minute, Shelly."

"Calm down? I ain't gonna calm down! You asked me to loan you two hundred dollars till payday! Well, dammit, payday was four months ago. Where the hell is my money?"

"Damn, baby, I thought you knew. Both my mother and father died in a car accident the day before payday. I'm still struggling to pay off their funerals."

"Do I look like I just fell off the stupid bus? Your daddy died in Korea and your mama lives in my buildin', asshole! Now, when am I gonna get my money?" She heard nothing but silence on the other end, so she shouted "It fucking figures!" before hanging up.

Tyrone stared at the phone in his hand and shook his head.

She didn't act that way when I had her ass climbing the walls a few months back. Well, there's always old faithful Jeannette. She wasn't much to look at, but the sex was always great and she was always available. Smiling, he dialed the number.

"Hello?" a soft voice answered.

"Hey, baby, how would you like for me to pour chocolate all over your body and lick it off until the sun comes up?"

"Mmm, that sounds good," the sexy voice answered, "as long as I can do the same to you."

Tyrone was happy. Jeannette, a short twenty-two-year-old, had always been horny. He figured it must have something to do with the acne all over her face, because in his experience, less attractive women always seemed more eager to please. When they were together, he was always careful to turn out the lights so the sight of her face wouldn't interfere with his arousal. In the dark, with her lips working their magic, she was the most beautiful woman on earth as far as he was concerned.

"Damn, baby, what you waitin' for? Why don't you catch a cab on over here?" he asked.

"I'd love to Tyrone, but . . ."

"But what? I plan on making you come ten times before I even take my clothes off."

Tyrone's confidence in his ability showed in his voice, and he could hear Jeannette begin to breathe heavily. But before he could continue to seduce her over the phone, he heard a loud smack.

"Who the fuck is this? If I catch you fuckin' with my girl, nigga, I'm 'onna kill your black ass!"

Tyrone wasted no time hanging up the phone.

He sighed deeply. *Shit!! I hope that girl ain't got caller ID. When the hell did she get a man anyway?*

Desperate now, Tyrone flipped through his phone book and decided to dial one more number. Stacey Preston, the neighborhood slut, was blessed with incredible curves and the sexual instincts of a prostitute. Known for giving the men she liked blowjobs for a can of beer, Stacey had always been Tyrone's safety valve when he'd needed quick, discreet sex. He dialed her number, figuring it was a sure thing.

"Hello," Stacey answered sweetly.

"Stacey, what's up, baby? This is Tyrone."

"Tyrone? Oh, what's up, baby! It's been a long time, boo." She sounded excited.

"Yeah, well, you know I've been a little busy. But I've been thinking 'bout you a lot." He lied, opening his nightstand drawer to see if he had any magnum condoms.

"You have? So when we gonna get together?"

"We can get together right now if you like, baby. All you have to do is bring your fine ass over here."

"I'm on my way. Oh, Tyrone, do you think we can get a little something to jump-start our party?" Tyrone didn't notice the desperation in her voice.

"Don't worry, baby, I've got two forties of Old E on ice as we speak."

"Oh, that's great," she answered weakly. "But I was thinking maybe we'd try something a little stronger."

"Sure, baby, no problem. Why don't you come on over? I'll slip out and get us a bottle. What you got a taste for, rum? Maybe a little gin?"

"Naw, man, I don't wanna drink. What I really wanna get is some crack."

Stacey's words hit Tyrone like a ton of bricks. The last thing he had expected from her was that she wanted drugs. He hadn't even known she smoked the stuff.

"You serious?" he asked.

"Yeah, I'm serious." Her voice became very animated. "You act like you never had sex after you smoked crack. That shit is the bomb!!"

Yeah, it is the bomb. He thought about how good it would be to hold a stem and take a long hit of some really good crack. Just the thought of that first hit reaching his lungs made his forehead perspire.

"Come on, boo, let's get a few dimes." Stacey's voice was becoming even more desperate. "I promise you, I'll suck your dick until you pass out!"

Tyrone didn't care about having sex now. His thoughts were on getting high. There was nothing any crack addict wanted more than to obtain that first high, and he had a chance to get there. It had been almost four years since he'd smoked crack, and he figured he could get high, get that feeling again, and then stop smoking the next day. His palms were sweaty as he reached on his nightstand for his wallet. Opening it, he saw two ten-dollar bills. He knew it wasn't enough for both of them to get a good high.

Glancing across the room, he spotted two one-hundred-dollar bills on his desk. They were supposed to be deposited into his checking account to cover his child support checks.

"Ay, Stacey, you got any money?" He knew the answer to the question before he asked it.

"Hell no! Don't tell me you ain't got no money, Tyrone."

"I got money." He walked over to the table, pocketing the two one-hundred-dollar bills.

"Good, I know some guys right by your building that got slammin' dimes." Stacey's voice was a mixture between relief and excitement.

Tyrone was getting really worked up now. His mouth was dry and he couldn't wait to feel the warm smoke fill his mouth and lungs. He didn't want to talk on the phone anymore. He just wanted to get high.

"Look, Stacey, we're wasting time talking on the phone. Just bring your ass—" He stopped himself in midsentence as he caught sight of the picture of his two daughters on the wall.

"Tyrone? You there, baby? I'm on my way over now, Tyrone." She could sense something was wrong. There was a long silence before he answered.

"Stacey, don't come over here. Don't come over tonight or any other night, 'cause I don't get high no more."

Tyrone hung up the phone quickly before she could try to change his mind. He sat on his bed and stared at the picture of his girls. Opening the Bible that was lying on his desk, he said a silent prayer, thanking God for one more day of sobriety.

As he lay on his bed, his thoughts wandered to Alicia and Kevin. He wondered what his life would be like if Alicia had been with him instead of Kevin. Imagining her in the sexy red dress she had worn when they first met, he knew he would be the envy of many brothers with a woman like that.

What the hell am I doing! he thought, opening his eyes. *Oh, man, times are really bad when you start dreaming about your friend's woman.*

Determined to change his luck and get some play, he picked up the phone and dialed 1-900-BLACK-LUV. He contemplated leaving a sincere message to attract a serious woman but couldn't bear to expose his emotions that way. He had spent so many years as a player and couldn't change easily, so he made his message short and to the point.

"What's up? My name is Tyrone. I'm a six-foot-three, dark-skinned brother. I'm lookin' for a woman who wants to put all the BS aside and have great sex. You must be drug and disease free. Serious inquires only. Please leave a message at Box twenty-nine eighty-eight."

6

ANTOINE

Antoine sat in his recliner, smoking a nineteenth-century curved pipe as he read *The Selected Poems of Nikki Giovanni.* Slowly drawing on the strawberry tobacco, he allowed himself to relax for the first time in weeks. As he removed his glasses to rub his tired eyes, his leisure was interrupted by a knock on the door. Taking a long drag from his pipe, Antoine set it down and stood to answer the door.

"Hi, Antoine." Keisha seemed excited and quite drunk.

"How are you, Keisha?" He didn't move to invite her in.

"I'm fine," she slurred as she slid past him into the apartment. "Mmm, what's that smell? Incense? I just love incense."

"No, it's the strawberry tobacco from my pipe."

"I didn't know you smoked," she said as she took a book from the coffee table. *"Selected Poems of Nikki Giovanni.* I read this. This is good, but you should read *Langston Hughes, Shakespeare in Harlem."*

Antoine gave no response but stared at Keisha, amazed at how rude she could be. He also assumed she was lying about the book, and the doubt was evident on his face.

"Bet you didn't know I love poetry, did you?"

"Keisha, did you come by here for any particular reason? I'm about to go to bed."

"Go to bed! It's only nine o'clock! Why you goin' to bed so early?" She replaced the book and approached him.

"If it's any of your business, I have a meeting with the editor of my book tomorrow morning."

"Oh, well, I just came by to see if you wanted that drink," she said sadly. "But if you're going to bed, I'll see you tomorrow."

Antoine breathed a sigh of relief as she left. Had it been any other woman with Keisha's looks and a different personality, he would have been happy to invite her in for a drink. But he couldn't seem to get past her aggressiveness to appreciate her. In his estimation there wasn't anything romantic about a woman so abrasive and straightforward. He preferred his women more refined. Yawning loudly, he put out his pipe, turned out the light, and headed for the bedroom.

Looking at his empty bed, he realized he was pretty lonely. It would have been nice to have someone to cuddle up to in that bed. As his thoughts wandered to the lack of women in his life, it crossed his mind that he had left his poetry on the 900 number line, and he wondered if anyone had responded. He tried to convince himself he was calling only to check for critiques of his work. But as he dialed the phone, he began to fantasize about a beautiful woman falling in love with his poetry and then with him. The first message he heard was as far from that fantasy as could be.

"Hi, my name is Tonya," a soft, sweet voice said, "and I wanted to thank you for your poem. After I heard it, I wrote it down and sent it to the boy I just broke up with. Now we're back together, and he's already promised to take me to the homecoming dance at my high school. Thanks again, and I hope you become real famous someday."

Although it held no prospect of love for himself, Antoine was flattered. "Young lady, you made my day," he said aloud. "I just hope your parents still let you go to that dance when they get these 900-number calls on their bill."

The next message began. "Hi, Antoine, my name is Robin. I just listened to your poem and found myself wishing that you were interested in meeting someone for a relationship. Your words just knocked me off my feet, not to mention that sexy voice of yours! I just thought you should know how special you are. I guess I'll just have to keep searching for a man with your unique qualities. Have a good day now, and stay blessed."

Antoine listened to Robin's message a second time. He had to admit Kevin might have been right. Maybe it was possible to meet a quality woman on a date line. If Robin had left a number, he would have been tempted to call her. As the next message began to play, he hoped it was another call like Robin's. It wasn't even close.

"Ay Antoine!" hissed an angry female voice. "Who told ya you could write anyway? You sound like a white boy to me. No real black man would ever leave a sissy-ass message like that on a date line. You better take that white shit back to Long Island. Hey, Oreo cookie, check this poem out. Roses are red, violets are blue. Antoine can't write, and he's a fool."

A raucous laugh and then an abrupt dial tone followed the poem. Antoine jumped out of his chair and nearly threw the phone across the room, shouting obscenities into the air until he realized he was still holding the phone and there was a voice on the line.

"To delete this message, press three." He quickly erased the hateful message, tempted to hang up. But the beautiful, sultry voice on the next message made him glad he hadn't.

"Hello, Antoine. I hope this message finds you in good spirits. As for me, I'm doing well. Your poem has left me truly inspired and convinced that there are still beautiful souls walking the earth. I have read many poems in my day, but it is rare to find one that moves me like yours did. I know you said that you are not interested in meeting someone, but I'd love to get together with you even if it's just to hear more of your poetry. If you're interested, give me a call at home before eleven P.M. My number is 555-7988. Oh, and my name's Shawna."

"Shawna," Antoine repeated aloud as he scribbled her number on the back of the book he was reading. He immediately hung up the phone and dialed her number. As the phone rang, doubt began to creep into his mind.

"I don't even know this woman, what in the world am I gonna say to her?" Reality had slapped him in the face, but it was too late. Before he had a chance to think again, he heard the sweet sound of Shawna's voice.

"Hello," she said for the second time, bringing him back to earth.

"Uh, hi. This is Antoine, is this Shawna?"

"Oh, hi, Antoine. I am so glad you decided to call me back. I was beginning to worry that I wasn't going to get the privilege of speaking to the talent behind that beautiful poetry."

Suddenly he felt bold and returned the flattery. "I had to return the call. When a man hears an angel speak, it's usually in his best interest to answer."

"Well, well. A poetic genius, and a master sweet-talker." Shawna was blushing on her end of the phone. "I guess that proves it."

"Proves what?"

"Proves that you have a woman, because in my experience, men like you are either gay or taken." She laughed. "You're not gay, are you? Because I just got finished reading E. Lynn Harris's book, and he's got me believing every man out there is a closet homosexual."

"No, I'm not gay, and I'm not taken either. I've just been too busy with teaching and writing to meet someone special. But who knows, maybe I've found what I'm looking for?"

"Maybe you have," Shawna flirted. "I like a man who puts the important things ahead of his sexual needs. You're not the love-'em-and-leave-'em type, are you?"

"No, not by a long shot." He hoped she knew he was sincere. "Personally I think that's a major part of what's wrong with society today. People spend too much time trying to get laid instead of trying to get to know each other. I could never live like that. For me it's love first, sex later."

"God, are you perfect, or what?" Shawna sighed. "Maybe I'm old-fashioned, but I think people are having sex much too soon in relationships. Antoine, can you keep a secret?"

"Sure," he told her, though he was suddenly nervous.

"I'm a virgin."

"Really? I think that's admirable in this day and age. I have to admit I'm impressed. I didn't think there were any virgins left." He smiled to himself. He had always fantasized about meeting and marrying a virgin.

"You know, Antoine, I have a good feeling about you. You're the kind of person I want to be around. Do you think we could get together sometime for coffee? Or maybe I could hear some more of your poetry?"

"Sure. I had hoped you would ask. Why don't we get together tomorrow, Shawna?"

"I'd love to, but I have to work tomorrow. Maybe you can come see me at the store."

"What store?" He picked up a pen to write directions.

"Have you been to the African American bookstore in the Gertz Plaza Mall?"

"No, I didn't even know there was one in that mall."

"Well, I'm the manager. Why don't you meet me there about three?"

"Sounds good, Shawna. I'll bring some more of my poetry."

"I can't wait, Antoine. Good night."

"Good night, Shawna." He placed the phone back on the receiver and smiled with anticipation. Sitting back in his chair, he lit his pipe again.

He wondered about Shawna's appearance. Normally he was a man who cared more about a woman's substance than her looks, but he could not help but wonder if she was as sexy as she sounded. He imagined her as tall and dark-skinned with long, sexy legs. And he hoped that she would have a large, shapely butt that swayed when she walked.

The following afternoon Antoine entered the African American bookstore nervously. He noticed a heavyset woman working at the register, and he assumed she must be Shawna. His nerves didn't allow him to approach right away, so he smiled at her and then walked through the aisles of books in an attempt to contain his apprehension.

He kept stealing glances over a small bookcase. Though she looked nothing like he had imagined, he still found her attractive. He pretended to be reading a copy of *Shakespeare in Harlem* as he tried to gather his confidence to speak to Shawna. He laughed to himself as he noticed the thickness of the book.

That Keisha is such a liar. There is no way her hairdressing self read this.

A sense that he was being watched overcame him, and Antoine looked back over the bookcase to see if Shawna was still at the register. She was still there, ringing up a sale, and Antoine decided it was time to put the book on the shelf and introduce himself. As he turned to the shelves, he nearly bumped into a tall, brown-skinned woman. She giggled as they made eye contact. She was taller than Antoine was, so he had to look up slightly to see the woman's exquisitely made-up face.

"That's a great book, isn't it?" She had a sultry voice.

"That's what I've been told," he answered before recognizing the voice. "Are you Shawna?" He looked at the woman with a big smile. She was so much like the woman he had pictured the night before.

"Yes, I'm Shawna. I had a feeling that was you, Antoine. I know most of our regular male customers. Well, at least the cute ones." She smiled flirtatiously. "Let me go tell Shirley I'm taking my break, and we can go across the street to the coffee shop."

Antoine watched her walk to the desk, admiring the sway of her hips.

In the coffee shop the two of them sat in a booth facing a window, drinking lattes. After about fifteen minutes of small talk Antoine brought up the subject of how they met. He was still a little embarrassed that he had resorted to a date line but was in awe that he could meet someone like this.

"You know, Shawna, I have to confess. I'm really surprised that you're so pretty. I always had the idea that everyone who called date lines is overweight or unattractive."

"Are you calling my friend Shirley unattractive, Antoine?" Shawna teased. "I saw you looking at her when you walked in."

"Actually I thought she was cute. But she doesn't compare to you. So why would a woman who looks like you call a date line anyway?"

"I grew up in Peoria, Illinois, and my parents kept me pretty sheltered. It took me twenty-five years to gather the courage to leave home. I've spent the last two years in New York, discovering who I really am. So who had time to be dating?"

"So now you know yourself?"

"Well, let's say I'm just about there. But that, handsome, is a conversation for another time. My break is over."

"A woman of mystery." He smiled. "I like that. Do you think I could see you tonight? There's so much I want to learn about you, and you haven't even read my poetry." He smiled as he lifted his briefcase.

"Oh, Antoine, I really would love to see you tonight, but I have a night job. How about tomorrow?"

"Definitely. There's a poetry reading tomorrow afternoon in Flushing Meadow Park. Would you be interested?"

"It's a date. I'll call you from work tonight to make arrangements."

Shawna gathered her purse and waited for Antoine, who left a generous tip on the table and walked her back to work. The short break he spent with Shawna had been just enough to pique his interest, and he went into the store to buy a book just to be able to spend a little more time with her. He left the store humming happily.

7

MAURICE

Dawn was freezing as she walked south down I-95 in Vermont in the frigid night air. Sticking her thumb out as a car sped by, she continued to cry. Tears had been streaming down her face for what seemed like the entire ten miles she had walked.

God! How the fuck could I be so stupid to go all the way to Vermont with a man and not bring any money?

She wished she had let Maurice buy her a ski suit instead of a flimsy, short leather jacket. After walking for hours in the subzero wind chill, she truly believed she wouldn't make it home without some divine intervention. She said a quick prayer through her chattering teeth.

"God, if you can see it in yourself to let me make it home to New York, I promise I will be in the front row of church every Sunday."

Dawn's prayers were answered quickly. The next car she saw pulled over to the side of the road. She thanked the Lord aloud as a Vermont state trooper stepped out of his cruiser. Dawn rushed toward the man.

"Miss, you do know it's illegal to hitchhike in the state of Vermont?" the trooper scolded.

Dawn smiled when she heard his voice. She finally felt safe.

"Officer, I was abandoned about a two-hour walk from here. If you could just get me to Western Union, or even a phone, I'd really appreciate it."

"Let me guess. Light-skinned black guy, a little over six feet, green eyes, and drives an expensive car?" the trooper sounded as if he had met Dawn's date.

Her jaw dropped and her eyes were wide. "How did you know?"

"Why don't you step into my car, miss." The officer opened the passenger door. "You look a little cold. You can warm up while I explain."

Thawing out in the police cruiser, Dawn drank black coffee from the trooper's thermos as he drove.

"Excuse me, officer, but could you please tell me how you knew the man that abandoned me?" She was shaking. "I'm pretty scared he might be some kind of psycho."

"I don't think you have to worry about that, miss," he answered. "We had him pretty well checked out after the first couple of girls."

"First couple of girls! There are others?" Dawn cried out.

"Yes, ma'am. Fifty-two girls in fifteen years. That doesn't include you, of course, or anyone that might not have reported it." The trooper did not take his eyes off the road as he delivered this devastating news.

"This has to be a nightmare! He made me feel as if I was the only woman on earth." Suddenly she was angry. "If he's done this to so many women why haven't you arrested him?"

The trooper was aware of how upset Dawn must be. He had picked up so many women in the same predicament and was prepared for her anger. Counting slowly to twenty, he allowed her to shout at him for a while before he interrupted.

"Miss, there is nothing in the world my fellow troopers and I would like more than to arrest that man. But we don't have a charge. Unfortunately it's not against the law to leave a woman without a ride home, even if it's over fifty women."

Dawn was furious. She turned her head to face the trooper and put her hand on his arm.

"Yes, you do have a charge. What if I told you he raped me?"

"Miss, just drop it, okay?" The trooper seemed a little annoyed. "I'm going to take you to headquarters. The desk sergeant's going to give you money for a bus ticket home, and then it's over."

Dawn couldn't believe what she was hearing. "Wait a minute. Lemme get this straight. A black woman tells a white cop that she's been raped, and all he can say is take your black ass home? Fuck that! I want your badge number now!" She was waving her hands wildly as she yelled at the cop.

"You know, there's really no need for that kind of language." The trooper was not about to allow Dawn to continue this time. "This is not about race, miss. Both you and I know that he didn't rape you." His tone was matter-of-fact. "You must think you're the first person to accuse him of rape, but you're wrong. At least a dozen girls have said that he raped them. But we're not dealing with a stupid man."

"I didn't say we were. Just take me to the hospital or have a rape kit sent to your headquarters. I have his sperm in me, and I even have bruises."

"Look, you don't seem to understand me, miss. So I'm going to explain it to you in black and white." The trooper felt a headache developing. "This Maurice guy asked you to go skiing in Vermont, he probably tells you about the early snow we just got. He's handsome, intelligent, and rich too. Basically the man of your dreams. So you accept. Am I right so far?"

"Yes." Dawn's voice was weak.

"The two of you drive up in his big Mercedes or Lexus. Then he takes you skiing and buys you some expensive gifts. . . ." Glancing over at Dawn, the trooper continued. "Like that leather jacket. Then he takes you back to the cabin he owns. It's beautiful, isn't it, with the big bearskin rug and the huge fireplace? He serves you expensive wine, and the two of you make love on that bearskin rug. You probably even got those bruises you were talking about on that rug."

"That's a nice story, officer, but I got raped." Dawn folded her arms defiantly.

"Oh, there's something I forgot. After you make love and fall asleep, this Maurice guy goes into the next room and takes a videotape out of a camera concealed in the wall. Your whole night of passion is on that tape. He likes to have it on the front seat of his car just in case some dumb trooper like me pulls him over and accuses him of rape."

Dawn slumped down in her seat after hearing the end of his story.

"Look, miss. It could have been worse. One woman who insisted on pressing rape charges had the whole thing backfire on her and ended up doing thirty days jail time herself."

"Get the fuck outta here! For what?"

"Vandalism, destruction of property, and filing a false police report. You see, when she woke up and found Maurice had left her behind with no money and no phone, she trashed his entire cabin. Now, trashing his place would have been all right. I think he considers that the cost of playing his sick game. But when she insisted on pressing rape charges against him, that pissed him off."

Dawn sat there, thinking about all the things she had broken before she left Maurice's cabin and was glad that trooper Perkins had talked her out of pressing charges. The whole thing had been a nightmare, and she just wanted to wake up.

"So he's just a con man."

"Pretty much. Except he takes your self-respect instead of your money." The trooper pulled his vehicle into the headquarters parking lot.

"I think I'd much rather he'd taken my money." Dawn's voice was barely audible by then.

"That's what most people say," the officer replied, pointing at the building. "Just go in those doors there and ask for the desk sergeant. Tell him that Trooper Perkins sent you and explain your story. He'll give you bus fare back home."

"Thank you so much, Trooper Perkins." A single tear slid down Dawn's windburned face. She hugged the officer before she got out of the car.

Twenty miles up the road Maurice smiled at the elderly woman behind the counter as she poured his coffee into a paper cup. He had stopped at the small Vermont truck stop after leaving Dawn behind in the cabin.

Damn, I should have thought of using 1-900-BLACK-LUV years ago, he thought to himself, remembering how easy it had been to get the girl up to his cabin. *I never dreamed there were so many stupid women just a phone call away.* He felt two strong hands take hold of his shoulders. Looking up, he smiled as he saw a Vermont state trooper.

"Well, if it isn't Sergeant Landell." Maurice's smile became a devilish grin.

"I thought I told you to stay the hell out of Vermont, you son of a bitch!"

"You know, sergeant, you're becoming a real pain in my ass." Maurice straightened his shirt before putting on his ski jacket.

"Who the fuck do you think you're talking to, you son of a bitch?" The sergeant's pale white face was now beet red.

"I'm talking to you, sergeant. And if I remember correctly, the last time you tried that tough-guy shit with me, you were a captain. Now, the next time you or any other trooper fucks with me or pulls me over, I'm going to own this fucking state." Maurice calmly reached into his jacket and pulled out his cell phone as if the sergeant were no more than a nuisance. "Now get the fuck out my way. Or do I have to call my lawyer?"

The woman behind the counter was in shock. In thirty years knowing Landell, he had never let anyone disrespect him. Now out of nowhere he was letting some arrogant tourist curse and point his finger at him.

"You're one sick motherfucker!" the trooper growled, balling his fist up in his leather gloves but not taking a step closer.

"Give it up, Landell. You've been trying to catch me doing something wrong for fifteen years. I'm not doing anything illegal." He laughed. "Maybe you're just jealous, huh, Landell? You should have seen the one I was with this time Landell. Mmm-mmm, was she pretty!" Taking his container of coffee, Maurice grinned as he walked past the officer.

"I hate that fucking bastard," Sergeant Landell said, clenching both his fists as Maurice walked out the door.

"I don't like him much myself," the elderly waitress replied from behind the counter. "But he's a great tipper!" She took the twenty-dollar bill Maurice had left on the counter and put it in her apron.

The sergeant reached around and took his radio out of its holster.

"Base, this is Sergeant Landell."

"Go ahead, Landell," the dispatcher spat out.

"I just spotted Maurice Johnson leaving Chance's Truck Stop. You might want to send a trooper up Interstate Ninety-five to look for a girl."

"She's already been found, Landell. Base out."

"That asshole thinks this is some kind of fucking game!" He slammed his hand down on the counter as he sat down.

"Can I ask you a question, sarge?" the woman asked.

"Sure, Mary."

"I've been knowing you over thirty years, and I've never seen you back down to any man like that. What the hell is going on? Is he from the NAACP or something?"

"That son of a bitch and his high-priced lawyer are the reason I lost my captain's bars." Landell's hatred showed in his eyes.

"Him?" She was shocked.

"He happens to make large donations to the Vermont Democratic Party. One day about ten years ago, me and a few of the boys decided to teach him a lesson for abandoning some New York girls out near Interstate Ninety-five. Well, two days later that son of a bitch shows up with a lawyer and sues for police brutality. The state, the governor, I mean, he sued everyone."

"I think I heard about that," replied the waitress, recalling vaguely having heard something through word-of-mouth.

"Yeah, well, you're one of the few who heard. Those damn Democrats put such a tight lid on things, it never even made the news. They gave that son of a bitch three hundred grand to drop the lawsuit, then fired everyone involved but me."

"Why didn't they fire you?"

"Because that smartass lawyer of his said that it would serve as a better example if they busted me down from captain to trooper. It took me five years just to make sergeant again."

"That's a real shame." The waitress shook her head slowly. "But, you know, what goes around comes around. Someday that man's going to get what he deserves."

The trooper stood up to leave. "You know, I hope you're right about that."

At the same moment Maurice's wife was sitting by the phone in their bedroom, fuming. *This is the fifth time I've called that motherfucker! Where the fuck could he be at 3:45 in the morning? I should just forget his ass and go to sleep.* She had already tried to sleep but was too upset.

This was not the first time Sylvia had found herself in this position, waiting for her husband at all hours of the night. Over the years her husband had spent many nights out late, and while he was away she would pace the floors, certain that he was with another woman. Most times he would come home with the excuse that he had been with his childhood friend, David. Sylvia rarely questioned his reason, mostly to avoid a fight. After pacing around the bedroom for another ten minutes, she dialed his cellular phone again.

"I'm sorry, but the number you have dialed is out of calling range at this time."

Sylvia slammed the phone against the nightstand in a rage. Grabbing her robe from the back of the bathroom door, she walked downstairs into the study, thinking she might find some clue in Maurice's date book. On the page for that day, Maurice had penciled in "meet with David, 9:30 p.m."

"That motherfucking liar!" she screamed as her fist pounded the desk. She knew he was not with David this time, since David had called two days before and mentioned to Sylvia that he and his wife were going to the Bahamas the following morning. She lifted the date book, and a slip of paper fell to the floor. It was an index card with 1-900-BLACK-LUV scribbled on it.

Sylvia was puzzled for a minute, until she figured out what the number probably meant. The reality of the situation hit her like a ton of bricks. Years of denial had built a protective wall around her ego, but it was shattering in seconds.

Don't tell me that lowlife has resorted to using a date line!

Her shock quickly became anger. Not quite sure what she should expect to hear, Sylvia dialed the date line. She had to know if her husband had actually used the line to leave a personal ad. Sylvia listened to one man after another, amazed at the number of ads.

I can't believe all these men call this date line. What the hell has happened to the black male that they have to stoop to this?

For forty minutes Sylvia kept searching the ads for Maurice's voice. Each time she heard, "Hi, my name . . ." she'd skip to the next message, listening for Maurice's voice. She knew she'd been on the line a long time but was determined to keep listening until she'd found it. Her jaw dropped as she finally heard her husband.

"Hi, I'm Maurice. Are you sick of the typical guy who takes you to dinner and expects you to pay half the bill? Are you looking for someone who's actually going to take you to dinner? Then I'm the man for you. I'm a thirty-two-year-old romantic who would love to make every day Valentine's Day."

"Thirty-two, my ass!" Sylvia shouted at the phone, becoming angrier by the minute.

"I'm six foot one with light skin and blue-green eyes. If this appeals to you, leave me a message in box number twenty-nine sixty. I can't wait to hear from you."

Sylvia shook her head in disbelief, and the tears streamed down her face. Even after suspecting Maurice of cheating, she never actually expected such a slap in the face. She had stood by her husband through twenty years of marriage and was repaid with this kind of disrespect. She had done without for so many years so he could pursue his doctorate degree. She even wrote half his damn papers, and it was her daddy's money that had paid his tuition. She practically raised their daughter single-handedly, and this was what she got in return? Now that they were financially successful, he was out there, offering to spend their money on some phone-line bimbos. Sylvia was furious.

Realizing the phone was still in her hand, Sylvia came up with an idea born from her anger. Two could play at Maurice's game, and she was determined to get revenge. The BLACK-LUV line was her perfect opportunity. She continued to listen to the messages of these men until she heard a man who would be perfect for her scheme.

"What's up? My name is Tyrone. I'm a six-foot-three, dark-skinned brother. I'm lookin' for a woman who wants to put all the BS aside and have great sex. You must be drug and disease free. Serious inquiries only. Please leave a message at Box twenty-nine eighty-eight."

Sleeping with another man would be the best way to hurt Maurice's overblown ego. At that moment she wasn't even concerned with the idea that she was lowering herself to his level. She just wanted to hurt him like he had hurt her. Punching in the numbers, she responded to Tyrone's ad in a dead serious voice.

"Hi, Tyrone My name is Sylvia. I'm a married woman with a cheating-ass husband, and I'd love to get with you for some great sex, not to mention a little revenge. Call me on my cell phone, and I think we can help each other out. It's 555-6523."

Satisfied with her plan, Sylvia went back to bed. Unlike before, she fell right to sleep and slept like a baby. She never even heard Maurice sneak into the bed hours later.

8

ANTOINE AND SHAWNA

Keisha had been up since 6:00 A.M. braiding Mrs. Williamson's hair for her daughter's wedding. As she cracked her knuckles to relieve the tightness, all she could think about was a hot bath and her warm bed. She stood back and admired the job she had done, then patted her customer on the shoulder.

"Looks like we're done here, Mrs. Williamson. Now, you best get home so you don't miss your own child's weddin'!" Walking to the front of the store, the two women chitchatted about the wedding while Keisha made change from the register.

"Listen, congratulations again, and please give my regards to Helen. She's gettin' a real catch in that Rob Dash." She smiled.

Keisha walked Mrs. Williamson to the front door and held it open for her, waving good-bye. Outside she turned to lock up the shop and was startled by a voice behind her.

"Excuse me, miss." Keisha turned to see a very tall woman standing close to her. She was not in the mood for any more customers.

"Look, miss, I'm sorry, but we're closed on Sunday except by appointment." Then she took another look at the woman and thought she might reconsider. *That woman's braids look like something out of a creature-feature movie.*

"I'm not here to get my hair done." Shawna smiled, looking at a folded-up piece of paper. "I was hoping you could tell me which apartment Antoine Smith lives in. He gave me this address, but the apartment number is really unclear."

"And who are you, his sistah?" Keisha said with attitude. "I don't give out that type of information to just anyone."

"No, I'm not his sister. My name is Shawna, and Antoine and I are supposed to go out on a date."

Shawna could see the shock and hurt on Keisha's face. Automatically she assumed the woman must be involved with Antoine or maybe an ex-girlfriend. She didn't want to cause a scene.

"Look, never mind. Is there a pay phone around here? I'll just call him."

Keisha didn't reply at first. She was still upset that Antoine was going on a date. But she snapped out of it when Shawna spoke again.

"Does he have a girlfriend or something?" Shawna didn't like the look Keisha was giving her, so she backed up a bit.

"Yeah, he's got somethin', and it's me! Why? You got a problem with that?" Keisha took a step closer, looking like she was ready for a fight.

"Oh, no. I'm really sorry. He told me he was single. I didn't know he had a girlfriend, I swear. This is one really big misunderstanding. When you see Antoine, tell him that he should lose my phone number." Keisha smiled as Shawna turned to walk away.

Damn. Why the hell would Antoine go out with a bitch like that when he could have me? That chick's so tall, she could eat a bowl of soup off his head.

Antoine had been watching the exchange between Shawna and Keisha from his bedroom window, hoping Keisha would leave before he went downstairs. He couldn't hear their conversation, but their body language said enough. It was obvious Keisha was trying to start trouble. He rushed down the stairs to break up their little meeting, arriving just as Shawna was stomping away.

"Shawna. Where are you going? I thought we were supposed to go out." He caught up to her and grabbed her arm to slow her down.

"Look, don't touch me! Don't speak to me! Don't call me! Just run over there to your little girlfriend, where you belong!" she yelled, shaking her hand to free herself from his grasp.

"Girlfriend! What girlfriend?" He turned to Keisha, who was doing everything she could to avoid eye contact.

"Antoine, I don't know what she's talkin' about." Keisha pointed at Shawna. "I never told her that I was your girlfriend."

"Oh, you dirty liar!" Shawna shouted.

Antoine looked directly into Shawna's beautiful eyes. "Do you really think I would have asked you to come to my apartment if Keisha was my girlfriend? That woman is not my girlfriend. She's my landlord."

She wanted to believe him. Looking smugly at Keisha, she decided Keisha was jealous and had made up the story. Antoine definitely wouldn't have chased after her if Keisha were his woman. She decided to go on her date after all, even if it was only to get revenge on Keisha.

"Okay, Antoine, I believe you."

Without taking her eyes off Keisha, Shawna took Antoine's arm and led him down the street to her car. As they drove past Keisha, she was shouting something and shaking her fist. They couldn't hear through the windows, but they both knew it wasn't a friendly goodbye.

"I've had my eye on that man for too damn long to let you have him. This ain't over yet you gorilla-haired bitch!"

In the car Antoine and Shawna avoided discussing the incident but made lots of small talk. A half hour later they were in Flushing Meadow Park. Antoine spread a blanket out as Shawna unpacked the picnic basket. Amazed at the spread she had prepared, Antoine could not help thinking he had found a pot of gold.

"Most women throw a couple of sandwiches, some fried chicken, and a six-pack of beer in a shopping bag and call it a picnic. But, Shawna, you've outdone yourself. Look at all this great stuff. Shrimp cocktail, crackers with Brie and pâté, kiwi, and my favorite chocolate-covered strawberries. My God, you even have a wicker picnic basket. I don't know anyone who has a wicker picnic basket."

"You do now, handsome." She handed him a bottle of white wine and a corkscrew. "Will you open this?"

Antoine opened the bottle of white wine and poured it into two crystal goblets. He handed a glass to Shawna, who raised hers in the air.

"I would like to propose a toast," she said gleefully "Here's to the start of something beautiful."

"I'll second that," he replied, gazing in her eyes as he dipped a chocolate-covered strawberry into some whipped cream and fed it to her. Unfortunately their romantic moment was soon interrupted by an obnoxious voice.

"Shawna, is that you, girl? Girl, I hardly recognized you with them braids in your hair. What you doin' out here?" A large, voluptuous woman walked toward them. "Henry, Henry, come on over here, sweetie. You remember Shawna, don't you?"

A very short, baldheaded black man approached and greeted them in an unusually high-pitched voice. Before Shawna could answer, his female companion was talking again.

"Girl, I ain't seen you since the coon died. You still workin' at the club?" She shook her hips and breasts for emphasis. "Thank God I don't need to work in there no more. My Henry takes good care of me. Don't you, sweetie?"

She spun around, not waiting for Henry to answer. She was showing off her new skintight tiger-print jumpsuit.

What a hootchie, Antoine thought, noticing her outfit was two sizes too small and accentuated bulges in all the wrong places.

"You know, Henry bought me the matching bra and panties too. But he don't like me to wear the bra." She laughed as she shook her large breasts.

Unable to take any more, Antoine stood up to introduce himself. He hoped to shut the woman up for a few seconds. The large woman never gave him a chance, because as soon as he stood, the woman looked Antoine up and down.

"Mmm! Mmm! Mmm! Girl, where did you find this handsome man? Damn, he's fine. You done gone and found yourself a triple-A number-one stud, haven't you?"

Embarrassed now, Shawna finally interrupted her friend by introducing her to Antoine.

"Antoine, this is Lola and her friend Henry. They're friends of mine from work."

Lola interrupted once again. "Friend? Henry ain't my friend no more, girl. He's my fiancé. We're getting married, ain't we, sweetie?"

"That's right, baby. But we got to go now. I need to get home for my treatment." Henry squeaked in his cartoonlike voice.

"That's right. This man got asthma so bad, when he wants to get some, I gotta always be on top." She patted Henry's balding head. Henry pulled on Lola's arm to signal it was time to leave, but before he could make a step, Lola's eyes fell on the feast spread out on the picnic blanket.

"Shrimp! I love me some shrimp. You don't mind if I have some, do you?" She had already poured half the bowl into her greedy hand. With her mouth full of shrimp she said, "Well, girl, I gots to go. You take care of this here fine man. Oh, and good luck with your operation, girl."

Shawna cut her eyes at Lola as she walked away. For a few seconds both Shawna and Antoine sat in silence. Neither was quite sure what to say, until Antoine broke the silence.

"What operation, Shawna?" he asked, needing to have an answer.

"It's nothing to worry about, Antoine. I'm just having some minor cosmetic surgery done in the spring." Shawna tried to reply as casually as she could. Their date had already had such a rocky start, she didn't want her surgery to become a major issue. She put both hands on her breasts. "They're a little small, don't you think? So I'm having breast implants put in."

Imagining Shawna with larger breasts made Antoine smile. She was already so beautiful, he could just imagine how perfect she would be with implants. He leaned over to give her an understanding kiss, figuring they could discuss it later. Shawna was relieved that he had not made a bigger deal out of her revelation. The rest of their picnic was picture perfect.

9

TYRONE AND SYLVIA

Slamming the door as she stepped out of the taxi, Sylvia rushed across the parking lot of the Sheraton Hotel in Flushing. She was nearly forty-five minutes late for her sex date with Tyrone and was cursing under her breath. Traffic had been terrible coming from Long Island. She hoped Tyrone would still be waiting for her.

She entered the hotel's elaborately decorated lobby and maneuvered herself as carefully as she could, considering the slight buzz she had. She'd purposely had quite a few cocktails trying to calm her nerves before meeting with Tyrone. Heading straight for the bar, she scanned the faces of the bar patrons, hoping to recognize Tyrone from the description he'd given her over the phone. The memory of their conversation brought a smile to her face. He'd seemed so sweet and genuinely interested as she talked about her daughter and her life. It also impressed her when he spoke with such great love about his own girls.

As Sylvia scanned the men in the room, she saw only two black men. One was short with light skin and freckles and was with a woman, so Sylvia assumed he was not Tyrone. The other black man was tall and thin, just as Tyrone had described himself. She liked what she saw.

Tyrone had been watching Sylvia since she walked into the bar. He knew it was her right away, because she was wearing a lavender dress, as she said she would. He noticed how flattering the dress was on Sylvia's curvaceous figure and smiled approvingly. She wasn't the overweight housewife he had expected her to be and was relieved. As Sylvia approached, he leaned back against the bar and smiled nonchalantly.

"Well, hello, pretty lady. I'm glad you made it. Can I buy you a drink?"

Although she knew she had already had enough, Sylvia decided one more drink might just make things less awkward for her. She asked the bartender for a gin and tonic, then sat next to Tyrone at the bar.

"I'm very sorry I'm late, Tyrone. I had to attend a cocktail party at the Ridgewood Estate." The bartender arrived with her drink, and she sipped it before continuing. "I really planned on being out of there on time, but I had to stop Bernard from chasing Councilwoman Jordan's son." Tyrone put his drink down and stared at Sylvia in disbelief.

"You know Bernard Ridgewood, as in Bernard Ridgewood of Ridgewood Galleries? As in owner of the largest African American art gallery in the country?"

"Yes," she answered matter-of-factly, taking a long swig of her drink. "Although, his gallery's actually the second biggest. Walter Black's out in L.A. is bigger, but he carries the work of white artists too."

Tyrone still couldn't believe his ears. This woman he was about to sleep with knew someone who quite possibly could change his life.

"You know, Sylvia, I'm an artist myself. I've been tryin' to get Bernard Ridgewood to look at my work for years. Do you think you could hook a brother up?"

The alcohol had made her a lot bolder, so she teased him. "I don't know, it depends on how much a brother hooks me up. Take care of me and I'll take care of you."

Of course, she had no way of knowing if Tyrone's artwork was any good, since she had never seen it. But she smiled wickedly, thinking that if he was any good in bed, she might be willing to pull a few strings for him.

Tyrone liked the naughty smile on her face and decided to continue this little flirtatious game with her. He leaned close as he asked, "Penny for your thoughts?"

"Honestly?" She sighed. "I was just thinking about how much you reminded me of my high school sweetheart."

"Is that good or bad?"

"Oh, it's good. It's definitely good. I was thinking maybe I should take you upstairs and get from you what I should have gotten from him twenty years ago."

"What if I refuse to go upstairs with you? Maybe I'm not that kind of guy," he teased.

"Well, Tyrone, I guess I would have to convince you that you are that kind of guy," she said, placing her hand on his upper thigh and caressing him.

"So you think you can convince me, huh? Well, give me three good reasons why I should go upstairs with you." Tyrone's breathing became a little faster as Sylvia's hand rose a little higher on his thigh. Things were moving a lot quicker than he expected.

"Three reasons, huh? Okay, number one, tonight might be the only chance you get to sleep with me. Number two, I'm horny as hell and might just do anything you ask. And number three, your little friend is not so little anymore." She laughed as her hand slid between his legs.

"Oh, boy." He sighed, removing Sylvia's hand and placing it on top of the bar. "Those are pretty damn good reasons, especially number three. But we have plenty of time for that. Why don't we have some dinner, then we'll take our little party upstairs."

Sylvia regained her composure and realized she might be going a little too fast.

"You're right. I haven't eaten all day, and I could use something other than alcohol in my stomach. I would hate to be so drunk that I miss something." She took Tyrone's hand and led him to the restaurant on the other side of the lobby, requesting a quiet table in the corner. They studied the menus silently for a few minutes.

"So, what do you think you'd like to have?" she asked.

"Shoot, I really don't know. I mean, I know what I'd like to order, but these prices are a little steep."

"Go ahead and order whatever you want, honey. My husband's paying for dinner and our room." She pulled out a gold MasterCard and they both laughed. When the waiter returned to take their orders, Tyrone asked for filet mignon and Sylvia ordered a pasta dish and the most expensive wine on the list.

While they waited, the two exchanged some small talk about Tyrone's job, and he shared several funny stories about his students. Before long their dinners arrived, and once he started eating, Tyrone barely lifted his head from the plate. Sylvia, on the other hand, was too nervous to touch her food, so she tried to engage him in conversation.

"So, why does a good-looking guy like you need to use a date line?"

Tyrone barely looked up from his dinner as he spoke. "Don't take this wrong, but I'm a player." He swallowed another bite of the tender filet. "The date line puts variety in my life."

"Why do I have the feeling you're not telling me the entire truth?" She chuckled. "Come on, Tyrone. What's your real story? I promise it won't change my mind about sleeping with you."

Finally putting down his fork, Tyrone looked into Sylvia's eyes and answered honestly. He had barely admitted his true reasons to himself until then.

"Okay, a friend of mine met what seems to be the perfect woman from the line the other night. I gave him all kind of shit about it, until I met her. I guess now I'm jealous. I'm gonna be thirty years old, and I haven't had a meaningful relationship since I was seventeen. It's about time I grew up and maybe even settled down."

"So, you're looking for the perfect woman, are you?" She was taken aback by the sincerity of his answer. They were strangers. He didn't owe her anything, but he was already being more honest than her husband had been in years.

"Well, I don't know if I'm looking for perfection. I just want to find someone I'm compatible with. Someone I can share my art with. Someone who's going to grow with me. You know what I mean?"

"Yeah, I suppose I do," she practically whispered as her eyes welled up with tears. "I suppose once upon a time my husband and I were compatible, but we drifted apart a long time ago. I just never realized it until now. We were never really meant to be together anyway."

"I don't understand. What do you mean?" Tyrone felt genuine sympathy for the pain Sylvia's marriage was causing her.

"I met my husband on the night of my senior prom. I had been with my boyfriend, Keith, since the first week of high school." She smiled, amazed as she noticed again the remarkable resemblance between Tyrone and Keith. "The night of the prom was supposed to be our big night. I was finally going to give him my virginity. I was pretty nervous, so I was giving Keith a really hard time most of the night. When the prom came to an end, we went to this beach party over in Far Rockaway. Keith was really impatient and kept pestering me to leave so we could finally make love. I was too nervous to go, so I told him I was having a good time. I suggested he should get a motel room and I would be ready to leave when he returned."

"So did he leave you there?"

"Are you kidding? He was so happy that he'd be getting some soon, he jumped into his car and sped off to the motel in about two seconds flat. I went back to the party. It could not have been ten minutes later, I felt someone cover my eyes. I assumed it was Keith. Then he kissed me, but it wasn't like Keith had ever kissed me before. You know the kind of kisses that make you weak in the knees?"

"Mmm-hmm. I sure do. So your boy Keith was trying out some new moves, huh?"

"It was like a movie or a dream or something. I opened my eyes, and there he was, the most gorgeous man I had ever seen. I will always remember the way the full moon shone down on his shoulders. He looked like some kind of mythological god."

Sylvia paused. She could tell by the look on Tyrone's face that he was in suspense.

"Who was this mystery man, Sylvia?"

Sylvia was enjoying his attention, so she kept him in suspense a little longer and continued her narrative.

"So there I am with my arms around this gorgeous man I've never met before, making out in the moonlight, and he whispers in my ear, 'Come on, let's go for a ride.' Well, now I'm speechless. I can't believe this hunk wants me to go for a ride with him. Somehow, though, I manage to say yes, and the rest is history." Her voice was flat.

"What do you mean, history?"

"I lost my virginity and conceived my daughter all on that very same night," she replied.

"Damn! Ain't that a bitch," Tyrone said, his eyes bugged out. "So that's how you met that no-good fool of a husband, huh? What ever happened to your boy, Keith?"

"Keith died two years ago from AIDS."

"Oh, damn. You mean the brother turned gay after you left him?" Tyrone nearly shouted.

"At first I thought so, but I spoke to him years later and found out I was wrong. Even in high school Keith thought he might be gay but didn't want to face it. That's why he wanted to make love to me. He thought it was a way to prove to himself that he really liked women. So after I left him for my husband, he just admitted to himself what he had known all along." Sylvia had a faraway look in her eyes as she recalled her friend.

"That's deep." Tyrone wasn't sure what else to say. It was clear that this man had meant a great deal to Sylvia, and he didn't want to upset her. "At least you got to clear the air with him, huh?"

"Yes, actually we became good friends after a while. It was he who introduced me to Bernard Ridgewood. They had been lovers for years before his death."

"I'm sorry for your loss."

"Thank you," Sylvia said, noticing his plate was empty. She was eager to end this depressing conversation. "I don't know about you, but I'm ready to go upstairs. Would you like to join me?"

He knew he would regret his words when he got home, but Tyrone could not go through with his original plan. Sylvia was not just another screw for him now. She had shown him a little bit of her soul, and he didn't want to use her.

"Sylvia you're a beautiful, intelligent woman whose had some really bad experiences with love. You don't need to sleep with me for revenge."

"But, Tyrone, I want—" He put his finger to her lips to hush her.

"I do too. But that's not what you need. You need someone to make love to you, to treat you the way you deserve to be treated. Most of all, you need a friend."

Sylvia sat in silence as a single tear slid down her cheek. She tried to wipe it off, but his words stopped her.

"I don't know who your husband is, but he's a fool, and I honestly feel sorry for him. If he could see you the way I see you now, he would hold you and never let you go."

Sylvia couldn't help it now. The tears were streaming down her face.

"I'm about to ask you something that I really have no right to ask, especially since you're married." He walked around to her side of the table, and she stood up so that they were face-to-face. "Let me show you how fun life is again, Sylvia. I don't want you to give in right away. I want to earn the privilege of making love with you."

They embraced delicately. After a long pause she leaned forward and whispered to him.

"Tyrone, what you just said has to be the most beautiful thing I have ever heard from a man in my life. I want to thank you for not letting me make a foolish mistake. It's good to know someone who can be honest."

"I'll always be there for you." He slowly began to kiss away her tears until his lips found hers. Sylvia sighed. In her twenty years of marriage she had never felt a kiss so tender and caring.

10

KEVIN

Kevin was happy to find a parking space in front of his house but not surprised. He had taken Antoine's advice on how to solve his personal New York City parking crisis. He made an anonymous call to the city parking violations bureau. Looking around, he saw that the old junkers his landlord seemed to collect were no longer taking up all the available parking around the building. They were all gone, probably towed by the city. He was sure he was not the only tenant who would be happy. This parking solution was like a bonus at the end of an already wonderful day.

Shutting off the car's engine, he closed his eyes and replayed the day's events. He had been nervous for his date with Alicia, unlike their previous eight. After two months together Alicia had decided it was time for him to meet her son, Michael, and Kevin was not quite sure he was ready. Fortunately his worry had been unnecessary. Michael was a nice, respectful kid and they had gotten along well. The three of them went to church, then went to see *Wild Wild West,* the adventure movie starring Will Smith.

Kevin realized he was happy for the first time since he'd left basketball behind. He had a job that he was starting to enjoy and a beautiful woman he planned on spending a lot of time with. As he placed the key in the lock, he heard the phone ringing inside his apartment. He glanced at his watch and knew exactly who was calling. He raced inside and grabbed the receiver.

"Hi, Mama. Sorry I didn't call you earlier," he panted.

"How'd you know it was me? And why you so out of breath, boy? You got some woman over there?"

"No, Mama. There's no one here but me. But I did go on a date with my new girlfriend." Kevin laughed, feeling like a teenager again.

"You got yourself a new girlfriend? Thank you, Jesus. What's she like, Kevin? She ain't one of them easy girls like you used to go with, is she?"

"No, Mama, she's not fast." He couldn't help but add, "Actually Alicia's a nice, churchgoin' girl. We went to church together this morning before we went out."

"Hallelujah! That girl done got my boy back in church? I like her already," Mama said seriously. "Now, baby, you better be careful, 'cause even those church girls can be bad news. You remember Bertha Mae Washington's two girls, Emily and Anna, don't you?"

"Yeah, I think so," Kevin mumbled, remembering how wild they were in bed. He'd had them both.

"Well, they got seven children between them, by five different daddies, and ain't neither one of them married! And got the nerve to be Sunday-school teachers! Now, how you gonna be a Sunday-school teacher acting like that?" Mama sucked her teeth in disgust. "At least I got sense 'nough to keep your sistah Whitney and my cute little grandbabies, Joe and Martha, home on Sunday!"

Kevin shook his head as he grinned. His mother could be such a hypocrite.

"Don't worry, Mama, she's already made it known that sex is not in our near future."

"You see? That's good. You done found yourself a real woman, Kevin. She respects herself." Mama was happy. "You don't find too many girls that respect themselves these days. You just treat her right, like your mama taught you, and you two will have a nice family."

Suddenly Kevin was nervous but figured now was as good a time as any to approach the subject of Michael.

"Speaking of family, Mama, before you go tellin' everyone at church about Alicia, there's something you should know."

Mama gasped. "Oh, Lord, baby. Please don't tell me the girl's married. Mimmie Wilks's grandbaby's been strayin' on her husband. There is nothin' worse a woman can do."

"No, Mama, Alicia's not married. She has a seven-year-old son. A wonderful seven-year-old son. I just met him today, Mama, and he's really a great kid."

"Well, if she's got a baby, where's her baby's daddy? And why ain't she married to him?"

Kevin considered making up a story that would please his mother but decided against it. "Things didn't work out with her child's father, Mama. He was beating her so bad, she finally had to leave."

"Dear Jesus, that poor child. Nobody should have to go through that," Mama said with compassion. "But, Kevin, you be careful. You don't know these women like I do. Just make sure she ain't after you to raise her son."

Kevin was amazed at how quickly Mama's emotions could bounce back and forth. "Don't worry, Mama, Alicia and I both want to take things very slowly. I'm being careful, but I know she's not looking for anything more than companionship right now."

"All right, baby. Mama's glad you're not rushin' things. Well, I guess I won't be meeting her anytime soon. But you're still comin' home to see me during your Christmas break, aren't you?"

"Yes, Mama, I'm coming down on Christmas morning," he said, imagining himself sitting at her table for Christmas dinner with his friends and family.

"Are you still bringing those boys with you? What's their names? Anthony and Tony?"

Kevin laughed, "Antoine and Tyrone, Mama. And, yes, they're coming with me. We're gonna try to drive my car. I just hope the car makes it down there. I can't wait to see you."

"Don't you worry. Your car will make it, because I know the Lord would not make ol' Mamie Brown miss her son on Christmas Day."

Kevin was tired. He suppressed a yawn. "Okay Mama. I guess it's time for me to go, so I can get up for work in the morning. I love you."

"I love you too, baby, but now that you mention work, there's something I want to talk to you about before you go."

"What is it, Mama?"

"There's another letter here from that Mr. Hirschfield. Ain't he that sports agent who's been trying to help you out?"

Kevin rolled his eyes. "Yes, Mama. He's the one who got me the tryout with the Charlotte Hornets."

"So, baby, why won't you answer his calls? I'm gettin' tired of making up excuses for you to all these coaches who call here."

"Mama, I don't need you to lie for me. Why don't you just tell them I'm not interested? My life is different now. Basketball is my past."

"Now, baby. I know you better than that. You love basketball more than the air we breathe. I know you had your heart set on the NBA, but why you gonna let that stop you? These people from the foreign teams really want you. Why don't you just go over there and try it?"

Kevin lost all confidence. "First of all, Mama, who's to say I'd even make the team if I went? And what would you do if I moved off to Europe?"

"Oh, baby." Mama laughed warmly. "Your old mama has already survived your move to the big city. I'll be just fine. I just want you to do what makes you happy."

"Mama, you're the best. But I'm working on being happy right now. I really think Alicia could be the key."

"All right, baby. I love you, and I hope you're right about what you're doing. But I'm going to hold on to this letter for you, and I want you to promise me you'll keep thinking about this. We can talk about it more when you come down here for Christmas."

"I'll think about it, Mama. I love you."

"Kevin?"

"Yes, Mama?"

"I'm glad you're not lonely anymore."

Kevin put the receiver back on the phone and headed into the kitchen, switching on the light. He stared at the picture of him and his mother hanging on the refrigerator. It was taken at his college graduation as Mama adjusted his cap and gown. Her face was glowing with pride. Kevin's heart swelled with love as he looked at the photo. He said a quick prayer that someday he would have children of his own so he could give them all the love and support that Mama gave to him. As he went off to bed, Kevin imagined himself with Alicia and Michael as a family.

11

KEVIN AND ALICIA

Kevin and Alicia flirted with each other across the table as they finished their meal. They had been together for three months to the day and had been celebrating with Antoine and Shawna. Shawna had left them at eight-thirty so she wouldn't be late for work. Antoine tried to play the gentleman by leaving with her, but Alicia knew from the expression on his face that he wasn't a happy camper.

"You know, Kevin, Shawna seemed a little weird, and your friend Antoine has a major attitude problem. Why was he so angry at her for having to work?"

"What do you mean? He didn't have an attitude."

"Oh, please, Kevin. You men never notice these things, do you? It was written all over his face."

Finishing the last bite of beef and broccoli, Kevin pushed his plate away. "Yeah, I suppose you're right. He didn't seem too happy. But look at it from his point of view. Shawna's always working. They've been going together as long as we have, and Antoine's never spent a Friday or Saturday night with her where she hasn't rushed off to work."

"Damn, that is a bit much. But what's she supposed to do? Quit her job? It's not like he's going to support her."

"Nobody's asking her to quit her job, baby. But Antoine would like her to take a night off every once in a while. I mean, she does have a day job too."

"I didn't know that." Alicia realized she really hadn't learned much about Shawna in the two hours they'd spent with the couple. "Now that you mention it, she was awfully quiet when I asked her what she did for a living. What does she do?"

Kevin laughed. "Well, during the day she works as a manager at a bookstore. But Tyrone's got me convinced she's a stripper at night."

Alicia's eyes got a little wider. "A stripper!! I knew there was something strange about that woman. She kept staring at me all through dinner."

"She probably thought you were cute. Most strippers go both ways. You're not going to leave me for her, are you? Damn, baby, that would really be embarrassing." Kevin couldn't help but laugh.

"Baby, let's get one thing straight. I know I haven't given you any yet, but I'm strictly dickly. Got it?"

"Okay, okay. Don't take things so serious." Kevin laughed. "Get this. She's been telling Antoine that she works as a makeup and costume lady at a strip club called the Men's Club. But she also told him that she's a virgin."

As the waiter approached, Kevin pushed his chair back so he could clear their table, then asked the waiter to bring their check. Alicia was silent until the waiter left the table.

"I'm tellin' you, Kevin, there's something strange about that woman. I can't put my finger on it, but I'm telling you that woman is weird."

"You might be right, baby, but all I know is ain't no virgin working in a strip club."

"Shoot. I'm no virgin, and I'd still be too modest to work in a place like that. But you never know. She's weird enough to be both. Maybe she really is just doing makeup. Besides, don't all those dancers have to have huge breasts? Shawna was kind of small up top." Alicia smiled.

"Only in white strip clubs. You've got to remember, brothers are into asses. And Shawna does have a nice enough ass to make some good money," he teased.

"What were you doing looking at her ass anyway?" she teased him back.

"You know, I never said her ass was nicer than yours." Kevin laughed as he placed some money on the table.

"Thanks. Maybe I need to go over to the Men's Club and make a little extra money myself."

"If you wanna take off your clothes, do it in the privacy of your own home. I'll be your biggest and only customer." They both laughed as they left the restaurant.

Wrapping their coats tightly around themselves as protection from the cold December air, they walked four blocks from Mr. Wong's restaurant to Alicia's apartment. The storefronts were lit with Christmas decorations, and Christmas music was playing from the bodega next to her building.

"I love this time of year." She sighed. "I always thought Christmas was magical, and now that I have Michael, I love it even more. You should see his face when he opens his presents. There is nothing like the joy of a child at Christmas." She beamed. "I really wish you could be here to see it."

Putting his arms around Alicia, he pulled her close. "Now, baby. You know my mama would never forgive me if I didn't go to church with her on Christmas morning. She told you that herself on the phone last week, didn't she?"

"Yes, you're right. She even tried to get me to come down there with you." Alicia smiled.

"So why don't you?" He loved the idea of spending his holiday with both women.

"I can't. You know my whole family comes together at Christmas. Besides, I thought you said we could take Michael down there in February, during your school break."

"Okay. But you can't blame a brother for trying one more time, can you?"

Alicia gave him a big hug. "Well, at least we have two more days together before you have to leave. You know Michael's home from school on vacation now."

"I know. What would you like to do for the next couple of days?" Kevin planned to spend every possible second with them until he had to drive down to Virginia.

"Actually I was hoping you could spend a couple of hours with Michael tomorrow. I have some last-minute shopping to finish, and it's easier without him in the mall."

"Sure, baby. What time do you need me?"

"How about from eleven until three?" Alicia was appreciative that he was so willing to help her out.

"That's perfect. That way I can leave your place and go straight to the school to meet the bus with the basketball team."

"Where is your team going on December twenty-third? Aren't you already on vacation?"

He rubbed his hands together to keep them warm. "We're done with classes, but the team has one more weekend tournament to go to on Long Island. It's an annual thing."

"Oh, Kevin. They are so lucky to have someone as dedicated as you are." She took his hands to warm them.

"Baby, I'm really dedicated to only one thing, and it's you." He pulled her close and kissed her lips.

Alicia returned his passion, opening her mouth to let his tongue explore hers. Because of the intense heat building between them, both had forgotten they were standing in the frigid temperature. Their tongues and hands continued to explore each other, and Alicia's breathing was getting very heavy. Kevin noticed her excitement and thought the time might be right for them to take the relationship further.

"Do you think I could come upstairs tonight?" he asked breathlessly.

Suddenly Alicia's passion subsided, and she looked very seriously at Kevin.

"Oh, Kevin. I knew I shouldn't have let that go so far. Things got out of hand for a second, but I know I'm still not ready to go to bed with you."

"What else do I have to do to prove myself to you, Alicia? You know I love you."

Kevin's hands dropped to his sides. His body language expressed his hurt. Alicia felt terribly guilty but kept the promise she made to herself.

"I'll know when the time is right, Kevin. I promised myself a long time ago I wouldn't sleep with another man until I knew I was emotionally ready."

"So are you planning on filling me in when that time comes? Just how long do you think it will be for this thing to be right?"

Suddenly he realized how angry he had become and knew he better cool out. She had already had enough bad experiences with angry brothers. He didn't want to blow this. He laughed, trying to lighten the mood.

"A man can take only so many cold showers, you know."

"I'm sorry, Kevin." She looked at him, her eyes filled with sincerity.

"I know, baby, and you just take all the time you need. I'll be here when you're ready for me." Kevin took Alicia into his arms for a final embrace before she went upstairs.

"Alicia?"

Yes, Kevin."

"I love you."

"I love you too." Alicia believed him, and it made her feel safe.

12

ANTOINE AND KEISHA

Antoine and Shawna stood arguing in front of the two-family house where she lived. They'd been carrying on since they'd left the restaurant, and Antoine was getting fed up.

"I'm not going to say this again, Shawna. I want you to quit that fucking job at the Men's Club." The frustration showed on Antoine's face as the rare curse slipped through his lips.

"Look, Antoine, I'm not quitting my job," Shawna replied, angry. "And another thing, don't curse at me. I'm not that uneducated hussy Keisha that follows you around."

"I didn't curse. And why are you bringing her into this anyway?"

"Yes, you did curse. And I'm bringing her into it 'cause I don't like her, that's why. I don't like any woman who's trying to take my man. Matter of fact, I think you should move out of that apartment!" Shawna's voice was getting louder as they spoke.

"I'm not moving out of my apartment," Antoine said firmly. " I pay only five hundred dollars a month. Do you know how cheap that apartment is for a two-bedroom?"

"I really don't care, Antoine. If I have to quit my job, you're gonna move!" Porch lights came on as Shawna's volume increased.

"Some of us are trying to sleep!" a voice reminded them.

Shawna turned to see her sixty-five-year-old landlord standing in his doorway.

"Sorry, Mr. Good," she apologized sheepishly.

"I think it's about time you two took this inside, don't you?"

"Antoine, I have to get ready for work. Please don't be mad at me. I promise I'll call you during my break." She tried to kiss him, but he turned his head so her lips met his cheek.

"I'm not going to be home during your break. I'm going over to Benny's Bar to have a drink."

"Isn't that where Keisha hangs out? Please don't go over there, Antoine," she pleaded.

"Look, you don't have anything to worry about. I'm just gonna have a drink or two to relax. You never know. Maybe I'll run into some of the fellas."

He could tell she was jealous by the look on her face. Shawna was truly paranoid when it came to Keisha. He had no intention of cheating on her. He just hoped that now she'd understand how he felt when she went to work at the Men's Club every night.

The two of them spent a few more minutes trying to smooth things out, until Antoine felt comfortable enough to part. Then he caught a cab home, spending most of the ride brooding over his relationship. He was honestly looking forward to a nice stiff drink. After paying the cabdriver, Antoine walked directly to Benny's. Once inside, he took off his coat and searched the bar for some familiar faces. Seeing no one he recognized, he strolled over to the bar to order a drink.

"How you doing, Benny? Can I have a glass of your best brandy?"

"Sure, Antoine. I haven't seen you around in a while," the bartender replied. "Life got you down?" He handed Antoine his drink.

"Yeah, woman problems, Benny. You ever have a relationship with a woman who's never around?" Antoine took a sip before he continued. "My girlfriend's always working, and when she's not working, she's sleeping, 'cause she's too damn tired from work."

"I feel for you, brother. What's your girl do anyway?" Benny handed a drink to another customer, then turned back to Antoine.

"Well, she actually has two jobs. She works in a bookstore during the day. But at night she works in East Elmhurst. You ever heard of the Men's Club?"

"Yeah, I suppose I've been there once or twice." Benny chuckled.

"Well, she works there at night as a makeup artist."

"A makeup artist, huh? Now, ain't that original!" Benny laughed, turning to another bartender. "Hey, Jake, you ever heard of a makeup artist at the Men's Club?"

"Hell no! And I tended bar there for years," Jake shouted from the other end of the bar. "What they need makeup for? Ain't nobody looking at their faces."

Antoine gave Benny and Jake a fake smile after that crack and walked back to his table. Although he was a little angry about Jake's comment, he realized he shouldn't be upset. He'd thought the same thing himself when Shawna first told him she did makeup at the club. In fact, Tyrone had made it a part of his daily comic routine at work. Antoine was reminded daily that nobody seemed to believe the girls at the Men's Club had their faces done by an expert.

As he sat at his table, Antoine had a crazy idea. Maybe he should just go find out for himself what she was really doing there. He bit his lip and smirked, imagining her surprise when he walked in. Taking a long swig of his brandy, Antoine envisioned the confrontation they would have.

But the more he thought about it, the more he decided it really wasn't such a brilliant idea. His grandmother had always told him, be careful what you look for, 'cause you just might find it. His rational self had returned, and he decided he could wait until the time was right to work things out with Shawna. They had been dating for only a few months. There was always the possibility that she was telling him the truth. And even if she wasn't, he hoped that when she was comfortable enough with the relationship she would tell him everything he needed to know. Antoine wanted desperately to believe in the relationship.

After nursing his brandy and smoking his pipe for about ten more minutes, Antoine still wasn't feeling relaxed. He stood to walk over to the bar for another drink and was surprised to see Benny standing before him, drink in hand.

"Thanks, Benny. That's some service you provide here."

"This one's compliments of the lady at the bar." Benny pointed in the direction of the bar.

Antoine didn't remember seeing any ladies at the bar. Curiously he adjusted his glasses to see through the smoke-filled room. As his eyes began to focus, he saw Keisha. She was wearing a skintight red dress that revealed all of her ample cleavage.

"Here, Benny, send it back to her," Antoine told the bartender seriously.

"The lady wants to know if she can offer you an apology." Benny refused to take the drink out of Antoine's hand. "If I were you, Antoine, I'd stop worrying about that chick at the Men's Club and start thinking of a few ways Big Red over there can apologize. If you know what I mean." He winked at Antoine.

"What the hell. I wasn't going to be able to relax anyway," he said, gesturing for Keisha to walk over. "Besides, I have a few things I want to say to Ms. Keisha myself."

Keisha approached Antoine nervously. She left her usual attitude behind and was genuinely prepared to apologize. Antoine sensed the change in her body language and was confused, to say the least. He was prepared for another confrontation when he invited her over to the table.

"Hi, Antoine, it's been a long time since we spoke. I was hoping we could bury the hatchet. I really hate it when you walk away every time I try to talk to you," she said timidly.

Antoine figured Keisha was just putting on an act, so he ignored the sweetness in her voice and snapped at her.

"Yeah, well, I've been pretty busy with my new girlfriend, Shawna. Things are working out pretty well. No thanks to you." He rolled his eyes at her.

"I know, I know. That's what I wanted to apologize about." Keisha took a step closer and had trouble looking Antoine in the eye. "Do you mind if I sit down?"

Antoine pulled out a chair. "Keisha, why the hell did you tell Shawna I was your boyfriend?"

"I was jealous," she admitted, still avoiding eye contact. "I been trying to get you to go out with me for three years. You always said you were too busy. But you made time for her, Antoine. You're always making time for her, and that really hurt me. How come you couldn't make time for me?"

Antoine was blunt. He was not in the mood to be sympathetic. "I don't know, Keisha, but I really don't think you're my type. I'm really a pretty low-key guy, and you're a very vocal woman. I don't think I could date a gossip."

Keisha leaned forward in her chair and looked Antoine in the eye for the first time.

"I'm a businesswoman, Antoine. Part of running a successful beauty shop is being the local gossip. What do you think keeps all those girls coming back every week? Now, you're a smart guy. I would think you'd be able understand that."

"Hmm, I never thought of it that way." His frown softened just a bit.

"Well, it's a fact in my business. But when it comes to my personal life, I'm very discreet. And as far as being your type, that really hurts. One of the things I always admired about you was that you were honest. If you didn't want to go out with me, you should have just said so. It's not as if I'm the kind of person who would fly off the handle."

"Oh, you're not that kind of person, huh? Is that why I have fifteen stitches in my head from your hair dryer?" He rubbed the spot where she had cut his head.

"Listen. I'm not normally that crazy, but my cousin LaSondra is always doin' something stupid, and she just set me off that day. I worked on that woman's braids for six hours and *personally* went to Brooklyn to get the hair she wanted. Well, that bitch had the nerve to try to pay me in food stamps. Honey, I'm sorry, but I tried to shove that hair dryer straight up her ass."

Keisha's language made Antoine shake his head disapprovingly. "That still doesn't explain why you went off on me. I was trying to help you. Mrs. Dinkins in Three B was calling the police. But the next thing I know, you're on top of me, banging me in the head with that hair dryer."

"Antoine, when you came running up behind me, I thought you were LaSondra's man, Jeffrey, coming to beat me up. By the time I realized it was you, you were already knocked out cold." She couldn't help but let out a small laugh.

"Well, you sure can be dangerous." Antoine lightened up, rubbing his head as he laughed.

"Look, I just wanted to say I was sorry. I know your girlfriend's probably on her way, and I don't want to cause you any more problems." Her voice was kind as she stood to leave the table.

"Thanks, Keisha. I appreciate that, but Shawna's not coming over tonight." Keisha's apology had begun to change Antoine's opinion of her. He didn't really want to be alone and thought Keisha deserved a little kindness. "Listen, why don't I buy you a drink? It took a lot of courage to apologize like you did."

"Sure, I'd really like that." She smiled as she sat back down and moved her chair a few inches closer to Antoine's.

Time passed quickly as Keisha and Antoine enjoyed each other's company. Antoine was grateful for the chance to laugh, considering the mood he was in when he first arrived at Benny's. Now he was feeling relaxed as Benny approached the table.

"I'm getting ready to close in ten minutes. If you two would like one more round, now's the time to ask."

Keisha answered for both of them. "No thanks, Benny. I think we're getting ready to leave." Then she gathered the courage gained from a few drinks. "You know, Antoine, you should come back to my place for a nightcap."

During the course of their two hours together, Antoine had consumed several drinks and was not concerned with good judgment. He had been too busy admiring Keisha's cleavage. Although he still considered himself Shawna's man, his drunken state had weakened his defenses considerably.

"You don't have to tell me twice," he slurred, standing to help with her coat. They left Benny's arm in arm, helping each other stumble to the door.

Walking out into the frigid night air, Keisha leaned against Antoine, telling him they could keep each other warm. Antoine, hunched over against the wind, wrapped his arm around her as they walked toward the apartment building.

As she rummaged through her purse to find her keys, Keisha heard a horn from the street behind her. Turning around, she saw Shawna rolling down her car window.

"Antoine! Antoine! Over here, baby!"

Keisha couldn't believe her bad luck but followed Antoine to the car nonetheless.

"Hey, baby." Antoine gave his girlfriend a kiss as she stepped out of the car. He had all but forgotten about their earlier fight.

"Phew, you tryin' to get my man drunk and take advantage of him?" Shawna looked at Keisha, gritting her teeth.

"No, actually she was telling me how happy she is for us," Antoine replied.

Keisha was happy that Antoine had corrected Shawna but knew her plan to seduce him was ruined for the night. She took a few steps back and listened angrily to Shawna's love babble.

"Antoine, honey, I had to leave work early. I couldn't take you being mad at me. I love you so much, baby, and it's gonna kill me when you go to Virginia in two days."

Antoine took Shawna's hand, and Keisha was disappointed to see the happiness on his face. He turned to face her and didn't notice the disappointment in her eyes.

"Keisha, I want to thank you for tonight. I had a wonderful time," he said sincerely.

Antoine kissed Keisha's hand and let it go. As he headed for the door, he realized Shawna was not following. He turned around to see where she was.

"Come on, baby, let's get in the house out of this cold."

"I'll be right there, honey. I just have to get my bag out the car."

Shawna smiled and winked at Antoine. She waited until his back was turned, then looked Keisha straight in the eye. Her voice sounded evil as she hissed, "You better keep your hands off my man, bitch."

Keisha was stunned but tried to keep her voice down as she replied, "What you need to do is put those gorilla braids back in your hair and get rid of that ten-dollar weave, hooker."

Shawna gave her a sickeningly sweet smile and walked to her car. "If you'll excuse me, my man is waiting."

"You got him, let's see how long you can keep him." Keisha growled her challenge.

13

MAURICE

Maurice Johnson pulled his white Mercedes sports car in front of the Tropicana Casino Hotel. As he stepped out of his car, he handed the keys and a twenty to the head valet. "Good to see you again, Clif." He winked at the balding man.

"Good to see you too, Mr. Johnson." Clif watched a beautiful young woman step out of the passenger side. As she straightened her tight black miniskirt, he couldn't help but notice her ample breasts, which seemed even larger in proportion to her tiny waist. Clif thought she must be a model or something. He was impressed. Mr. Johnson always showed up with the finest women.

Champagne strutted in her spike heels to the front door and waited for Maurice, who was having a brief conversation with the attendant. She was in awe as she gazed at the elegant facade of the hotel. Maurice had the kind of money to visit a place like this so often that even the parking attendant knew him by name. She made a mental note to grab some matchbooks inside, because nobody back home would believe she had been there.

Catching a glimpse of herself in the mirror, Champagne made sure her long weave was still impeccable and opened one more button on her silk blouse. She wanted to be sure he saw enough to stay interested, because he was just the sugar daddy she'd been looking for. As she was checking herself out, Maurice walked up behind her and slipped a hand around her waist.

"You look beautiful," he whispered, grinning. Champagne couldn't help but notice he was staring at his own reflection in the mirror as he said it.

Taking her hand, Maurice led her through the door and into the stunning lobby. Captivated, she admired the lush floral arrangements placed throughout the huge room. She ran her hand over the back of the velvet sofa and admired the huge Oriental rug at her feet. The hotel was a far cry from the dingy old Men's Club where she worked.

"Shall we, my dear?" Maurice guided her up the escalator and into the casino. It seemed to Champagne that glamorous people filled every corner of the room. She stood tall with pride, walking in on the arm of this handsome man.

I wish that fool guidance counselor could see me now, she thought. *He had the nerve to tell me that every dropout becomes a welfare mother. Well, this dropout is about to be set for life.*

"Have you ever gambled before?" Maurice's question snapped Champagne out of her fantasy.

"I played a little twenty-one with my girls, but I've never gambled in a place like this." She tried not to sound as inexperienced as she was.

"Well, pretty lady, let me show you how to play craps. And I just know you're going to be my little good-luck charm."

"Now, Maurice, you know I'm just a working girl. I can't afford to be gambling my hard-earned money away." She giggled, batting her long eyelashes.

"No need to worry. I think this will get you into the game." He pulled a wad of bills from his pocket and handed two hundred dollars to Champagne. Squeezing her waist, he guided her toward the black-jack tables.

Champagne smiled to herself. With two hundred dollars in her hand, she was starting to like Maurice more and more, and the night was still young.

After an hour of gambling she discovered two hundred wasn't much in a casino. Maurice left the table with fifteen hundred dollars more than when he started. Champagne had not been so lucky. She lost the two hundred dollars in a matter of minutes.

Maurice took her hand. "I'm sorry your first try at the tables wasn't more successful, baby."

"That's okay. I'm not worried about me, 'cause I came here with nothing. I'm just sorry I lost your money."

"But I want to make sure you leave here with something to remember our first date, so why don't we go and find you something nice in a lobby store?"

They strolled arm in arm to the dress shop, where she halted, staring at an elegant black cocktail dress.

Maurice noticed the dress and also noticed that the shop was closed for the evening. He plotted his next move. As usual, his plan was falling into place almost too easily.

"Champagne, you really like that dress, don't you?"

She turned to face him.

"That is the most beautiful dress I have ever seen."

"You are the most beautiful woman I've ever seen, so I think that dress is made for you." He touched her face lightly, and his eyes wandered down her voluptuous body. "Why don't we go get that dress?"

"Maurice, do you realize how much that dress costs?" she asked, wide-eyed. "It's a Versace dress. I saw Naomi Campbell modeling one like it in *Vogue* last month. It's got to be at least a thousand dollars!"

Patting the breast pocket of his suit, he smiled. "I just happen to have fifteen hundred dollars right here. The only problem is, it looks like the shop is closed until tomorrow morning."

Champagne's pout let him know he had the fish on the hook. She couldn't hide her disappointment but didn't want to ruin the fantastic evening.

"Don't worry about it. Let's just go check out the gift shop." She tried not to sigh.

"I do have another idea, sweetheart. We could get a room, order room service, and pick up the dress tomorrow morning as soon as the dress shop opens."

Champagne's face brightened to a smile. She didn't hesitate to wrap her arms around Maurice's neck and plant a big kiss on his lips.

"Thank you so much, Maurice." She pressed her body against his.

"Oh, baby, this is nothing. Nothing at all." He slid his hands a little lower around her hips.

As they finished the last few bites of their lobster dinner, Maurice poured another glass of white wine for himself and Champagne. He took a sip and gazed at her.

"So tell me. Why did you become a stripper?"

She put down her glass and looked him straight in the eye.

"I'm a high school dropout with two choices. It's either work a minimum-wage job and always be struggling, or strip for a hundred dollars an hour. Which would you choose?"

"Fair enough. It's not that I have a problem with it, it's just that I don't know much about it. I've never really been to a strip club," Maurice fibbed.

"Get outta here! I didn't think there were still men like that. So if you don't know that much about it, what do you want to know?"

"Well, why don't you just show me what you do?" He gave her a sly smile. He knew it was time to make his final move.

Without missing a beat she walked to the radio next to the bed. She searched for a station that played R&B and stopped the dial when she heard the first few lines of Marvin Gaye's "Sexual Healing."

"This is perfect." She laughed as she turned and took a few seductive steps toward Maurice. He pushed his chair away from the table and took a seat on the bed, where he had a full view of Champagne as she started to gyrate her hips.

Loosening his tie, Maurice showed his approval as she began to slowly unbutton her silk blouse.

"Mmm, baby, you sure know how to turn a man on."

"You ain't seen nothing yet," she purred as her blouse slid down her shoulders and dropped to the floor. She ran her hands up her hips, then over the fullness of her breasts, which were covered by a black lace bra. Reaching behind her back, she unhooked the bra and bent over slightly, so Maurice could see her breasts swinging as the bra fell forward.

As she continued the seductive sway of her hips, Champagne caressed her long, smooth neck and loosened the clip in her hair, which fell in soft waves to her shoulders. She adjusted to the beat of a new song and reached to unzip her skintight skirt. Maurice sat up a little on the bed.

"Goddamn! You're not wearing any panties. That's so fucking kinky."

"You like it, don't you? Well, you haven't seen kinky yet." She danced closer and shook her full hips in front of him.

He put his hands on her hips and pulled her nearer. She kissed him full on the lips, letting her tongue explore his mouth as she stood straddling his legs. Reaching down, she unzipped his pants and released his throbbing penis. He leaned back and let out a sigh of pleasure. Sliding herself down onto Maurice, Champagne began to gyrate in his lap.

When I get done with him, she thought, *he's gonna wanna give me the world.*

Two hours later Maurice woke and glanced across the bed at Champagne to be sure she was still asleep. He was reassured by her deep breathing. She would be asleep for hours. He slipped out from under the covers. Tiptoeing across the room, he dressed in the bathroom. He inspected his image in the mirror to be sure there were no lipstick stains, then checked his watch.

Shit. It's almost two, and it's going to take me at least two hours to get home. Sylvia's going to have a fucking fit.

Sneaking past the bed, Maurice stopped to take one more look at Champagne. Even in her sleep she looked good. He considered waking her for round two and maybe even giving the girl a ride home. The thought passed quickly.

Nah. Let her get herself home. She's just another whore willing to do anything for a guy with some money.

He slipped out of the room, hoping his wife would be sound asleep by the time he got back to New York.

14

KEVIN AND ALICIA

Kevin and Michael had spent an enjoyable afternoon at Laser World playing laser tag and eating pizzaburgers while Alicia went shopping with one of her girlfriends. Although the prospect of becoming attached to this child was very frightening to Kevin, he had become very fond of his girlfriend's son. All his worries about Michael trying to make things difficult for his "daddy's replacement" turned out to be unfounded. Michael hadn't shown a hint of anxiety about his mother having a new boyfriend and actually seemed happy to have a man to spend time with him. This was something his own father didn't seem too interested in doing, so Kevin was glad to fill that void. He was looking forward to introducing Michael to Mama in the near future.

The two sat contentedly in Alicia's living room, waiting for her to return from the mall. As they waited, they played video games. Kevin's lack of skill was evident in the number of times Michael had beaten him in less than an hour. Each time he beat Kevin, Michael would do a victory dance. After his final win he immediately dropped the game's joystick, jumped up on the sofa, and raised his hands triumphantly.

"I'm the greatest! The greatest of all time!" he yelled, laughing at Kevin.

Kevin tackled the boy, and they began to play-wrestle on the sofa until the phone rang. Michael jumped up when he heard the phone.

"Hello?"

"Hey, baby," Alicia said, "have you been a good boy?"

"Yes, Mom."

"What'd you guys do today?"

"We went to Laser World. Then Uncle Kevin bought me this cool video game called Legends of the Boxing Ring. And my Mike Tyson beat the shit out of his Muhammad Ali."

"Michael! What did I tell you about using that kind of language? Wait until I get home. I'm gonna tear your butt up."

"But, Mom, Aunt Teresa uses that word all the time," he pleaded.

"And if you were her son, I'm sure she'd let you too. Now put Kevin on the phone and go to your room. I'll be home in about an hour."

Taking the phone, Kevin watched the boy mope to his room. "I hope you're not as mad with me as you are with him."

"I'm not mad at him." She sighed. "I'm really mad at myself for letting my sister talk like that around him. But that's neither here nor there. How'd it go today?"

"It went very well until about half an hour ago."

"Oh?" she asked, concerned. "What did he do?"

"He didn't do anything except hurt my ego."

"Kevin, what the hell are you talking about?"

"I was trying to explain to Michael how much better Muhammad Ali was than Mike Tyson. But your son wouldn't believe me. He kept saying his friend Theo had Legends of the Boxing Ring and Mike Tyson always beats Muhammad Ali. Well, to be brief, he conned me into buying Legends of the Boxing Ring, and, as your son so eloquently put it, 'Mike Tyson beat the shit out of Muhammad Ali,' eleven damn times."

"Oh, you poor dear." Alicia chuckled. "Listen, I'll be home in about an hour. I'm going to pick up some Chinese. Are you gonna stay for dinner?"

"Damn, I wish I could. But . . ."

"But!"

"Baby, I told you I had to go to that basketball tournament."

Alicia relaxed. "You're right, I forgot. Well, what time are you coming back? We should get together after that."

"I can't, baby. I figured that since I would be back late, we wouldn't be able to see each other. I made plans with the fellas to work out and go to a bar over in Antoine's neighborhood."

"Dammit, Kevin. You're going to spend the whole Christmas break with them." She didn't mean to sound whiny, but she really wanted to see her man.

"I know, baby, but a promise is a promise."

"Okay, then, make me a promise. Promise me that you'll spend tomorrow evening and New Year's Eve with me."

"No problem," he answered without hesitation.

"All right, let me go before this cell phone bill bankrupts me. Don't let Michael eat any junk food before I get home, okay? Oh, and, Kevin, I love you."

"I love you too, honey." He paused before clearing his voice to continue. "Ah, Alicia, one more thing before you hang up."

"What is it, sweetheart?"

"Your ex, Trevor, called twice." His voice was flat. The calls had disturbed him, inciting his jealousy, and he hoped there was a valid explanation to allay his fears.

Alicia nearly dropped the phone. "What the hell did he want?" she barked.

"I have no idea, baby. He just said he wanted to talk to you."

"I hope he's calling to tell me he has half the money for Michael's bike. I'm getting tired of him neglecting his son!" Alicia realized she was yelling at Kevin. "I'm sorry, baby, I shouldn't be yelling. That triflin' nigga is not your problem. I'll see you in a bit. Bye."

"Bye," Kevin said, slamming the phone down. Alicia's reaction, although not favorable toward Trevor, didn't do much to relieve his anxiety. He wished he had asked Alicia how Trevor got her number in the first place.

Michael was looking through a comic book when Kevin walked into his room.

"You okay, kid?" Kevin asked, concerned.

"I'm okay," Michael whined. "I just hate my mom sometimes."

"Come on, Michael," Kevin said in his best fatherly tone. "You don't mean that. Your mother loves you more than life itself."

"Oh, yeah? Then how come she's gonna give me a beatin' when she comes home?"

"Maybe because you deserve it, Michael. You know better than to curse like that."

"I said I was sorry. But you watch. She's still gonna get me." Michael pouted.

"Well, that's what mothers do sometimes to teach their children lessons."

"Uncle Kevin, people shouldn't teach lessons by hitting, right?"

"I think it depends on the situation. Why? Who told you that?"

"My mom. She said it right after my dad gave her a beating for coming home late once."

Kevin winced at the thought of Alicia being hit. "I understand where you're coming from, little man. But this is a little different.

What your dad did to your mom was abusive." Kevin hesitated, not wanting to overstep any boundaries. "Look, I promise not to let your mom spank you this time, but you have got to stop cursing. All right?"

"Okay," Michael said with a devilish grin. Suddenly Kevin felt as if the boy had manipulated him.

"Uncle Kevin, are you and Mommy going to get married?"

"Right now your mom and I are just very good friends trying to get to know each other." The question had surprised Kevin. "Why? Would you like it if we got married?"

"Yeah. You're pretty cool, and you don't treat me like a little kid." Michael smiled.

"And you think that's good enough reason for me to marry your mom?"

"That, and the fact that you're big enough to protect my mom and me from my dad." As he said this, goose bumps formed on Michael's arms.

"Your dad really scares you, doesn't he?"

"Sometimes. What about you, Uncle Kevin? Does he scare you?"

Michael seemed to be searching for some reassurance. He was at that stage when young boys start imitating the behaviors of grown men. He wanted to act grown, but when it came to his father, he was still a scared child.

"No, he doesn't scare me, Michael, but if I ever get the chance to have five minutes alone with him, I bet he'd be pretty damn scared of me," Kevin spat out rather confidently. "Now, enough about your father. Why don't you give me another chance to beat you in the boxing ring?" Kevin stood up and headed toward the living room.

"Can we open the ice cream you brought now?" Michael asked.

"I'm sorry, little man. Your mom said no junk food before she gets home."

"Uncle Kevin, are you going to let a girl tell you what to do?"

Now Michael was testing the male-bonding thing. Kevin couldn't believe the young boy was doing this. It was obvious he was trying to manipulate Kevin.

"Look, Mike, don't try to play games with me, all right? Your mother said no junk food, and that's final."

"My name's Michael, not Mike," he huffed. He folded his arms across his chest and stuck out his lower lip in a pout, hoping Kevin would give in. When he didn't, Michael tried another approach.

"What if I tell you about Mommy and Daddy having sex last night after you left?" he said suddenly. "Will you give me some ice cream then?"

"I can't believe you just said that about your mother." Kevin shook his head in disbelief. "Maybe you do need that spanking after all. Lying is one thing, but lying on your mother? That's unforgivable."

Michael was frightened by the way the veins in Kevin's neck popped out as he spoke. In a panic, he jumped up.

"I'm not lying to you, Kevin! I can prove it to you."

Running into his mother's room, Michael searched through his mother's dresser drawers. Kevin leaned against the wall and watched, figuring Michael was just trying to find a way to cover his lie. Pulling something out of the dresser, Michael approached Kevin.

"Here. I told you." He handed Kevin a small box of opened condoms.

"Michael, this doesn't prove a thing. You probably don't even know what this is used for." An angry frown spread across Kevin's face.

"Yes, I do. My dad told me last night when he baby-sat me. He told me to make sure I use one if I'm gonna have sex. He doesn't want me to make the same mistake he did."

Michael had actually heard those words from Trevor in the past, and recalling them now brought up the same pain. His father thought he was a mistake. The significance of such a statement was lost on Kevin though, who was busy thinking jealous thoughts.

Damn, so that's why she didn't want me to come up last night, he thought, wishing he had insisted more forcefully to be invited up the previous evening. He could feel a pit growing in his stomach as he began to worry he was being played for a fool by this woman. Still, he couldn't be sure, so he pumped Michael for more information.

"This still doesn't prove they had sex," he said to Michael, not so confident anymore that Alicia was innocent.

"Yes, it does. When Dad showed me the box, it had six rubbers in it. When I got up this morning, it was on Mom's dresser, and there were only four in the box," Michael said, wishing Kevin would stop looking so mad.

Kevin's thoughts and feelings were now written all over his face as he tried to make sense of what he was hearing from the young man. He raced through various possible explanations for the opened condom box, including that the box had been in her dresser for ages. Still, he could not shake the growing suspicion that Alicia was still sleeping with her ex. After all, he did call the apartment two times just that afternoon. For all Kevin knew, Alicia's anger at Trevor was just a cover-up, and the two were together every night.

Michael sensed Kevin's increasing disturbance but in his childish, self-centered way continued his quest for the junk food.

"Well, Uncle Kevin, you gonna give me some ice cream if I tell you the rest?"

"Yeah," Kevin muttered, slumping his shoulders as they walked to the kitchen.

Kevin watched Michael spoon ice cream into his mouth. He prayed Michael was lying about the whole thing. After a few minutes he couldn't stand the suspense and pulled the bowl of ice cream away.

"All right, Michael, I could get in a lot of trouble with your mom for giving you this ice cream. And I'm not convinced you're telling me the truth, so talk now."

Pulling the bowl of ice cream back in front of him, Michael tried to remember what had happened three days before when he spent the night at his aunt Teresa's house. He planned to use that memory to fabricate a story about his mother and father. For a brief moment he contemplated admitting that he was lying, but he could see by Kevin's growing agitation that it was too late to back out now without getting in lots of trouble.

"Well, first Mommy put me to bed," he said, looking up from his bowl to see if Kevin was paying attention. "Then I could hear them close the bedroom door. At first I thought they were fighting, because Aunt, uh, I mean Mommy, started saying 'No, No, No!'" Michael stuffed his mouth with another spoonful of ice cream, silently praying Kevin had not noticed his slip-up with the names in his story. When Kevin did not question it, Michael continued.

"Then I heard her yelling 'Yes! Yes! Don't stop!'" Michael did his best imitation of a woman's voice. "I wasn't sure if they were having sex until I heard the bed start moving. You know like you see on the Playboy Chan—"

Michael was cut off midsentence by Kevin crushing his empty Pepsi can with his bare hand. Mad and hurt, it took all of Kevin's pride to hold back the tears from his eyes.

"Michael, if you're lying, please tell me the truth now. You had your ice cream and I promise I won't get mad. But if I find out you lied, I'm gonna beat your butt myself." He was struggling to keep his temper under control.

Just then Alicia and her girlfriend walked into the apartment, their arms filled with packages. Scared, Michael picked up his empty bowl, put it into the sink, and ran to his mother. He wrapped his arms around her neck and kissed her as she put down her packages.

"I'm sorry, Mommy. I'll never say a bad word again. Honest," he whispered in her ear.

"All right, son, now go get cleaned up for dinner," she whispered back, nudging him toward the bathroom. He ran out of the room, grateful for the chance to escape the hole he had just dug for himself.

Alicia was surprised by the strength of Michael's apology over what she thought had been a minor incident. She meant to question Kevin about it but was distracted by the sight of him sliding into his coat.

"Where do you think you're going without giving me a kiss?" she asked, playfully grabbing his collar and puckering her lips.

"I told you I had to meet the basketball team at the school," he replied with attitude, avoiding her kiss.

"Okay, baby," she said, taking a step back. His tone of voice confused her. "You're still going to spend Christmas Eve with me, right?"

"Yeah," he grumbled, ready to explode. "When was the last time you slept with Trevor?"

"Kevin! I can't believe you just asked me that in front of Shannon." She looked at her friend, embarrassed.

"I don't give a shit about Shannon. I want to know when was the last time you had sex with Trevor." Kevin folded his arms and stared at her angrily.

"Look, Kevin, I think you need to go to meet the basketball team. We'll talk about this later." Alicia opened the door for him so that he could leave. She was not about to discuss this in front of her friend and was so angry that she just wanted Kevin out of her face.

"You need to think about who you want to be with, Alicia!" Kevin glared at her angrily, then stomped out the door.

"Damn! What's with your man?" Alicia's girlfriend sucked her teeth with attitude as Kevin closed the door behind him.

"I guess he's a little mad about Trevor calling. But that's all right. I've got something I guarantee is going to put a smile on that handsome face of his." She held up a package from Victoria's Secret, and the two women laughed.

Outside, Kevin slammed the door to his car and sped off. He couldn't wait to see Tyrone and Antoine later to clear his head after what he just learned about the woman he loved.

*   *   *

Kevin met Tyrone and Antoine outside the school when he returned from the basketball game. Since he was a security guard, Tyrone held the keys to the entrance in case of an emergency over the school holiday. He had cleared the use of the weight room with his superiors, who agreed he could use it during his daily check of the school grounds. The three friends decided to take advantage of the opportunity rather than buy a temporary gym membership that none of them except Antoine could truly afford.

As they walked down the empty halls, the sounds of their footsteps echoed loudly. Occasionally Tyrone or Antoine would try to strike up a conversation, but Kevin was strangely silent. It made both of his friends uncomfortable, but they decided that if he had something on his mind, he would tell them whenever he was ready. They all trusted their friendship enough to give one another that kind of space.

Inside the weight room Kevin was still silent except for the loud screams he released while struggling with more weights than he typically piled on. He had quite a bit of aggression to release. His friends saw how hard he was pushing himself, but neither commented until a two-hundred-fifty-pound weight crashed just inches in front of Tyrone's foot.

"What the fuck is wrong with you?" he screamed at Kevin.

"Sorry, Ty," Kevin said with a dazed look. "I really didn't mean it."

"Sorry ain't good enough, Kev, man. You damn near broke my toe." Tyrone was serious. "What the hell's crawled up your ass anyway? That fine-ass girlfriend of yours fucking Wesley Snipes on the side?"

"You're not far from the truth." Kevin glared at him.

"Oh, shit," Tyrone exclaimed.

"Hold on, Tyrone," Antoine barked sharply as he turned to Kevin. He didn't want Tyrone to turn this situation into another one of his joke fests. "What's going on between you and Alicia?"

"She had sex with her ex last night." Kevin tried to stop it, but a single tear rolled down his cheek.

"I find that hard to believe, Kevin. Shawna and I were with you two last night, remember? The two of you looked like something out of a romance novel." He placed his hand on his friend's shoulder sympathetically.

"Dammit! Will you let him tell us what the fuck happened?" Tyrone pushed his way back into the conversation. "Obviously something happened. The man's got tears in his eyes."

Shaking his head as he wiped his eyes, Kevin explained the afternoon's events. Stunned, his two friends sat on gym mats and listened intently as he told them all he knew about Alicia's affair.

"Damn, ain't that a bitch. If I told you once, I told you a thousand times, Kev. Don't love them hos." Taking a quick look at Antoine, he smirked as he continued. "If you had listened to me, instead of Mr. I'm-not-having-sex-till-I'm-married over here, and put some pressure on her to give you some ass, you wouldn't be in this predicament."

"You're right," Kevin whispered.

"I say, never trust a woman who can hold out that long. She has to be getting some from somewhere else." Tyrone was on a roll. He fancied himself something of an expert on women and loved to offer his advice.

"Wait a minute," Antoine said hopefully. "You said yourself you thought the kid was lying at first. What makes you so sure he wasn't?"

"You know, maybe Ty's right about you being a little naive, Antoine. What kid his age knows about condoms and sex with the kind of detail he does? On top of that, why would he lie? He likes me." Kevin sat on the weight bench and waited for an answer.

"I'm naive? I think you're the one who's naive, Kevin." Antoine folded his arms. "This is the nineties. A kid his age could find out anything he wanted to know about sex on television or the Internet. And as far as lying goes, you said he wanted ice cream. Some kids will lie for anything."

"You think Michael's lying, Antoine? Maybe Alicia's not cheating on me." The contrasting advice from his two friends was making his head spin, but Kevin was searching for any glimmer of hope.

"I don't know if he was lying or not," Antoine answered. "But I do know that the woman I met last night had the look of someone in love. You need to sit down and talk to her. This whole thing could be one big misunderstanding. You never know. Maybe this kid's afraid you're going to replace his father."

"You can listen to Dr. Ruth over there all you want." Tyrone jumped back into the conversation. "But I'm telling you, women have needs just like us. And one of the easiest things to do is to sleep with someone you already did, especially if it was good. But don't take my word for it. How many exes have you slept with over the years?"

Tyrone's words hit Kevin hard. He knew he was right. "It is easy to sleep with an ex. You already know exactly what you're getting. God, this woman's going to give me a nervous breakdown," he moaned.

"Kevin, don't listen to Tyrone. You need to keep an open mind and sit down with Alicia. Communication is what makes a relationship work."

"This from a man whose woman won't admit she's a stripper!" Tyrone laughed as Antoine shot him a dirty look.

"Okay, that's enough!" Kevin glanced at each of them seriously. "I feel as if I've got the devil on one shoulder and an angel on the other."

"Who you calling the devil?" Tyrone said quickly.

"If the shoe fits," Antoine retorted.

"Will you two stop it? Damn!" Kevin blasted them. "Antoine's right, Ty. If Alicia and I are truly in love, we have to talk about our problems."

Tyrone place his hand on Kevin's shoulder. "Hey, Kev. If it means anything, I hope I'm wrong. You're like a brother to me, and the last thing I want to see is you getting hurt." Kevin wrapped his arm around Tyrone in a brotherly hug.

"I love both of you like brothers." He pulled Antoine in with his other arm. "Now let's finish this workout, because I could use a beer."

15

KEVIN AND ALICIA

Kevin was glad he had put the previous day's events behind him. After a long talk with his mother, he decided not to confront Alicia. Mama's advice was very similar to Antoine's.

"You know, your nephew is only eight, and he's already had his birds-and-bees talk with his mama. They're learning younger and younger now," she told her son.

"So you think Michael could actually know enough to make up those kinds of details?" Kevin asked hopefully.

"Sure I do. And I also think kids will lie about anything these days. He wanted the ice cream, so he did what he had to do. And once he started, he probably couldn't see a way out even if he wanted to stop lyin' to you."

"I hope you're right, Mama. Antoine saw me with her that night, and he said he could tell how much she loves me."

"I know, son. I know how much you want this to work."

"I do. I just can't believe she would leave the restaurant and go up to her apartment to be with him." The thought made him shudder.

"Well, Kevin. She probably didn't. But it's up to you what you wanna do about it. Do you think you'll talk to her about it?"

"I don't think so, Mama. It is the holidays, after all. No need to start something major with her, especially since the kid probably made it up. Things are just starting to get good. I don't want her to think I don't trust her now," Kevin concluded.

Later that evening Kevin sat with Alicia in her apartment. He had apologized to her for his behavior the previous evening, although he did not tell her about Michael's involvement. Alicia just chalked it up to a rare display of jealousy on Kevin's part, thinking maybe he was just stressed after a full day with her child. Both of them were grateful just to put the incident behind them and enjoy their first Christmas together.

They had finished a wonderful candlelit dinner Alicia had lovingly prepared. Michael had been sent to his grandmother's house for the night. Sipping on his glass of wine, Kevin motioned for Alicia to move from the kitchen table to the couch. He kissed her lightly as they sat down.

"That was the most incredible meal any woman has ever made for me," he whispered.

"Does that include your mother?" she teased.

"No fair. That's a trick question." He tried to change the subject by nibbling on her neck. She wasn't having it.

"Yup." She laughed, moving him back gently. "Now answer the question."

"Your honor, I plead the fifth. But I would like to plea-bargain my case." He reached into his sport coat pocket and handed her a small box. "Merry Christmas, baby."

"Oh, my God, Kevin! This must have cost you a fortune." Alicia opened the box and tears welled in her eyes.

"Well, let's just say it didn't come from one of the Asian brothers selling watches on Parsons Boulevard for ten dollars." He flashed a grin, helping her to put on the elegant quartz watch he had brought.

"Oh, Kevin, thank you." She wrapped her arms around his neck, kissing him. "Are you sure you can afford this?"

"MasterCard, baby. Fifty dollars a month for the rest of my life, and it's paid for." Kevin chuckled. "My mother told me not to buy you this watch."

"Why? I thought your mother liked me."

"Old superstition," he explained. "Buy a woman a watch and your time is up. But I like to think of it as my time's just started."

"Oh, Kevin." She sighed happily.

"You know, Alicia, when I lost my spot in the NBA, I didn't think I could ever truly be happy again. But you restored some joy to my life, and I want to thank you for being so special."

Overwhelmed with emotion, Alicia couldn't say a word. She just wrapped her arms around the man she loved and kissed him passionately. Kevin, feeling a little daring, began to massage Alicia's breasts over her silk blouse as they kissed. Her breathing became more rapid, and it boosted Kevin's confidence. He began to slowly unbutton her blouse as he kissed her neck.

Alicia purred as she felt Kevin placing warm, soft kisses over her neck and shoulders. She moaned as her breathing became even heavier. She helped him unhook her bra from the front and he caressed her breasts with his soft hands. As his kisses traveled down to her breasts, Alicia let out a long, low moan. She massaged his head and neck to let him know how much she loved what he was doing. Chills ran up her body, emanating from the pleasure she was feeling between her thighs. Suddenly the shrill ringing of the phone interrupted their pleasure.

Ignore it. Please ignore it, Kevin begged silently.

"Phew! Getting a little hot in here." Alicia gently pushed Kevin off her. She fanned herself with one hand and closed her blouse with the other. *Don't get ahead of yourself, girl,* she thought as she stood up to answer the phone.

"Don't think I forgot about your present, sweetheart." She winked at Kevin. "This is probably my mom calling about Michael. It will take only a minute." She pushed the button on the cordless.

At midnight? Kevin thought, looking at his watch and listening to Alicia's side of the call.

"Oh, hello." Alicia was frowning. "Look, Trevor, I appreciate what you did for me the other day. But now is not a good time. I have company."

As soon as Kevin heard Trevor's name, he shot Alicia an evil look. "What's he calling about?" he asked, folding his arms.

Alicia shrugged her shoulders as she listened to her ex. Kevin was getting angry. What the hell was he calling about at midnight? And why didn't she just hang up on him? He was beginning to think maybe Michael had told the truth.

After listening to Trevor briefly, Alicia knew the conversation could get ugly. She placed her hand over the phone and asked Kevin to excuse her for a minute. Without waiting for his answer, she walked into the bedroom and shut the door behind her. In reality she didn't want Kevin to hear her arguing, because she knew Trevor usually made her mad enough to curse. She was unaware of what Kevin was thinking as he sat fuming in the living room.

No, she didn't! No, she didn't walk out of this room to talk to her baby's father! All the anger from the day before resumed. *She's sleeping with that guy. I know she's sleeping with that guy.*

In the other room Alicia was well aware she shouldn't keep Kevin waiting long. But before she could return to him, she had to straighten out Trevor.

"Motherfucker. Just because you finally caught up with your child support and gave me a few dollars toward a bike don't mean you can call my house at midnight. How the hell did you get my number anyway? I don't need this shit, Trevor. I got a man. Repeat, I got a man!" Alicia could have lots of attitude when she needed it. This was exactly what she had not wanted Kevin to hear.

Trevor waited for Alicia to finish patiently. Then, in the sinister, soft voice he used right before he used to beat the hell out of her, he said, "Listen to me. Listen to me real good, because I'm not going to repeat myself. If you ever talk to me that way again, I'm gonna come over there and kick your ass and that nigga's ass. You got the nerve to take my loot and think I'm not going to call? You think you can play me or something? I own you, Alicia. Ever since I popped that cherry of yours, I've owned you. That nigga might rent the pussy, but both of you remember who owns it. Oh, by the way, it was your drunk-ass daddy who gave me your number. For a can of beer."

Alicia slipped out of her clothes as she listened to Trevor rant. Her mind was on getting back to Kevin to finish what they had just started. Admiring the picture of Kevin on her dresser while she listened to Trevor shout, she realized that he no longer had any power over her.

"You don't own anything, not even the shirt on your back," she calmly told him when he finished his tirade. "Trevor, the only reason I got your money is because Child Support was gonna lock your ass up. What you need to do, Trevor Raymond Hill, is grow up and be a father. Oh, yeah, and about my man. He's built like a brick shithouse. So if you're gonna bring your coward ass over here, bring it now, because we plan on making love for the next few hours. That's hours, not minutes, like you." Alicia waited a few seconds for a response, then hung up when there was none.

Aware that her man was still waiting in the other room and probably upset by then, Alicia slipped quickly into her teddy and a pair of red high-heeled shoes. She checked herself in the mirror. "You look good girl." She laughed.

Slipping into a robe, she frantically began looking through her dresser drawers for the condoms she bought. Giving up, she finally went to an old goody bag from a bachelorette party and found one. She placed it in a small jewelry box and smiled broadly, whispering, "Merry Christmas, Kevin."

Kevin was still sitting on the couch, steaming, when Alicia yelled from her bedroom, "I'm going to turn out the lights so I can bring out your present."

"This is not a time for presents, we need to talk!" he shouted from the living room.

"We can talk all night after I give you my present." She turned out the lights and walked into the living room, stopping about three feet in front of him. "You can see, can't you?" she teased.

"No, I can't," he said honestly, "but I really need to say something to you."

"Kevin, your eyes are going to adjust to the light in a minute. Will you just relax and let me give you your present?" She handed him the box and slipped out of the robe, trying to strike a sexy pose before the lights came on. "There are two parts to your present. One is in the box, the other's over here. There's a light on the coffee table to your right. Why don't you turn it on so you can see?"

"Alicia, I can't accept any present," Kevin said sadly.

"Why not?" Alicia was getting tired of posing and wished he would just stop it and turn the light on.

"Because I don't think we should see each other anymore."

Alicia's arms dropped to her sides. "Look, Kevin, I'm sorry about Trevor calling so late. I'll even change my number if it'll make you feel better. Just turn on the light, sweetheart, so that I can give you your present." Alicia was frustrated and really pissed at Trevor. With one phone call he had turned what should have been a perfect evening with Kevin into a fiasco.

"I don't want your fucking present, Alicia! And this is not about that phone call. This is about you fucking that motherfucker Trevor! How the fuck could you do this to me?" He slammed his hand down on the coffee table, breaking the glass.

Alicia was so shocked that she couldn't speak. Kevin had never acted like this, and she really didn't like this side of him.

"What's wrong with you?" she asked, reaching over to turn on the light.

Kevin looked up and saw Alicia's half-exposed body. For a brief second he let go of his anger and admired what he had lusted over for so long. The thought entered his mind to have sex with Alicia one time, then dump her. But he dismissed that thought knowing that if he slept with her once, he would want to do it again.

"Oh, my God, Kevin, you're bleeding!" She reached over to help him. But Kevin, not wanting to be touched, accidentally pushed her to the ground.

"Now see what you made me do," he apologized, offering her a hand up.

"That's the same shit Trevor used to say right after he beat the shit out of me."

Alicia looked with tear-stained eyes at the broken table and then at the blood on her cut hand. It was starting to seem like she'd gotten herself involved in another violent relationship. This time she was determined not to let it go on the way she had in the past. Alicia was crying as she walked to the kitchen phone.

"Now who the fuck are you calling?" Kevin took a paper napkin to stop his hand from bleeding.

"The police!" she shouted, trembling.

"Alicia, there's no reason to call the police. Look, I'm sorry I pushed you. I just can't believe you would cheat on me like this." Kevin looked down at the broken coffee table. He was in trouble if she called the police, and the last thing he wanted was to go to jail on Christmas Eve.

"Please, Kevin! Didn't nobody cheat on you. Why the fuck would I mess with Trevor when I love your stupid ass?"

"I love you too." Kevin followed her and was now crying himself. He was starting to think he had made a big mistake.

"You have a funny way of showing it." She placed the phone by her ear. "Now get out of my fucking house or I'm really calling the police."

Kevin's eyes pleaded with Alicia as he walked past her to the door. "Alicia, please. Let's sit down and talk like adults. We can work this out."

"Save it for someone who cares, Kevin. You're the one who wanted to break up." She held the door open to let him know she wasn't changing her mind. "Oh, and, Kevin, your mother was wrong."

"Wrong about what?"

"This watch." She threw it at him. "Your time isn't up. It never really got started. Stupid ass!"

He looked at her in the red teddy as she closed the door. "Goddammit. I think I just made the biggest mistake since I smoked that joint in North Carolina."

16

TYRONE AND SYLVIA

Sylvia gave her most seductive pose in front of the mirror as she admired her new Victoria's Secret thong. Across her bed were strewn several other pieces of lingerie she had also purchased. She planned to try on each and every one, enjoying how the soft fabrics felt against her skin.

She looked good, and she knew it, as she admired her womanly curves. While she had always known she was an attractive woman, she had a newfound confidence about her desirability. Tyrone's sweet flattery had convinced her that the sexual problems in her marriage were not hers but her husband's. He made her feel more desirable with his words than Maurice had done in bed in all their years of marriage. In past years especially, Maurice was a wham-bam-thank-you-ma'am kind of lover, and it made Sylvia feel like it didn't matter who she was or how she looked. If she was a piece of meat, Maurice would have been just as interested. But Tyrone seemed more interested in making her feel good than in getting her in bed. In fact, Sylvia had been the one trying to seduce him. Tyrone seemed more concerned with boosting her self-image, and she was falling for him quickly because of it.

She'd indeed come a long way in a short time. With Tyrone's encouragement she threw away all her old briefs and cumbersome bras and spent a fortune at Frederick's of Hollywood and Victoria's Secret. She now sported a sexy, short hairstyle and made a habit of borrowing from her daughter's closet. It was incredible the kind influence that Tyrone had on her, and it had loosened the grip Maurice had held on her emotions. As she drifted away from him, she felt herself more capable of loving, and her feelings for Tyrone grew stronger. She often thought of taking their relationship beyond friendship.

Unfortunately Tyrone didn't seem to be interested in taking things a step further, so they had met in person only two times. Both times Sylvia had tried to get him to make love to her, and both times Tyrone had declined. He would leave her with a lustful kiss and a promise that when the time was right, they would make love beyond her wildest imagination. Sylvia couldn't understand a man who didn't take it as soon as it was offered, and she hoped he wasn't just stringing her along.

In the meantime she had to be satisfied with the occasional phone sex they were having. As she modeled her lingerie in front of the mirror, she found her thoughts drifting to sex, so she picked up the phone to call Tyrone.

Tyrone smiled as he flicked on his cell phone. "Hey, baby, what's up?" It was 3:15, so he knew it would be Sylvia making her daily call.

"I'll tell you what I want to be up," Sylvia purred into the phone.

"Is that all you ever think about?" he teased.

"When it comes to you, yes!" she said, only half joking.

"Damn, woman! Can't you appreciate me for anything more than my body?"

"Sure I can. How about your tongue?"

"You're a trip. You know that?"

"Only because you make me this way. Oh, by the way, tomorrow's Christmas Eve and my family's left me home alone. My husband went skiing in Vermont, and my daughter's in the Bahamas. I was hoping we could spend some time together before you leave for Virginia. Maybe have dinner and exchange gifts?"

"Aw'ight, Sylvia, that sounds like a plan. Why don't you pick me up at the corner of Hillside and Parsons tomorrow at four?"

Sylvia could barely hold back her excitement. "I'll be there at four o'clock sharp. Bye, Tyrone."

"God, I want to make love to you," he told her in a sultry voice, sensing her anticipation.

He hung up the phone before he heard Sylvia reply, "Promises, promises."

Tyrone was whistling as he began his rounds, checking each hallway of the school. Not saying good-bye to Sylvia had been a deliberate act on his part. It was Tyrone's belief that lovemaking was really a game, and if you learned the rules to any game, you could win. Reaching into his wallet, he pulled out a worn piece of paper he had been carrying since his days in prison.

Tyrone's 10 Rules To Satisfy A Woman

1. *If you like her, hold out at least three months. (This will drive her crazy and make you more mysterious.)*
2. *Try to refrain from seeing her more than once a week. (Temptation is a hard thing to resist, especially in a beautiful woman.)*
3. *When you kiss her, make it count. (Give her an idea of what your tongue can do.)*
4. *While you're holding out, tell her what you plan on doing to her sexually. (Always best to do this by phone.)*
5. *Sex is at least 50 percent mental. The things you tell her should be stimulating to a woman. (You want to make her fantasize about you.) Remember, the more she wants it, the better it will be when she gets it.*
6. *Ask her questions. Find out what she likes and dislikes.*
7. *Any woman can make a man come, but not every man can make a woman come. (This means you do whatever it takes to get the job done and you'll be her hero.)*
8. *Take your time and use a lot of foreplay. (Slow and steady wins the race.)*
9. *Oral sex is the key to success. (Don't stop until she tells you to!)*
10. *If she's satisfied, you're satisfied. (No rule could be truer.)*

Damn, he thought. *I sure had a lot of free time on my hands in prison to be writing this.* Still, Tyrone believed there was truth in what he had written so long ago, and he smiled as he realized he had completed rules one through six. He was definitely looking forward to number seven through ten. Though he was making her wait, Sylvia had ignited a fire in him too.

It was about quarter to four Christmas Eve when Tyrone walked up the stairs from the F train. He had just spent a few hours with his two daughters and was truly feeling good about himself. He smiled as he looked in the bag of Christmas presents his girls had given him. His girls were growing up fast, and they made him proud.

Sylvia's Mercedes pulled up to the curb. Opening the door and sliding into the passenger seat, Tyrone grinned at Sylvia.

"Hey, baby." He moved a little closer and pressed his lips against hers.

"My Lord, what's put you into this mood? For kisses like that, I'll pick you up every day."

Tyrone chuckled as Sylvia pulled away from the curb. "Where are we headed, Sylvia?"

"To a Christmas party with some friends of mine. Do you mind rubbing elbows with the black elite?"

"Sure, why not? I can go for a little Grey Poupon." Straightening his tie, Tyrone faced Sylvia and sniffed his nose up in the air.

They laughed together as they headed toward the Long Island Expressway and the north shore of Long Island, home of some of the country's wealthiest individuals. Many of the homes in the area were once enormous estates, complete with a gatehouse, a separate residence for the housekeepers, and acres of land for bourgeois pleasures such as horseback riding. Even as the "old money" families sold off their estates to be broken into several parcels of land, the new owners still had enormous mansions set well back in the woods. Gated entrances with warning signs guarded most of the homes from tourists curious to see how the rich and famous were living on Long Island. For someone like Tyrone, the opulence and enormity of the homes was awe inspiring.

Holy shit! That house is bigger than my whole building. This thought crossed his mind not once, but with every home they passed on the narrow winding road.

"Nice, huh?" Sylvia smiled as she noticed how captivated he seemed to be.

Tyrone nodded and pointed to a huge Georgian mansion they were passing. "Is that really a single-family house? My God, Sylvia, that house must have five or six bedrooms."

"More like ten, actually, but yes, all the houses around here are owned by one person or a family." She pulled into the driveway of the Muttontown Country Club.

"Damn," Tyrone mumbled as he looked at the huge old mansion at the end of the driveway. "Is this somebody's house too?"

"Not anymore. That is what they call an old-money house, which was bought to make a new-money country club. It's all really confusing and doesn't make much sense unless you are white and have Donald Trump-type money."

"Wait a minute. Didn't you say this was a Christmas party for some black elite?" Tyrone was a little confused and definitely intimidated. "When did they start letting blacks into the country clubs?"

"When Reginald Lewis made his first billion. And in our host's case, when his gallery was appraised at a hundred million. Money can make the most prejudiced people color-blind. That is, until the money runs out."

"Our host has a gallery? Who is it?"

She turned and smiled. "I thought you might like to meet Bernard Ridgewood. Maybe you two could talk art or something?" she teased.

"Sylvia! I can't believe you didn't tell me this sooner. At least you could have given me some time to prepare." He was suddenly very nervous about meeting a man with so much influence in the world of black artists.

"Don't be ridiculous. Bernard is a good friend of mine. He's already heard lots about you, and he's eager to meet you. Just try to relax and be yourself, and I'm sure he'll love you."

He tried to do some deep breathing to calm himself, and smiled weakly at Sylvia. For her it was just another ritzy affair, but for him it could be the start of something big, or a complete dead end. He did not want to do anything to make himself look stupid.

Sylvia stopped the car in the circular drive at the front entrance of the club. She stepped out of the car, handing her keys to the young parking attendant. She held her hand out for Tyrone. He stepped out, a little wobbly in the knees, and they entered the foyer of the club.

Inside, a tall salt-and-pepper-haired white man in a tux greeted Sylvia and Tyrone.

"Dinner will be served in approximately one half hour in the dining room, and cocktails are being served in the living room now."

"Thank you, Frederick," Sylvia said as he helped her take off her mink coat.

"Excuse me, sir." Frederick took Tyrone's coat and folded it over his arm. "A sport jacket is required in the club."

Goddammit. I knew these white motherfuckers was gonna pull this shit. Tyrone thought before speaking. He was already so nervous, this one comment just set him off. The last thing he needed was to have some pasty-faced butler telling him he wasn't dressed appropriately.

"So what you want me to do, leave?" Tyrone clenched his fist as he got in Frederick's face.

Frederick took a step back, seemingly unfazed by Tyrone's aggressiveness. "Actually, sir, I was going to ask you if I could supply you with a sport coat."

"Oh." Tyrone was embarrassed to see a small crowd had gathered nearby when they heard the commotion. "Yeah. I'd appreciate that." He nervously smoothed the front of his shirt.

"Then follow me, sir." Tyrone followed with his head held low.

"Meet me in the living room, Tyrone," Sylvia called after him. He couldn't tell by her tone of voice if she was upset with him for his outburst.

Hopeful that no one would recognize him as the idiot from the foyer, he entered the living room of the country club wearing a suit jacket. Frederick had managed to find one that matched his pants and tie perfectly. Searching the room, Tyrone found Sylvia talking to a very unattractive elderly woman. He approached her sheepishly.

"Hi." He tried to sound apologetic.

"Hi, handsome. The jacket looks great."

Sylvia's smile let him know that he was forgiven already. She knew this was his first time in such surroundings and was sure her little surprise had set him even more on edge. It wouldn't have been fair to get upset with him for the incident in the foyer, since she felt partly responsible. Besides, it didn't seem like the onlookers were really even aware of what had happened, so everyone could just forget about it, including her and Tyrone.

"I apologized to Frederick and he seemed cool with it."

"Good. By the way, Tyrone, this is an old high-school friend of mine, Blanche Peterson." She gestured to the woman she had been speaking to.

"The pleasure is all mine, Mrs. Peterson." Tyrone thought to himself that there was no way this woman had been a classmate of Sylvia's. She looked thirty years older than Sylvia did.

"That's right, the pleasure is all yours." Blanche flashed a gap-toothed grin as she took his hand and rubbed the inside of his palm with her middle finger. "And do call me Blanche, sweetie. Mrs. Peterson is my mother. I'm a single woman, if you didn't know."

I could have guessed that, Tyrone thought, noticing she needed a breath mint. His stomach turned when he realized Blanche had made a pass at him. Ugly women had made passes at him before, he'd even slept with a few, but Blanche Peterson and her shit-for-breath had to have been the worst. Looking for an escape, he turned to Sylvia and offered to get her a drink from the bar.

"Gin and tonic, please. How about you, Blanche?"

"No, thanks, I have what I need right here." She eyed Tyrone as she took a sip of her drink.

Blanche watched Tyrone walk across the room to the bar, then turned to Sylvia. "I see you've got yourself a new boy-toy, Sylvia. Honey, he's good-looking too." She turned around to take another look. "Nice and tall, just like I like them. I find the tall ones always seem to fuck better for some reason. What do you think?"

"Let me tell you something. He is not my boy-toy. He's a very close friend whom I don't want hanging out with a whore like you."

She tried to be discreet but stood close to Blanche as she shoved her finger in her face and growled at her. For as long as she could remember, Blanche had been making passes at Maurice whenever they were at social functions together. It stemmed back to some incident in high school that had happened so long before that Sylvia couldn't even remember the details. She just knew that Blanche never seemed to let up. She was jealous of Sylvia and determined to get revenge. With her new-found confidence Sylvia was not quite so forgiving this time. But Blanche wasn't about to back down as she pushed Sylvia's hand out of her face.

"Listen, girl. All I wanted was a slice of the pie. But call me a whore again and I'll take the whole damn pie," Blanche threatened before storming away.

"Who the hell was that woman?" Tyrone asked as he returned with their drinks.

Sylvia rolled her eyes. "That sick woman is Blanche Peterson, New York and the country's number-one black madam. She can make or break most of the men and a lot of the women in this room. I suggest you stay away from her. She has a thing for younger men."

"Kinda like you?" He tugged her arm playfully, but Sylvia shot him an evil glance.

"Oh, Sylvia!" A high-pitched voice came from behind the pair.

"Bernard!" She turned, wrapping her arms around a very short, well-dressed, light-skinned man. "How was Europe?"

"Absolutely marvelous," he raved. The voice did not seem to fit him. "And the men! Child, the men were so sexy, I almost committed rape."

"You are too much." Sylvia shook her head and smiled.

"I'm too much? Look at you." He touched her hair with his hands. "I love this new look—the short hair, the short dress, the handsome man. You look so sexy, you make me wanna go back to women."

"Oh, Bernard, you lie so bad." Then she shot him a look and added, "About going back to women, that is. The part about me being sexy is so true." Sylvia did a little spin so he could admire her little black cocktail dress. She stopped her display and put her hand on Tyrone's arm. "This, Bernard, is Tyrone. He's the young man I've been writing you about. He's truly changed my life, and you can thank him for my new look."

"It's a pleasure to meet you, sir." Tyrone extended his hand nervously, hoping to make a good first impression.

"Call me Bernard."

"Bernard is our host tonight, and he owns Ridgewood Galleries." Sylvia wrapped her arm around Bernard's shoulder. She winked at Tyrone because she knew full well that he was already painfully aware of just who Bernard Ridgewood was and what he did.

"You know, Bernard, Tyrone is quite the artist himself. Maybe you should take a look at his work before he signs a contract with Walter Black."

"Walter Black's going to sign him?" Bernard searched Sylvia's face for an answer. He was intrigued.

Nodding to Bernard, Sylvia gave Tyrone a look that said "Don't you dare open your mouth." Tyrone willingly complied.

"Well, in that case, make sure you give Sylvia a copy of your portfolio to give to me. I wouldn't want Walter Black to steal some of my thunder."

He led them into the dining room, where the large staff of waiters had begun to place shrimp cocktail at each place setting. Sylvia and Tyrone were seated at a table with several other couples, most of whom were married. Blanche Peterson had somehow managed to get herself seated right next to Tyrone and spent most of the meal trying to monopolize his attention. As difficult as it was for him, Tyrone behaved politely to the woman.

Aside from the seating arrangement, Tyrone found dinner to be magnificent. Each of the seven courses seemed to be better than the one before. Tyrone tasted caviar for the first time and decided he could live without it, but the salmon entree was perfect. He thought he could get used to this lifestyle.

By the time dessert was served, Tyrone was absolutely stuffed. Once the chef's special apple strudel was brought to the table though, he found a little more room and bit into the buttery crust. As the smooth dessert melted in his mouth, Tyrone felt a hand caressing his inner thigh.

"This has been a perfect Christmas Eve," he said to Sylvia with a smile.

"Yes, it has, and I hope it gets better." She squeezed his thigh suggestively before removing her hand from his lap to taste her apple strudel.

Well, perfect except for that bitch Blanche sitting next to you, Sylvia thought anxiously as she glanced at the woman and gave a fake smile. Blanche lifted her wineglass in a toasting gesture and gave Sylvia the same fake smile.

Five minutes later Tyrone was eating what was left of Sylvia's strudel as he listened to the various conversations she had with Bernard and the other guests. He was impressed by her knowledge, and content to listen rather than participate in the conversations, though she did try to include him periodically.

Tyrone smiled when he felt Sylvia's hand back on his lap. He winked at her. Sylvia returned the wink and smiled. Tyrone was getting an erection as she continued to massage him through the thin material of his pants. He marveled at her ability to arouse him and carry on her conversations at the same time. Glancing around the table, he felt sure that no one else was aware of what was going on beneath their dessert plates. He struggled to maintain his composure as his breathing quickened a little.

Sylvia noticed his breathing and glanced at Tyrone oddly. He took the hint and tried once more to get himself under control. This became almost impossible, though, as she unzipped his fly and released his throbbing penis. Tyrone gasped, then covered his mouth with a napkin to conceal the small moan that escaped as her soft hands manipulated him.

He was astonished at the expertise she was using. He began to wince in ecstasy and had to pretend it was a smile as a woman across the table looked at him.

"Oh, my goodness, Tyrone. Are you all right? You look a bit uncomfortable," she exclaimed. All eyes turned to him.

Tyrone could barely get the words out but managed to reply, "No. Everything's fine." He took another bite of his strudel. Mercifully the guests returned to their conversations.

Tyrone could feel himself nearing a climax. He was so hard by this point that he was tempted to finish the act right there at the table. His better judgment told him to stop though, because several people kept looking in his direction. He had continued eating the dessert and tried to appear engrossed in someone's conversation, but it was nearly impossible at this point for him to conceal his rapture. He reached between his chair and Sylvia's to stop her. To his surprise, he did not find her arm, so he nonchalantly glanced over at her, only to see both her hands resting on the dining room table.

"Holy shit!" he gulped, quickly turning to his right to see Blanche Peterson's hideous snaggletoothed yellow smile six inches from his face. Her breath burned his nostrils.

"Feel good, honey?" she whispered as she expertly squeezed his penis to ejaculation.

Horrified, Tyrone began to choke on a piece of apple strudel. *Oh, God,* he thought in a panic. *I'm gonna die with this bitch's hands around my dick!* Afraid to stand up because of the predicament he was in, Tyrone struggled to remove Blanche's hand and zipped up his pants just as Frederick rushed to the table and applied the Heimlich maneuver. Struggling for air, he gasped once the strudel had been dislodged, then he nearly gagged again as he watched Blanche wipe the evidence on her linen napkin. She dropped it on the floor with a satisfied grin.

"Are you all right, Tyrone?" Sylvia reached for her napkin to wipe the apple strudel from his chin.

Tyrone was doubled over, clenching his stomach. *Hell no, I'm not all right. I don't think I'll ever be all right,* he thought. He looked up to see Blanche exposing her crotch to him under the table.

Tyrone stood upright and said in a whimper, "Maybe you better take me home. I am feeling pretty nauseated." He was eager to put as much distance between himself and Blanche as possible.

Sylvia was upset that her special night was coming to an end, but she could see by the look on his face that something was seriously wrong. Bernard approached their table as Sylvia and Tyrone prepared to leave.

"Phew, I'm glad to see you're all right." He laughed. "For a minute there I thought your family was going to have one hell of a wrongful death lawsuit."

Tyrone chuckled and glared at Blanche, who was also preparing to leave.

"The way I feel now, I probably would be better off dead," he told Bernard.

"Let me make it up to you." Bernard offered. "A few of us are going to sneak off to the club's smoking lounge for a cocktail before the show. I would love it if you two would be my personal guests."

Sylvia desperately wanted to prolong her evening with Tyrone, so she pleaded with him. "Can we stay just for a short time? Bernard's having a wonderful African art show and auction in the club's gallery later, and I really wanted to buy you a piece for Christmas."

Tyrone agreed, since Blanche was no longer in the room. He had never been able to see an art auction, even when he worked security at the Manhattan Gallery. And if she wanted to buy him a piece of art, who was he to stop her?

After thanking Frederick for his lifesaving heroics, Tyrone followed Bernard and Sylvia into a windowless room. He sat down on a small couch next to the door, explaining that he still needed to recuperate. Sylvia joined seven other guests who sat on the floor in a small circle.

This sure don't look too elite to me, Tyrone thought to himself.

Bernard stood near the circle of guests and opened a brown cigar box he was holding. He removed a large, clear plastic bag filled with white powder. "This is pure Colombian cocaine," he told the group as he poured some into a glass pipe. A few of the guests nodded their approval at the quality of the drug.

Oh, no. Tyrone thought to himself, shaking his head in disbelief. *This motherfucker's about to free-base right here.*

An attractive, dark-skinned woman from the circle handed a lighter to Bernard and he lit the pipe. He smiled as he took a hit and proclaimed, "I feel like a new man already."

As angry as the whole scene was making him, Tyrone began to perspire. The cocaine was calling him with a longing he had not felt for quite some time. He silently cursed his weakness.

Bernard took one more hit, then bent to hand the pipe to Sylvia. She accepted it without even looking in Tyrone's direction.

Unable to watch Sylvia smoke, Tyrone closed his eyes. Smoke from the pipe seeped into his nostrils, and the cocaine angels began to sing his song. *"Tyrone, come to me. Tyrone, come here."* A vision of his two daughters entered Tyrone's mind, and he regained his willpower. He stood up and walked out the door, bumping into Frederick, who had been standing guard.

"Is there somewhere I can get a cab around here?" he asked Frederick desperately.

"No, sir, but I can have the club limousine take you anywhere you would like to go," Frederick answered. "Excuse me, sir. I don't mean to intrude, but is there something wrong?"

"Is something wrong?" Tyrone pointed to the door he had just come through. "Frederick, do you know what's going on in there?"

"Unfortunately, sir, I do," he answered shamefully. "And to be quite frank, it sickens me."

"I know what you mean," Tyrone said, still in disbelief. "I've worked too hard to fuck up my sobriety now."

"You're in recovery," Frederick said with a smile. "That's good. I picked up a nasty heroin habit in Vietnam. I've been clean now almost twenty years. But I must admit, I always feel uncomfortable when they have these private parties in the smoking lounge."

"So why don't you call the cops, or, even better, say something to management?"

Frederick smiled kindly. "They don't pay me eighty thousand dollars a year to run and tell their secrets. I have three children in college who depend on me."

Instantly Tyrone could relate. "Eighty gees, huh? For that kind of loot I'd keep quiet too." He handed Frederick some keys. "Look, Frederick, I'm gonna catch that limo back to Jamaica. But I want you to hold Sylvia's keys for me and make sure she gets home safe."

"I will take care of it personally, sir."

Tyrone turned to walk down the hall, and Frederick called after him, "Oh, sir! The young lady. Miss Sylvia?"

"Yeah." Tyrone was standing by the front door, hanging up the jacket that Frederick had lent him.

"This is the first time she's been in the smoking lounge." He gave Tyrone an understanding look.

"Thanks," Tyrone said as he walked out the door. "And you have a Merry Christmas."

17

KEVIN AND ALICIA

It was four days after Christmas. Kevin and his friends had just finished a delicious southern dinner prepared by his mother. She had insisted that all of them take a second serving of collard greens, candied yams, and turkey wings. The air in the kitchen was heavy with the scent of fresh-baked rolls and the tangy barbecue they had all enjoyed.

"Mrs. Brown, this food is so good, it makes me wanna go back to New York and smack my mama," Tyrone joked, sucking on a turkey wing so he could get every last drop of the delicious flavor.

"Did you say smack your mama? Why in the world would you wanna do that, Tyrone?" She looked over at him with her hands on her hips.

"Yes, ma'am, I did say smack my mama. I need to smack her, 'cause she can't cook this good."

Mama joined in as they all laughed. She had enjoyed having Kevin's friends over for the holidays. It had given her a chance to cook some of the special things the doctor said she couldn't have because of her high blood pressure. A big southern woman, Mama stood about five foot nine with black hair heavily streaked with gray. Sixty years old, it was not unusual for people to ask if she was Kevin's grandmother instead of his mother. But Mama took it in stride. She had always been mistaken for older than she was, and for her it was just a part of life.

At the age of thirteen Mama dropped out of school to help care for her ten brothers and sisters. Two years later she was nicknamed "Mama" by the local townspeople because she always had at least one small child following behind her. Now she was still known as Mama to most of the residents of the small southern town of Hopewell, Virginia. And just like the old days, she still had her two grandchildren in tow wherever she went.

After dinner Tyrone and Kevin moved their stuffed selves into the living room, where they played spades with Kevin's two sisters, Phyllis and Whitney. Antoine and Mama moved into the parlor. He was reading *The Philosophy and Opinions of Marcus Garvey* and she was working on a needlepoint design that she planned to donate to the church for their New Year's bazaar.

In the living room Phyllis and Whitney laughed as Tyrone teased Kevin.

"Damn, what the fuck did you play that card for? Can't you see I'm cutting diamonds?"

"Watch your mouth," Kevin scolded, hoping Mama hadn't heard his cursing. "Look, brother. You play your cards and let me play mine," he told Tyrone.

"That'd be fine, 'cept that I bet your sister Phyllis dinner and a movie, remember?" Tyrone looked at the score sheet with disappointment. "With you as a partner, it looks like I just might be paying up, huh? And somebody I know was bragging that he invented the game of spades." He cut his eyes at Kevin, and his sisters giggled.

Before anyone could play another card, Tyrone's cell phone rang. Kevin grew impatient as the phone rang for a fourth time.

"Aren't you going to answer it?" he pleaded.

"No, they'll call back later." Tyrone dealt the cards. "Right now I got to take care of some of the damage you done."

"Don't you think that's a little rude?" Kevin sounded desperate. His sister Phyllis gave him a strange look.

"Yo, Kev. I know who it is, aw'ight? I really don't want to talk to her. Just chill."

"Look, Tyrone, answer the phone," Kevin demanded. He was tempted to grab the phone and answer it himself. "I left your cell phone number on Alicia's answering machine in case we went out."

Pulling his cell phone out of Kevin's reach, Tyrone frowned and answered the call.

"Hello?" The expression on his face changed. Kevin's sisters felt the tension from both men. He was practically shouting into the phone. "Listen to me. I don't want to hear your apologies. This is the third time you've called today, and you're really not saying anything new. I'll talk to you when I get back. Bye."

Without wasting a second he disconnected the call. Tyrone looked at Kevin and shook his head.

"Yo, man. You need to get a grip. You been calling Alicia ten times a day, leaving messages all over New York. If she hasn't called you back by now, buddy, she ain't callin'."

"You know what, Tyrone?" Kevin's voice was angry but quiet, because he knew Mama was still in the next room. "When I want your fucking advice, I'll ask for it."

He stood up so fast that he knocked over the card table, then stormed out the front door. His sisters looked at each other with eyebrows raised, then turned to Tyrone for an explanation.

"Well, ladies, looks like our game is over" was all he could say.

Outside, Kevin sat on the steps of Mama's porch and whistled for the family dog, Blue. The golden retriever had been Kevin's dog since long before he left for college. Blue came running around the house, and as he patted the dog, Kevin smiled for the first time since he had been home.

"You still love me, don't you, Blue?" Blue gave him a lick on the face as a response.

"Blue's not the only one who loves you, Kevin." Mama startled him as she opened the screen door. She sat next to him on the step and put her arm around her son's shoulders. "This old dog of ours has been around a long time, hasn't he?"

"Yeah, almost twelve years. I remember when he was a puppy and knocked over that can of blue paint."

Mama laughed. "Your daddy said right then and there that we was callin' him Blue."

"Yeah, Daddy didn't even get mad that day." Kevin smiled as he remembered his father.

"Those were good times. Your father couldn't get mad. He had just finished this here house. That can of blue paint was the last bit of trim for this house." Mama looked up at the two-story colonial that her husband had built fifteen years earlier.

"I still can't believe Daddy built this house all by himself." Kevin looked up at the house in amazement.

"Yeah, he started the day you was born, and it took him eight years to finish. But he promised me that his son was going to live in the prettiest house on the block. And he did it too."

"Yeah, he did, didn't he?" Kevin touched the blue trim of the porch. "You know what, Mama? It's still the prettiest house on the block."

"I know, son, I know." Mama sighed, then became serious. "You and Alicia having problems, aren't you, son?"

"Yeah, we broke up. I know I should have listened to you about her son lying, but when her ex-boyfriend called, I just lost it." He watched Blue run into the bushes and return with a ball. "I really hurt her, Mama."

"Sometimes we hurt the ones we love, Kevin." Mama took the ball from Blue and tossed it. "Your daddy used to hurt me every day when he went out drinkin'. But I know he loved me, and you children too."

"I know, Mama, but you had to see the look on her face when she slammed her door on me. It was as if all the love she had for me had turned to hatred."

Blue came back, dropped the ball, and lay down at Mama's feet. She stroked his fur.

"Alicia will get over it, son, and so will you. If there is one thing I've learned in my years on God's green earth, it's that time heals old wounds. She's hurt now, Kevin. You have to give her a chance to be hurt."

"Yeah, but, Mama, she won't even return my phone calls." Kevin knew there was wisdom in Mama's advice, but he was still longing for Alicia.

"Kevin. Are you listenin' to me? Leave that girl alone for a while. I promise you, son, when she's ready to talk, she's gonna let you know. Even if it's just to curse your ass out."

"I'm sorry, Mama, but I can't leave her alone. Not until she tells me to my face that she doesn't love me."

"Son." She sighed sadly. "You're a grown man and you're capable of making your own decisions. But if you really love this girl, let her go."

"No way, Mama. There is absolutely no way in the world I'm gonna let her go." He wiped a tear. "If you could feel the emptiness I have inside right now, you wouldn't even suggest that to me."

As Mama hugged him, Kevin heard the phone ring. Jumping up, he ran inside to answer it. Breathless, he ran into the kitchen to find his sister Whitney already holding the phone to her ear. When he realized the call was not for him, Kevin walked into the living room, where Antoine and Tyrone were talking to his sister Phyllis.

"Pack your bags, fellas. We're leaving for New York in an hour."

Back in New York, Kevin could hardly wait to see Alicia. He called her several times on the day after his return but could not get her to return his calls. In desperation he decided to go to her office, hoping to clear up their misunderstanding. He drove to Brooklyn as fast as traffic would allow, weaving among the cars and praying he would not be pulled over.

At first he planned on waiting outside until Alicia left her office. But as he stood staring at the building, he grew impatient. He decided to call from a pay phone and ask her to meet him at a nearby coffee shop.

"Hart, Jacobs, and Hill law offices. Can I help you?" the receptionist answered the call.

"Hi, this is Mr. James. I wanted to know if Ms. Alicia Meyers is in?" Kevin lied, hoping she would not recognize his voice from the other ten calls he had made earlier in the day.

"Yes, Ms. Meyers is in, but she's on another line. Would you like me to put you on hold?"

"Ah, no, thank you, I'll call back later." He hung up the phone and looked up toward the fifth floor, where her office was.

Damn. All I want to do is talk to her. That's not too much to ask for, is it?

Kevin leaned against his car for almost an hour, debating whether he should go up to Alicia's office. He wanted her back, there was no question about that. But he was afraid that she would reject him, or, even worse, speak to him the way she did on Christmas Eve, when they broke up. He also couldn't decide if he should tell her about Michael's involvement. After all, he was just a kid, and Kevin should have known better than to listen to a kid.

Kevin looked over at the entrance to the building and watched a young couple embrace. His heart ached for the tenderness he had shared with Alicia. He couldn't stand it anymore. It was absolutely necessary that he make her understand that their relationship was special and deserved another try. He walked across the street and entered the well-decorated law offices of Hart, Jacobs, and Hill.

The reception area was large and the walls were covered with expensive-looking paintings of horses. All the furniture and desks were made from a heavy, dark brown wood, shellacked until it shone like a mirror. He gave the receptionist a friendly smile.

"Good morning. Can I speak to Alicia Meyers, please?"

"Sure. Let me ring her desk. And your name is, sir?"

"Mr. Brown, Kevin Brown." He tried to sound as professional as possible, waiting patiently as the receptionist dialed Alicia's extension.

"Hi, Alicia, this is Janice from the front desk. I have a Mr. Kevin Brown here to see you." She was silent as she listened to Alicia's response. "Okay, Alicia. I understand."

Looking at Kevin, the receptionist gave a phony smile. She delivered her message without changing her expression.

"Ms. Meyers said she's unavailable, and that she would appreciate it if you would no longer call or come by her home or place of business."

Kevin stepped back. "She actually said that?"

"Well, her choice of words were a bit stronger, but I think I expressed her thoughts."

She picked up a pen and started to work on something on her desk, fully expecting Kevin to leave. His plans were a little different. He got closer to the woman's desk and gave the woman a command.

"I don't believe this. Call her back. Tell her I'm not leaving until we talk!"

The receptionist's demeanor remained calm. "Sir, I'm going to have to ask you to leave, otherwise I'm going to call security."

"I don't care if you call President Clinton. I'm not moving a damn step until Alicia comes out here."

Kevin walked over to a chair and sat down, crossing his arms defiantly. After several minutes he came back to his senses and realized how stupid he must look.

I need to take my black ass home, he thought, standing up to leave. As he headed for the door, two white men in uniform approached.

"You're going to have to leave, sir," the larger security guard said politely as Kevin stepped toward the elevator.

"Yeah, no drug deals going down here, bro!" The other guard laughed, spinning his nightstick. He muttered his racist insult quietly since there were witnesses in the reception area.

"What did you say?" Kevin spun to face the men in anger.

"He didn't say anything, sir. We'd just appreciate it if you'd leave." The polite guard tried to hold his partner in check.

"I said you better get your black ass on that elevator before I crack open that coconut you call a head." He gripped his nightstick threateningly as Kevin took a step closer.

"Come on, John, we don't need no problems. Let the guy go," the bigger guard pleaded.

Kevin looked around and noticed that the commotion was beginning to attract a crowd. People were standing in their office doorways, probably hoping to witness a fight. Then to the left of the crowd he saw Alicia standing with her hand over her mouth. She was wearing a conservative navy-blue pinstripe suit, and Kevin was mesmerized for a moment. Was it possible she was even more beautiful than before?

"Sir, would you please leave?" The big guard was barely holding back his partner.

Kevin paid no attention as he took two steps closer to Alicia.

"Alicia, honey, we need to talk," he begged. The entire office turned to look at Alicia as if she were the cause of all the commotion.

"Kevin, I don't have anything to say to you." Her face was flushed and upset as she felt the stares of her coworkers. "How could you embarrass me like this?" She turned and walked back toward her office.

"Let go of me, Harvey. I'm going to teach him a little respect for our uniform." The smaller guard pointed his nightstick at Kevin as his partner held him back.

Kevin snatched the nightstick out of the guard's hand. He gripped the nightstick hard, looking dead into the eye of the now-terrified guard. Then he threw the nightstick to the ground. A wicked smile came to his face as he savored the fear that had paralyzed the bigoted guard.

The receptionist sat stunned at her desk. As Kevin stepped onto the elevator, he said to her, "Tell Alicia we need to talk, and that I'll be back."

18

KEVIN AND DENISE

It had been five days since the turmoil at Alicia's office. Kevin, Antoine, and Tyrone were lifting weights in the school gym when two men dressed in cheap suits walked into the gym. Maurice and Miles, head of school security, followed them.

"Mr. Brown, these two men would like to have a word with you," the principal said, clearly annoyed.

"They're cops, man. Miles would have never come out of his office if they weren't cops," Tyrone whispered to Kevin. He had seen men like these in the school before.

Kevin gave Tyrone a quick nod to show that he understood, though he had no idea what the police would need to speak to him for. As he placed his weights back on the rack, he prayed they didn't have bad news about Mama or his sisters.

"How can I help you gentlemen?" Kevin asked, wiping his face with a towel.

"Mr. Brown, we're with the police. Maybe we should discuss this in private. It's a personal matter." The tall black officer pointed to the door.

"No, we can talk right here. These guys are like brothers to me. I don't know what this is about, but I don't have anything to hide." He tried to sound confident but was actually quite nervous.

"Well, suit yourself," the smaller white cop responded. Reaching into his coat pocket, he handed Kevin a folded document. "Mr. Kevin Brown, you are being served with an order of protection: This order of protection states that you are not to go within five hundred feet of Alicia Meyers or her son, Michael Hill; you are not to go within five hundred feet of her home or place of business, you are not to call, write, or use electronic means to contact her. Do you understand what has just been explained to you?"

Kevin was in shock. He couldn't believe what was happening to him. He clenched his jaw to stop himself from exploding in anger. Alicia had actually gone so far as to get an order of protection against him, and the pain was unbearable.

"He understands, officer. He won't go by there." Antoine spoke for him, seeing that his friend was too distraught even to give the officer an answer.

"It's very important that he understand this, sir. Otherwise he can be arrested under the stalking laws of New York State," the black cop warned them.

"He's not going to go by there. I'm going to make it my business to make sure he don't," Tyrone guaranteed, in disbelief himself.

Miles led the two officers out of the gym as Antoine handed Kevin a towel to wipe his eyes. Suddenly he became aware that Maurice had not left with the other men.

"Well, Mr. Brown, I hope you realize that you made a fool not only of yourself, but of the school too."

"Look, Maurice, give the kid a break. You don't even know what the hell's going on," Antoine said in defense of his friend.

"I don't have to know, Mr. Smith. Just the fact that some woman would take out an order of protection against him makes me think he could be dangerous. I'm going to have Miles keep a closer eye on you, Mr. Brown. A man like you might get out of control around the students."

"Wait a minute, Dr. Johnson. If you think I would hurt one of the boys, you're crazy!" Kevin insisted. "This is all one big misunderstanding, and all I have to do is make one call and straighten this whole thing out. Give me your cell phone, Tyrone."

"I hope you're not planning on calling that young lady, Mr. Brown. That is, unless you plan on going to jail." Maurice shook his head at the young man's stupidity.

Kevin rifled through Tyrone's gym bag, searching for his cell phone. He ignored the disapproving stares of his friends. Tyrone finally moved to stop him.

"He's right, Kevin, you've got to let her go."

"I don't know if I can, Tyrone. I love her so much, it hurts."

Tyrone gave him a sympathetic one-armed hug, and Kevin slumped down on the weight bench.

"Mr. Brown, I want you to understand something. If the police come by here again looking for you, you'd better start looking for a new job, because I'm going to fire you. I suggest you get a hold of yourself." Maurice straightened out his suit jacket and walked out of the gym.

"Kevin, I don't give a shit how you feel. Don't you fucking call Alicia." Antoine jabbed his finger in the air near Kevin's face.

"I don't care what those cops say. I need to talk to her and get this straight!" Kevin knocked over a chair in anger as Antoine shouted at him.

"Are you fucking listening to me? Don't fucking call her!"

Tyrone stared at Antoine in disbelief. It was the first time Antoine had ever gone off. Usually Antoine was the one who remained calm and dignified in every situation. He realized that Antoine must feel very deeply about his friendship with Kevin to let his emotions escalate like this.

"Aw'ight, Antoine, I'll wait till she calls me for now. But I'm telling you, order of protection or not, Alicia's going to find out how much I love her if I have to lose my job and my freedom to do it."

Three weeks later Alicia still had not contacted Kevin. He had tried to be as patient as possible, still holding out hope that she would change her mind and listen to his apology. He waited every evening at home by the telephone, wondering where Alicia was and what she was doing. The order of protection sat on the counter in his kitchen, and each time he walked by it, it served as a reminder of his pain. Every day his emotions ran the gamut from deep sadness to rage.

On this day Kevin was particularly angry and confused by Alicia's actions. He had been sitting in his living room for two hours since he came home from work, brooding over the chance meeting he had with Alicia's sister Teresa. The television was on, but he barely noticed it as he recalled the conversation they had in front of a diner where Kevin had eaten lunch alone.

Teresa had noticed Kevin as she walked out of the restaurant with one of her girlfriends, talking loudly and laughing. When she saw Kevin, the smile quickly disappeared from her face, and she took a few steps to steer clear of him.

"Hi, Teresa," Kevin said, refusing to let her ignore him. He was desperate for any news of Alicia.

"Oh, hi," she answered, and kept walking.

"Wait, please. Just let me talk to you for a minute," Kevin begged.

Teresa rolled her eyes and told her girlfriend to wait for her. Kevin thought he heard Teresa say something like "He might get crazy, girl," but he ignored it, just grateful that she would stop to talk.

"What do you want? Aren't you supposed to stay away from Alicia's family?" Teresa put her hands on her hips and cocked her head to the side.

"I don't want to bother you, Teresa. I just need to know what's going on with Alicia. I really messed up."

"Mmm-hmm. You sure did," Teresa replied with no mercy.

"Listen, I know I was wrong about her and Trevor being together. I never should have accused her of that. I just want to tell her I was wrong, but now I can't even call her to apologize. Could you just tell her I'm sorry?" The words poured out as Kevin felt some slight sense of relief. This was the closest he had been to actually speaking to Alicia since their fight.

"Sorry, Kevin. You're too late." A strange, wicked grin came across Teresa's face.

"What are you talking about?"

"Well, when you accused her of being with Trevor, you must have pushed her back into his arms. You really hurt her, you know. And Trevor was there to soothe her. They're back together, and I think this time it's for good."

Teresa checked her watch to let Kevin know she was finished talking to him.

"But how could you let her go back with the man who beat her?"

"Look, Kevin. That's her life, not mine. And if she tells me she's okay, then I just have to stay out of it. Besides, who are you to talk about someone being violent?" Teresa's friend approached and told her it was time to go.

"But . . ." Kevin started to protest.

"But nothing." Teresa sighed. "She has moved on, Kevin, and it's time that you do the same. Just accept that you fucked this one up." With those harsh words Teresa and her friend walked away.

As he recalled the conversation and the heartless way Teresa had treated him, Kevin was angry with her and with Alicia. Now he was resolved that he would move on with his life.

She had let Trevor beat the shit out of her for years. But Kevin left a few messages on her answering machine and she had him humiliated with the order of protection. Now, after all that, she was dating Trevor again. He thought she must be crazy. How the hell could she choose Trevor over him?

He pounded his fists angrily into the arms of the chair. There was nothing he could do to clear up his mistake. He hadn't felt this helpless since that one lapse in judgment had ruined so many years of hard work to get to the NBA. Back then he had escaped his pain by moving to New York, running away. This time he decided to find another woman to ease his anguish. And in a fit of jealous anger he hoped that news of the other woman would get back to Alicia and hurt her the way he was hurting now.

Fuck this shit, man! I'm done with her. I should have known better than to fall into her trap in the first place. I bet if I had kicked her ass a few times, she'd be with me right now!

He grabbed the telephone and punched in the numbers for 1-900-BLACK-LUV, searching through the ads left by women rather than leaving one of his own. He was in a hurry to find a woman, and he needed a specific type. No way was he interested in another one like Alicia, who seemed so afraid of relationships. Kevin wanted a woman who sounded desperately in need of a man, and when he came across an ad left by a woman named Denise, he knew she was the right type. He left a short, no-nonsense message, hoping to get a reply soon so he could run from his past once again.

Denise listened to three cornball messages left in her 1-900-BLACK-LUV mailbox, erasing each one with a laugh.

"That guy has got to be kidding! He doesn't have a chance with a line like that!" she remarked more than once. But she had several more messages to listen to, and she hoped at least one would have some potential. Her wish came true as she heard a smooth baritone voice with a slight southern twang. Instantly she was attentive.

"Hi, Denise. My name is Kevin. Your message said that you're interested in athletic, dark-skinned men who love to have fun. Well, I happen to be six foot one with ebony skin. I work out every day, and I'm all about fun. My interests are sports and reggae music. Uh, look. You didn't really say much about yourself other than you're five foot eight and a hundred and twenty pounds. If you don't mind, I'd like to get to know you better. Maybe we can have some fun together. So here's my number: 555-9876. Call me."

Quickly memorizing Kevin's number, Denise began to fantasize. Something about Kevin's straightforward message attracted her. Most of the other men who left messages sounded like they were trying too hard to impress her, but Kevin's take-it-or-leave-it attitude was the kind of challenge Denise found very attractive.

She wished she had a face to place with that sexy voice. In her mind she envisioned every dark-skinned man she had ever seen on MTV or in the movies. She settled on an image that was a cross between Wesley Snipes and Michael Jordan. Unable to wait to talk to this man she had just created in her mind, Denise dialed Kevin's number.

Kevin was in the bathroom, shaving, when he heard the phone ring. Since his fight with Alicia he had not shaved, vowing to keep growing a beard until they resolved their differences. Tonight he had given up that hope and was removing the heavy beard. He put his razor on the edge of the sink and ran to answer the phone, his face still covered with shaving cream.

"Hello?" he answered, a bit breathless.

Chills ran up her back as she stammered, "Oh, uh, hi. Can I please speak to Kevin?"

"This is he." Kevin tried to remember if he had paid his Visa bill, since they were the only people who called during the dinner hour. "Who's calling, please?"

"Hi, Kevin, this is Denise from 1-900-BLACK-LUV. You left a message in my box. I hope I'm not interrupting anything."

"No, I'm not doing anything. How are you?" Shaving cream was smearing on the receiver as he shifted it to his other ear. He was amazed to be getting the call so soon, since he'd just left the message twenty minutes before. Either it was a coincidence or this woman checked her messages every half hour.

"I'm fine. The reason I'm calling is I was wondering if you'd like to go out tomorrow night?"

"I'd like that." He sat down in his recliner to get comfortable. "But I was hoping you'd tell me a little about yourself before we go out." This woman was even more desperate than Kevin had expected.

"Oh, I'm sorry. I hope I didn't give you the impression that I didn't want to talk to you. The truth is, I'm just dying to know what you look like."

"Well, not to brag, but I've been stopped by people who thought I was Tyson. You know, the model?"

"People mistake you for Tyson?" She picked up the latest issue of *Jet* from her coffee table and stared at Tyson Beckworth on the cover. "Oh, my God, I think I've died and gone to heaven."

"What did you say?" Kevin wasn't sure he had heard her correctly.

"Oh, nothing," she lied. "So, anyway, what do you do for a living?"

"I'm a teacher. I teach physical education at a high school in Queens," he answered. "What about you?"

"I'm a partner in a large malpractice law firm. It's a family-run business."

She always added that last part in case she was talking to a man intimidated by successful women. It usually made them feel better if they could think she got the job only because it was her daddy's firm. In truth she had a very sharp legal mind, but they could learn that about her later. But that didn't matter to Kevin. He was only curious why she was so eager to meet a stranger.

"A lawyer, huh? What makes a high-paid lawyer need to call a date line anyway?" He immediately assumed she must be pitifully ugly.

"Well, to be honest, I just find it hard to meet good black men. What about you? Why did you call the line?"

"This is actually not my first time. I met my ex-girlfriend on the line."

"By the tone of your voice, I guess you still care for her."

"I don't care for her. I love her. But I also realize it's time to move on."

Denise jumped at the chance to soothe his aching heart. "Would moving on include going with me to tomorrow night's Knicks game?"

"It would if the game wasn't sold out. But this is Shaq and Kobe's only Madison Square Garden appearance this year. The nosebleed seats are being scalped at five hundred bucks."

"My dad has season tickets. It shouldn't be too hard for me to get them." Denise silently thanked her father, who was always too busy to attend the games. "So what do you think? Want to go see Knicks with me?"

"Yes. I'd like that a lot." Even if nothing worked out with Denise, Kevin was happy for a distraction for at least one night.

"Great! Meet me in front of the Garden twenty minutes before the game. I'll be wearing a white hooded leather jacket and white pants."

"That sounds great, Denise," he said as a blob of shaving cream fell in his lap. "Look, I've got to go take care of something, so I'll see you tomorrow, okay?"

"Sure, Kevin. Good night."

Denise hung up the phone and rushed into her room to decide

which shoes to wear with her white outfit. She eagerly anticipated the next evening.

On his end Kevin hung up and wiped the shaving cream off his leg. He stomped into the bathroom to finish removing the remainder of his beard and hopefully any reminder of his problems with Alicia.

The following night Denise sat contentedly in the Seventh Avenue Diner, waiting for Kevin to return from the rest room. The two had come to have coffee after the game. As she waited alone, Denise thought about the evening. She had been having minor feelings of regret about lying to her father. He was under the impression she was using the tickets to entertain clients for the law firm. After spending a few hours on her date, Denise had forgotten about her father completely. Kevin had been so polite and charming, he swept her right off her feet. And his looks just completed the package as far as she was concerned. She smiled to herself, amused that this whole phone-date experiment had turned out so well.

Sliding into his chair, Kevin noticed her smile and gave her one back.

"Did the waitress come yet?"

"Yes. I ordered you coffee and a slice of cheesecake. Is that okay?"

"Thanks." He had hardly heard what she had told him. He was busy admiring the clothing on a man who had walked into the diner. "Look at that coat he's wearing. Now, that's hot."

"You like it, huh?" Denise admired Kevin's taste.

"Yeah, I like that style. You can probably tell I'm into fashion."

"I'm pretty sure you can find a coat like that one in Bloomingdale's," Denise suggested.

"Not on a teacher's salary. That's a Tommy Hilfiger leather. I bet it cost at least a grand."

"Who knows? When's your birthday? Maybe someone might buy you one." She winked.

"Only if my mama hits the lotto." Kevin joked as the waitress set down their order.

"Hey. What did you think about Kobe Bryant?" Denise stuck her spoon in Kevin's cheesecake. "Wasn't he incredible?"

"Anyone who scores fifty-three points in one game is pretty impressive. But I have to admit, I was more impressed that you got seats right next to Spike Lee."

"I'd love to take credit for that, but my father has had these seats for years. It's more like Spike got his seats next to my family." Denise noticed a strange look come across Kevin's face. "Kevin, is something wrong?"

"No, not exactly." Then he gave her the truth. "Well, yeah, I guess there is. See those two women over there?" He nodded his head in the direction of a nearby table.

Denise glanced at the two black women seated at the table. "Yes, what about them?"

"They're staring at us."

"Oh, my God, Kevin, that's not your ex-girlfriend, is it?" She was suddenly very self-conscious.

"No, that's not Alicia." He was amazed that she hadn't figured out why the women were staring. "Denise, can I ask you a question?"

"Sure, Kevin, ask me anything you like." She was beginning to suspect where this was headed.

"You seem a little unaware of what's really going on here. Why would a white woman call an African American date line anyway?"

"Like I told you last night on the phone, I find it hard to meet good black men."

"But why do you want to meet black men anyway? Why didn't you call one of the hundreds of white date lines?"

He had been shocked when he met Denise at the Garden and discovered she was a white woman. At first he thought she was probably some rich white girl looking to hook up with a brother to fulfill a jungle-fever fantasy. He didn't mind this, because in truth, he thought a one-night stand might be just what he needed. But now he was suspicious about her true motives. Her actions during the evening were not the typical flirtatious advances of a woman looking for easy sex. Kevin was beginning to worry that this woman was looking for a relationship, and he knew it was something he did not want just then. He waited for Denise to explain her intentions, hoping she was not interested in anything too deep.

"Honestly, Kevin, because I have no attraction for white men, and very little attraction to light-skinned black men. My therapist thinks it has something to do with the dark-skinned chauffeur who drove my father's car and dropped my brothers and me at school every morning until I was a teenager. He gave me more fatherly affection than my own dad."

Kevin had to stifle a laugh as he thought: *Those damn therapists will say anything to convince their patients they need more treatment. That's why black people don't go to them.*

"But to tell you the truth, I think it was more simple than that. I saw Wesley Snipes in the movie *New Jack City,* and he was so hot, I saw it fifteen times. Then I saw him make love in *Mo' Better Blues.* I don't think it's complex. I just have a strong attraction for dark black men."

Kevin listened to every word intensely. The majority of white women he'd ever known who preferred brothers were either super-fat or trashy. This woman didn't fit his stereotype. She was beautiful and classy, with her blond hair and flawless makeup. He supposed it was possible that it was just some sexual fantasy brought on by a few too many Wesley Snipes films.

"Okay, Denise, what's the real deal? Your Park Avenue boyfriend not turning you on under the sheets? Thought you'd go find a big black stud to put out that fire between your legs, then go back to the country club and brag to your friends about how you let some black savage ravage your body?"

"*No.* This isn't a game to me, Kevin, and I'm not some cheap one-night stand. I just like dating black men." Denise gave him a serious look. She was surprised by his affront. It was such a sudden change after how polite and gentle he had been toward her all evening.

"All right. If you're so into brothers, why didn't you tell me you were white on the phone last night, or at least say it in your message?"

"Would you have agreed to meet me if I told you I was white?"

"No, I probably wouldn't have even responded to your ad." He wanted to be sure this woman knew there was no chance of a relationship.

"Well, you don't feel that way now, do you?" As uncomfortable as she was, Denise was glad that the color issue was out in the open.

"Denise, I hope I didn't just give you the wrong idea." Kevin knew it was important to clear this up quickly. "I don't believe in interracial dating. We can be friends, but this is the last date between us."

"Why? Aren't you having a good time?"

Kevin thought she might actually be ready to cry, and that was definitely not the scene he wanted. She had treated him to a great time, and the thought of going to more Knicks games definitely appealed to him. He decided to steer her down the friendship road.

"I'm having a great time, and you're a beautiful woman. I swear, if you were black, I'd probably end up marrying you and having kids. But there are too many black women looking for a good black man for me to go out like that. I'm sorry." He imagined his mother fainting on the spot if he walked into her house with this white woman.

"You're not even going to give it a chance?"

"No, I'm not." Kevin tried to sound sympathetic. "But I could use a new friend, okay?"

"Okay." Denise gained her composure. Her lawyerly instincts took over and she didn't want this man to see her get emotional. She forced a smile. He was the handsome, sincere, and honest man she had sought for a very long time. There was no way she was going to give him up just because she was white. She was determined he was going to be hers, and she was accustomed to getting what she wanted. They could play the friendship game for a little while, if that's what it took.

19

MAURICE

Maurice walked into his bedroom a little wobbly, sipping on his fourth brandy. He sat on the bed and loosened his tie as Sylvia walked out of her bathroom. She strode past him without a word and stood facing the full-length mirror. She let her robe fall to the floor, exposing a pair of thong panties, silk stockings, and a garter belt.

Maurice tried to adjust his eyes. He stared at the glass in his hand, thinking he ought to buy this brand of brandy more often. He never would have imagined he could be turned on by his wife the way he was then. It had to be the brandy. Placing his glass on the nightstand, he stood up and walked over to his wife. He pressed his body against hers from behind, wrapping his arms around her waist.

"Happy birthday, baby," he murmured in her ear.

She thanked him without a trace of emotion in her voice. She hurried to put her earrings on as Maurice kissed her neck.

"Could you stop that, please? I really have to get ready to meet Vivian for this show." She shrugged her shoulders and wiggled away from his grasp.

"You don't have to be there for an hour and a half, sweetie." He moved closer and started nibbling on her neck again.

Unfazed, Sylvia pulled away and moved over to her dresser to select a necklace from her jewelry box. Maurice followed her and ran his hand along her thigh, taking a long look at the erotic underwear Sylvia had on.

"When did you start wearing such sexy underwear? It makes me want to do naughty things to you, you know." He figured his wife would be flattered by his rare compliment. Instead, she whirled to face him angrily.

"I can't believe you just asked me that. For your information, I've been wearing this kind of lingerie for months. If you were interested in getting some, you would have figured it out a while ago. Goddammit, Maurice, it's the middle of February. I can't believe it took you two months to notice. Am I supposed to be flattered now?" she ranted.

This was definitely not the reaction he had expected. Usually she was so compliant when he asked for sex. He didn't know what her problem was but figured he would have to fake an apology now if he wanted to get anything. He gave her a weak hug.

"I'm sorry, honey," he began feebly. "Why don't you lie down and let me make it up to you?" He took off his suit jacket, fully expecting her to comply.

"No, thanks, I'm really in a rush."

"Hey, Syl, it's your birthday. Don't you want to get a little before you go out?" He had never come so close to begging.

"Maurice, I just got my hair and nails done. And to tell you the truth, I think I'm getting my period. These cramps are killing me." She didn't even bother to look at him as she slid into a fitted black dress designed to reveal lots of cleavage.

"I guess there's nothing you can do about that. So why are you wearing thong panties if you're going to get your period?" He was disappointed and becoming a little suspicious. Sylvia could hear the doubt in his voice, and that amused her.

"I don't know, Maurice. Maybe they just make me feel a little sexier. God knows you don't do that for me."

"You need to put on some regular panties before you go out," he demanded. If he couldn't coax her into giving him something, he sure as hell was going to at least put her back in her place.

"Look, Maurice, why the hell are you telling me how to dress all of a sudden? I'm dressing to make me happy. You don't seem to care about my self-esteem, so I'm doing what makes me happy. Now, if you want to talk about underwear, why didn't you have any on when you came home two nights ago?"

That shut him up. When he didn't respond, she turned around and finished dressing. Maurice sat brooding. He knew he couldn't push her too far, because his own indiscretions were becoming more frequent. As he learned how easy it was to find unsuspecting young women on the date line, Maurice had begun taking more risks. Where he used to stay out perhaps once a month, it was becoming more like once or twice a week. His libido was satisfied, but it was becoming harder and harder to keep his alibis straight. On several occasions he had slipped, as she pointed out, by forgetting his underwear once, and missing a smear of lipstick on his collar on another occasion.

Before this night Maurice believed wholeheartedly that he could do anything and Sylvia would still be right by his side. She had been almost pathetically devoted to him for so many years, regardless of how badly he treated her, how much he belittled her. Her devotion had given Maurice a strong sense of invincibility, but Sylvia had shocked him during this fight. He had no idea she had even noticed the night he came home without underwear. Now he knew that if she had noticed that and not mentioned it, there were probably other things she was withholding. Sylvia would just throw this all back in his face if he started accusing her of too much. It was as if they were in some kind of bizarre tactical war, and she held the upper hand at the moment. After a long silence he made his last-ditch attempt to get some play from his wife. He needed it to feel like he was still in control.

"Well, wake me up when you get home, Syl. Maybe I'll let you go down on me."

Not on your life, sucker was what she wanted to tell him, but she played it cool to avoid a fight. She wanted to get out of there on time.

"Sorry. I'm spending the night at Vivian's." Admiring herself in the mirror, she smoothed the fabric of her black dress over her hips and gave Maurice one more jab. "But talk to me in five or six days and maybe we can work something out, okay?"

Maurice slumped back on the bed, defeated.

Kissing him on the forehead, Sylvia walked out the bedroom door, telling him over her shoulder, "I'll see you tomorrow after work."

Maurice sat on the bed and pouted for a while after Sylvia left.

What the hell was that all about? he wondered angrily as he finished his brandy. *Since when does she turn me down?*

This side of Sylvia was completely foreign to Maurice, and he certainly didn't like it. He preferred his wife when she was totally compliant to his wishes. Now he felt challenged by her, and it upset him.

He considered going downstairs to get the bottle of brandy and finishing it off but couldn't stand the image of staying home to get drunk alone. He sat around thinking about how Sylvia had changed. The thought that she could be cheating on him crossed his mind, but he just couldn't make himself believe that she would want anyone but him. His place as the most important thing in her life had been cemented so many years before, he doubted that would ever change. Now his job was to figure out this metamorphosis she seemed to be experiencing and stop it before things became more difficult for him. He didn't want things at home to become so unbearable that he was forced to divorce Sylvia. As much as he didn't love her, he needed a respectable wife for social functions. And he definitely needed her family money, which had helped them achieve their present status. Maurice knew he had some serious work to do to bring his wife back to her old compliant self.

In the meantime though, he was still horny. His plan to straighten out his wife would have to wait until he was a little more sober and a little less horny. He pulled out his wallet and cell phone. Inside his wallet he searched for and found a business card from a tattoo parlor on Jamaica Avenue. He called the parlor and asked to speak to Janet, one of the tattoo artists.

"This is Janet," a woman with a deep, sexy voice answered.

"Hi, Janet, this is Maurice. We met yesterday afternoon, remember?"

"Oh, yeah." She laughed. "You're the straitlaced rich guy I met from 1-900-BLACK-LUV. I can't believe you pretended to be interested in getting a tattoo."

"Actually, if I remember correctly, you seemed pretty interested in working on me."

"Yeah, I liked you." Janet was pleased that he got right to the point. She found aggressive men very attractive. "I like older men, okay? I never did get much attention from my daddy, being the youngest of nine kids. So maybe I have some kind of complex," she joked. "Got a problem with that?"

"A complex, huh? Well, I think I could talk to you and help you work some of that out. How about going up to the Poconos with me tonight?"

"The Poconos, huh? No, I don't think so. I've gotta work tomorrow. But if you want, we can grab a cup of coffee."

"I was really thinking the Poconos would be nice." He tried painting a very romantic picture. "You know. A log cabin, a fire, and a bottle of wine. Come on, we'll have fun. It might be just what you need to get over your little father-figure problem."

He was determined to end up in bed with this woman, not sipping coffee and pretending to be interested in her conversation. Janet knew what he was trying to do. But she was at work and couldn't continue this little flirting game for too much longer.

"Look, Maurice, I can't stay on this phone and discuss this all night. Your offer sounds really nice, but I'm not in the mood to go all the way to Pennsylvania. Let's just go have a cup of coffee. I promise it will be worth your while."

"All right. Where do you want to meet?" Maurice reluctantly agreed. He figured he could convince her once they were face-to-face.

"Meet me at the Van Wyck Diner on Queens Boulevard and Eighty-seventh Avenue. I get off in about forty-five minutes."

Maurice tried to remember the last time he was in a diner. He couldn't keep his mouth shut. "A diner. That's a little cheesy, isn't it? Why don't you let me take you somewhere nicer than that?"

"Oh, my God. Don't be such a snob. Just meet me there, Maurice." She hung up the phone without even saying good-bye.

Her attitude turned him off. He considered not even going to meet Janet, but when he remembered her tight body, he stood up to change his clothes and splash on a little cologne. Within ten minutes he was in the car. Maurice drove past the Van Wyck Diner three times before he stopped. During the car ride he once again had doubts about meeting Janet for coffee. Something just didn't feel right. Something about their earlier conversation rubbed him the wrong way, but he couldn't figure out what it was. As he drove past the diner once more, he noticed that the Jet Motel was directly across the boulevard. He put aside his reservations and pulled into the diner parking lot.

Man, this is not my style. I've got to get this little bitch up to the Poconos.

Waiting in the diner, Janet had seen his black Mercedes drive past four times and was beginning to think Maurice was not going to come in. She smiled when he finally walked through the door. He walked over and kissed her cheek. She decided not to mention that she had seen him circling in his car.

"You look nice," he told her, examining her outfit, which consisted of ripped jeans and a halter top. He liked the way she revealed so much of her gorgeous body. It was covered in various places with piercings and tattoos. He silently counted the large number of piercings in her ears and nose. She was one hell of a freak but sexy in an exotic kind of way.

Standing five foot eight, Janet was a very pretty woman. She sported a short, nappy bleached-blond hairstyle that highlighted her African features and bronze complexion. Although muscular, her body was very feminine, and her tattoos almost seemed like an invitation to touch.

Sitting beside Janet in the booth, Maurice tried one last time to convince her to go away with him. "Come on, Janet. We can jump in my car and be in Pennsylvania in ninety minutes."

"No." She licked her lips and looked boldly into Maurice's eyes. "All you want to do is get me up there and fuck me."

"I didn't say that. I just want to show you a good time." Maurice had an uncomfortable feeling that the conversation was out of his control. This was definitely not what he needed after his argument with Sylvia.

"You didn't have to say it, man. I knew what you wanted as soon as you called me today." She leaned across the table. "Let's keep it real. Why else would a man like you want to date a girl like me? Look at you. You're what, forty? Maybe forty-five? You wear designer suits and drive a Mercedes-Benz. I bet you're even married."

Maurice gulped but didn't say a word.

Janet continued. "What other reason do you have for dating a twenty-year-old woman with thirty-two piercings and this on my neck?" She pointed to a tattoo on her neck that read BITE ME HERE AND I MIGHT CUM.

"So what else would you want except to fuck me? It's not like you could take me to one of your stuffed-shirt social events." She leaned back and folded her arms across her chest, waiting for an answer.

Maurice was totally flustered. From the moment he had sat down, Janet decided the direction of the conversation and taken charge of the date. This was something he had not experienced in all his years of womanizing. He wasn't sure how to deal with it, and he sure as hell didn't like it. Trying to regain his composure and some control, he put his fists on the table.

"Look, Janet. You've got this all wrong—"

"Just answer the damn question! Do you want to fuck me, or what?" Janet interrupted him loud enough for the whole restaurant to hear.

"Yes, Janet." Maurice leaned close and whispered, "I want to make love to you. But I don't want the whole diner to know."

"Then what the hell are we sitting around here for?" She dangled a key from the Jet Motel in front of his face. Throwing five dollars on the table for the coffee they had never even ordered, Janet ordered Maurice, "Let's go!"

Still a little flustered, Maurice followed as he was told. He was careful not to make eye contact with anyone as they walked past the tables and out of the diner. As soon as they entered Room 18 of the motel,

Janet threw her coat on the bed and stripped off her jeans and halter. She stood proudly by the bed as Maurice stared. He had barely begun loosening his tie when he stopped in fascination as he noticed that Janet's body was pierced in other places as well.

"Wow, you really do like to pierce things, don't you?" He walked closer to touch the rings hanging from her breasts.

"It makes things more sensitive," she said, arching her back as he massaged her breasts. She pulled Maurice close and slid her tongue into his mouth. He felt the metal ball that was piercing her tongue. Slowly she pulled him on top of her as they fell onto the bed.

After a few seconds she found herself getting bored. She was definitely not impressed with the way Maurice kissed, so she slowly pushed his head down below her belly button. Maurice resisted, but Janet just kept pushing until he got the idea and went to work.

"Ow!" she blurted out not long after, pushing him away. "Damn! For an older man, you don't have much experience pleasing women, do you?"

"My wife's pretty frigid. She doesn't like oral sex," Maurice answered flatly as he sat up. As soon as the word "wife" left his mouth, he regretted it.

"Ha! I knew you were married," she said matter-of-factly. "This wife of yours, she does like to fuck, doesn't she?"

"Yes. She does like that."

He was humbled but also relieved she didn't care that he was married. Janet was beginning to hope she hadn't wasted fifty dollars on a room.

"Then take your clothes off and let's see what you can do."

She reached for his belt buckle to speed him along. Maurice's embarrassment changed to anger at the way Janet spoke to him.

Who the hell does this little bitch think she's talking to anyway? he wondered, wishing they had gone to the Poconos so he could leave her arrogant ass behind.

"You want to get fucked? I'm going to fuck the hell out of you!" he shouted at her as he ripped off his shirt.

Janet liked this new side of the old man. She sat eagerly on the bed, watching him undress. When he took off his boxers, she was thankful for small favors. At least he was well endowed.

Practically lunging on top of her, Maurice entered her with the confidence of a man on a mission. He wasn't wasting any time on foreplay with this woman.

"Oh, yeah," he growled as he listened to her moan. "Talk shit now, you little bitch."

Turned on by Maurice's aggression, Janet wrapped her thighs tightly around his back. Within seconds Maurice moaned loudly and fell on top of her.

"What the fuck?" She was stunned. "What the fuck was that? I've had vaccinations that lasted longer than that. Get the fuck off me!"

She shoved him off her and sat up in the bed. Maurice had enough of her attitude.

"I'm tired of you talking to me like I'm some child, bitch. What the fuck is your problem?"

"My problem, Five-Stroke Charlie, is I paid fifty bucks for this room and you're gonna give me that money and carfare too. Damn! I been with virgins that fuck longer than you, old man."

Maurice crumpled a hundred-dollar bill and threw it at Janet as she hurried to get dressed.

"You should have told me your fee before we took our clothes off, whore."

"You're right, motherfucker! At least then it would have been worth my while!" Janet shouted, picking up the money on her way out the door.

At the same time that Maurice had been home brooding about her changed behavior, Sylvia was in her car heading for Tyrone's apartment. She was happier than she had been in a long time to have this second chance with him. After several weeks of begging and pleading, Tyrone had finally agreed to speak to her so they could clear the air about the incident at the country club.

As she gripped the steering wheel, she cursed under her breath. How could she have been so stupid as to smoke crack that night? Especially when she knew he had a drug problem.

She pulled in front of Tyrone's building and smiled when she saw him standing there. He had been waiting nervously for twenty-five minutes. She grabbed her purse from the front seat and hurried across the street to get to him.

"Long time no see," he murmured, wrapping his arms around her and kissing her gently. Both of them had missed being in an embrace like this. He opened the door to the building and held it for her as she entered.

"Do you meet all your lady friends at the front door?" Sylvia asked coyly as they walked up the stairs.

"No, but you're the first one brave enough to park a Mercedes in my neighborhood. So I thought I would make sure you made it into the building alive."

They reached the fourth floor and stood at the landing while Tyrone unlocked the door to his apartment. Sylvia got to the point immediately.

"I want to apologize again for what happened at the club Christmas Eve. I don't know what got into me. I'm not a drug addict, and I'm usually not a drug user." She wished she could find a way to express how truly remorseful she felt.

"Listen, let's just forget it, okay?" He left the key in the lock and turned to her sternly. "You've probably apologized a thousand times since then. So let's not get into it, because the thought of that pipe in your mouth is going to really piss me off. I don't know what the fuck you were thinking about that day."

"Okay, Tyrone, I'm sorry."

Looking around the hallway to avoid his eyes after the tense moment, she couldn't believe the condition of the apartment building. The walls had obviously not been painted in over a decade, aside from the graffiti that covered them. Litter was piled in every visible corner, and one apartment had four bags of trash piled next to the door. The odor made her shiver.

She wondered how a man so neat could stand to live among such filth. A roach ran down the stained wall. She jumped slightly. Tyrone unlocked the door and held it open for Sylvia.

"I'm sorry about the way I spoke to you a minute ago. I just care about you so much. I don't want anything to happen to you." He stroked her face.

"I know, Tyrone. I deserved every word. I don't know why I was so stupid."

"Let's just put it behind us. Come on in."

He stepped aside to let her enter. As Sylvia's eyes took in the incredible scene before her, Tyrone spoke.

"I didn't have a chance to give you your Christmas present, so what's inside is both your Christmas and birthday present. I hope you like it. I don't have a lot of money like your friends, so I tried to use my creativity. Welcome to Tyrone's heaven on earth."

She walked into the studio apartment in awestruck silence. The small place, which consisted of a bed, a couch, a television, and a small kitchenette area, was aglow with what seemed like thousands of scented candles. The floor and bed were covered with dozens of small white balloons, while the ceiling was covered with helium balloons with long white ribbons.

"Oh, Tyrone. This does look like heaven." Sylvia walked over to the bed. Lying on the bed was a large rectangular gift wrapped in plain white paper with a huge red bow. Sylvia knew it must be a painting. "Can I open it now?" she asked excitedly.

"Of course you can, baby." He stood beside her as she reached for the gift.

Anxiously ripping the paper off, Sylvia gasped as she uncovered a stunning painting of an angel. In the corner was Tyrone's signature.

"I used you as the model for her face. I would wake up at all hours of the night thinking about you and use my memory to paint a little each night."

"Oh, Tyrone, it's absolutely beautiful. A true work of art. " She put the painting down and turned to wrap her arms around his waist.

"I guess I was God inspired, living here in heaven." He smiled.

"You are the most romantic man I've ever met."

"Baby, it's all about you. My job is to make you happy," he murmured, kissing her deeply.

This was truly all he did want. There was something about this woman, who had been denied any real affection for so long, that made him want to work twice as hard to please her. Even the drug incident had been forgiven, and he didn't think he could ever excuse someone else's drug use again in his lifetime. But over the weeks that he thought about it, he realized he couldn't push her away over one mistake. In his own life he had chosen drugs to escape, and perhaps as she was making all these changes in her life, she got a little scared and needed to escape. Whatever her ultimate reason was, he knew he was crazy about Sylvia and had missed her terribly, so he decided to give her another chance.

"Just being near you makes me happy," Sylvia told him.

"And you make me happy, Syl. I think we're really good for each other."

"Oh. Really? How am I good for you?"

She wanted to be told that she was important to someone. She desperately needed that kind of affection in her life.

"Sylvia, you've shown incredible faith in me, encouraging me to reach for my highest goals. Nobody's ever really done that for me before. You introduced me to the black elite and made me feel like one day I could get out of this place and be one of them."

"You would want to be like those people at the country club?" Her eyes widened.

"Not really." Tyrone laughed. "But it is a good feeling to think that your woman believes you have the potential to be accepted there."

She draped her arms over his shoulders, and they began to slow-dance as she softly sang, "Heaven, I'm in heaven . . ."

It was six o'clock the next morning when Sylvia awoke. Tyrone was across the room, ironing his shirt for work. She decided that the bathroom could wait a few minutes and lit a cigarette. After their long night of passionate lovemaking, she was a little stiff. Making love to Tyrone had been the most wonderful experience of her life. Not only did she have an orgasm, but she had multiples for the first time in her life.

"Good morning, how are you feeling?" Tyrone asked. He had stopped ironing and sat next to her on the bed.

"A little overwhelmed but good." Sylvia rested her head in his lap.

"Overwhelmed?"

"Yes, overwhelmed. I've been with my husband for twenty years, and until now I never realized how bad he is in bed."

This thought upset Sylvia, and she stood up and walked into the bathroom to avoid discussing it further with Tyrone. He watched her. The sight of her body made him smile as he remembered how appreciative she was each time he had made love to her that night.

"You want me to make you something to eat before you go to work?" she asked as she came back out of the bathroom. She wanted to do something nice for him.

"No." He kneeled at the edge of the bed and smiled naughtily. "I think I can find something to eat right here."

"Tyrone, you're going to get me started and be late for work." She giggled.

"No, I won't. You can drive me."

He nibbled on her ankle and kissed his way up her thigh, finding the spot Maurice never cared enough to look for. Forty-five minutes later the two of them climbed into Sylvia's car.

"Damn, I'm gonna be late." He sounded worried.

"Don't stress yourself." She was completely relaxed after Tyrone's early morning gift. "There's nothing you can do about it now anyway. I'll drive as fast as I can. Now, where are we going?"

"Springfield and Francis Lewis. The Alternative High School for Boys."

Her heart was in her mouth. As large as the New York school system was, it had never occurred to her that he might work at the school where her husband was principal.

This is going to get very complicated, she thought nervously as they drove away from Tyrone's building. She knew she would have to choose carefully the time to reveal to Tyrone who his boss really was. For the time being she just wanted to bask in the afterglow of their beautiful reunion.

20

KEVIN

"Two hundred and ninty-seven! Two hundred and ninty-eight! Two hundred and ninty-nine! Ahhh, Three hundred!"

Antoine barely got the words out as he finished the last sit-up. He and Kevin were doing their daily workout in the gym, fitting in one last session before the school closed for the midwinter vacation. Although he was starting to notice results from his workout and diet routine, Antoine would never have a physique like Kevin's. Yet every time they got together, he would push himself to match Kevin set for set. On this day Kevin decided to work a little harder to see if his buddy would really try to keep up with him. It was a friendly competition.

"You boys working up a good sweat?" Tyrone shouted as he entered the weight room with a wide grin across his face.

"Yeah, and you need to get out of that uniform and start sweating too," Kevin answered, giving his friend a light hug. "You're twenty minutes late."

"Bro, I got my workout last night."

He wished he could tell his friends about his relationship with Sylvia without ruining his reputation as a ladies' man. His relationship was definitely smoothing the rough edges of his personality, but there was no way he was about to let his boys know it.

"So you finally hit that little freak you been telling me about, huh?" Kevin gave him a high-five. "I hope you put it on her?"

"Let's put it this way." Tyrone hesitated for a second, trying to get his lies straight. "Tesha Walker asked me to be her baby's daddy last night." He laughed along with Kevin.

"What's so funny about that?" Antoine asked.

"I probably could have gotten some last night myself," Kevin interjected. He wished sometimes Antoine could just be lighthearted with them.

"You almost got some?" Tyrone grinned in mock amazement. "I thought your girl was trying to get you locked up for harassment."

"Don't go there, Tyrone." Now Kevin was the one becoming serious. "I was talking about that woman, Denise, I told you about."

"Oh, yeah," Antoine remembered. "That's the woman you went to the Knicks game with last night. How'd that go anyway?"

"Perfect, except for one thing."

"What's that?"

"She's white."

"What! Kevin, what are you doing going out with a white woman?" Antoine was not pleased at all.

"So what?" Tyrone exclaimed. "Was she ugly?"

"Not at all."

"Then what's the problem? You said she's a lawyer. That means she's got loot." Tyrone patted Kevin on the back to show his approval. "So, she was fine, huh?"

"You should have seen her, Ty. She's got this natural blond hair down to her shoulders, with these crystal-blue eyes and an ass like a black woman."

Even with his reservations about interracial dating, Kevin had to admit Denise was very attractive. She was the kind of woman some would refer to as a trophy.

"Damn, I always wanted to get with a natural blonde." Tyrone's voice showed a hint of jealousy. "I once dated this really cute blonde a few times. Then, when she took off her clothes, I found out she was a brunette. Damn, was I pissed."

"Yeah, I could see you getting mad. The thought of sleeping with a woman who's blond down there is kind of exotic." Kevin laughed as Tyrone continued his story.

"Man, that girl took off her clothes and I was like a kid whose parents bought him books for Christmas. The books were nice, but they definitely weren't what he wanted."

"I wonder if Denise is a true blonde?" Kevin asked himself.

"There's only one way to find out. Why didn't you hit that last night anyway?" Tyrone asked curiously. "I thought you said from now on, if a woman wants you to stay, they've got to give you some play."

Meanwhile Antoine's objections had practically been forgotten by the two friends as they bantered about sex with a blonde. Although

Antoine didn't consider himself to be prejudiced, he had strong feelings against interracial dating, feelings he had assumed Kevin shared with him. He sat listening to Tyrone and Kevin with displeasure on his face. He had to speak his mind.

"Kevin, what the hell are you doing going out with a white woman? I thought you were against interracial dating." He folded his arms and waited for an answer like an angry parent.

"I didn't even know she was white," Kevin protested.

"Oh, sure, she put a magic spell on you so you couldn't see she was white. Give me a break. I can't believe you would insult my intelligence like that."

"It was a blind date. We met on the 1-900-BLACK-LUV line, and she didn't tell me her race, so I assumed she was black. I had no idea what she looked like until we met at the Garden."

"Well, if that's the case, why did you go out with her once you saw her?" Antoine was about to start his pro-black speech.

"The woman had courtside tickets to the Knicks game. Do you really think I was going to miss that because she was white?" He was exasperated. He had struggled enough with his own conscience on this issue and didn't want to have to explain himself to Antoine. As long as he didn't plan to make this a steady thing, what difference did it make if he went to the game with her?

"Besides, Antoine," he continued, "if you had been in the same situation, I really wonder if you would have left the woman standing alone in front of the Garden. What can one night hurt? It's not like I'm taking her home to meet Mama."

"I never figured you for a sellout, Kevin. I really thought you were one of the righteous brothers. Dating a white woman just to see a basketball game? That's pathetic." He wouldn't even look him in the eye.

"Wait a minute, Antoine. Who the hell are you to call me a sellout?" Kevin was defensive. "Besides, I was fifteen minutes late. What was I supposed to say? 'Sorry, miss, I know you've been waiting in the cold for almost twenty minutes, but I can't go out with you now that I know you're white.' I don't care what your feelings are about whites, Antoine. My mama didn't raise me to be rude. Denise has feelings too."

"The hell with her feelings!" Antoine shouted. "Did you think about the feelings of the sisters that saw you with her?" He picked up his gym bag to leave. He was visibly upset. "If you really want blond hair and blue eyes, Kevin, you can find them right here in your own race. Black women come in any shade or hair color you want. All you have to do is look."

"Hold on, Antoine. You're getting this all wrong. I still don't believe in interracial relationships. I went out with her not to be rude. I told her that we couldn't see each other again." Antoine tried to hide a smile when he heard this. He dropped the gym bag, indicating he was staying to hear more.

"Don't listen to this fool, Kevin," Tyrone interrupted. "Antoine's got his own agenda."

"I don't have any agenda." Antoine hoped Tyrone wasn't going where he thought.

"Yes, you do." Tyrone smiled ear to ear. "I guess you never told Kevin your pops left your mom for a white woman."

Kevin was stunned. He had always thought Antoine's dislike for white women was a little obsessive. But now it made sense. Antoine had told him once that his mother had committed suicide five years earlier and that he didn't speak to his father because of it. Now Kevin saw the bigger picture. His mother's death must have had something to do with her husband leaving her for a white woman.

"Are you talking about my mother?" Antoine glared at Tyrone.

"No, man, I would never do that." He was serious. "I just think that you should let Kevin make up his own mind and not prejudice him because of the problems you've had. I mean, white people have done right by me."

Kevin watched his two friends during their disagreement. Both of them made good points. Tyrone was sold on the fact that a white counselor at his drug program was the one who had put him on the right track. The woman had gone above and beyond for Tyrone when she recognized his talent. Antoine, on the other hand, felt strongly that blacks and whites should be separated, because it would lead to the loss of identity for blacks. As the argument heated up, Kevin jumped in.

"I know the white people in your program helped you out a lot, Ty." Kevin got between his friends to separate them. "The truth is, I have a lot of white friends back home too. But this isn't about friendship for me. This is about the feelings of my mama, my sisters, and every other black woman who is offended by a brother and a white woman."

"Well said, young man." Maurice's heavy voice startled them. "Just think about how you feel every time you see a beautiful black woman with a white guy, Mr. Jefferson." Maurice didn't wait for an answer but headed straight into the locker room.

"Damn, I hate that guy. He's always creepin' around corners and shit, listening in on everybody's conversations," Tyrone whispered.

"Believe me. You're not the only one who can't stand him," Antoine chimed in. With Maurice in the vicinity, he knew they couldn't continue their debate. He would just have to trust that Kevin would do the right thing and stay true to his race.

"Anyway," he told them, "I need to ask you guys a favor."

"What's up?" Kevin was glad to be off the subject of Denise.

"You know I've been planning on buying Shawna an engagement ring." Antoine smiled with pride.

"Get out of here, big man. You're really gonna do it, huh?" Tyrone patted him on the back.

"Well, yeah, that's the plan. But I'm having some real problems with her Men's Club job." Antoine seemed embarrassed. "I was wondering if you guys would mind going over there with me some time this week? You know, to check the place out."

"That's cool with me. Saturday's the first day of midwinter break. I've got nothing planned all week." Kevin looked at Tyrone, expecting him to agree.

"Hey, I haven't been to the Men's Club in months." Tyrone nodded approvingly. "I was planning on going over there to see your girl's phat ass anyway . . ."

"Aarrrrr!" They were jolted by a scream from nearby.

"What the hell was that?" They turned in the direction of the sound.

"It sounded like someone screaming in the locker room," Antoine shouted.

"Post one, this is post three. We have a disturbance in the men's locker room." Tyrone spoke quickly into his radio as he ran toward the locker room with Kevin and Antoine in tow.

Searching through the rows of lockers, the three men found nothing until they heard the hideous scream again. It was coming from the adjoining rest room. Rushing into the bathroom, they were all shocked to see Maurice lying on the floor by a urinal. Almost unconscious from pain, Maurice opened his eyes as the three men helped him to his feet.

"What the hell is wrong with you?" he grunted, pushing them away. "You act as if you've never seen a man get his zipper caught on his dick!"

"Look, Maurice, we're just trying to help you." Antoine shot Kevin a raised-eyebrow glance. He couldn't believe the principal was angry at them for reacting to his shrieks.

"Just forget it," Antoine said to his friends. "Come on, guys, let's get the hell out of here."

No one bothered to ask Maurice if he was all right as the men left the bathroom. As they entered the weight room, the three men laughed out loud about how silly Maurice looked with his pants around his ankles and his penis in his hands.

"Oh, I wish I had a camera!" Tyrone was laughing so hard, he was almost crying.

"No! The funny thing was when he said he caught his dick in his zipper," Kevin cracked. "I wasn't sure he even had a dick."

"Hey, fellas." Antoine cleared his throat. "Calm down a little." He gestured toward the school secretary, who was approaching them with a large package in her arms.

"Good morning, Mrs. Rogers," all three said in unison. It was clear that they were fond of her.

"Mr. Brown." She smiled sweetly. "A messenger delivered this for you about an hour ago." The secretary handed him a package with an envelope attached.

"Thanks, Mrs. Rogers. That was nice of you to bring it down to the gym."

They watched her walk out of the gym.

"That Mrs. Rogers is one fine sister," Tyrone commented once she was out of earshot.

"She has a beautiful spirit too." Antoine didn't want to disrespect the woman, even though she was already out of the gym.

"Yeah, too bad she's married." Kevin handed the package to Tyrone and sat on the bench press to open the envelope.

Dear Kevin,

I wanted to let you know what a great time I had last night. I thought very hard about what you said, and I think you're right. We are better off as friends. As a friend, I wanted to ask you a big favor, because I'm really in a jam. A girlfriend and I were supposed to go to St. Thomas tomorrow for a week, but unfortunately her father was just hospitalized. I've called all my friends and nobody can get time off with such short notice. So I was hoping since both you and my girlfriend are teachers that you have the same winter break. Look, Kevin, I totally understand if you don't want to come, but the tickets and room are paid for. I just want to have a good time and enjoy a vacation with a friend. You do not need a passport, so don't worry about that. I hope to see you on the plane.

Your friend,
Denise

P.S. I hope you like my little surprise.

Kevin looked in the envelope and found a first-class ticket for 9:00 A.M. the next day. He wondered what "little" surprise she meant, because these tickets were no small thing as far as he was concerned. He turned around to see Tyrone wearing the Tommy Hilfiger jacket he had admired the night before.

"Kev, this jacket is so phat. When did you order this?" He took it off and handed it to Kevin.

"It's a gift from a very rich friend," he grumbled, handing Antoine the note, then trying the jacket on himself.

"This Denise must have money to burn," Antoine concluded after quickly reading the letter. "You realize she's trying to buy you, Kevin, as if you're a piece of meat?"

"Denise? Money? Don't tell me that white chick sent you this coat?" Tyrone said enthusiastically.

"Yep, and she wants me to go to St. Thomas tomorrow."

"So what you gonna do?"

"I'm not sure yet. What do you think, Antoine?"

"I think you should take off that coat and send it and the plane tickets back." He was serious. "You're not some poor nigger who can be bought with material things. Or have you decided to sell all our black sisters out like Tyrone?"

Kevin ignored Antoine's comment for the moment.

"Ty, what do you think?"

"All I got to say is, if you don't want to go, gimme the ticket."

"You two are my best friends, the closest thing I have to real brothers. You know I've gone through a lot the last few weeks with Alicia. Now I've got the chance at a week's vacation in a tropical paradise." Kevin looked at Antoine, took off the coat, and handed it to him. "You're right. I am going to give her the coat back."

"Thank God for small favors," he said nastily. "Now, what are you going to do about those plane tickets?"

"I don't know Antoine, you tell me. Should I give up a once-in-a-lifetime trip because you're going to be mad? If that's the case, tell me right now and I won't go."

"You know I'm not going to make a decision like that for you. But I know what I would do."

"Well, Antoine, I'm not you. So I guess you're going to have to trust that I'm going to keep this on the friendship level. But I can't pass up this vacation." He turned to Tyrone and smiled. "It looks like this time tomorrow I'm gonna be drinking piña coladas on the beach." He waved the plane tickets in front of their faces.

"Oh, and, Antoine, I'm not gonna be able to make the Men's Club this week."

"That's okay, man." Antoine was still angry but aware that his friend had to live his own life. "We'll just do it when you get back." He hoped he'd be cooled down by then, and that Kevin would keep his word.

21

MAURICE

Maurice thanked the secretary as she showed him into the doctor's office. He sat briefly in a comfortable leather chair in front of the doctor's desk, admiring the family photos prominently displayed throughout the office. When he heard the door open, he stood and turned, smiling as he saw his best friend of thirty years walk in. Dr. David Jackson grabbed Maurice's right hand and hugged him.

"It's good to see you, man," David said joyfully.

"It's good to see you too, buddy. How are Rita and the kids?"

"Good, real good, thanks. And what about Sylvia and that goddaughter of mine?"

"They're fine. Jasmine made the dean's list again. Look, Dave, I appreciate your seeing me on such short notice. I know you're busy."

"Give me a break. You're my best friend, for Pete's sake," David chastised as he settled his chubby frame behind the large mahogany desk. "Why didn't you come up earlier? I would have had Charlene set us up with a tee time at the club."

"Like I said when I called earlier, I just needed to talk."

Sensing that something was seriously wrong, David motioned for Maurice to have a seat. Maurice sat down in front of David's desk and stared at the many plaques and certificates on the walls. He was stalling, unsure of where to start. Instead of beginning with the truth, he just engaged his friend in more small talk.

"Your new office is beautiful, Dave. You've really come a long way in twenty years." Unlike his friend, David had made it on his own, without the help of a wealthy father-in-law.

"Hey! This is me, David. Enough with the fucking pleasantries. What's going on that you had to come all the way to Westchester to talk? They no longer have phones in Queens?"

Maurice bit his top lip, hesitating.

"I didn't come here just because you're my best friend and I needed to talk. I came here because you're my doctor also."

David raised an eyebrow as he listened intently. In fifteen years of practice, Maurice had never come to his office for anything other than a yearly physical. Whatever was bothering Maurice, David knew it must be something serious.

"Dave, I think I have V.D.," Maurice answered directly.

"Oh, shit!" David said, covering his mouth with his hand. "How the fuck did this happen?"

"I don't know. I think it was this slutty freak I fucked last week."

"I told you that fucking date line was a bad idea." David shook his head in disbelief. "When did you first notice the symptoms?"

"Friday. I went to take a piss and almost passed out because of the pain." He grimaced at the memory. "Now there's pus coming out of the head of my dick."

"Friday! You waited six days before calling me? What are you, fucking stupid?" David stood and leaned over his desk toward Maurice. "You didn't fuck Sylvia, did you?"

"No, I'm pretty sure she's okay."

"Thank God for small favors." David stared at Maurice in disgust. He pointed to the door to his private examination room. "All right. Go in there and take your pants off."

David purposely had Maurice wait in his examination room for almost forty minutes while he saw other patients. While he conducted the exams, he pondered the nature of his friendship with Maurice. He realized he didn't really know the man. He had always been Robin to Maurice's Batman. A short, average-looking man, he had been Maurice's sidekick, taking the women he rejected over the years. He had even met his wife that way. Sure, they had been in each other's weddings, been godfathers for the other's children, but he really didn't know Maurice.

David was shocked by Maurice's revelation. He believed that most men fooled around on their wives a little, but his friend took it to the next level. Even David was carrying on an affair with his secretary, but he couldn't understand why Maurice wouldn't grow up. He was such a successful man in so many ways, but he refused to stop playing this dangerous game.

When he thought he had made Maurice wait long enough, he returned to the examination room where Maurice was waiting in his boxer shorts on the examination table. Maurice looked nervous but turned his apprehension into aggression toward his friend.

"Where did you go? I've been waiting almost an hour."

Maurice was angry. He was accustomed to David fawning over him as if he were a rock star and David was a groupie.

"Don't go there, Maurice. I have paying patients who keep their dicks in their pants," David growled as he put on a pair of rubber gloves. Picking up a cotton swab, David gently took hold of Maurice's penis, pulling the foreskin until yellowish-brown pus seeped out, running down the shaft.

"I can't believe you're taking this attitude with me, David. It's not like you haven't had more than a few affairs of your own, my friend."

He spat out the last words with plenty of sarcasm. He had come there looking for some sympathy, and David was offering him judgment. David ignored Maurice's last comment and continued the examination.

"Yep, definitely infection there. Looks like gonorrhea," he declared, taking the swab and rubbing the opening of the penis.

"Arrrr! You son of a bitch, that hurts!" Maurice screamed in pain. "What the hell is your problem? Are you trying to kill me?"

"You're lucky I don't treat you the way they did in World War One. Back then they would stitch the head of your dick up and send you back to fight until the pus hardened all the way down your shaft. Then you would go back to see the medic and he would put your dick on the table and smash it hard with a rubber hammer until all the hardened pus cracked. Then he would give you a pint of beer so that you could piss it out."

David grinned as he watched Maurice's body contract. He handed him a wastepaper basket just as Maurice began to throw up.

"Still got a weak stomach, huh?"

"You son of a bitch, they didn't do that," Maurice mumbled as he wiped off his face.

"No, but in your case they should." David's back was turned as he dipped the swab in a culture dish. "Now get dressed. We have a lot to talk about."

Five minutes later Maurice sat in front of David's desk as he walked in with the results of the culture test.

"Well, it's definitely gonorrhea. But I won't be able to tell if you have chlamydia until the lab results come back tomorrow." He handed Maurice a bottle of pills. "Take these. The instructions are on the bottle. And for Pete's sake, Maurice, please don't have sex with Sylvia for at least two weeks. I suggest you have an AIDS test before you leave too."

"Okay, Dave, I want you to know I really appreciate what you have done for me."

Maurice stood. He couldn't even respond to Dave's suggestion of an AIDS test. He felt like his whole world was crashing down around him. He just wanted to get out of there as quickly as possible.

"Sit down, Maurice." David's voice was commanding. "You're not going anywhere until you give me some answers."

"What do you mean answers?" Maurice asked haughtily. He wondered who the hell David thought he was all of a sudden.

"You know what I mean by answers." David picked up the phone. "I wanna know why you've been treating women the way you do all these years. I may be your best friend, but I want some answers, or so help me, Maurice, I will call Sylvia right now and tell her everything I know."

Not sure if his friend was serious, Maurice glared silently at his childhood friend. *I'll be damned. I think he really might do it,* Maurice thought. *He'd really sell me out.*

"Okay, David, I'll tell you what you wanna know. I guess I owe you that much."

Unable to look his friend in the eye, Maurice settled himself in the chair again. There was an incredibly long silence as Maurice stared at the floor, wondering where to begin. He finally looked David in the face and sighed sadly before he began.

"Do you remember Ms. Diane Simon?"

"Yeah, she was the French teacher in junior high. She was the finest teacher I'd ever seen," David replied as an image of the beautiful woman entered his memory. "Wasn't she arrested for statutory rape a couple of years after we finished junior high?"

"Yep, that's her." Maurice lowered his head again. "Well, Ms. Simon was teaching me more than French when we were in school."

"Stop lyin'." David rolled his eyes, then glanced at the phone, letting Maurice know he wanted the truth.

"I swear, Dave," Maurice said humbly. "I was having an affair with Ms. Simon all the way through junior high." Something about the tone of Maurice's voice made David believe him. He'd never seen his friend seem so weak and uncertain.

"You're serious, aren't you?" David asked, leaning over his desk.

Maurice put both his hands together and nodded yes.

"You were having sex with her?"

"Yes, but it was more than just sex. I was truly in love with her. For two years I spent every possible minute with her. Think about it, those were the only two years I didn't play organized sports."

David laughed. "Because you were busy playing hide the sausage with the hottest teacher in the school." He couldn't resist joking, but there was a hint of envy in his voice.

"She was a wonderful woman, Dave. She taught me more about having fun than anyone I ever met. She's the only woman I ever loved, and for a time I think she loved me too."

Real tears began to roll down Maurice's face as he continued his story. He wiped them away with the back of his hand, and tried to compose himself. David couldn't believe his friend was actually crying.

"Do you remember at the end of eighth grade when my parents said that my grades were so bad they were going to send me to military school?"

"Yeah, I remember that. I couldn't believe they were really gonna send you away like that."

"Well, neither could Diane. She freaked. She kept ranting and raving about how nobody could separate her from her man. Then one afternoon she tells me to sneak out for what I thought was going to be a quickie. By that time I was grounded, but I found a way to see her."

"You always were good at sneaking out the house," David mused.

"So when I got to Diane's place, she pulled me inside the door and said, 'I can't lose you. We have to run away together so they can't separate us.'" Maurice got a very faraway look in his eyes, and then the tears started again. "I was so in love with her. I would have run away to the moon if she asked me to."

"So you were with her? I thought you ran away because your old man was kicking your ass. How come you never told me you were with Ms. Simon?" That whole period of their youth was starting to make more sense to David as the story unfolded.

"Come on, Dave, would you have believed me? You called me a liar when I told you I got to second base with Monica Smith. If I had told you I was getting laid by a teacher, you woulda laughed in my face. Hell, I was there, and I'm still having a hard time believing it."

"Yeah, I guess you're right."

"Thirteen years old and getting laid every day. Sounds like every boy's dream, huh?"

"I suppose it does, man."

"Well, that dream became a nightmare when I woke up alone three months later in a motel in Gary, Indiana."

"Get the fuck outta here! You mean you woke up and she was gone?"

"Yep. She didn't even leave me any money to get home."

"So she just left you in Indiana, a thousand miles from home?" David was in awe. He handed his friend a box of tissues and waited as his friend cried quietly. Finally Maurice was able to continue.

"Yeah, believe it or not, she took off with motel manager's twelve-year-old kid. Can you believe she was doing him too?"

"Damn, she was a real pedophile, wasn't she?" David stated.

Maurice didn't answer his friend. He just stared at the ceiling. As far as he was concerned, Diane hadn't done anything wrong other than cheat on him.

"So what happened after that?"

"I thought Diane was gonna come back, so I tried to hide out in the motel room. Then I got caught and the police got involved. They called my parents and my pops told them to keep me, but Mom came and got me on the bus."

"Never could understand your old man's attitude."

"He's a jerk."

"I don't even know what to say, Maurice."

"There's nothing to say, Dave. After I found out Diane was with that other kid, I decided to live life for one thing, to do to all women what Diane had done to me."

"Damn, that's deep. Now it makes sense, all those hearts you broke in high school. I could never understand why you were so cold."

"My heart was frozen after Diane left me. I knew I could never love another woman. I felt nothing but anger toward them all."

David felt pity for Maurice and also for his family.

"But what about Sylvia? You must have loved her if you married her."

"That was nothing more than a marriage of convenience. She needed to marry the man who made her pregnant so her family name wouldn't be tarnished."

"I never knew Jasmine was conceived before you were married!"

Maurice answered with pride as the memory of Diane was replaced with the anger he had come to live with.

"Shit. I left Sylvia's ass in a grassy field in Flushing Meadow Park that day I took her virginity. She was supposed to be just like all the other hos, until that fuckup Jonathan Sparks told her where I lived."

David's mouth opened as if he wanted to say something, but he was too disgusted to respond. He cared about Sylvia. And Maurice was turning out to be a real Jekyll and Hyde.

"Sylvia's daddy offered me a whole bunch of money to marry that girl, so I figured, what the hell? I took the money and went on my merry way. She's my wife for appearance's sake, but there is no love there, Dave."

David couldn't take any more and decided to put an end to the sordid story.

"Look, man. This whole story has totally blown me away. I'm really worried about you, Maurice. I think you need to see a specialist who can help you deal with all of this."

He flipped through his Rolodex and scribbled some information on a sheet of paper, which he handed to Maurice. He couldn't wait to get this man out of his office.

"This is the number for Dr. Jerome Stanley. He's a friend of mine, and a hell of a good shrink. You need to do whatever it takes to stop this behavior before you get yourself killed."

He leaned over and spoke into his intercom.

"Charlene? I want you to talk to Mr. Johnson about making another appointment. He needs to have some further blood work done. He'll be out to see you in a minute."

Sighing loudly, he turned to face his lifelong friend.

"Maurice, I mean it, man. You need to stop having sex with all these women. And don't touch your wife until you've had that AIDS test."

Maurice was back to his usual self and not in the mood for David's sermon. He faked sincerity to get the man off his back.

"You're right, Dave. I need to try to make some changes in my life."

The men embraced, and Maurice walked out of the office with no intention of making that appointment for an AIDS test.

22

KEVIN AND DENISE

Kevin sipped his piña colada as he sat admiring the peaceful sunset from the balcony of his hotel room. He was still drunk from the afternoon's booze cruise and swayed to the sounds of the reggae band floating up from the pool area. This had been a magical vacation for him, and he hated that it would end in two days. It had been exactly what he needed to take his mind off Alicia. He still loved her, but for the first time since they had broken up he realized he could live without her.

Denise and Kevin had been the perfect vacation partners. Both athletic, they played tennis in the mornings and water sports in the afternoon. They danced to reggae music until the wee hours of the morning. Kevin had really enjoyed Denise's company and was very happy with her behavior. She had not brought up the issue of relationships once. But as relieved as he was about that, there was still one slight problem that created a difficulty for his conscience. She seemed to have exhibitionist tendencies. Watching her prance around their hotel room naked day after day had caused him to struggle all week. Every time he tried to think of respecting his black sisters, Denise's bare breasts would tempt him to abandon his principles. It was enough to make even the most righteous brother want some play. If he had to take one more cold shower, he thought he might just run up the white flag and surrender.

Denise walked into hotel room and quickly removed her bikini. She wondered where Kevin was. When she heard him on the balcony, she made a little noise, hoping he would come into the bedroom. He didn't respond, so she walked into the bathroom to shower the salt off after her swim.

Denise had been purposely walking around Kevin nude for five days, and he hadn't seemed to notice. He even insisted on sleeping on the couch every night, though she had offered many times to share the bed with him. It was as if he were practicing for sainthood or something. Unable to stand it any longer, she resolved to go to Plan B. This time she would hold nothing back. Stepping out of the shower, she slid on a pair of bikini panties and strolled onto the balcony.

On the balcony Kevin sat in his chair and slurred the words to a Bob Marley song. Denise positioned herself directly in front of him so he could get a full view of her practically naked body. She smiled devilishly when she realized he was still drunk.

"Hi!" She plopped down on his lap.

"Hi." He held her gently so that she wouldn't fall. He tried to avert his eyes from her bare breasts, but the alcohol was making it difficult for him to control himself.

"Can I ask you a personal question?"

"Sure."

"When was the last time you had sex?"

"That's a good question." Without realizing he was doing it, he moved his hands low enough to feel the curve of her hips. "I think it was at a fraternity party in Chapel Hill, North Carolina, while I was trying out for the Hornets."

"You were in a fraternity?"

"Yeah, I'm an Omega, a Q-dog, as we like to call ourselves."

He proudly displayed the horseshoe on his right arm. Denise stared at the symbol. Whatever it was, she thought it marred his otherwise perfect body. She reached out to touch it.

"What is that, a tattoo?"

"No, it's a brand."

"A brand! What the hell do you have a brand for? You take this fraternity shit pretty seriously, don't you?" She jerked her hand away.

"Well, yeah, I do take it pretty seriously. You would be serious about it, too, if you pledged for six weeks."

"Six weeks! I thought white frats were stupid pledging two weeks. Why the hell would you let someone do that to you?"

"I don't know how to explain it, except that when you're pledging, they break you down to build you up."

"Come on, Kevin, that's ridiculous. Are you trying to tell me that getting the shit beat out of you made you a better person?"

"Look, Denise, I'm not asking you to believe me or understand me.

All I can tell you is I started freshman year a very insecure young man. But after I pledged Omega, I was confident and ready to take on the world."

"If you're so confident, why haven't you had sex since college?" she asked, not wanting him to go on a nostalgia trip back to his college days. "Are you some kind of born-again Christian who's saving himself till marriage?"

"Trust me, I believe in God, but he's not stopping me from getting some." He shifted Denise so she wouldn't notice his growing manhood. "I'm probably the horniest guy you've ever met. But after I was cut by the Hornets, I went into a depression and didn't want sex."

"I didn't think it was possible for a man to not want sex."

"Oh, it's possible all right. I had no interest in women until Alicia and I got together." Kevin was enjoying the way she was squirming on his lap.

"So why didn't you have sex with her?"

"Alicia had just gone through a rough time with her child's father before we met. So she wanted to get to know me better before we made love."

"Wow, that must have been pretty frustrating." She wiggled her buttocks against his manhood.

"Oh, yeah! Every time we kissed I had to go home and take a cold shower."

"I don't get it, Kevin. Why didn't you find yourself an F.B.?"

"F.B.? What in the world is an F.B.?"

"An F.B. is a fuck buddy. Somebody who expects no emotional ties but gives you great sex. You know, someone you can call anytime you're horny, but they don't get offended when you don't call for a while. Or maybe even someone who's married and lives out of town, but when you see each other, you can't resist sneaking off for a quickie." As she spoke, Denise squirmed some more on Kevin's lap to make sure he kept his erection.

"So that's what you call it! Yeah, I used to have a . . . what do you call it? An F.B., when I was in Virginia. Crystal was one hell of a woman. She would do anything if she thought it would get me off."

"So what happened to her? She's not still around, is she?"

"She dropped out of school with some light-skinned guy with a receding hairline. I haven't seen her in over a year."

"Oh, that's too bad. A man like you should have a way of releasing all that pent-up anxiety and tension." She leaned forward so that both of her large breasts jiggled in his face. "You know, Kevin, it's too bad you're not attracted to white women, 'cause I would make one hell of an F.B."

He stared at her and smirked. In his alcoholic haze he had finally realized where the conversation was headed.

"Listen, Denise, stop beating around the bush. What are you trying to say?"

Denise sighed. *Do I really need to spell it out for him?*

"I would love to be your F.B. You wouldn't have to worry about taking me out, so technically you wouldn't be in an interracial relationship. And I'd make myself available to you at all hours of the night except when I'm on an important case."

"I don't know, Denise . . ."

"Look. Just try it until the end of our vacation." She bent over and kissed him.

"I'd just be using you for sex. That's not right."

He couldn't help but think about how nice it would be to be intimate with her right there on the balcony with the setting sun behind them. He had always heard that white women were willing to do anything to please their men, and just then his defenses were so weak that he was tempted to test the theory. The buildup of a week of temptation and the piña coladas were clouding his better judgment.

Denise sensed him weakening. She leaned in closer to him, pressing her breasts against his chest as she whispered in his ear.

"We would be using each other, Kevin. The truth is, you're not half as horny as I am."

She lowered her head and rested it on his warm chest. Kevin had to admit it felt good holding Denise close, and it had been so long since he'd been with a woman physically. The only thing really holding him back was his love for Alicia and the thought that somehow they might reconcile.

I can't live like this, he rationalized to himself, *maybe sleeping with Denise is the only way my feelings for Alicia are gonna go away.*

"Well, what do you think? Are we going to let this night go to waste, or are you going to carry me into the bedroom and show me how you make love?"

He didn't waste a second lifting her into his arms and carrying her to the bedroom.

*   *   *

Two hours later Kevin sat at the end of the bed. Perspiration slid down his shaved head onto his broad shoulders as he watched Denise fan herself, gasping for air. No longer drunk, he was fully aware that she had manipulated him into having sex with her. But he wasn't upset with her. He was grateful. She had reminded him how wonderful sex was, and as a reward he sent multiple waves of pleasure throughout her whole body.

"You okay?" He grinned.

"Yeah, I just need a little air. Can you open that window?" She watched him stand up and put on his shorts before opening the window. "Are you going somewhere?"

"I was thinking about going for a run before dinner."

Denise looked at him in amazement, and between breaths she asked, "Are you serious? You mean to tell me that wasn't enough exercise for you?"

"I'm sorry. I didn't hear you. Did you want some more?" He jumped playfully on the bed beside her.

"No! No! Not right now, Kevin. Don't you ever get tired? We just made love for almost an hour and a half!" She backed away, putting both her hands up to keep him away. "Besides, we don't have any more condoms. Why don't we wait till after dinner?"

"I told you I was a horny guy. But if it'll make you feel any better, I'm gonna go sit by the pool and listen to the band until you're ready for dinner. While I'm down there I'll pick up some more condoms."

She watched him finish dressing. After he left, she rolled over, picked up the phone, and dialed her secretary's home number.

"Hello, Ruth? This is Denise. I have something I need you to do before I get back. Get a hold of the private investigator the firm has on retainer. Tell him I want to know everything there is to know about an Alicia Meyers. She works for a criminal law firm near the Brooklyn courthouse. Oh, and, Ruth, I don't want this getting back to Daddy."

She hung up the phone and dialed her best friend's number.

"Hey, Liz," she shouted, hearing the answering machine. "This is Denise. He finally gave in and it was great. Now it's time to get rid of the competition."

"Yo, hold on a minute, Denise." Liz turned off her answering machine.

Liz Trendle had been Denise's best friend ever since their second year of high school. They were both raised in Port Washington, Long Island, a small community close enough to Manhattan that it attracted many of the city's high-powered professionals who sought suburban surroundings for their families. Denise, who was born with a silver spoon in her mouth, had teased Liz in school, an overweight white girl who lived in the small, subsidized housing project located on the border of the town's richest neighborhood.

As the girls reached adolescence, a time when boys became important to them, Denise realized she and Liz actually had something in common. Since Liz lived in "the projects," most of her neighbors were black, and many of those neighbors were her friends. As Denise began to recognize her own attraction to black men, she knew that an acquaintance with Liz could gain her acceptance among those black boys she wanted to date. Over the years the time she spent with Liz yielded many dates for Denise. Most of her dates, of course, had to be kept a secret from her family and her upper-middle-class racist friends. Denise soon learned that Liz was one of the few friends who understood and supported that side of her, and the two cemented a friendship that lasted beyond their high school years.

"What up, girl? So you finally got you a little sum'in, sum'in?" Liz asked, excited.

"Oh, did I! Liz, the man is so skilled."

"Damn, I must need to dye my hair blond or something. 'Cause as much as I love the brothers, I can't find me a nigger to do me right if my life depended on it."

"Liz, you know I can't stand it when you use that word!" Denise's voice was serious.

"Damn, girl, will you relax? Black people call each other nigger all the time."

"Contrary to popular belief, Liz, you're not black," Denise reminded her.

"Well, I ought to be." She and Denise always had arguments about Liz's wanna-be behavior. "So what's this about getting rid of the competition? You want me to kick some bitch's ass?"

Denise had to chuckle when she heard Liz's words. She was twenty-six years old, but Liz still loved to fight and was good at it. She had saved herself and Denise from quite a few beatings by jealous black women over the years.

"No, I don't think a beating will work. He's still in love with her. I can tell. Would you believe he screamed out her name when he climaxed?"

"Get the fuck outta here! I know you was pissed."

"Yeah, but to be honest, I was just happy to get some." She sighed. "Besides, the sex is so good, I don't want to confront him and blow it. I finally got him where I want him."

"Well, you can always get pregnant, girl. If he's the kind of guy you think he is, he'd never leave his baby's moms. Plus that other chick won't want anything to do with him if he gets a white girl pregnant."

"Hmm, that's a good idea, but let's use that as a last resort. I've got a private detective looking into his ex's past. And like Daddy always says, everyone's got skeletons. You just have to find out what closet they're in."

"I hear you, girl, just let me know if you want me to kick that bitch's ass."

"Okay." Denise laughed. "I'll talk to you later."

"Okay, girlfriend. You get some for me, you hear?"

23

ANTOINE AND SHAWNA

Kevin parked his car in the jam-packed parking lot of the Men's Club. He had driven there with Antoine, Tyrone, and Tyrone's uncle Billy in his Honda. Stepping out of his car, he was unimpressed by the looks of the large Victorian house that had been converted into a strip club. The illuminated sign was about to fall off the building, which was in bad need of a paint job.

"Don't judge a book by its cover," Tyrone's uncle Billy told them.

Billy reached into his pocket to check his thick wad of one-dollar bills as they walked to the entrance. There were already enough bulges on Billy's three-hundred-pound frame, and the wallet protruded obviously in his back pocket.

"I don't care what you say. This place looks like a dump to me," Kevin told Billy, frowning when Antoine pointed out a used condom on the sidewalk.

"I cannot believe Shawna works in a place like this." Antoine shivered at the thought. He had just proposed to Shawna two days before, and they were still fighting over her night job. So with a little encouragement from Tyrone, he decided to pay Shawna and the Men's Club a surprise visit to know for sure what she did there.

"What's up, Tiny?" Billy laughed at the six-foot-seven security guard who frisked him.

"Nothing much, Billy. It's your world. I'm just trying to live in it."

"It's not my world, Tiny. All I'm trying to do is get a nut." Billy laughed.

"Well, you came to the right place." The man laughed, letting Billy pass so that he could frisk Tyrone. "You touch, you pay," he announced to the group.

"Yeah, no problem." Tyrone walked past the man.

After being frisked and paying the ten-dollar admission fee, Antoine and Kevin entered the club. They were surprised by the sharp contrast between the outside and the inside. The club was clean and well kept, and Kevin at least looked forward to his first experience in a strip club. Following Billy and Tyrone, he could not help but laugh as he watched Antoine's head follow the totally naked women's breasts as they passed.

"Damn, Antoine, don't stare so hard. They're not going to fall off," Tyrone teased.

They seated themselves at a table in front of the main stage.

"Now, this is beautiful, isn't it?" Billy exclaimed, grabbing a young Latina girl by her buttocks and slipping a dollar into her garter. "Four black men with the opportunity to look and touch over a hundred naked women. Heaven, wouldn't you say?"

"You can touch them?" Antoine asked, upset.

"You've been going to those white strip clubs too much, son." Billy laughed as he gently stroked a woman walking past. "This is a black club. You can touch anything you want if you're willing to pay for it."

"Tell him about the table and lap dances, Uncle Billy," Tyrone said excitedly. Billy pointed to another table for the men to see.

"Now, you see that sister dancing in front of that brother over there? See the way she's dancing in front of him, rubbing her stuff up against his leg? Well, that's a table dance. Not bad for five bucks, huh?"

Kevin felt sorry for Antoine. He had never seen his friend so upset. Maybe coming to the club was a bad idea. There was no way Shawna could win in a situation like this. Antoine was already angry because she worked in the dump. But if she really turned out to be a stripper, he'd probably break off the engagement in a second.

"Now, look over there." Billy pointed across the room to about twenty-five women sitting on men's laps, grinding their bare crotches into them as if they were having sex. "That's a lap dance. You don't see those in too many clubs anymore, because brothers would offer the girls a little more than the ten dollars to slide up in there and the club wouldn't get a cut."

"Now I understand why so many women don't want their men going to strip clubs," Kevin said seriously.

"They really have sex with these guys?" Antoine asked in disbelief.

"What planet did you get this guy from?" Billy nudged Tyrone.

"Antoine's just upset, Uncle Billy. That's why we wanted to meet you here." Tyrone explained everything about Shawna to his uncle.

"Aw'ight, now I understand." Billy looked at Antoine sympathetically.

"Big Daddy Bill-Bill," a tall, half-Asian sister purred, wrapping her arm around his neck. "How you doing, Big Daddy? You haven't had a VIP with anyone yet, have you?"

"No, baby, I was waiting for you." He playfully grabbed the girl's buttocks with both hands for the other men to see. "Fellas, this here is China Doll. She's gonna take me upstairs and give me the VIP treatment. But when I come back, I'm going to get to the bottom of that problem for you, Antoine."

The three men watched Billy follow China Doll up the spiral staircase.

"What's the VIP treatment?" Kevin asked Tyrone.

"Oh, that's when you give the woman of your choice a hundred bucks and she takes you upstairs to knock the boots."

"No way! That's prostitution, isn't it?" Kevin replied.

"Yep."

The three friends watched the show for about fifteen minutes until Billy and China Doll walked back over to the table and sat down.

"Do me a favor," Billy said, patting China Doll on the rear. "Go find Amed and tell him to come here." The men watched as China Doll walked away.

"That girl's got some good pussy," Billy remarked. "And, Kevin, she told me she'd like to see you outside the club."

"Damn, Kev, that means you can get that stuff for free anytime you want," Tyrone said excitedly.

"Thanks, Billy, but I'm not into sloppy seconds."

"Or thirds, fourths, fifths . . ." Antoine mumbled.

"You got a lot of nerve for a guy that needs my help," Billy chastised Antoine. "Do you realize there's almost a hundred girls working the floor and another thirty or forty in the locker room? You might not ever find out if your lady dances here."

"I'm sorry." Antoine realized that he could use Billy's help.

"Now, listen, here comes Amed. Don't nobody say a word except me. I spend a lot of money in this place, and they usually give me what I want," Billy commanded, smiling as Amed approached the table and shook his hand.

"Good to see you, Mr. Big Daddy. However can I help you?" Amed asked graciously in an Indian accent.

"I'm doing fine, Amed." Billy slipped the man a twenty. "A friend of mine told me about a real beauty you have working here. I was hoping maybe I could get a VIP with her."

"Sure, Big Daddy. What is her name?"

"I don't know her stage name, but her real name is Shawna. Shawna . . . ?"

"Dean," Antoine interjected.

Amed looked surprised by the request. "Ah, yes, Shawna. I did not know you were into her type, Big Daddy?"

"You're right, I usually go for the light-skinned ones." Billy recalled that Tyrone had described Shawna as tall and dark-skinned. "But I think it's time for a change. What do you think?"

"It is entirely up to you. With me, the customer is always right. However, Shawna is already booked up with VIPs tonight. But I have a beautiful girl named Roberta who is along the same lines as Shawna. Would you like me to—"

"Booked up with who?" Antoine shouted before Kevin could cover his mouth.

"You have to excuse my friend. He was looking forward to meeting Shawna," Billy said smoothly, cutting his eyes at Antoine. "Listen, why don't you let me buy all her VIPs for the next two nights? The truth is, I just want one good round and then she can go back to work."

Amed quickly ran the figures through his head and smiled greedily.

"But, Big Daddy, that's over a thousand dollars."

"You take Visa, don't you?" Billy smiled back.

"We certainly do. Let me go see what I can arrange for you, Big Daddy." Amed walked away, counting the profits in his head. Billy sat at the table, certain he would never have to spend that money. He knew that if Shawna ever came out to the table, there'd be a scene, and no money would ever end up changing hands.

"What the hell is wrong with you? That man's job is to protect his girls from husbands and boyfriends!" Billy yelled at Antoine. "I'm trying to help you out. Don't fuck up my thing here!"

"Look. I'm out of here. There is no way I'm going to watch my girlfriend walk out here naked in front of you guys," Antoine shouted angrily. As he stood, he knocked all their glasses to the floor.

"Come on, Antoine, sit down. We're gonna leave in a little bit."

Kevin put a hand on his friend's shoulder, trying to calm him. "I just don't want you to make the same mistake I did."

"Yeah, Antoine, you need to talk to her, man, before you do anything rash," Tyrone added.

"I'm telling you, if she walks out here nude, I'm going to lose it!" He was in a jealous rage, and Kevin could barely hold him down.

"Look, you guys are going to have to calm down, or I'm going to have to ask you to leave the club," a beefy bouncer demanded, flexing his huge biceps.

"Fuck you! And fuck this whorehouse of a club!" Antoine put his finger in the bouncer's chest. Billy stood up between the two before the bouncer could react.

"Listen, Jake, my friend over here's a little drunk. He didn't mean no disrespect."

Billy motioned for Kevin and Tyrone to escort Antoine out as he handed Jake twenty dollars. The two friends grabbed Antoine's upper arms tightly and rushed him toward the door. With each step Antoine struggled more and his cursing became louder. He had never felt the desire to hurt someone the way he did at that moment, and if his friends had not been there to escort him out, he knew he would have ended up in jail.

Shawna had four girls waiting in line as she transformed an average-looking brown-skinned woman into a raging beauty.

"Hold still, Nutmeg. If you want to make some money tonight, you're gonna have to look extra good. Amed hired about fifteen white girls this week, and you know some o' these no-good sellout brothers are gonna give them all their money."

"That's right, girl. I saw one of them bitch's take two of my regulars upstairs to the VIP room. That bitch might as well have went to my house and took my baby's Pampers and milk, 'cause that's two hundred dollars I'll never see."

"Why would Amed do that shit anyway?" another woman asked. "When I first started working here, you could make some good money. Now there's so many girls, you got to haggle with the price to go home with anything after that Indian motherfucker gets his cut."

"Well, girls, you better get used to it. Mayor Giuliani is closing down all the clubs in Manhattan, and those girls are gonna make their way here in order to feed their families. The word on the street is that he's gonna shut us down too."

"I hope not, Shawna." Nutmeg admired herself in the mirror. "I just started to pay off my bills."

"I know, girl. Not only do I have to pay off my operation, but my wedding also."

"You're getting married?" Nutmeg squealed, giving her a hug.

"Yes, a couple a months after my operation." Shawna displayed her engagement ring.

"Congratulations!" Amed said, startling the women. "Shawna, may I speak to you in private, please?"

"Sure. I'll be right back, girls."

She followed him to his office. Inside Amed's cluttered office Shawna sat down. Amed got straight to business.

"Shawna, outside I have Big Daddy Bill-Bill and he is very interested in a woman of your, how do you say it, qualities. He's willing to pay handsomely for a VIP, I might add. Six hundred big ones, minus my cut, of course. What do you think? You think you might do me this one favor?"

She looked at him in amazement. Even if she was interested, she knew he was lying about the price, as he did with all of the girls.

"Hell no! My boyfriend would kill me. He's having a hard enough time with me being a makeup girl. If I was a stripper and a prostitute, he'd kill both of us. I suggest you go talk to Roberta." She stormed out of the office.

While Antoine fumed outside in Kevin's car, the other men sat and waited for Amed to return with Shawna.

"Excuse me, Mr. Big Daddy," Amed said, smiling sheepishly. "I am sorry, but I am unable to get Shawna to do a VIP with you."

"Why is that? My money no longer good here?"

"She is just very backed up with her regular clients." Amed handed him four tickets. "These are four Men's Club VIP passes. Give them to any girl, and you and your friends will get free VIPs. That includes the room fee and condom."

"Well, that's mighty nice of you, Amed."

Billy loved to watch Amed squirm. He shook the Indian man's hand and dismissed him with a wave of his hand. He handed Tyrone and Kevin each a pass.

"You boys take your time and pick the right girl, you hear?"

Kevin handed the ticket back to him. "Look, guys. I'm going to drive Antoine home. I'm pretty sure he's gonna want to talk to someone. You mind calling a cab?"

"Suit yourself," Billy said, shaking his hand. "It was nice to meet you, son." He stuffed the extra ticket in his pocket to use later.

For about ten more minutes Tyrone laughed and joked with his uncle and two women they had called to the table. Surprisingly he found himself bored with the women.

"Uncle Billy, I'm gonna call it a night. I'll give you a call in a couple of days, okay?"

"All right, boy, but you don't know what you're missing. Does he, girls?" He squeezed them both.

Tyrone looked down at the women and thought about Sylvia. He placed his VIP ticket on the table and told his uncle, "Yes, I do."

24

TYRONE AND ALICIA

Tyrone and Sylvia left the Schomburg Library after spending the afternoon admiring an exhibit of Gordon Parks's photography. Tyrone had always wanted to go to the library because of its historical significance as a center for culture and education in Harlem. Since the consummation of their relationship, they had managed to spend some time together every day, and their day at the library's African American museum was just as enjoyable as every other they had spent together. After spending years with a husband who admired only himself and their money, Sylvia was thrilled to be with a man who shared her admiration for black artists.

And Tyrone was happy to be with a woman who shared his love of art. He had known women before who pretended to be interested just to attract his attention, but he learned quickly that there was no depth to their knowledge. With Sylvia he had someone who understood his passion and shared it.

With Maurice away on another overnight trip, the couple had planned to take advantage of his absence. They had been frustrated that so many of their meetings were cut short, so they planned to turn their afternoon at the museum into an evening of dinner at the world-famous Sylvia's soul food restaurant and whatever else developed.

Once they were inside the restaurant, they were seated at a cozy table. Sylvia looked around and reminisced. "I haven't been here in years. This used to be my favorite restaurant just because of the name. It didn't matter what was on the menu. I would eat it just because it came from Sylvia's. My dad would bring me here whenever I got a good report card."

"Yeah, this place is great all right," Tyrone added.

"So what do you want to do after we eat?" she asked with a suggestive wink.

"Well, actually, I was planning on taking a buggy ride downtown. But by the way you're looking at me, I guess you have something else on your mind."

"What do you expect? We haven't made love in three days."

Lately Sylvia seemed to have sex on her mind all the time. Since Tyrone had shown her the physical pleasures she had been missing her entire marriage, she couldn't get enough. She just couldn't keep her hands off the man she was falling in love with.

"I'll tell you what. If you don't mind a quickie, I promise you something so special, you'll remember it the rest of your life."

"Really? What?" Sylvia asked.

"Excuse me, Tyrone?" a woman interrupted, looking scared. She clung to her child, who was trembling.

"Alicia, what are you doing here?" He noticed the tears in her eyes. "What's wrong?"

She looked nervously at the front door. "Michael's father, my ex-boyfriend, Trevor, is outside, waiting to beat me up."

Tyrone stood up abruptly and pulled out a chair. He ordered Alicia and her son to have a seat.

"Relax," he said. "No one's gonna hurt you while I'm here. Now tell me, what's going on?"

"We were all going to the Apollo Theater to see the junior talent show, when Trevor says, 'Gimme a hundred dollars so I can pay for the tickets.' I knew he'd been drinkin' so I tried my best not to have an attitude when I told him I'm not going to pay for the tickets, he invited me. He smacked me right there, tellin' me who am I to tell him no in front of his son. Well, I wasn't going to wait around for him to hit me again. So I kicked him in the balls and ran in here. Thank God I saw you come in. I remembered Kevin telling me you were a black belt in karate when we went to see that Jackie Chan movie in the fall."

"Okay, Alicia. You did the right thing getting away from this guy. I'm gonna ask you one question, and if you want my help, you're not gonna lie." He gave her a serious look.

"Are you fucking this guy? 'Cause if you're fucking this guy again, I don't know if I wanna get involved with that kind of shit."

Sylvia was amazed to see Tyrone's street personality come out. "Tyrone! Watch your language. Can't you see she has her child here?" She placed her hand over Michael's. "Now, you help this woman!"

"Sylvia, you don't know the history between these two. He's been kicking her ass for years. If I get involved, she'll be back with him in a week. Maybe even tomorrow."

"I don't care. She needs help now. And if you're not man enough to do it, I'll go out there myself." She stood up, challenging Tyrone's manhood.

"Sit down, Sylvia," he said, disgusted. He reached into his wallet and pulled out his school security badge. "Alicia, does this guy carry a knife or a gun?"

"No, he really is a coward—except when it comes to women."

"I bet you wish you hadn't caused your mother and Kevin to break up now, huh, kid?" Tyrone said gruffly to Michael as he walked toward the door.

"What did he mean by that?" Alicia asked her son suspiciously. Michael slumped in his chair and didn't say a word.

"Oh, don't pay any attention to Tyrone. He's probably still upset that your son manipulated Kevin into breaking up with you." Sylvia waved her hand as if dismissing the incident.

"Michael didn't manipulate anyone," Alicia insisted rather forcefully. "Kevin is just an uncouth ass, like most men."

"Look, I'm just going by what Tyrone told me. Maybe you're wrong Alicia, and he's a different Michael, but I'm sure about what he told me."

Rolling her eyes, Alicia pulled her son in close.

"Well, what did he tell you?"

"Look, maybe Tyrone was right, maybe we shouldn't have gotten involved."

Sylvia was aggravated by Alicia's tone. Who was she to take an attitude with her after she'd just defended her and her son when Tyrone wasn't willing? She hesitated but decided to speak her mind to this arrogant woman.

"No, actually I think you should know this. Kevin's not the uncouth ass, you are. If you had raised your son properly, he wouldn't have told Kevin all those lies about you sleeping with that no-good nigger outside."

Sylvia was ashamed of herself for using the word "nigger" as soon as it left her lips, but she was furious. Sitting back in her chair, she folded her arms with the full intention of not saying another word until Tyrone returned.

"Who do you think you're talking to anyway?" Alicia raised her voice. "Michael didn't tell Kevin I was sleeping with Trevor. Did you, Michael?" Michael was silent, so she nudged him. "Did you, Michael!"

Sylvia reached over and touched Michael's hand. "It's hard to keep a secret from your mom, isn't it? Especially if you know it's going to hurt her." Michael nodded and Sylvia continued. "You need to tell your mother the truth, Michael. She deserves that much from you."

"Mom, I told Uncle Kevin you had sex with Daddy. I wanted to tell you, but you were so mad at Uncle Kevin, I just didn't want you to be mad at me." The boy's face was wet with tears. "Then when Dad started staying over, I didn't think you cared about Uncle Kevin anymore."

Alicia's embarrassment showed all over her face. Looking down at her son's tear-stained face, she realized she had made quite a few mistakes in the past few months.

"I am so sorry," she told Sylvia.

"Don't worry about it," Sylvia replied. "What are you going to do about Kevin? From what I hear, he's a great guy who still loves you."

Alicia placed her hands on the sides of her head and began rubbing her temples. "I don't know. I'm just so confused about things right now."

"Please, don't tell me you're in love with this guy outside."

"No, not anymore. But he is my baby's daddy."

Oh, God, not you too, Sylvia thought, regretting staying with Maurice all these years because of their daughter. "What about Kevin? Do you love him?"

"I don't even want to think about Kevin after what I learned today. He probably hates me. He was the nicest guy I ever dated."

"From what I hear, he's still in love with you."

"Really?" Alicia replied excitedly before lowering her head. "I don't even know what I'd say to him."

"How about starting with I'm sorry?" She gave Alicia a smile. "You did have him served with an order of protection."

"My God, I completely forgot about that." Alicia lifted her head and looked at Sylvia. "I guess I had the wrong person served, huh?" Sylvia nodded her head.

"Look, I'm not trying to get into your business, but don't you think it's time you got rid of Trevor?"

"Yes, but it's not that easy. I have a child with that man." She hugged her son tightly.

"I know, but if he's violent, you might end up dead one day." Sylvia took out a small pad and pen and wrote down a name and number before handing it to Alicia. "This is Jen Anderson's number. She's a really good friend of mine. She runs a place called Standing on Your Own."

"Look, I know you mean well, but I'm not going to any battered women's shelter. I made my own bed, so I have to lie in it." Alicia lowered her head.

"It's not a shelter. It's a club where women can get free counseling and learn self-defense."

"Counseling? I don't need counseling. I just need Trevor to leave me the hell alone."

"Look at you, Alicia. Are you always going to be the damsel in distress, always looking for some man to bail you out of trouble like Tyrone is doing now? You went right from Kevin's arms into Trevor's, and now you're thinking about going back into Kevin's, aren't you?"

Alicia stared at Sylvia without saying a word.

"Look, just give Jen a call. After she explains the program, if it's not what you're looking for, you don't have to go."

"Aw'ight." Alicia placed the number in her purse. "I'll call her, but I'm not promising anything."

Sylvia nodded her head. "That's all I can ask."

Tyrone smoked a cigarette as he watched Trevor peek inside the window of the restaurant. Sizing up the five-foot-six man, he couldn't believe that this little guy was Kevin's competition. For some reason, he had expected him to be taller. Tyrone ran his plan through his head again quickly. He knew he could pull it off as long as he was real smooth.

Trevor was still hobbling a little from the shot in the groin he had taken from Alicia.

"Wait till I get my hands on that bitch. I'm gonna kick her ass all the way home," he mumbled, peeking through the window again right before he felt a sharp pain in his kidney.

"Police!" Tyrone yelled, rabbit-punching Trevor again from behind as he twisted Trevor's arm behind his back. He flashed his badge to the crowd to ward off any Good Samaritans. Tyrone quickly moved Trevor to the nearby alley.

"I didn't do anything, officer. I was just standin' there, waitin' for my girlfriend," Trevor pleaded in a frightened voice. Tyrone slammed him into the brick wall.

"Assume the position, asshole," Tyrone snickered, remembering how it felt to be harassed by the police. He had guessed right. Trevor, like most black men, was afraid to question the credentials of a police officer. He was sure Trevor would cooperate just to avoid a nasty beating, but he never dreamed Trevor would be so polite.

"Excuse me, officer, is it possible for you to tell me what I did wrong?"

"There is a young lady inside this restaurant who says you tried to rape her." He punched Trevor in the ribs hard. "I don't like rapists. My sister was raped last year."

"Ahhh! I didn't try to rape her, officer. I swear," Trevor whimpered. "She's my girlfriend."

"You know, for some reason I'd like to believe you." He punched him in the ribs again. "But attempted rape is a serious crime. I'm going to have to arrest you anyway. Don't worry though. A few days on Rikers Island and we will have this whole thing straightened out."

"Please don't arrest me, officer." Trevor began to cry. "I'm on probation and my probation officer will violate me for sure."

"Wow, I'm really sorry about that, but I can't just let you go. I want to, but my shift's over and I could really use the overtime pay. My wife's pregnant and I just can't make ends meet on a detective's salary. So I'm going to take you in."

"I can pay. Look in my wallet," Trevor begged desperately. "There's two hundred dollars in there. Take it out, it's yours."

"Is this a bribe or a baby shower gift?" Tyrone pulled Trevor's wallet out of his pants and took out two crisp hundred-dollar bills.

"It's a baby shower gift!"

"Man, that's really nice of you . . . What's your name?" Tyrone put the bills in his pocket.

"Trevor. Trevor Hill."

Okay, Mr. Hill, this is what I'm gonna do. I'm gonna tell my partner inside talking to the lady and the kid that you got away. But so help me, if you go and bother that lady one more time"—he opened Trevor's wallet and looked at his address—"I'm going down to

167-98 Hollis Court in Queens and shoot your black ass myself. Now get the hell out of here!" He stuffed the wallet into Trevor's coat pocket.

Trevor didn't have to be told twice. Like a bat out of hell, he took off, never once looking back to see Tyrone's grinning face.

25

KEVIN AND DENISE

Denise kissed Kevin passionately before he rolled out of the bed to take a shower.

"You know we're going to have to do something about all these boxes you have lying around here." She laughed as he tripped over a basket of clean clothes.

"Yeah, I know. Maybe when I get my tax return I'll buy some bedroom furniture."

She knew he hadn't even bothered to file his taxes yet, even though the deadline was less than a month away. But she didn't want him to have to wait that long to get some dressers to keep his expensive clothes neat. Reaching for her bag on the side of the bed, Denise pulled out her daily planner. On her to-do list she wrote *Buy Kevin new bedroom furniture*. In her mind she began to redecorate his bedroom until the phone interrupted her. She answered it, thinking Kevin wouldn't mind.

"May I speak to Kevin?" a female voice asked.

"Can I ask who's calling, please?"

"Could you tell him Alicia's on the phone, please?" Denise put the phone down on the bed.

Shit, Denise thought, *I didn't expect her to call this soon. He's gonna go for this F.B. crap only so long if she's trying to wiggle her way back in.*

She tried to compose herself. Flipping through her planner, she found the notes she had written from the private investigator's report. Then she picked up the phone again.

"Alicia, how are you? This is Denise, Kevin's girlfriend."

"Girlfriend?" Alicia asked weakly.

"Oh, I'm so glad you called. Kevin has told me so many good

things about you and Michael. I just wish I were around to help when you left that battered women's shelter. That Big Brother program is wonderful, isn't it? And you really lucked out getting my Kevin as your son's mentor."

"Yeah, we really lucked out," Alicia mumbled.

Alicia had no idea what Denise was referring to, but she figured it was just a pack of lies Kevin had fed her. She decided not to bother to correct this woman's misconceptions of her. The original intent of this call had been to try to work things out with Kevin. She had experienced a change of heart, realizing she was still in love with him, and had called to ask if they could start over. Now there was this other woman on the line, claiming to be his girlfriend. Alicia was hurt and angry, especially to think that Kevin was telling lies about her. All she wanted now was to get him on the phone and cuss him out.

"Listen, Denise. Is Kevin around? I really need to speak with him about this Big Brother program," she lied.

"Oh, I'm sorry, he's not home. I think he's out with his friends, picking out my engagement ring. He thinks I don't know, so I'll just have to act surprised." Denise giggled.

"You're getting engaged?" Alicia paused and added flatly, "Well, congratulations to both of you."

"Thanks. That means a lot coming from you, Alicia. I really appreciate it. You know, I have to admit I was pretty jealous of all the time you and Kevin were spending together until he told me you were gay."

Alicia gasped but didn't say a word as Denise continued.

"I hope you'll be coming to our wedding?" Denise tried not to laugh and was saved when the call-waiting beeped. "Hold on a second, Alicia. I have another call coming in."

Alicia waited a few seconds, fuming. She couldn't believe she had called to ask for a reconciliation, and now she was finding out what a true dog Kevin was. She heard Denise's voice again.

"Alicia, I'm sorry, I have Kevin's sister on the phone, and it sounds pretty important. I'll have Kevin call you when he gets in, okay? Bye." Denise clicked the phone over just as Kevin walked into the room.

"Who's that on the phone?"

"It's your sister Phyllis. I think she's been crying." Denise handed him the phone.

"Phyllis? What's wrong, sweetheart?"

"It's Whitney, Kevin. She collapsed during breakfast," Phyllis sobbed. "Kevin, the paramedics couldn't wake her up!"

"Try to stay calm, Phyllis, where's Mama?"

"She's went with Whitney to the hospital in the ambulance."

After listening to Phyllis explain the situation again, Kevin told her that he would be there as soon as possible. Denise, who had been eavesdropping, immediately dialed her secretary's home number on her cell phone.

"Hello, Ruth? This is Denise. I'm sorry to disturb you on a Sunday morning, but I need something done right away. I need two first-class tickets on the next plane leaving out of Kennedy to Richmond, Virginia. Have the tickets waiting at the ticket counter in the names of Kevin Brown and mine. I also need a limo waiting for us going to—" She looked at Kevin, who stood beside her with a puzzled look on his face.

"Petersburg General Hospital," he mumbled numbly.

Denise repeated what Kevin had said. "Look, I have to go. I'll call you in a few minutes from my car."

"I don't have the money to pay you back right now," Kevin told her. He had planned on driving.

"Well, I guess I'll have to stick around until you do." She smiled. "Right now you just need to take care of your family."

Two hours later Kevin walked onto the floor of the intensive care unit of Petersburg General Hospital. He was greeted with a hug by his red-eyed mother. Mama noticed the white woman standing behind her son, but she was too emotional even to ask who she was.

"Kevin, they said she's gonna die if she don't have this operation, but them doctors ain't gonna give it to her." Mama sounded distraught.

"Don't worry, Mama. I'm gonna straighten everything out once I talk to the doctors. Where's Whitney's room?"

"She's in here." Mama pointed.

Realizing he had not introduced Denise to his mother, Kevin distractedly said, "Mama, this is my friend Denise. She's the one who helped me out with the money to fly down here so fast."

Mama nodded at Denise, but there was no expression other than sadness on her face, so it was hard for Denise to read her reaction.

"You two can get to know each other later, once Whitney is better," Kevin told them as he took Mama's hand and led her into Whitney's room.

"She's in bad shape, Kevin, real bad shape." Phyllis stood and whispered as they entered the room.

"I know, Phyllis, but she's gonna be all right." He walked over to his comatose sister and gazed down at her. *Please, God, don't take Whitney away. We need her,* he prayed.

"Excuse me, Mr. Brown?" A small, balding white man in a lab coat walked over to Kevin with his hand extended. "I'm Dr. Brand. I'm in charge of the ICU. Your mother said they were waiting for you before they could make any decisions about your sister's care."

Kevin glanced over at his mother. She tried to smile through her tears, but it wouldn't work. "You're the man of the house, Kevin. Take care of our business."

Kevin nodded and turned to the doctor.

"What is my sister's condition, Dr. Brand?"

"Not good, I'm afraid. Mr. Brown, your sister has severe heart disease."

"Heart disease? But she's only twenty." Kevin was shocked.

"Heart disease can affect the young as well as the old, Mr. Brown, and with your sister having had scarlet fever as a child, well, the risk factors were much higher."

"I didn't even know she had scarlet fever. Are you sure?" Kevin glanced over at his mother, who nodded that the doctor was right. "So what's wrong with her?"

"Well, Mr. Brown, to put it in layman's terms, your sister had a heart attack. Both the valves to her right ventricle and aorta are severely damaged and need to be replaced. I recommend that we operate as soon as possible, otherwise she might not make it through the night."

"What are you waiting for? Let's get this done."

"As a doctor, there is nothing I'd like more. But there is a problem that is out of my control," he said sadly, gesturing for Kevin and his family to follow him out of Whitney's room.

Standing outside were two well-dressed white men.

"Mr. Brown, this is Dr. Goldstein, our chief of staff, and Mr. Levin, our hospital legal counsel. I think your mother's already spoken to them." Mama nodded with a frown.

"I'm sorry about your sister's condition, Mr. Brown," Dr. Goldstein said solemnly. "I was wondering if you were aware of any health insurance your sister carried that your mother might not know of."

"Is that what you're worried about? If we can pay the bill? That's my sister in there, doctor. If I have to, I'll work three jobs." Kevin's voice was rising in pitch as he became more frantic.

"Well, Mr. Brown, why didn't you pay your father's bill after his death?" the hospital lawyer asked, pulling some papers from a folder. "I have here almost thirty thousand dollars in unpaid hospital bills." Kevin looked over at his mother as the lawyer kept talking. He had no idea Mama still owed so much money to the hospital. "Your sister's operation is going to cost almost sixty thousand dollars, and that doesn't include aftercare expenses. Who is going to pay these bills, Mr. Brown? Your mother says you're the only one in the family with a steady job."

"Are you telling me you're not going to give my sister this operation? 'Cause we're poor?" Kevin was about to punch the man.

Levin took a step backward, checking down the hall to be sure the security guard was at his post.

"Mr. Brown, you have to understand. We're not a public hospital. We're private, and we have bills to pay too. You can always have your sister transferred to MCV in Richmond. . . ."

"This woman cannot be moved. It took me two hours just to get her stabilized," Dr. Brand stated emphatically.

"You can't refuse a patient treatment because of past-due payment or lack of insurance in a life-threatening emergency," Denise said, stepping from behind Phyllis.

"Excuse me?" Levin demanded. "That's not true."

"I'm afraid it is," she told him confidently as she stood beside Kevin. "Jackson vs. Downston County General is the precedent, if you care to look it up."

"And who are you?" Dr. Goldstein demanded.

"I'm Denise Shwartz, their lawyer." She handed each of them one of her cards. "As you can see, I specialize in malpractice. Now, Mr. Levin, I think you need to bone up on Jackson vs. Downston County General. Because if Ms. Brown dies, I'm going to take pleasure in suing this hospital and both of you, individually, for wrongful death and discrimination."

Goldstein glanced at Levin, who was still looking at Denise's card with a frown. Denise was happy to see a look of fear cross the man's face as he realized she was serious. Even as Kevin and his family were experiencing the terror of his sister's possible death, Denise was plotting for her own satisfaction. She knew that if Kevin's sister received her surgery, she would always be a hero to Kevin and his family and elevate herself from F.B. status to true girlfriend. To her his sister's critical health was a perfect opportunity for advancement.

"Believe me, I'm going to work extra hard if my future sister-in-law dies," she told the hospital lawyer without looking at Kevin or his mother to see the shock on their faces.

"D-discrimination?" Dr. Goldstein stuttered.

"That's right. I can't wait to subpoena your records and find out how many African Americans you've denied treatment. Hey, you never know, I might end up with one hell of a class action suit. Oh, and, Dr. Goldstein, if you didn't know, discrimination is not covered under malpractice insurance."

"Now, Ms. Shwartz, I'm sure we can work out something that will be agreeable to all parties concerned." Dr. Goldstein smiled nervously. "Why don't you let me have a word with my colleagues?"

"Sure. We'll be waiting in Ms. Brown's room." She grabbed Kevin's hand and led him back to Whitney's room. His mother and sister followed in stunned silence. Mama was too numb with the pain of watching her child suffer to process everything Denise had said. But she was certain she had heard the word "in-law" and knew that at some point she would need to have a serious discussion with this young woman. After five minutes in which barely a word was spoken in Whitney's room, Dr. Brand came in with a wide grin on his face.

"What did they decide?" Kevin asked nervously.

"They said we're a go! I just beeped our best heart surgeon, and the O.R. team is prepping as we speak. We should have your sister on the table within the hour."

"Thank you, God, and thank you, Dr. Brand. I can see you had my sister's best interests at heart all the time." He shook the doctor's hand.

"Don't thank me, thank her." He pointed to Denise. "I don't know where you found this young lady, but she's the first person I ever saw frighten Josh Levin."

Denise sat in the hospital cafeteria, drinking coffee. It had been about three hours since Whitney had been taken to the operating room. She had not felt comfortable in the waiting room when the pastor and deaconess of Mrs. Brown's church demanded that they all get down on their knees for a prayer vigil.

Come on, Whitney, you have to make it, she thought selfishly. *If you make it, I'll always be a hero in his eyes.* At that moment Denise's cell phone rang.

"Hello."

"Denise, this is Liz. What's up? You paged me three times."

"Liz, you'll never guess what happened," Denise said in a conspiratorial whisper so that none of the other people in the cafeteria could hear. "I saved Kevin's sister's life."

"What the hell are you talking about? You're a lawyer, not a doctor."

"I'm sorry, Liz. Let me start from the beginning." Denise explained to her friend what had taken place.

"You have got to be the luckiest woman on the face of the earth. If his sister lives, he's going to worship the ground you walk on. Well, I guess you can start taking your birth control pills again, huh?" Liz joked.

"Yeah." Denise laughed. "Now I just hope my period comes next week."

"Excuse me. Denise, isn't it?" Mama startled Denise as she sat in the chair across from her.

"Mrs. Brown! You scared me. Any word on your Whitney?" She hung the phone up on Liz without saying good-bye.

"She's in the recovery room. Dr. Brand said the operation was a complete success. She's not goin' to be able to run any marathons, but she'll lead a happy life. Thank God she already has two children."

"That's great, Mrs. Brown. I'm so happy for all of you." Denise hugged her as she thought about how happy she was for herself too.

"I asked Kevin what you meant by callin' Whitney your future sister-in-law."

"Oh, I'm really sorry about that. I hope I didn't embarrass you or Kevin. The lawyer in me gets out of control sometimes. I wanted them to know how serious I was about getting care for your daughter."

"Is that so?" Mama raised an eyebrow. "Denise, what's goin' on with you and my boy?"

Denise was speechless for a second, so Mama continued.

"Look I'ma be honest. I appreciate what you did for Whitney, but I wanna know what you want with my Kevin?"

"I don't want anything from him, we're just friends," Denise insisted.

Mama smiled. *Who this girl think she's foolin'?*

"Honey, do you want us to get along?"

"Yes, Mrs. Brown," Denise said humbly.

"Then first of all, stop callin' me Mrs. Brown. For as long as I can

remember, people 'round here been callin' me Mama. You can too."
Mama sat back in her chair.

"Okay, Mama." The words sounded awkward coming from
Denise, and she smiled nervously. This was her moment of truth. If his
mama accepted her, Kevin would have no reason to refuse a relationship with Denise.

"Now, I seen the way you looked at Kevin. Those aren't looks of
friendship. Those was looks of lust and love. Pretty white girl like you
can get a black boy killed 'round these parts, lookin' at him like that."

Denise was at a loss for words. She had no idea what to say to this
woman without offending her.

"Mrs. Brown, I like Kevin, and one day I'd like to be his girlfriend.
But right now we're just friends. That's Kevin's choice, not mine."

"Well, I think you should talk to Kevin, 'cause he just told Phyllis
and me that you was his new girlfriend."

"Really?" Denise couldn't hold back an elated smile.

"That's what he said." Mama's face was expressionless.

"You don't look too happy about it," Denise said as she tried to
contain her own emotions.

"That's y'alls decision. I just want Kevin to be happy."

"I can make him happy."

Before Mama could respond, Kevin entered the cafeteria and sat
down next to Denise.

"What are you two talking about?" He smiled, placing his arm
around Denise.

"Oh, nothin', baby. I was just welcomin' Denise to the family."
Mama looked across the table at Denise. She had a bad feeling about
this girl.

26

ANTOINE AND KEISHA

It was warm for the middle of March. Keisha was sitting on the stoop in front of her building, rubbing Antoine's back sympathetically as he recounted the events at the Men's Club the night before. Although he had never actually seen Shawna dance, he was upset she spent so much of her time in such a raunchy place. Every time he had seen Billy grab a woman's breasts, he imagined some other sleazy man doing the same to Shawna. It hurt him deeply that she would not leave her job, and he was pouring out his heart to Keisha in hopes that talking about it might make it hurt less.

"I appreciate you listening to me, Keisha. I really needed to get a woman's perspective on this."

"Like I told you before, Antoine, I'm always gonna be here for you. But I can't believe that she's that type. Are you sure?" Actually Keisha was thrilled by the news, because it gave her a better chance with Antoine.

"I was in the club last night. And Kevin told me after I left the man said she was booked all night."

"Damn, she sure fooled me." Keisha shook her head. "I thought she was a schoolteacher like you."

"She fooled a lot of people," Antoine said angrily, "but I'm through letting her make a fool of me."

"If you really mean that, here's your chance." She pointed to Shawna's car, which was pulling up. "Antoine, please don't be trippin' outside the building."

Antoine rolled his eyes. Keisha had made enough scenes of her own in front of this building. Besides, he intended to break up with Shawna calmly and rationally.

"I'm just gonna end things with her, that's all. I'll be cool." He walked over to meet Shawna at her car, but she was already storming toward the stoop.

"Antoine, how come every time I come over here, this wench has her hands all over you?" She gestured wildly toward Keisha, who sat with an amused grin on her face. "Didn't you tell her we're getting married? You'd think she'd have some respect!"

"Calm down, Shawna!"

"That's right, Antoine, you better shut her up before I put my foot in her ass!" Keisha shouted.

"Antoine. Are you going to let that bitch talk to me this way?" Shawna glared over at Keisha.

"She's a grown woman, and she can say any damn thing she pleases."

His reply sent Shawna into a state of total confusion. He had never defended Keisha in the past. The only thing she could think of was that Keisha had told him some more lies.

"You think you can take my man, bitch?" Shawna took off her earrings as she challenged Keisha. "I don't know what the fuck's going on here, but I'm gonna kick your ass before I figure it out!"

"You're not going to kick anyone's ass," Antoine said sternly, stepping between the two women. He turned to Keisha. "Would you please stay out of this?" Keisha sat back down on the stoop so she could hear their conversation.

"Why are you acting like this, Antoine?" Shawna wailed. "What did I do?"

"It's your night job, Shawna. I love you, but I can't stand the fact that you don't want to leave that sleazy dump. If you quit that job right now, I could forget you ever worked there, and we could still get married. But if you insist on working there, I can't be with you."

"I need that job to pay for my operation!" she pleaded.

"I don't really care about your breast size. I love you for the person you are inside. If you really want the operation, Shawna, I'll give you the money. Just leave that place."

He wished he could make Shawna understand she was beautiful just the way she was, but she seemed obsessed with getting her breasts enlarged.

"Antoine, I'm not quitting my job. I love my job. My job makes me feel like a woman."

"So, what are you trying to say, being a prostitute makes you feel like a woman?" His eyes got small with anger. Then he felt the sting of pain as Shawna smacked him across the face.

"Don't you ever talk to me that way again! You hear me, Antoine?" She swung at him again.

Keisha jumped up, deciding she couldn't watch anymore. She practically flew through the air as she tackled Shawna.

"You know he ain't gonna fight a woman, bitch. But if you want a fight, you got one!" Keisha got in a few good swings, and Shawna fought back, scratching Keisha's neck with her long fingernails. Antoine grabbed Keisha and pulled her off Shawna, shouting loudly.

"Shawna, I think you'd better go home." He was still holding Keisha, who tried to lunge toward Shawna.

"But, Antoine, we need to talk," she pleaded, trying to catch her breath, and straightening out her clothes.

"There's nothing left to be said. It's over." He turned his back to her as he struggled to hold Keisha, who still wanted to continue the fight.

"Let me go, Antoine! That bitch scratched my neck!"

Shawna walked to her car, tears streaming down her face. She turned one last time to look at Antoine, who wasn't even glancing in her direction. Sadly she got into her car and drove away.

Releasing Keisha, Antoine turned to watch Shawna's car as it turned the corner. Keisha stood breathing heavily. She couldn't resist one more insult, even though Shawna was already gone.

"You know, my grandmother always used to say something about girls like her."

"What's that?" Antoine was annoyed.

"You can make the housewife into a whore. But you can never make a whore into a housewife."

"Do me a favor, Keisha. Don't speak to me again. Ever. I'm just gonna put the rent check in your mailbox." Antoine turned to leave.

"What did I do?" Keisha asked in amazement.

"You did everything. This whole thing would have gone a hell of a lot smoother if you had stayed out of it like I asked." He stomped up the stairs to his apartment.

"I'm sorry . . ." she tried to tell him as the door slammed shut.

Keisha was at a loss for words as she returned to her beauty shop. She couldn't understand why Antoine was upset with her. It was her personality to attack when she felt threatened, and Shawna had been a threat to her since the first day she showed up in front of the building. Shawna had something that Keisha had wanted for a long time.

But Keisha actually thought she had been pretty good until then, restraining herself every time the bitch said something to her. It was only when she saw her hit Antoine that she couldn't hold herself back anymore. Why couldn't he understand that she was only fighting for him?

Keisha was confused. She wanted Antoine to accept that she would fight when she had to. But she knew he never resorted to physical violence to solve his problems, and that was exactly what she liked about him. He was so refined compared to most of the men she knew. He wanted to solve his problems with his mind rather than his fists. She knew that she and Antoine could learn a lot from each other and their differences, and she was determined that someday she would make Antoine understand this.

Upstairs in his apartment Antoine grabbed a bottle of rum and nearly finished off the entire bottle in one gulp. For two weeks he stayed in a drunken stupor. He left his apartment only long enough to get more booze. His head was reeling from all the alcohol and from the rush of emotions that he still could not contain. He threw an empty bottle of rum at his telephone when its ring invaded the silent room. He missed.

"Who the fuck's calling me?" he slurred, picking up a brandy bottle and trying to drink the remaining few drops.

"Antoine, pick up! Antoine, this is Kevin. Listen, I just got back from Virginia, and they say you haven't been to work in over a week. I don't know what's going on over there, but I'm worried about you, bro, and so is Tyrone. Look, gimme a call when you get this message. It doesn't matter what time."

"Fuck you *and* Tyrone! You don't give a shit about me. Nobody does," Antoine screamed, throwing the brandy bottle at the answering machine. It hit the message button, which activated the machine.

"You have four messages," the machine barked. "Message number one: 'Yo, Antoine, this is Tyrone. Where you been, man? Kevin's sister Whitney is in the hospital.'"

"Message two: 'Mr. Smith, this is Dr. Maurice Johnson. You haven't called in sick or notified us about any personal time you needed. It is imperative that you give me a call at the school so we can make arrangements to cover your English Regents review class.'"

All that son of a bitch cares about is those fucking test scores. I could be dead for all he cares.

"Message three: 'Hello, Mr. Smith, this is Mrs. Rogers, the school secretary. I was just calling to let you know that the staff and I were thinking about you. I hope whatever it is keeping you out is not serious. Have a blessed day.'"

Mrs. Rogers's message sobered him slightly, just enough to realize how recklessly he had been acting. The breakup with Shawna had hurt him more deeply than anything he could remember, but he knew this was not like him to spend practically two weeks in an alcoholic fog. The more he thought about it, the more disgusted he became with his behavior. He had to get himself together.

He staggered over to his desk to find his rent check, which was a week late. Once he discovered it under a pile of unopened mail, he stumbled down the stairs to Keisha's apartment. As he tried to open her mailbox, he tripped over his own feet and fell. Too drunk to get up, he soon passed out in front of her door.

Antoine awoke with blurred vision and a headache that felt as if an anvil had been dropped on his temples. Blinking several times to focus his eyes, he finally made out what appeared to be a naked woman. She was large but shapely and hummed softly as she toweled herself dry. Antoine was sure he must have been dreaming. As the woman turned around, he recognized her face. He was surprised that Keisha would be the woman in his dream, but she sure looked good. He laughed, thinking she would be flattered to know he was dreaming about her.

"It's good to see you're among the living." Keisha smiled, wrapping the towel around her body.

"Keisha? You mean I'm not dreaming?" He took both his hands and placed them on the sides of his head, hoping to ease his headache.

"No, Antoine, you're not dreaming. It's me in the flesh." She smiled again.

"You're not kidding about that." Antoine rolled over and groaned as the pain in his head intensified. "What time is it anyway? I don't want to be late for work."

"You're already late." She pointed to the clock, which said 12:47 P.M. "I hope you don't mind. I called your job and told them you'd be in tomorrow."

"No, I don't mind. I need to get myself back on track. I really appreciate it." He sat up at the edge of the bed and noticed that he was wearing only underwear. "How long have I been here? What happened?" he muttered.

"I found you passed out in front of my door yesterday morning.

You were covered in your own vomit. It took me about three hours to clean you up and get rid of the smell." She walked into the bathroom to put on a robe.

"Damn, my head hurts. You wouldn't have any aspirin, would you?"

"That doesn't work on hangovers, trust me. I'll get you something that will."

She walked out of the room, headed for the kitchen.

Antoine sat up on the bed and looked around Keisha's bedroom for the first time. The room was much larger than his, and instead of pictures the walls were lined with decorative bookcases, all filled with books. He walked over to one of the cases and read the brass-engraved label. BLACK HISTORY: FIRST PRINTINGS. He took a book off the shelf and opened it up, looking at the copyright.

"Damn, this is a first printing of J.A. Rogers's *Superman to Man*," he said out loud, astonished.

"Great book, isn't it?" Keisha had returned, handing him a glass with a red mixture in it. "Drink this. It will help knock out your headache." He quickly gulped down the mixture and made a face at the horrible taste.

"Don't worry. It tastes like crap, but it'll fix your head in no time."

"Where'd you get all these books, Keisha? This one must be worth a couple of hundred dollars."

"Three hundred to be exact. I've been collecting rare books by African Americans for years. That's one of the things that attracted me to you in the first place."

"Why do you say that?"

"When you first moved in, one of the boxes broke, and I saw all the poetry books you had. Right then and there I knew you were the kind of guy I wanted to get with."

"Why didn't you ever tell me this, Keisha?" He was flattered.

"I don't know. I guess you never really gave me the chance. I think you decided you had me all figured out as soon as you saw me working in the shop, gossiping with my girls."

Somehow, in the midst of a pounding headache, Antoine had a moment of clarity. There was much more to Keisha than he had ever imagined, and he was ashamed that he had judged her so harshly all this time. For all of her tough street talk and aggressive behavior, Keisha had a big enough heart to take him in when he was at his lowest, passed out on her doorstep. And now that he was in her apartment, she had not displayed one bit of anger for all of the times he had written her off as not worthy of his standards. He was humbled.

At the same time, he was also becoming aware that this wonderful woman was standing in front of him wearing only her bathrobe. The hangover and the rawness of his emotions made him very bold, and he put his hands on Keisha's hips, drawing her closer to him.

"Well, Keisha, I have been a fool. Why didn't I notice the real you sooner?" He pressed his lips against hers. She sighed contentedly and snuggled against him as they kissed again.

Making their way onto the bed, Antoine fell back and pulled Keisha on top of him. He opened her robe and caressed her. Keisha arched her back and breathed a deep, satisfied sigh. This moment was exactly what she had dreamed about with Antoine for so long, but she didn't want it to happen for the wrong reasons. Sitting up, she took both her hands and closed her robe tightly.

"I'm sorry, Antoine, but I have too much self-respect to be a one-night stand."

"Who said anything about a one-night stand?" He tried to open her robe again.

"You men are all alike, aren't you? Yesterday you were ready to commit suicide because your precious Shawna wasn't pure as the driven snow. Now I'm supposed to think you want me just because you found out I have some good books? Be for real, man. I know you're just looking for some pussy." She tried to get up, but Antoine held her.

"Look, I'm not saying I'm fully over Shawna, but I see now what you've been trying to make me notice all along. You and I could really have something, Keisha."

"What, like some fun in this bed? No, thanks, I don't need that kind of misery. Guys on the rebound never stay with the next chick."

"No, Keisha, books. Think of all the hours of enjoyment we can have, sharing and talking about books. I'm willing to make this work if you'll give it a try," he pleaded.

"Okay, I'll give it a try. But, Antoine, there are some conditions if I'm going to trust that you want more than some rebound sex."

Keisha sensed his sincerity. Besides, she couldn't resist his cute round face. But her streetwise side told her that she'd better not fall too quickly. There was still that chance that Shawna could come back, and he might have another change of heart. She decided to be cautious and let him know he was not going to be able to dive right in without proving himself.

"Go ahead, I'm listening."

"First of all, I'm not giving you any sex until I'm ready. Second, you're going to wine and dine me just like you did her. And third, I don't want to see her whorish ass around here if you're going to be my man. I live and work here, so both of you are going to show me some respect. Do you think you can handle that?"

She practically barked out her list of demands, but this time her aggression wasn't a deterrent to Antoine. He understood that this was only one side of Keisha, and he was willing to look beyond it for the chance to know the rest of her. He looked up at her with a smile.

"If you're willing try this, Keisha, I promise to make every day better than the last."

She hugged him tightly, looking forward to making sure he kept that promise.

27

ALICIA

Alicia picked up her gym bag and said good-bye to the women in the locker room. She had just finished a karate lesson at the Standing on Your Own club that Sylvia had told her about, and Alicia was feeling really good about herself. She had been attending the club's self-defense classes for a little over a month and had just started attending group counseling sessions for battered women. Making the decision to seek counseling was a giant step for Alicia. Originally she was too ashamed that she had let Trevor back into her life, and she wasn't about to admit that to some stranger who wanted to analyze her. But after meeting some of the women in her karate classes and hearing their stories, she learned that she was not alone. Many women were in similar situations, and they convinced her she would have to be willing to seek help from every possible source if she wanted to start putting her life back together.

As she left the locker room, she stopped to watch the advanced karate class for a few minutes. *That's gonna be me one day,* she thought, watching a five-foot woman flip the six-foot instructor flat on his back. *I'm not gonna let anyone intimidate me anymore.* She picked up her gym bag and strode over to the area that had been set aside for child-care.

Inside the room were almost fifteen children mesmerized by a television. Alicia approached a light-skinned woman in her late forties who sat behind a desk.

"I'm here to pick up my son, Michael," she told the woman as she reached for a pen and the signout sheet.

"I don't know what it is about that Pokémon, but it's the best baby-sitter I've ever seen," the woman remarked.

"Tell me about it. All I have to do is threaten to throw out my son's Pokémon cards and he does whatever he's told."

"So how long you been comin' to the club?" the woman asked.

"About a month. What about you?"

"I opened the club with Jen Anderson five years ago. My name's Laverne Jackson." The woman smiled.

"Nice to meet you, Laverne. I'm Alicia Meyers." Alicia offered Laverne her hand, but Laverne stood up from her chair and walked around the desk.

"We don't shake hands when we make new friends around here. We give them a hug." Laverne opened her arms and wrapped them around Alicia, embracing her tightly. "I don't know what you're looking for, Alicia, but if you stick with the club, I'm sure you'll find what you need."

"I hope so, Laverne, I really do hope so." Alicia hugged Laverne back.

It had taken Alicia and Michael a little more than thirty minutes to get home from the club. Alicia had decided to order a pizza and have it delivered for dinner. She rented a video game for Michael and a romantic movie for herself. As she placed the key in her door, she was looking forward to ordering their dinner and putting her feet up for the evening for some peace and relaxation. A voice startled her from behind.

"Hi, Alicia." The voice gave her chills. She spun around to face Trevor, holding a small flower arrangement.

"Trevor, what are you doing here?" She pulled Michael closer to her.

"I just wanted to talk." Trevor's tone was lacking its usual aggression. He actually sounded humble, though it didn't matter to Alicia. She was still scared.

"Why'd you change your number?" Trevor asked.

"Isn't it obvious? I did it 'cause I don't wanna have anything to do with you." Alicia reached in her handbag, taking hold of the pepper spray she'd been carrying since she'd started taking self-defense classes. Now she prayed she would have the nerve to use it if things got out of hand.

"Come on now. Why you gonna act this way?" Trevor pleaded. "I told you I'm sorry. Y'know I act a little stupid when I get drunk." He could tell from Alicia's expression that she didn't want to hear it, so he tried his best to sound even more sincere. "I swear, I haven't even had a drink in over a month and I'm gonna start goin' to AA meetings next week, aw'ight?"

"Yeah, right." Alicia took a step toward her door, but Trevor matched it.

"Come on, baby, you know I love you." Alicia could see the frustration on Trevor's face, so she tightened her grip around the pepper spray in her bag.

"Stay away from me, Trevor!" He froze in his tracks, looking around for anyone who might be watching them.

"Why you actin' this way? You know I ain't gonna hurt you." Trevor tried to hand her the flowers. "Take 'em. I know how much you love flowers."

"I think I've seen enough flowers to last a lifetime."

"Well, I got some money for you and Michael too." He reached into his pocket and pulled out some folded bills, handing them to Alicia.

"Only reason I'm taking this money is 'cause your son needs new clothes." Alicia took her arm from around Michael to get the money. She didn't want to have to let go of the pepper spray in her handbag.

Trevor smirked. It had been his experience that whenever she took his money, he was on his way back into her life.

"Look, Alicia, we need to sit down and talk. Work things out for Michael's sake. Do you really wanna raise him without his daddy? Without his family? Come on, baby, just give me one more chance." Trevor lowered his head to look humble. "Hey, Mike, tell your mom to give me another chance. Come on, man, remember how much fun we had going to that Nets game together? If your mom takes me back, we can go to some more games and go to Disney World this summer, like I promised."

Michael tugged on his mother's coat. "Give him another chance, Mom, please?"

Alicia looked down at her son. "I'm sorry, Michael. I can't do it. Your father has a lot of problems, and until he's really willing to deal with them, I don't want anything to do with him." Alicia turned her attention to Trevor. "I appreciate the money, Trevor, and I pray that what you said about the drinking is true, but it's been all about you in the past. Now it's about me." Alicia turned the key and opened the door to her building.

Trevor stuck his arm in front of her to prevent her from entering the building. "I know I fucked up in the past, but I'm gonna change this time, I promise. I'm willing to do whatever it takes to make this work. I just want my family back. I swear on my dead grandmother I'm gonna change."

Alicia stared at Trevor. She was softening a bit, starting to believe that he really meant what he was saying. But the short time she had been at Standing on Your Own had taught her that it would take more than a few promises for an abuser to truly change himself. She was not ready to let him back into her or her son's life.

"I'm sorry, Trevor, but words aren't good enough this time." Alicia braced herself as she pushed her way past him into the building. "Get some help, Trevor, then we'll talk."

"You promise?" He practically sounded like a child.

"Yes, I promise."

"I'm gonna prove to you we need to be together, Alicia," he said as the door shut behind her.

Alicia held Michael's hand tightly as they walked down the hall to their apartment. She felt an incredible sense of relief as she reached her door and realized they were both safe. What she thought was going to end up as a physical confrontation turned out to be a sincere offer of reconciliation from Trevor. It was one that she probably would never accept, but it made her feel that she and Trevor might possibly be friendly one day. That would be the best thing for their son.

"Alicia," she heard her next-door neighbor call.

"What's up, Cathy?" Alicia turned toward her neighbor's door. Cathy, a woman in her early thirties, strolled out of her apartment wearing a housecoat and slippers. Her hair was wrapped up in a scarf, and Alicia knew it hadn't been done in days.

"The florist delivered something for you again today." She walked back in her apartment and returned with a vase filled with two dozen roses. "Damn, girl, this is the third time he sent you flowers this week."

"I know," Alicia said without emotion. "He was just outside with more flowers a minute ago, but they didn't look anything like these." Alicia touched one of the flowers and then opened her door. Michael ran inside with his video game and disappeared behind his bedroom door.

"Girl, if you don't want that man, let me have 'im. That nigga's cute, and he got a nice car too." Cathy's tone was serious as she followed Alicia inside.

"Cathy, how many times I gotta tell you? Trevor is abusive."

"If a man don't smack you, he don't love you. That's what my mama use ta say."

"Yeah, mine too," Alicia said quietly. "But I'm not like my mom. I don't like getting hit, and I swear, ain't no man gonna hit me again."

"Uh-huh, sure." Cathy rolled her eyes. "You still sweating that fine-ass gym teacher, that's your problem. But he ain't perfect. Didn't you say he had a girlfriend the whole time y'all was goin' together?"

"Yeah, that's what she said, but I'm not sure I believe Kevin would do that."

"Why not, he's a man, ain't he?" Cathy sucked her teeth.

"You don't know him, Cathy, so please don't talk about him." Alicia handed the flowers to Cathy. "Here, you can have these. I don't want any more flowers."

"Look, don't no woman answer no man's phone unless she with that man. Now, you better stop worryin' about somebody else's man and love the one you with." Cathy pulled the card from the flowers and handed it to Alicia.

Alicia read the inscription on the card.

Dear Alicia,
I can't explain how much I miss and need you. Please give our love another chance.

I love you,
Trevor

She dropped the card on the coffee table, where it landed next to a vase of lilies that had been delivered the day before. Trevor had delivered his message loud and clear; now only time would tell if he really meant it.

28

DENISE, KEVIN, AND ALICIA

Denise sat in her Park Avenue office, entrenched in a pile of law books. She had been working eighteen-hour days on her present case. In that time she had seen Kevin only once, and that was for a quickie in her office at two in the morning. Setting the book facedown on her desk, she leaned back in her leather chair and closed her tired eyes. Things were going pretty well between her and Kevin, she thought, except for the occasional nasty comment or bold look a racist gave them. Both she and Kevin were learning to expect comments from time to time from both blacks and whites and handled it by ignoring them. The only thing that worried her was Kevin's habit of talking in his sleep. Often the things he said were about Alicia, and it made Denise nervous that this woman was still on his mind. Lately she had become obsessed with doing everything in her power to make him forget about his ex.

Picking up the phone, she dialed his number.

"Hey, Chocolate Star, this is Snow White. I hope you haven't forgotten about me. Listen, I really need to see you. I have this terrible itch that needs to be scratched, and you're the only man for the job. So I'm coming over tonight and I'll do some work while you watch the game. Try not to eat, because I'm going to stop by BBQ's on the way over. See you about eight. Love you."

She hated answering machines. Picking up a pen, she scribbled *Buy Kevin a cellular phone* on her to-do list.

"Denise." Her secretary's voice startled her.

"Yes?"

"Mr. Nunn and Mrs. Jones are here to see you."

"Good. Could you send them in, please, Ruth?"

Ruth left to direct the visitors to Denise's office. Dominic Nunn was a tall, well-built Italian man, and his partner, Lisa Jones, was a tall, thin black woman who looked as if she could be Whitney Houston's sister. Both ex-cops, they now worked as private detectives, usually for very wealthy clients. They were known for their discretion. Denise stood and smiled as the detectives entered her office.

"Well, how are my two favorite private detectives?"

"Good, Ms. Shwartz," Dominic answered as he helped his pregnant partner sit down.

"How about you, Lisa? You're not going to have that baby anytime soon, are you?"

"No, Ms. Shwartz, I'm only seven months, but I am going on maternity leave right after we get paid." She patted her large stomach contentedly.

"Good for you." Denise settled herself behind her desk. "So, what have you got for me?"

Lisa opened her bag and handed Denise a small file.

"Ms. Shwartz, it looks like your boyfriend is squeaky clean. In the last two weeks I've had four very beautiful African American women approach him. He was polite but nonresponsive to all of their advances."

"Yeah, that's him, polite. Where did they try to come on to him at?"

"Grocery store, subway, Benny's Bar, and one of the girls even pretended to be a parent of a student. He just wasn't interested."

"Did he accept any of their phone numbers?"

"The only phone number he took was from the girl in the bar, but he handed it to his skinny friend when she left."

"Okay, so what's your professional opinion?"

"I suspect at this time the guy's pretty happy with his life. As far as him cheating on you? I don't think you have to worry about that right now."

"Well, that's good news, don't you think?" Denise smiled, looking at the two of them. "What about you, Dominic, do you have any good news for me?"

"Actually, Ms. Shwartz, I do." He reached into his briefcase and handed her a bill. "We sent Alicia Meyers over a thousand dollars worth of flowers, candy, and gifts in the last month under the name Trevor Hill. It was our hope that the gifts would help get the two of them back together."

"Well, did it?" Denise asked as she perused the bill for all the gifts that had been sent to Alicia.

"At first I didn't think it was going to work, because the guy showed up at her apartment only once and left pretty quickly. But lately things seem to be improving between them. He's even spent the last few nights at her apartment."

"That coincides with what I did," Lisa added.

"What's that?"

"Well, as per your instructions, Alicia received a visitor at her apartment. You said you wanted a black woman to approach Alicia, pretending to be you."

"Yeah, so did you send someone?"

"Actually, I went myself, just to make sure the job was done right."

"Oh, my God! What did she say when she saw that you were pregnant?"

Denise had a delighted expression on her face. These two were even better than she had expected.

"I think you should let her explain from the beginning," Dominic added. "It's really a pretty good story." He turned to Lisa as she described their meeting.

"Well, I caught her just as she and her son were getting home one evening. I could tell she was tired, so I waited in the car a few minutes so that she could get herself settled. Then I went to her apartment and rang the bell with my arms full of gifts for her son.

"As soon as Alicia opened the door, I was as sweet as I could possibly be. I told her I was Kevin's girlfriend and explained that he had spoken a great deal about Michael. I told her Kevin wished he could still be in the Big Brother program because he missed the boy. I think she was too flabbergasted even to speak. She finally just asked me directly what exactly I wanted from her.

"Just as she asked me, her son came running to the door. He nearly jumped out of his skin when he saw all the toys I was holding. He wanted to know what they were for, and I told him his uncle Kevin wanted him to have them for his birthday. Well, that kid grabbed those toys and took off faster than lightning.

"Once the packages were out of my arms, Alicia was able to see my stomach, and her jaw nearly hit the floor. She tried to play it cool, but all of a sudden she had a thousand questions for me. She even invited me in to sit down so she could hear all about me and Kevin.

"I sat with her in the living room for about half an hour and told her all about my 'relationship' with Kevin. I laid it on real thick too. I told her we'd been dating for two years, and I could see that hit her hard. But she held herself together and just kept digging for more information. I finally had to tell her I had an appointment at the obstetrician's office and that Kevin would be worried if I was late. I didn't think she was ever going to let me go."

Denise interrupted Lisa's story, impressed at what a thorough job the woman had done.

"I can't believe you were able to do so much work in only half an hour. Alicia's head must still be spinning."

Denise let out a huge sigh, amazed at the job Lisa had done. "You guys seem to have covered every base, that's for sure."

"We sure did," Dominic replied.

Lisa laughed. "The truth is, from what Dominic tells me, we should have put Trevor on the payroll."

"I don't understand." Denise was puzzled.

"The day after I went to her apartment was when she went to the Alcoholics Anonymous meeting with Trevor."

"And?"

"You should have seen him crying and testifying in that meeting about how he lost his family to alcohol and he'd stopped drinking to get them back. Ms. Shwartz, the guy put on an Academy Award–winning performance. There wasn't a dry eye in the place. Especially not Alicia's. She was so moved by his words, she let him spend that very night at her apartment, and he's been there ever since," Dominic concluded.

"That's great," Denise said, then paused and remembered to be realistic. "But are these two going to stay together? I really don't need this woman popping up to ruin my life."

Even with the quality performance Lisa gave, Denise was concerned that something might destroy everything she had worked to build with Kevin. Their relationship still felt strangely fragile to her.

"Ms. Shwartz, we can't be a hundred percent sure about anything as far as this couple's concerned. The police records show constant domestic violence, but so far they are still together," Dominic replied.

"In other words, as long as we keep her away from Kevin, these two will end up breaking up and getting back together until she's dead or he's locked up?"

There was a vicious tone to Denise's question that alarmed both of them. They both nodded in unison, trying not to reveal their true feelings in their facial expression.

"Well, I guess we're going to have to keep them together, then." Denise smiled.

"Ms. Shwartz, there's something I didn't tell you," Dominic said with concern.

"What's that?" Denise looked worried.

"This guy, Trevor, he's still drinking. Which means he could snap at any time."

"That, Dominic, is none of your business."

"Aren't you the least bit concerned about what Trevor might do to her? He's already broken her nose twice in the past!" Lisa couldn't keep silent about her concern.

"No, as far as I'm concerned, this case is over. I might call you to do some follow-up work in the future, but for now we're done. And I want both of you to forget the names Alicia and Trevor. Got it?"

Lisa gave her partner a strange look, but all he did was rub his two fingers together as if it were time to get paid.

"Got it, Lisa?" Denise repeated herself.

"Yeah, I got it," Lisa replied.

The three of them stood up and shook hands. Denise reached into her desk and pulled out two thick stacks of neatly bound hundred-dollar bills.

"I think this will take care of your fee. Five thousand dollars each, plus expenses. And I must say, you've earned every penny."

It was almost 9:30 when Kevin walked into his apartment, covered in automotive grease. From the look on his face, Denise could see he was totally disgusted. He went into the bathroom and stripped off the stained clothing, dropping it on the floor. Putting her law book face-down on a table, she followed him into the bathroom.

"Kevin, honey, is everything all right? You're not mad I'm here, are you? I charmed your landlord into letting me in." She admired his firm butt as he slid into the shower.

"It's not you. That fucking car of mine died on the Belt Parkway. It took me almost an hour and a half to walk home. What the hell is it with you New Yorkers? You see someone needs help and you run the other way. I must have asked ten people if I could get a ride, and not one of them would let me in the car."

"Welcome to New York, home of the Good Samaritan," Denise joked as she began to take off her clothes. She hung her conservative business suit and silk blouse on the back of the door. "What's wrong with the car?"

"I don't know. It could be anything at this point. That whole car's nothing but a piece of shit anyway. I'm gonna go down to the auto auction by the Van-Wyck Expressway tomorrow. I can probably pick something up for around a grand." He smiled when Denise stepped into the shower.

"I don't think you should go to one those auctions." She took the soap from him and began to wash his chest. "I read in the paper that most of those cars are real problems for the new owners. Why don't you lease a new car? Didn't you say you really like the Ford Expedition?"

"Baby, you must be confusing me with Michael Jordan. I'm the *poor* black guy you think is cute."

"I wasn't going to tell you this until your birthday next month . . ." She started soaping his back. "But I was going to give you money toward a down payment on a new car anyway. If I give you enough, we can probably get your payments down to three hundred a month."

She turned Kevin around to kiss him on the lips. She loved the fact that material things always made him happy, since she could buy him anything he ever wanted.

"What do you think? Could you afford that monthly payment?"

"Hell, yeah, I could afford that. Baby, I pay that much in repairs on my Honda each month now."

He pulled Denise in close and kissed her under the warm spray of the shower. She always seemed to know how to make things better. First with his sister Whitney, then with any kind of financial trouble. Of course, he liked to think he was taking care of her too.

He lifted her up and walked out of the shower, carrying her into the bedroom. Laying her wet body down on his new bed, he explored her neck and shoulders with his mouth. She moaned loudly when she felt his soft tongue. Kevin continued to travel across her body, placing kisses everywhere. Her breathing grew heavier as she eagerly anticipated his arrival at the final destination. The sudden jarring sound of the phone tore her from her ecstasy. He stood up to answer it.

"No! What are you doing? Don't stop!" She pulled him back on top of her. The answering machine kicked in, and Kevin heard his mother's voice.

"Kevin, this is your mama. Would you call me when you get this message?" Mama sounded depressed. Kevin jumped up to answer the phone.

"I'm right here, Mama," Kevin panted into the phone.

Denise got up from the bed, cursing, and put Kevin's robe on. Looking back at her lover, who had not finished the job he started, she walked into the living room to look through her law books and pout. Experience had taught her that he and his mother had meaningless two-hour conversations, and to sit there and wait was pointless.

"What's up, Mama?" Kevin asked.

"Your uncle Kenny died this morning," she said sadly.

"Oh, Mama, I'm sorry to hear that. Uncle Kenny was good man."

"Yeah, Kenny lived a good life. I just pray God lets me stick around till I'm ninety-five."

"Mama, you don't have nothin' to worry about as long as you take your blood pressure medicine." He knew Mama always became depressed when family died. It was the only time she thought about her own mortality.

"Yeah, I guess you're right. Well, I'll call you when I know more about the funeral arrangements." She paused before changing the subject. "So, what you doing? Denise over there cooking you some more of that Jewish food?"

"No, but we were trying to do a little celebrating when you called."

"Celebrate! What you two got to celebrate? I hope you ain't asked that girl to marry you, son. You haven't even met her mama and daddy yet." After a moment's silence she thought to ask, "Why is that anyway?"

"We're not getting married, Mama." He laughed. For some reason he was unable to even picture himself and Denise married. Especially since he still thought about Alicia almost every day "We're just celebrating because I'm going to get a new car in a few days."

Kevin smiled at the thought of getting a new Ford Expedition. As long as he could remember, no one in his family had ever owned a brand-new car. After so many months of feelin' like a failure, driving a status symbol might restore some of his pride.

"Oh, baby, I'm so proud of you. What are you getting, something new or used?" Mama assumed he would be getting a compact car.

"I'm going to get me one of those new Ford Expeditions. You know, the big sports utility trucks. That way when I have summer vacation we can take trips down to Georgia and Florida and visit your sisters." He thought this would make his mother happy but learned he was mistaken when he heard her stern reply.

"Where you gettin' the money for this big fancy truck? Them things are expensive. Lord, boy, don't you tell me you're gettin' the money from Denise."

Kevin didn't say a word. He knew his mother was upset; he just didn't understand why.

"Boy, I thought I raised you right. Don't you have any shame?" Mama's voice was getting louder with every word. "That girl done bought you a bedroom set, a living room set, and Lord knows what else. And you got the nerve to ask her to buy you a car? You ought to be 'shamed of yourself."

"Mama, I didn't ask her to buy me a car. I'm the one buying the car. She's just helping me with the down payment. Besides, what's wrong with her giving me expensive gifts? She can afford it." He couldn't believe his mother was so upset.

"Boy, if you was here right now I'd knock you upside your head. You think I'm stupid? I know how much them trucks cost. You gonna needed at least eight thousand dollars to get the payment so's you can afford them."

He had not thought about how much he was going to have to get from Denise as a down payment until Mama brought it up. But she was wrong, Denise wouldn't have to give him eight thousand. It was more like twelve to fifteen thousand. Still, he didn't see the problem with accepting the gift Denise was offering. If his damn basketball career hadn't fallen apart, he would be spending his *own* money on things like this.

"Mama, why you gettin' all upset? Denise knows what she can afford. Why can't you just be happy for me? This is going to be my first brand-new car ever. And I'll still be making all the payments by myself."

This was not the first time his mother had protested the gifts Denise had been giving him. In fact, every time she bought him something, Mama would let him know that she was displeased. He couldn't understand what her problem was, but it was starting to become tiring. As far as he was concerned, she was his girlfriend, and she liked spoiling her man. If he had the kind of money she had, he'd do the same thing for her.

Mama had never fully explained her objections to Kevin. A part of her felt she should respect Denise for the help she gave in getting

Whitney medical treatment. But now, she thought, things were getting out of control. Her son was getting sucked in by the lure of so many big-ticket gifts, and she needed to give him a dose of reality.

"Kevin, you listen to me, because I have something very serious to say." Mama hesitated for a second, gathering her thoughts. "You know I like Denise. But if you think that girl is giving you all this stuff out of the kindness of her heart, then you are one stupid-ass man. That girl is up to something. I don't know what, but she's up to something. I can feel it."

For the first time in his adult life, Kevin was ashamed of his mother. Denise had proven herself to him. The fact that she saved Whitney's life should have been enough to convince everyone of her intentions, but it wasn't. He couldn't understand how his mother could be so ungrateful, and he exploded on the phone.

"Mama, how could you say that? Denise saved Whitney's life. I would think you would be praising her instead of trying to develop conspiracy theories. Is this only because she's white?"

"You can call it whatever you want, son. But if you're not careful, one day you're gonna wake up and find that everything you have really belongs to her. And that you ain't a man but an unimportant little nigger following behind your white massa, waiting for her to throw you a crumb. Is that really a position you want to be in?"

"Mama, that's uncalled for."

"Is it? When was the last time you bought her a present? Can you remember when you last paid for the two of you to go out? Kevin, I don't know what's going on up there in New York, but something stinks, and I'm starting to think it's Denise. I don't care how much money she has. No one buys this many presents for a new love unless there's another motive."

"Mama, you don't know what the hell you're talking about." Both of them were silent.

He was tired of defending his relationship with a white woman. It was bad enough when total strangers judged him on the street, but hearing it from his own mother pushed him to the breaking point.

"I'm sick and tired of you constantly giving me shit about my girlfriend! You should be kissing her ass after the way she got those doctors to give Whitney that operation."

"Who the hell do you think you're talking to?" Mama replied in a scream of her own. "You're going to respect me, Kevin Raymond Brown! I swear before God you're going to respect me, or so help me

I'll have Phyllis drive me to New York and put my big toe straight up your ass! Now, you tell that girl that you appreciate it, but you won't be needing her money for a new car."

"Mama, I'm a grown man. You can't tell me what to do anymore. I want that car, and if Denise is going to help me get it, that's none of your goddamn business." He hung up the phone in anger.

After he took a minute to calm down, he realized what he had just done to his own mother. Never before had they had such a volatile argument. Even after he messed up with the NBA, Mama had always been by his side. He knew this issue must be extremely important for her to be as adamant as she just was. He dialed her number but decided he still wasn't ready to face the whole issue again and hung up. He would apologize to her another day and hoped that she would relax her opinion just a bit.

In the living room Denise pretended to be reading her book but had listened to every word of his conversation. Her pout was gone, replaced by a subtle grin. She was happy that her plan was working, and Kevin was becoming more fiercely loyal to her every day. She put down her book and joined him by the phone, hoping to convince him to finish what he had started earlier.

29

MAURICE

Carol Davis sang the words to Lionel Richie and Diana Ross's "Endless Love" as she sipped her red wine. She gazed out at the beautiful azure-blue water of Jamaica. A light breeze blew the wind chimes that were hanging on the patio, filling the air with their sparkling sounds. The music and the wine made her feel exquisite as she stretched out on a lounge chair to admire the pastel sunset.

She placed her wine on the table beside her chair and picked up a bottle of almond-scented lotion. Generously she smoothed the cream over her long, sexy legs, which were exposed beneath the ultra-short skirt she had chosen to wear for her first evening with Maurice. The intoxicating scent of the rich lotion made her feel both romantic and sexy, and she couldn't wait for Maurice to arrive from the airport so she could properly thank him for this vacation.

In front of the condo complex Maurice stepped out of his rental car and smiled approvingly at the luxurious accommodations. He had flown Carol in earlier so that he could tie up some loose ends at work without making her wait to start her vacation. She had happily accepted the ticket for the earlier flight and promised him she would spend all day in anticipation of his arrival.

He liked that idea. He figured if she was waiting all day on the heavenly island, she would be even more eager to please him by the time his plane arrived. He checked his watch and smiled. He was right on time and sure that Carol would be primed and ready for him after a day in paradise.

The past month had been good to Maurice. His school was up twenty percent in English S.A.T. scores, so he no longer felt like his job was in such jeopardy. He had been with just as many women as he had before he contracted the venereal disease, and although he wasn't having intercourse with them, he was still able to get his sexual satisfaction. Even more important, his wife had stopped pestering him for sex. For Maurice, life was good and about to get much better. He was going to enjoy the evening with Carol, the twenty-eight-year-old interior decorator with gorgeous lips. During his flight he imagined what she could do with those lips.

As he approached the front desk, Maurice could not help but notice the strikingly beautiful woman at the check-in desk. He smiled confidently at her, all thoughts of Carol fleeing from his mind as he poured on the charm for this woman. He was like some type of predatory animal, always on the hunt for fresh meat.

"Hi, I'm Maurice Johnson." He admired her shapely figure without trying to conceal his stare. "I have a condo rental. I think my associate already checked in."

"Yes, Mr. Johnson. We have you confirmed for one week in a two-bedroom oceanview condo," the stunning woman replied, looking up from her computer screen. She returned his flirtatious glances as she told him, "Ms. Davis has already checked in."

It's a shame this man is not here alone, she thought, *I have some ideas about how I could welcome him to Jamaica.*

"Good, but there's been a change in plans. We're going to be checking out first thing tomorrow morning, so I'd like to close out my account now, if you don't mind, Miss"—he read her name tag—"Warner."

"No problem, Mr. Johnson. I can do that right now." She took his credit card.

"Please call me Maurice."

"Only if you call me Debra." She smiled, handing him a key.

"You know, it's too bad I have to catch a five-thirty A.M. flight, otherwise I'd talk you into going back to the States with me for a couple of days." He winked at her.

"I don't think your associate would appreciate that, Maurice." She smiled. He had a naughty side to his flirtatiousness, and she liked that. She batted her long eyelashes to continue their game.

"She's just my secretary. She won't mind." The wheels were turning in Maurice's devious mind. He was hatching a plan to get this woman back to New York with him after he was through with Carol.

"In that case, I get off at two A.M. Maybe we can have a drink before you leave." This time she did not bat her eyes but stared him down directly, as if challenging his honesty.

"Maybe," he teased as he walked toward the elevators. He was planning on seeing this woman again before the night was over.

At the door to the condo he had rented, Maurice straightened his tie and smoothed his hair before he knocked. Carol opened the door with a smile on her face that would have flattered even the biggest player.

"Well, well, well, what do we have here?" he said.

He stared admiringly at Carol as he entered the condo. She had dressed in a micromini skirt and a halter top to reveal as much of her baby-smooth skin as she could. He couldn't wait to get his hands on her well-toned body. She was perfect from her long, shiny hair to her delicate painted toenails.

"Since you said you'd like to dine in, I thought I'd dress for comfort more than show. I hope you don't mind." She could tell by his appreciative gaze that he didn't.

"Mind? No, I don't mind at all." Maurice couldn't take his eyes off this striking woman. "Carol, you look better casual than most women look with an Oprah makeover."

As he flattered her, he was imagining how she looked underneath her revealing outfit. He thought the ring in her belly button looked incredibly erotic. Carol felt Maurice's stares slowly undress her. She contemplated making the first move. She figured if she was bold enough to wear a skirt the size of a Band-Aid, she might as well be forward.

Stepping closer, she massaged his neck seductively. Brushing past his lips, she blew in his ear and nibbled on his lobe. She took a step back when she felt his stiffness against her warm thighs. Maurice let out a long, low moan.

"Whew! Excuse me." She stepped back, trying to compose herself. "I'm really sorry about that. I've kind of got this thing about sucking on a man's ears when I'm excited annnn—"

"Oh, you're excited, huh?" He raised an eyebrow.

"Oh, my God! Please don't get the wrong idea. It's just that I've been lying on this romantic island, daydreaming about you, and I got a little ahead of myself. I'll try to behave now, and at least let you in the condo first."

"Relax," he said with a huge grin. "Why don't you show me around the condo? I'd like to see what three thousand dollars a week looks like." Dropping his suitcase just inside the front door, he followed Carol as she took him into the living room. The condo was beautifully decorated with a mix of modern art and antiques. They walked through the rooms, chitchatting about the different decorating changes Carol would make if the place were really hers. They ended their tour in the kitchen, where the room was filled with the aroma of a wonderful meal Carol had prepared. He grabbed her and kissed her passionately.

"Thank you," she said tenderly, accepting his kiss. "Are you ready to eat?"

"Always." He licked his lips seductively.

"Dinner! Are you ready to eat dinner?" She lifted the cover off a steaming pot. The wonderful scent coming from the pot told Maurice's taste buds and stomach that it was time to stop being a Mack daddy and eat.

"Mmm, that smells delicious. What is it?"

"It's Italian seafood. There's fresh lobster, shrimp, clams, oysters, and crabs in there. I hope you like seafood."

"I probably love it more than anyone you've ever met."

He sat down at the table and opened a bottle of red wine. They quietly traded small talk as they dined. Maurice mostly listened as he savored the delicious meal Carol had prepared. She seemed to have no problem carrying on a conversation by herself.

"Can I get you some more, Maurice?" she asked, picking up the serving fork. "My mama always said the best way to get a man is through his stomach."

"No more, thanks. But I would like a cup of coffee and a slice of that delicious-looking pie over there."

"Coming right up. Why don't we have our pie and coffee in the living room?"

"That sounds great. It will give us a chance to play a game I brought along with me." He settled himself comfortably on the couch while Carol went to the counter to slice the pie.

"What game? I didn't see you come in with a game." She placed the dessert down on the coffee table in front of him. As she sat on the sofa next to him, he reached into his pocket and produced a small deck of cards.

"Oh, no, Maurice, I'm horrible at cards. Why don't we take a walk on the beach?"

"Relax, baby." He handed her the small box of cards. "I brought these along because I thought they might help us get to know each other better. We're going to be here a week. We can spend all day on the beach."

Carol took a good look at the box and read the words printed on the back of each card. THE DATING GAME, A FUN WAY FOR ADULTS TO GET TO KNOW EACH OTHER.

"Well, what do you think? Would you like to play?" he asked impatiently. Now that his appetite was satisfied, he was ready to get on with his conquest.

"You're gonna have to explain the rules first."

"Okay. They're really pretty simple." He opened the box. "Each one of us takes a card from the top of the deck. Then when it's your turn, you read the question for the opposite sex. If you want, you can ask another question to find out more information. I'm gonna warn you, some of the questions are a little bit risqué."

"I'm a big girl, don't worry about me," she giggled. "Now, you go first."

He smiled, picking up the top card from the deck, and read the question out loud.

"What is the largest number of times you have had sexual intercourse in one night?"

Carol blushed as she answered, "Four."

"Was that with one partner or more?" Maurice questioned playfully.

"One!" She shook her head and reached for the top of the deck. "It's my turn now. Do you feel obligated to perform oral sex on a woman if she performs it on you first?"

"Yes."

"Why?"

"Experience."

"You mean to gain more experience, like practice?" She was worried he didn't know how to take care of a woman.

"No, I just mean a woman taught me a long time ago that it's very important to give when you receive. Now it's my turn."

He pulled another card while she thought about how much she liked his answer. She knew that not all men were interested in pleasing the woman as well as themselves, and she was relieved to know Maurice was different.

"How old were you when you first had sex?" Maurice read from the next card.

"Eighteen," she said, thinking the question was kind of weak. Picking up the next card, Carol smiled before she read it aloud. "What is your favorite sexual position?"

He didn't hesitate to answer when he heard the question asked.

Then again, why should he hesitate? He had prearranged the cards while Carol was in the bathroom earlier.

"Having someone go down on me has got to be my favorite," he answered with confidence.

"Really? Why is that?"

"Selfishness," he said, folding his arms and tightening his bottom lip as he thought, *You can't get gonorrhea from a blowjob.*

"Selfishness?" she repeated quizzically. She had been expecting an erotic answer.

"That's right. All our lives, men are under stress and pressure during sex. The only time we have to relax is during oral sex."

Carol laughed out loud. "I'm sorry, Maurice, but I've never met a man stressed out over sex. Furthermore, if I did, I think I'd be concerned whether or not he's a real man."

"Is that so? Well, I guess you've never met a real man. Because a real man's always concerned about your sexual satisfaction. A real man's always worried about whether or not you had an orgasm."

"I never thought about it that way, but I think I like that."

"Okay," he said with devilish grin. "Answer this question for me. How do you know if a man had an orgasm?"

"He shoots sperm. What kind of a question is that?"

"And as a woman, how do you feel when he has that orgasm?"

"Really good. Like I know he's satisfied and happy."

"Now let's switch places for a minute. I'll be the beautiful woman for a minute, you be the man."

"Okay." She was intrigued.

"You've just made love to me." He sprawled out all over the couch. "Two minutes before I was moaning and groaning your name, telling you how I was having an orgasm."

"I really did a job on you, didn't I?" Carol laughed, thinking about how much fun it must be to be the man.

"Oh, yeah, I won't be able to walk for a week," he answered, still lying on the couch. "But how do you know I really had an orgasm?"

"You told me you did."

"Exactly." He sat up quickly. "There is no way any man can be one hundred percent sure that his woman had an orgasm even if she said she did." Taking both her hands in his, he smiled and delivered his punch line. "Oh, and, Carol, I just put on an Academy Award—winning performance. I never had an orgasm."

She frowned when she heard him say that. Of course she knew she was not a man and they didn't just have sex, but somehow she felt inadequate next to him.

"Now you know the pressure and stress a man's under during sex."

Carol nodded. "I still don't understand why you said selfishness is the reason you like oral sex so much."

"To be honest with you, Carol, having someone go down on me is the most gratifying experience imaginable. It's the only time I can truly concentrate on nothing but my own satisfaction. There really is no way to describe the pleasure."

"I have noticed men seem to have a weakness for oral sex," she commented as he massaged her hands.

"Well, that's enough about oral sex. Whose turn is it now?" He was satisfied with where the conversation had gone. He had laid the groundwork for his conquest.

"Your turn, I believe." She handed him a card.

"Would you like the other player to give you a passionate French kiss?" he improvised, ignoring what was really printed on the card.

"Yes." She opened her arms and lay back on the couch, waiting for Maurice to kiss her.

It was 6:25 A.M. when Carol awoke, still lying on the couch in the condo living room. Sitting up, she slowly picked up her bra, halter top, and miniskirt. Half asleep, she searched for her panties before realizing she was still wearing them. Standing up, she walked into the bathroom and sat on the toilet to relieve herself. Her jaws were killing her, so she reached for her bag and a bottle of Advil.

Walking from the bathroom to the bedroom, her knees gave out on her when she realized Maurice was not in bed. Quickly gaining her composure, she checked the other bedroom, which was also empty. She bolted first to the living room, then to the kitchen, desperately searching for his suitcase, which was nowhere to be seen.

"Goddamn you motherfucker," she screamed, crying as she slid down against the front door. "I went down on your ass three times last night and you couldn't even leave a note." She couldn't even begin to imagine how she would get herself home from Jamaica. Maurice had been holding both of their plane tickets.

Maurice smiled as he handed Carol's ticket to the ticket agent.

"Hi, I'd like to exchange this ticket for another one. It's an open ticket. I paid for it on my credit card."

"Sure, sir. I just have to void this ticket out and print you a new ticket. What name would you like on the new ticket?"

Maurice turned around and looked at Debra, who was still wearing her desk-clerk uniform from the condo.

"Debra, honey, what's your last name again?"

"Warner," she said to the ticket agent. She was ecstatic to be going to New York City with this handsome man. Little did she know that she would be left stranded by him in the biggest city in the world less than fifteen hours later.

30

TYRONE AND SYLVIA

Tyrone sat on a bench in Roy Wilkins Park watching his two daughters, Donna and Kim, play on the monkey bars. Sylvia sat beside him, resting her head on his shoulders.

"Look at me, Daddy," his younger daughter, Kim, shouted. "I can hang upside down."

"I can do it too, Daddy." His elder daughter didn't want to be outdone.

"You girls are amazing," he told them, wrapping his arm around Sylvia.

"They're really good kids," Sylvia told him softly.

"Yeah, I know." He gave her a hug. "Hey, Syl, you okay? You seem a little bit down. The girls aren't stressing you out, are they?"

"No, they've been great. I'm just concerned about Bernard. He's been complaining a lot about being tired. Then his secretary told me he's been freebasing a lot of coke. I'm really worried. He's been my best friend for years."

"I wouldn't sweat it. Bernard's a big boy. But I'll tell you what. After our meeting with him, I'll have a little talk with him about the drugs, okay?" He looked down at Sylvia. "I know you didn't forget about our meeting with him tomorrow, did you?"

"No, I didn't forget. Matter of fact, I was planning on going back to your apartment with you and working on your portfolio."

"Working on the portfolio or working on me?" he joked.

Sylvia looked at him very seriously. "I know, I usually laugh at your jokes, but this is serious, Tyrone. You're never going to get another chance to impress Bernard. He has a personal rule. He never looks at an artist's work more than one time. So your portfolio can be the difference between imported champagne and that disgusting Old English ale you like so much. We have a lot of work to do if we're going to get you an exclusive showing."

"I know, Syl." He shrugged his shoulders as if it were no big deal.

Sylvia shot him an annoyed look. "I don't think you do. This is your future we're talking about. Don't you see, Tyrone? If Bernard signs you to an exclusive, your girls won't be playing in a broken-bottle-filled park. They'll be playing on their own swing set in the backyard of your five-acre home in Long Island."

"You really think so?"

"I know so," she answered confidently as both girls jumped into their father's lap.

"Daddy, can we get some ice cream? Please!" they said in unison.

"Sure, we can get some ice cream on the way home. It's about time I take you two home anyway." He hugged them both. "Aunt Sylvia and I have a lot of work to do on my future tonight."

Tyrone dropped off his daughters and walked back to Sylvia's car. He thought about what she had told him. She was right. With an exclusive contract from Bernard, he could do so much more for his girls. He might even help their mothers move out of the projects. He was hopeful as he got back in the car. Opening up the driver's side door, he slid in behind the wheel and turned toward Sylvia to get a quick kiss.

"What's is it? What's wrong, Sylvia?" he asked, seeing her eyes full of tears and her cell phone in her lap.

"It's Bernard. His secretary just called me. He's in the hospital, Tyrone. He has pneumonia."

"Damn, is he aw'ight?" Tyrone placed his hand on Sylvia's back to comfort her.

"No, they think he might die." Sylvia burst into tears.

"It's all right, baby," Tyrone said with sympathy, "I had pneumonia. Doctors can treat it."

It was hard for Sylvia, but somehow she looked up through her tears and said, "Bernard has AIDS, Tyrone. Pneumonia might kill him."

"Oh, shit." Tyrone was worried, not just about Bernard's health, but about what effect this might all have on his art career. "What hospital is he at?"

"North Shore University Hospital in Manhasset. Take the Long Island Expressway east."

It had been two days since Tyrone and Sylvia had visited the dying Bernard Ridgewood in the hospital. Tyrone stepped out of the cab in front of his apartment building very upset. Bernard had passed away a few hours earlier. Taking a deep breath of the spring air, he sighed. He had not lost a dear friend, as Sylvia had, he had lost what he figured was his only chance at a career in art. He knew he was being selfish, but he couldn't help it.

The day after the guy's supposed to look at my work, he ups and dies. Dammit, I can't catch a fucking break, he thought. Standing in front of the entrance to his apartment building, he pulled out his keys to open the door.

"Remember me?" A voice startled him from behind.

Quickly he turned around in a martial-arts stance before realizing it was his ex-girl.

"Shelly! Don't do that shit, girl! You could have got kicked in the head." He suddenly remembered that he owed her money. "What you doing here anyway?"

"I saw you walking through the projects earlier today, so I thought I would come over and get payment for the money you owe me."

Reaching into his pockets, Tyrone pulled out a twenty-dollar bill. "You can have this twenty, but it's all that I have. I swear." This was the final straw to this devastating day.

Shelly snatched the twenty dollars, then kissed his lips. "I said I wanted payment. I didn't say anything about money." She caressed his crotch before putting the money back in his pocket.

"Shelly, you don't know how much I want to . . ." Shelly had began to feel his butt with both her hands. "But I'm kind of seeing somebody."

"I don't give a shit about some other chick. I just want to get some tonight. Tomorrow you can be all hers again."

Tyrone's facial expression didn't give Shelly the answer she was looking for, so she grabbed his hand and placed it under her pantiless skirt. "Do you mean to tell me that you don't want any of this?"

He felt the intense heat between her legs, and it was definitely enticing.

"No, I'm not saying that I don't want some. I'm just saying maybe I shouldn't take some 'cause it's wrong. It wouldn't be fair to my girl."

Shelly laughed hard. "You didn't think it was wrong when you were screwing me behind my husband's back. Shit! If it wasn't for you, I'd probably still be married. Besides, who has the best stuff you ever had?"

"You do," he said honestly, remembering how good she was in bed.

"And who gave you the best head you ever had?"

"You did." He didn't need any more convincing. He grabbed her hand and led her up the stairs.

They stood at the edge of his bed, kissing. She had stripped off her blouse and bra as soon as they entered the room, not allowing him a chance to change his mind.

"My girlfriends and I were talking last night about the best lover we ever had. I was telling them how you were the only guy who ever wore me out." Shelly massaged his neck and shoulders. "Do you know one of those bitches had the nerve to ask me if I still had your phone number?"

"Damn, and I thought brothers were cutthroat."

"I ain't gonna lie. All that talk about sex had me horny as hell. So when I saw you dropping off your daughter Donna, I decided I was gonna forget all about that two hundred dollars for some really good sex."

She reached down and stroked him through the thin material of his pants, disappointed to find that he was not even aroused yet. She decided to remedy the situation. Slowly kissing down his neck to his chest, she worked her way to his belt buckle, fumbling to unlatch it. Before she could even open his fly, Tyrone grabbed her gently and pulled her up off her knees.

"I can't do this. I'm sorry, Shelly. I just can't do this." He buckled his pants and sat on the edge of the bed, handing her the blouse and bra she had dropped on the floor.

"I don't care how good you are in bed. I'm in love with Sylvia. I'm sorry, but I'm just going to have to pay you twenty dollars a week until my debt is paid. Now, if you don't mind, could you please get dressed?"

Shelly left without an argument, wondering why Tyrone hadn't been this faithful when she was the woman in his life.

Kevin walked into Ridgewood galleries, holding Denise's hand as he looked around at the stunning, lavish lobby. They were at the gallery to attend an art auction held in memory of Bernard Ridgewood, who died four weeks before from pneumonia. The proceeds of the evening were going to be donated to AIDS research. Tyrone had asked Kevin to attend because the auction was to be a special evening, and he wanted all his friends there. He had gladly accepted and called Denise so that she could clear her calendar for that evening.

There was no longer a question about the two of them going out together in public. Since Denise had done so much to help save his sister's life, Kevin had endured the stares and remarks from strangers without a comment. Whatever their reasons for disapproving of the interracial relationship, Kevin was sure those people had no idea what a difference she had made in his life. He no longer cared what color her skin was, because she had shown herself to be nothing but generous and helpful toward him. She had planned her act very carefully and never once slipped to reveal her scheming side to him.

Kevin smiled as his friends entered the lobby. Antoine held the door for Keisha, Tyrone, and his daughters. Dressed in evening wear, the men looked incredibly handsome. Denise wore a sexy black cocktail dress that complemented her gorgeous legs, and Keisha wore a tight red evening dress that revealed plenty of cleavage.

Kevin pulled Antoine and Tyrone to the side as soon as they approached. The three had a long talk earlier in the day, and Kevin finally told them about his relationship with Denise. As expected, Antoine was upset and actually called him an Uncle Tom. However, he soon apologized when he heard how instrumental she had been in saving Whitney's life.

"Antoine, I hope you're not going to be uncomfortable with Denise around. If seeing the two of us together is going to be a problem, we can leave."

"Don't worry about me, Kevin. You're my brother. If you're happy, I'm happy." He gave him a hug. "Plus I really like what she did for Whitney. She's all right with me."

"Well, bro, this is your big night." Kevin playfully punched Tyrone's shoulder.

He was right. This was Tyrone's big night. Somehow Sylvia had used her influence to get one of his paintings included among the art to be bid on at the First Annual Bernard Ridgewood Memorial Charity Art Auction. It was virtually unheard of for an unknown artist to be included in such a prestigious event, but Sylvia had faith that his talent was worthy of the evening. Black artists from around the country had donated art for this event, and buyers and critics from all over the world were expected to be in attendance. This was indeed his big break.

Walking down the wide corridor toward the main gallery, the group oohed and aahed at the magnificent African paintings and sculptures.

"Wow, this is incredible. I'm not into art, but this stuff is awesome." Antoine touched a large mahogany statue of a bushman.

"This is the cheap stuff," Tyrone told him. "You should see the stuff they sent out on tour from the main gallery, which we're using for the memorial service. Now, that, my friend, is art."

"Daddy, did you do all these pictures?" his daughter Kim asked.

"No, honey. Daddy did only one of the paintings." He handed their tickets to the woman standing outside the main gallery.

"Good evening, Mr. Jefferson. We've had quite a few people ask about your painting so far. I'm quite impressed." She pointed them in the direction of Tyrone's painting, then handed him their seating assignment.

"Tyrone, Denise and I are going to the rest rooms. Would you like me to take the girls? Your little one is dancing in place," Keisha asked, taking the girls' hands when Tyrone nodded. She and Denise led them toward the ladies' room.

Kevin and Antoine gave each other a hopeful glance when they saw the small crowd gathered around Tyrone's painting. He had painted a picture of what appeared to be an African goddess surrounded by children. Each child represented the different shades, hairstyles, and features of children of African descent. The artwork was something all African Americans could relate to.

"Look, Jim." A woman pointed at the painting. "That little girl looks just like Michelle when she was a baby."

"I think we should put in a bid for this one," another man whispered to his wife.

The three friends stood at the periphery of the small crowd and listened to the positive feedback for several minutes without saying a word. Sylvia approached them, grinning.

"I hear you're a big hit," she whispered, kissing Tyrone on the cheek.

"Well, we have to sell it first, but I've overheard some good things from the crowd."

"Don't worry about that. When I start the bidding at three thousand, my rivals will take it from there," Sylvia promised, wondering why Antoine was staring. "Excuse me. Do I know you?" she asked him politely.

"I was just thinking the same thing." He extended his hand to her.

"I'm sorry," Tyrone cut in. "Sylvia Johnson, this is Antoine Smith. He and Kevin work with me."

Sylvia shook both their hands graciously, but inside she was panicking. It hadn't occurred to her that Tyrone had friends from work who might have been introduced to her as Maurice's wife at one function or another.

"Excuse me, Tyrone?" It was the museum curator Joan Jemerson. "You don't mind if I introduce you to the crowd, do you?"

"Not at all." Tyrone smiled.

She turned around to the crowd in front of the painting. "Excuse me, everyone. I'd like to introduce you to the artist of this marvelous painting we call 'Children of Color.' This is Mr. Tyrone Jefferson."

The crowd circled around Tyrone and his friends to congratulate him on his wonderful painting. Sylvia stood to the side, hoping that Joan's announcement had created enough of a distraction so that Antoine wouldn't make the connection and remember when they'd met. Tonight was Tyrone's big night, and she didn't want to ruin it by having it revealed that she was married to his boss. She had planned on waiting until the time was right to share that information.

As Tyrone accepted the compliments of the crowd, Sylvia stood admiring him in his handsome tuxedo. He had come so far since they had first met. Shaking hands and offering commentary on his painting, Tyrone carried himself with the confidence and poise of a professional. Yet, he was still able to hang on the streets with his boys. There was nothing fake about him, and she loved him for that. She was determined to do everything possible to help him sell his first painting and get his career off the ground.

"Your painting is marvelous," an elderly woman said gracefully. "I'm really thinking about placing a bid on it."

"Thank you very much, miss, and I hope your bid is successful." Tyrone shook the woman's hand as he searched the crowd for Sylvia. Noticing her leaning against a large column, he winked. He smiled when she winked back, then watched her walk toward another part of the gallery. A few more well-wishers had approached, so Tyrone turned to work the crowd a bit more. He gladly shook hands with all his new admirers but nearly screamed when he saw his own worst nightmare coming toward him. It was Blanche Peterson, and her snaggle-toothed grin brought back hideous memories of Tyrone's dinner at the country club.

"Well, I'll be damned. Look what the cat done dragged in." She smiled, licking her lips. "Tyrone, what has it been, three, four months since I had my fingers wrapped around that thick, long dick of yours?" Blanche took two quick steps closer, then grabbed Tyrone by his balls, applying just enough pressure that moving would have caused excruciating pain. With a smile she wrapped her free arm around him as if they were hugging. Then she drew her body close to his as if they were lovers, to conceal her little game from the crowd.

Antoine's eyes bugged out of his head as he turned to Kevin, whispering in his ear, "Did she say what I think she said?"

"Yeah, but even I didn't think Tyrone was that desperate," Kevin whispered back, his eyes never leaving the hideous woman. "She's uglier than my great-aunt Spooky, and she's been dead ten years."

"Blanche. Let go of me now," Tyrone demanded in a soft, high-pitched whisper that only she could hear.

"What's wrong, Tyrone, aren't you glad to see me?" She paused, taking a tighter grip on his balls as she smiled at the other guests. "Well, if I was you, I'd make nice with Blanche, otherwise you're going to leave this place without your jewels."

She squeezed again. Tyrone gulped, standing on tiptoe to avoid the pain.

"I've been waiting a long time to see you again, Tyrone. You really should have kept that little hand job I gave you on Christmas Eve to yourself. That high-yellow bitch of yours has been making things pretty damn difficult for my girls and me lately. I lost a lot of business because of her goddamn mouth."

"Sorry about that, Blanche." He coughed, hoping an apology would make her loosen her grip.

"That's all right, baby. You're forgiven. Now, I want you to deliver a message to your mistress for me. Tell her if she ever tries to pull strings and have one of my brothels closed again, I'll kill her. You got that?"

"Yesss," he groaned as she squeezed him more tightly.

"Good. Now give Blanche a big, juicy kiss and introduce her to your handsome friends."

There is no way I'm gonna kiss this ugly bitch. She's just gonna have to rip my nuts off, he thought. He grimaced at the ugly woman.

Blanche smiled at Tyrone as if she could read his thoughts. Squeezing him until he gasped for air, she stood on tiptoe and slid her snakelike tongue into his open mouth for all to see.

Kevin and Antoine both cringed as they watched their friend tongue-wrestle with the Creature from the Black Lagoon. Sliding her tongue out of his mouth, Blanche licked her lips, then led Tyrone toward his friends.

"Hi, I'm Blanche Peterson." She finally released his balls to shake Kevin's hand. Tyrone bent over in relief.

"Hi, I'm Kevin Brown, and this is Antoine Smith." Kevin was afraid to look Tyrone in the face for fear he would burst out in laughter at his friend's choice in women.

"It's a pleasure to meet you, Ms. Peterson," Antoine said, actually managing to sound sincere.

Turning to see if Tyrone had recovered, Blanche smiled at his two friends. "Well, I've got to go." She scurried away into the crowd, cackling.

"Where'd that bitch go?" Tyrone asked, finally getting himself together.

"Oh, now she's a bitch? Two minutes ago you were slobbing her down, but now she's a bitch." Kevin laughed.

"Wait a minute, Kevin. Technically he's right," Antoine joined in. "If ever a woman looked like a female dog, that ugly wench Tyrone was just kissing does." Both of them laughed hard.

"What's so funny?" Denise asked, walking up with Keisha and the girls.

"Nothing," Tyrone replied, grabbing his two daughters by the hands and walking away.

"What was that all about?"

"Just a personal joke between us guys," Kevin answered, taking her hand and walking to view the painting up close for the first time.

"So, this is Tyrone's painting?" Keisha said, admiring his work. "I have to admit, I like his style."

"Yeah, I knew he could draw, but I never knew he had this kind of talent." Antoine wrapped his arm around Keisha, then kissed her cheek. "You know, if this painting sells, Tyrone's entire life will probably change."

"Don't tell him I told you this, but he said his entire career as an artist depends on how well this one painting sells today," Kevin explained.

"He's right." Denise joined the conversation. "Only one percent of artists are given the chance to have their work shown in a gallery of this magnitude. If this painting doesn't do well, chances are your friend will never be asked to show art here again."

They were all silent as they looked at the painting and considered how monumentally important this night was to Tyrone.

Tyrone searched through the crowd for Sylvia with his two daughters in tow. He wanted to find her before word of his incident with Blanche reached her. Spotting her in conversation with a woman across the room, he approached her.

"Thanks, Jen, I really appreciate hearing it from you," she said to the woman as Tyrone neared. The woman looked at Tyrone strangely as she walked away.

"Donna and Kim, you see that door over there?" They both nodded. "Well, in that room are a bunch of kids eating ice cream and playing games. Would you like to go in there and play?" Both girls agreed, eagerly looking up at their father for permission.

"Go ahead. But not too much ice cream."

He watched them run toward the door, holding hands. Then, just as he was about to tell Sylvia about Blanche, she glared at him, and he knew enough to shut up.

"What the hell is this? Jen Anderson tells me you've been kissing Blanche Peterson in front of everyone in the gallery." There was venom in her voice.

"I didn't kiss her, Sylvia, I swear. That bitch had a vise grip on my balls so hard that when I went to scream, she stuck her tongue in my mouth."

Sylvia bit her bottom lip. She knew Blanche well enough and trusted Tyrone enough to know that he was probably telling her the truth. Blanche had played the same games with Maurice when they had first married, and Sylvia had had enough of the woman's disrespect.

"That's the last damn straw. Blanche needs a good kick in the ass," she steamed.

She ran through the litany of insults she had prepared for this unruly heifer and left to find her, marching like a woman on a mission. Tyrone followed. They walked through the gallery searching for Blanche until they found her standing by the bar. Sylvia grabbed Tyrone by the hand and looked at him very seriously.

"I don't care what happens or what is said. Do not get physical with Blanche. Do you hear me?" She sighed. "The last thing your career needs is bad press."

"Yeah, I just hope you take your own advice."

"Don't worry about me. I have everything totally under control, sweetheart. But you can believe that woman is going to hear my mouth." She walked toward Blanche, smiling and waving at the other guests until she was face-to-face with Blanche Peterson.

"Blanche, what the fuck is your problem?" she hissed.

"Sylvia, what the hell are you talking about?" Blanche did a very bad job of trying to sound innocent.

"You know what I'm talking about. You need to keep your creepy-ass tongue to yourself."

Blanche looked over Sylvia's shoulder at Tyrone with no fear whatsoever.

"Well, Tyrone, I guess you had to call your massa to protect you, huh?"

"Leave him out of this, Blanche, this is between you and me."

"Ohhh, yeah. You definitely have more balls than him, Sylvia. Trust me, I just had them in my hands." Blanche laughed as she looked at Tyrone. "Hey, Tyrone, I bet if I reached between Sylvia's legs, I'd find more than a handful. What do you think?"

"Listen, you ugly bitch, if you put your hands on him ever again, I'm gonna . . ." Sylvia was ready to explode and turned her back on Blanche to calm herself. The last thing she wanted was to make a scene at Bernard's memorial. She was ready to smile and walk away, when Blanche pursued her.

"You're gonna what? You're not gonna do shit now that the drug-addicted fruitcake is dead." She whispered confidently to Sylvia. "That fag motherfucker was your power base, bitch. Without him, nobody important gives a shit about you."

Sylvia knew what Blanche was saying was not true. She was well liked among the elite. But what Blanche had said about Bernard was unforgivable. Bernard had been one of the few people kind enough to try to help Blanche improve her image. And now she repaid him with such ungrateful defamation of his memory. All the pain of losing her best friend erupted from deep within her. She could no longer maintain her composure.

"You fucking bitch! How dare you talk about him like that at his memorial?" Sylvia reached across and snatched Blanche's dangling earring off, ripping her earlobe open so that it began to bleed.

Oh, my God! What have I done? she thought, looking at the earring in her hand.

"I'm bleeding, you fucking yellow bitch!" Blanche screamed as she grabbed her ear. She lunged at Sylvia, swinging as hard as she could.

Ducking out of the way of Blanche's punches, Sylvia grabbed her hair and rammed Blanche's head into the bar. It was as if years of pent-up frustration had surfaced, and now Sylvia found herself in the middle of the first physical confrontation of her life. She was in such a rage, she had totally forgotten about the crowd of socialites in the room to witness the altercation.

Blanche was down but not beaten. Holding on to the bar, she kicked Sylvia hard in the ribs with the spike heel of her shoe. Then, grabbing Sylvia's blouse, she threw her into an unoccupied table, which broke under her weight. Sylvia grabbed hold of a saltshaker that was on the table, quickly unscrewed the top, and threw the salt in Blanche's eyes, lunging toward her.

"Ahhrr!" Blanche screamed, trying to scurry away blindly.

"You must!"—punch—"think!"—punch—"I'm!"—punch—"playing!"—punch—"with!"—punch—"you bitch!" Sylvia yelled as she pounded her fists into Blanche's head.

Blanche ran frantically toward the crowd that had formed. Following Blanche through the crowd, Sylvia caught her fifteen feet away from where Kevin and Antoine were standing.

Keisha, nibbling on an hors d'oeuvre, tugged the sleeve of Antoine's tuxedo.

"Damn, baby, they sure have good entertainment at these high-society parties, don't they?"

"Yeah, I guess they do at that." Antoine laughed.

Tyrone was pulling Sylvia off Blanche and hugging her.

"It's over, Sylvia. Let's go into the auction room." Tyrone pointed to the two security guards helping Blanche to her feet, and another two headed their way.

"All right." She was trying to fix her clothes as she gasped for air.

As she struggled from a guard's grip, Blanche was mumbling, "I can't believe I let that yellow bitch embarrass me like this. Nobody makes a fool out of Blanche Peterson and gets away with it."

"You okay, miss? Are you sure you're all right to walk?" one guard asked.

"I'm fine, thank you," Blanche watched as Sylvia and Tyrone embraced. Unable to stand the sight of the two of them, she darted toward Tyrone's painting. Grabbing it from the easel, she ran toward Tyrone and Sylvia, lifting the painting high in the air. Baring her blood-stained teeth in a maniacal grin, she slammed it over both of their heads as she laughed uncontrollably.

"What the hell!" Tyrone screamed, hearing the canvas rip as it hit his head. Grabbing Sylvia tightly, he was not sure of what had happened until he saw the frame from his painting hit the ground. "Ohhhhh, no!" He let go of Sylvia and stepped out of the frame, heading for Blanche, when the two security guards stepped in front of him.

"Let us handle it from here, sir. I think we've had enough violence for one day, don't you?" one of the guards addressed Tyrone as two others escorted Blanche out of the gallery.

Tyrone sat on Sylvia's Mercedes, drinking a can of Old English 800 ale. Kevin and Denise had volunteered to take his daughters home, so Tyrone was waiting outside the gallery for Sylvia. She was still inside the building, trying to smooth things over with Raul, Bernard's secretary, who had organized the memorial fund-raiser.

"Fuck!" Tyrone shouted, throwing the can. "Even Old English tastes like shit after you get used to Dom Pérignon. Why the hell did I ever think I could be a gallery artist?"

"Because I told you that you could," Sylvia answered, approaching the car. "And I still believe you can. This was not your fault, Tyrone. It was mine."

"What did Raul say?"

"Exactly what I thought he would say. As executor of Bernard's estate, he has to run Ridgewood Galleries the same as Bernard would. He suspended both of us from the gallery for one year."

"Damn! By that time all the name recognition I built up tonight will be gone."

"That's not definite. And besides, he did promise to let you do next year's memorial. That gives you twelve months to paint the perfect picture."

"I just don't know, Syl. With all that's happened lately, maybe someone's trying to tell me this just isn't meant to be. I mean, first Bernard dies right before he's going to review my work, and now this. Maybe I need to stop dreaming and get on with my life."

Sylvia held him tightly, determined to find a way to keep his dream alive until it became a reality.

31

SHAWNA AND KEISHA

Shawna pulled her Volkswagen Beetle out of the Gertz Plaza Mall parking garage onto Archer Avenue. She had spent the day shopping with her friend Roberta, happily looking for outfits to accentuate her new breasts. After the surgery had healed, she was determined to celebrate her bigger and better chest, showing as much of it as she could without getting arrested. She had worn a baby-blue halter that exposed her expensive cleavage, and men had been ogling her all day.

Roberta looked over at her. "I have to admit, Shawna, I'm jealous. You look good, girl."

"All you have to do is save your money, Roberta. How long have I been tellin' you? A nice C cup beats an A any day."

"It's just hard for me to save money. You know I'm a clothes freak, girl. When I die, just go ahead and bury me in Macy's, 'cause that's what I call heaven!"

"Well, you know the men seem to like bigger breasts."

"Speaking of men. Have you talked to Antoine lately?"

Shawna hesitated. "No, I think he's screening his calls."

"I told you what to do when you first started dating him. If you had listened to me, you two would be together right now."

"You're right, but I hate to think sex is that important."

"Well, it is. The sooner you realize it, the sooner you'll get your man back."

"You think so, Roberta? You don't know how much I miss him."

"Well, go over there and handle your business, girl. There's more than one way to satisfy a man."

"Yeah, and I'm good at that."

"That's right, girl. Virgin or not, a woman's gotta do what a woman's gotta do to keep her man. Listen, lemme borrow the car while you're over there."

"No problem. I plan on being there for quite a while." The two women laughed, then spent the rest of the ride in silence as Shawna planned Antoine's seduction.

Keisha sat behind the register of her beauty shop, cracking jokes about how ugly Blanche Peterson was at the memorial auction.

"I swear to God, y'all, after that Sylvia kicked her ass, that bitch was fugly."

"Fugly? What the hell is fugly?" a customer asked.

"Well, she was ugly to start with. But after that Sylvia got to her ass, she was fucked up. So she was fucked up and ugly. You know, fugly!"

The entire beauty shop fell out laughing until Terri looked out the window and gasped.

"Speaking of ugly, isn't that your man's ex-girlfriend knocking on his door?"

The shop became quiet. Keisha jumped out of her chair and ran to the window. Antoine was gone for the weekend, fishing with his friends, so at least she knew he couldn't have planned to meet Shawna here. But she still had to know what her competition was doing outside *her* man's door.

"Terri, go get my sneakers out of the back room," she told her friend.

She took off her earrings and jewelry, then reached into a cabinet and pulled out a large jar of Vaseline.

"What's that for?" Terri asked, handing Keisha her sneakers.

"It's an old street trick. You take Vaseline and put it all over your face and arms like this." She smeared it liberally over herself. "Then she can't scratch you or get a good grip if you have to wrestle."

"Gimme some so I can help you kick that bitch's ass," Terri offered.

"No, little sister, you stay here. This is between her and me. I don't want you to let anyone out of the shop until this is over." She sat in the chair and put her sneakers on, then tied her hair in a ponytail. Taking a deep breath, she walked outside to face her competition.

Shawna looked at her watch. Antoine was usually home at this time on a Saturday. She was disappointed he wasn't answering. Reaching into her bag, she pulled out a pen and paper.

"Ain't no reason to leave a note, bitch! He's not gonna call you."

"How the fuck do you know?" Shawna asked, surprised by Keisha, who was standing at the bottom of the steps.

"Because he's my man now. And after I gave him some, I'm sure he doesn't want your ass."

"You know, Keisha, you're pathetic. You're lying just like the first time I met you."

"Oh, yeah? Remember that lingerie he bought for the first time you gave him some?" Keisha could see Shawna's eyes become smaller with anger. "Good thing we wear the same size, 'cause I wore it last night when he made love to me." She laughed hard as Shawna came running down the stairs.

"I'm sick of you interfering with Antoine and me. I'm gonna kick your ass all over this goddamn block if I have to, but you're gonna leave him alone," Shawna screamed.

"You still don't get it! He's ain't your man. I've been goin' with him almost two months." Keisha backed into the street, then landed a hard right hand to Shawna's jaw.

Shawna was so angry, she barely felt the blow. Swinging wildly, she tried to scratch Keisha's eyes out.

"I'm gonna kill you, bitch! I swear I'm gonna kill you."

"I knew you was gonna try and scratch me." Keisha laughed as Shawna's wild swinging made her fall on the ground. "You ain't gonna kill shit!" She kicked her ribs.

Bending over to catch her breath, Keisha waited for Shawna to get up, then ran at her as fast as she could. Shawna hit Keisha with a blow harder than she had ever felt from another woman.

"You don't know how much I hate you," Shawna screamed, punching Keisha repeatedly. "You've brought out a part of me I've tried to hide for years."

Keisha fell backward from the barrage of blows to her head. Grabbing Shawna's hair to soften her fall, she hit the pavement hard when Shawna's weave ripped out of her head.

"Damn, you look like a man with no hair," she jeered.

"Just 'cause I don't fuck around don't make me less than you. I'm just as much woman as you and more, bitch!" Shawna was enraged now. She dove on top of Keisha.

Roberta sat in Shawna's car, laughing, as she watched the fight.

If that chick knew what I know, she wouldn't be fucking with Shawna. Damn, she's getting her ass kicked!

Still recovering from the punches she had taken, Keisha closed her eyes when she saw Shawna leap to finish the job she had started.

Damn, this bitch fights just like a man, she thought. Defensively she stuck her foot out to try to soften the blow of Shawna's weight and accidentally caught the tall woman in the groin. Surprised when she no longer felt Shawna's punches, Keisha opened her eyes and tried to get up. Catching a glimpse of Shawna balled up on the ground, she limped over to a metal trash can and grabbed the lid.

"Get up, bitch!" she screamed at Shawna, who had her hands between her legs. "I wanna see your nappy ass smile when I knock you out!" Taking hold of what was left of Shawna's hair, Keisha drew back the trash-can lid and pounded it into her head. She was about to hit her again with the lid but was stopped when Roberta grabbed it from her, throwing it in the street.

"That's enough! Can't you see she can't defend herself after you kicked her in the nuts?"

Keisha froze. *"Nuts!* What the fuck are you talking about?"

"Oh, Roberta, what have you done?" Shawna moaned weakly, trying to stand.

Roberta helped her friend up. "Girl, you ain't got nothing to be ashamed of. Even with a dick, you look better than this bitch."

Terri and a few girls from the shop came running out when they saw Roberta. "Keisha, you all right? I see her big-ass friend had to save her."

"This ain't over by a long shot, Keisha," Shawna said as Roberta helped her into her car.

"Oh, it's over. I can't wait for Antoine to get home tomorrow so I can tell him what you really are!" Keisha threatened before Roberta closed the car door and sped away.

"What was that all about?" Terri asked.

"Nothin'. I just got myself mixed up in some Jerry Springer–type shit." Keisha walked slowly into her shop. Every bone in her body ached.

Later that night Keisha sat in her bed, thinking about the day's events. She had soaked for an hour in Epsom salts, so her pain had lessened a bit, but she knew she would be sore for days. And to top it off, she missed Antoine. She was wearing his sweatshirt as a nightgown and lit his pipe so that the room would feel as if he'd been there. She frowned. This had been the first time they had not slept together since they made love a month before, and she was lonely. Things had gone so well for them in the past two months. He had courted her in the most romantic way, taking her to shows and poetry readings all over the city. He even joined her book club to spend more time with her. But the thing Keisha considered most romantic was that every afternoon he would come home from work with something special for her. There were days he brought flowers, and on others just a special poem, but no matter what he brought, she waited like a schoolgirl for him to come home.

Keisha had given much thought to her discovery about Shawna's true identity. She had come to the conclusion that this news was a million times worse than if she had just been a stripper. Now Keisha was worried about what the revelation of Shawna's true gender could do to Antoine's ego. After much indecision, she thought it would be best to keep it a secret. She hoped she was doing the right thing.

While she was resting her bruised body, she tried to figure out how she would explain her injuries when Antoine returned from his fishing trip. The doorbell rang, and Keisha walked slowly to the door, feeling twinges of pain with each step.

"Who is it?"

"Shawna."

"What the hell do you want?" Keisha was just too tired to fight anymore and couldn't believe Shawna was back for more.

"We need to talk, Keisha. Please let me in."

"We ain't got shit to talk about, mister." Keisha took hold of the baseball bat she kept by the door, then opened it. She made sure Shawna could see the bat.

"I didn't come here to fight." Shawna was watching the bat very carefully. "We need to talk about Antoine."

"There is nothing to talk about. After I tell him you're a man, he's probably gonna wanna blacken that other eye for you."

"That's what I want to talk to you about. Look, can I come in and explain? You have my word I won't cause any trouble."

Keisha thought about it a second and figured Shawna was probably just as sore as she was. She probably wouldn't be much of a threat even if she did try to start something. She stepped back and let Shawna enter her apartment.

Shawna groaned in pain as she seated herself in the recliner in Keisha's living room. Keisha positioned herself on the arm of the couch so she could get a good swing just in case she tried to get funny.

"Well, you wanted to talk, so talk." Keisha folded her arms.

"Look, Keisha, I know you don't like me. The truth is, I can't stand you either. But the one thing we have in common is that we both love Antoine. I don't want to hurt him."

"Don't you think you should have thought about that before you let him get involved with your transvestite self?"

"I don't know, maybe you're right. But I fell for him so fast, I couldn't stop myself. I just never found the right way to tell him, and then things just got too deep."

Keisha shuddered at the thought of Antoine with another man, but she could understand why Shawna had fallen for him so quickly. It had been the same way for her, and in a strange way she almost had sympathy for Shawna. Quickly she banished any kind thoughts from her head and confronted Shawna.

"So what does your fucked-up story have to do with me anyway? As far as I see it, I don't owe you anything, and we really have nothin' to say to each other."

"Well, Keisha, I was hoping you could understand how much I love Antoine."

"Mmm-hmm. But he's mine now. I thought we already discussed this on the sidewalk."

"No, no, no. I'm not here to fight about him anymore. I love him more than anything, but I know how much it would devastate him to find out he was living a lie. I'm here to beg you not to tell him about me."

Keisha was skeptical. "Sure. I keep your little secret, and you try to get right back into his life behind my back. Is that how it works?"

"Not at all." Shawna sounded defeated and tired. "My only concern is sparing Antoine any pain. So if you keep this secret, I swear to you, I'll leave him alone. I'll just disappear, and neither one of you will ever hear from me again."

"Nothing would make me happier." Keisha grinned wickedly. She was not about to tell her she had already made that decision not to tell Antoine, especially when Shawna was promising to get lost for good.

Shawna stood up to leave. "Well, Keisha, I wish things were different, but if I can't have Antoine for myself, I just hope you do everything you can to make that man happy. He really deserves it, you know."

"I know that." Keisha opened the door for Shawna. "Can you answer one question for me before you go?"

Shawna nodded.

"Why did you accept his wedding proposal if you knew you couldn't marry him? I mean, you're a goddamn guy, for crying out loud. Sooner or later he was gonna find out you don't have the right equipment."

"You don't understand. I could have married Antoine. My enemy wasn't you, or even this penis between my legs. My enemy was time. If I could have kept our relationship together for three more months, I would have been just as much a woman as you. I'm scheduled for my operation on August twenty-ninth. Then I could have quit my job at the Men's Club and married the man I love." Shawna touched her crotch. "But even if I can't have him, I still can't wait to get rid of this thing for good!"

"You're gonna get a sex change?" Keisha couldn't believe that this just kept getting deeper.

"I don't expect you to understand this, Keisha, but I am a woman. A woman trapped in this hideous masculine body." She began to cry. "I can't explain how much I hate myself. I wake every morning afraid to look in the mirror because I might see some hair growing on my face. Sometimes I can't even leave my house. All I've ever wanted was to be a woman and find some man to love me for me."

In a strange way Keisha felt sorry for Shawna. No one should have to live life that confused. But as she said good-bye and closed the door, she was glad it was the last time she would ever have to see Shawna Dean.

32

KEVIN, DENISE, AND ALICIA

It was 1:30 when Kevin walked into the Court House Bar and Grill in downtown Brooklyn. Normally the restaurant would be packed with lawyers, court stenographers, and the like on their lunch breaks. But it was a Saturday, and Kevin was impressed that the place was still so crowded. He figured it was either a testament to the quality of the restaurant, or all of the patrons were workaholics who were in the area even on a Saturday. Squeezing his way down the crowded area by the bar, he found Denise and her friend Liz chatting with two rather preppy white guys.

"Hey, baby." Denise wrapped her arms around him and kissed him passionately. She made sure both men had a good view when their tongues met. "Kevin, this is Bradley and Ken. Bradley's a partner at the Wilks and Barnes law firm, and Ken's one of his associates."

Denise grinned devilishly as Bradley reluctantly shook Kevin's hand. He and Ken had been trying to put the moves on her and Liz for almost forty-five minutes, running up a tab of almost a hundred and fifty dollars on expensive champagne. In most cases when men showed interest in Denise, she would politely let them know that she was involved in a relationship. But Bradley had rubbed her the wrong way from the start as he bragged about how many "murdering brothers" he had helped set free on technicalities.

"Oh, Kevin, Bradley just invited Liz and me to his summer place in Bridgehampton next weekend. I'm sure he wouldn't mind if I brought the love of my life, my little chocolate star. Would you, Bradley?" Bradley's face became beet red, but before he could answer, Liz chimed in.

"Wait a minute now. If you get to bring Kevin, I know Bradley won't mind if I bring my new boyfriend, Malik." Liz looked directly at

Kenny, a short, stout, balding man, as she poured another glass of champagne. "You're gonna love him, Kenny. He looks just like Busta Rhymes, the rap star."

"Well, look at the time," Bradley announced, pretending to consult his watch. "We have reservations at the Chelsea Piers driving range. Come on, Kenny." He reached into his pocket and threw two hundred-dollar bills on the bar. "Listen, we'll give you two a call about next weekend." Both he and Kenny disappeared into the crowd.

Denise and Liz looked at each other and burst into laughter. Both of them knew that was the last time they would hear from either one of the men, and they were glad.

"I don't know what just happened, but somehow I think those guys got the bad end of it." Kevin joined in on their laughter as Liz poured him a glass of champagne.

After sharing small talk for about ten minutes, Liz checked the time on her beeper. "Yo, it's been great hanging out with y'all. But I think it's about time I went home and checked on my man." They hugged their good-byes, and she left the bar.

"Well, I guess it's just you and me," Denise whispered, kissing Kevin's ear. "How about we find a table and have some lunch?"

They walked into the dining room to be seated. As they waited for their meals to arrive, Denise told him about the new truck she was going to pick up for him. Originally she had agreed to help only with the down payment, but things had changed. When he had argued with his mother, Denise knew that it was time to make her move to separate him even more from his family. She sensed that there was still some underlying pressure from his mother and sisters for him to find a black woman. The only way she could be sure to stop this pressure was to get them out of Kevin's life completely. So far the financial route seemed to be doing the job, so she continued on that track. Without telling Kevin she had prepaid a three-year lease on a customized Ford Expedition in his name.

"So why don't we pick up the truck around noon tomorrow?" Denise's voice was filled with excitement.

"Look, Denise, I've been giving it a lot of thought, and I don't know if I can accept the truck."

"Why not?" The excitement had left her voice. "Please, don't give me that crap about you don't wanna use me, okay?"

"Denise, it's just that people are starting to ask if I'm dating you for the money."

"People, or Antoine and Tyrone? You know your friends should mind their own damn business." Denise threw her napkin on the table.

"It's not just them, Denise. I'm not even speaking to my mama 'cause of this truck."

"I can't help it if I have more money than you, Kevin. What am I supposed to do, sit back and let my man live out of boxes or drive a car that's gonna break down when he drives around the corner? I'm sorry, I can't do that."

Kevin became quiet. He had to admit, her argument was sound. Denise took hold of his hand.

"I love you, Kevin. You're the most kindhearted man I've ever met. If you want me to stop helping you, I will. But look me in the eye and tell me you wouldn't do the same for me if you had the money." Denise smiled when he didn't answer. "I thought so. You know what your problem is? You need to talk to me about our problems instead of your friends."

Suddenly Denise's face became whiter than snow as she noticed a tall, well-dressed man in his late fifties standing near the door, helping a young woman put on her coat. Denise really panicked when he started to walk toward their table.

"Oh, shit! What is he doing here?" The words escaped her mouth before she could stop them.

"What's going on?" Kevin asked, preparing himself for some type of physical confrontation as he turned to see the man.

"Denise, honey, is that you?" her father asked.

"Hi, Daddy. I didn't even see you walk over," she lied, smiling falsely at her father. "What are you doing here anyway? I thought you were going down to the Jersey Shore to play golf."

Stephen Shwartz glanced nervously over at his twenty-year-old mistress standing by the door. The last thing he wanted was for his daughter to mention this to his wife.

"To be honest, pumpkin, I just said that to your mother to get away. I needed to work on the Samson case and I didn't want your mother nagging me about working too hard." He gave his daughter a fatherly smile, then turned his attention to Kevin, giving him an obvious glare. "I thought you and Liz were headed for the mountains."

"Oh, yeah, well, I had to meet with a client myself." Denise looked at Kevin sadly, knowing that the words she was about to say would hurt him. "Daddy, this is Kevin Brown. Remember? I told you about representing his family down in Virginia." She raised her eyebrows as she looked at Kevin, pleading with him to understand, though she knew he wouldn't.

"Oh, yes, pleased to meet you, Mr. Brown." He offered Kevin his hand, oblivious of his daughter's lie. "I'm really glad Denise was able to help your sister with her insurance problem. It's always the charity work my firm does that seems the most rewarding. Isn't that right, sweetheart?" Stephen Shwartz smiled proudly at his daughter.

"Of course, Daddy. You always said we have to help the little guy."

Denise's words were like a knife in Kevin's heart. He was starting to think Mama had been a little more on the mark with her assessment of Denise than he once believed.

He shook Denise's father's hand firmly as he glanced angrily at Denise. He had every intention of berating her as soon as her father was gone. He watched with no expression on his face as she kissed her father good-bye. Mr. Shwartz hurried to the door and was careful not to put his arm around the woman waiting as he escorted her outside.

"What the fuck was that all about?" Kevin hissed at her, smashing his two fists down on table as soon as the door closed behind Denise's father. "Is that what I am, the little guy?"

"What are you talking about?"

"I don't fucking believe you, Denise. I can't believe you're going to sit right here in my face and pretend you don't know what the fuck I'm talking about." Kevin's voice rose steadily, and other patrons were staring in their direction.

"Kevin, will you calm down? You're embarrassing me," she whispered, trying to clean up a glass of water that spilled during his tirade.

"*You're* embarrassed! How about me? I finally meet my girlfriend's father, and she introduces me as one of her clients! What the hell am I, Denise? Some insignificant little boy-toy that you pay for with expensive gifts?"

"Kevin, it's not like that at all! I love you. You just don't understand Daddy."

"It's not your daddy that I don't understand. It's you!"

Denise tried to reach across the table and hold his hand, but he pulled it back.

"I haven't talked to my mother in three weeks because I was defending you and this relationship. And now you're too embarrassed to introduce me to your father. You know what, Denise? I knew this interracial shit wasn't gonna work out," he declared with finality.

"What are you trying to say?" She was truly worried for the first time. "Are you trying to say you don't want this relationship because I didn't introduce you to my father as my boyfriend? What are you, a baby?"

"Yeah, I guess I am a baby. You sure as hell haven't treated me like a man, have you?" Kevin stood up, disgusted, and walked toward the door.

Denise had planned for many things in her pursuit of his unconditional love, but this was not one of them. She never planned on him meeting her family until they were ready to marry. Especially not her father. He was always too busy working or having meaningless affairs to be concerned with his children's relationships. He certainly never bothered to ask who his children were involved with, but it was an unspoken law in the Shwartz household that they would never date outside their race. It was just deemed below their family status.

She had figured she could hold off telling her family until she was able to make herself an invaluable part of the law firm. She was just starting out but had won quite a few very lucrative cases. Her father respected her work, and she figured once she was making enough money for his firm, he wouldn't be willing to let her go even if she did marry a black man. When she saw her father approaching their table, Denise saw her little plan crumbling before her eyes, and she panicked. She couldn't think of a lie that would not offend Kevin. Now she was paying the price as she watched her man walking away. She raced after him.

"Kevin, where are you going?" She grabbed his shirt to stop him at the door. "Listen, I'm sorry. Please don't leave. It's not me, it's my father. He's prejudiced."

"Let go of me!" he shouted, trying to loosen her grip from his shirt. "Look, Denise, my family was willing to accept you for the person you are. My mama and my sisters had to put aside their pride to judge you as an individual, not as a white woman. If your father and the rest of your family can't do the same, well, then, you and your family can kiss my ass." He tried to walk out, but Denise blocked the doorway.

"Kevin, please don't do this. Just come back to the table so I can talk to you." She was sobbing, the mascara running down her face. "Please, honey, just let me explain. This whole thing's a little more complicated than you think."

"This had better be good, Denise, or I swear it's over between us." Kevin could see Denise wasn't going to move without a physical confrontation. He smiled with an embarrassed look at the ten people behind him waiting to leave the restaurant. He gently escorted Denise back to their table, and they sat down.

"Why the hell didn't you tell me your dad was prejudiced?"

"Look, Kevin, I'll be right back. I have to go the rest room and clean up my face."

"Just go," Kevin barked, rolling his eyes. He knew she was just stalling for more time.

Denise looked a wreck. Her mascara was smudged all over her face and her eyes were totally bloodshot from crying, all of which the other patrons were whispering about. On top of all that, she needed time to think of a creative lie to pacify Kevin. Her father was far from prejudiced, although Denise was pretty sure he wouldn't be happy about her dating a black man. Especially one who was just a physical education teacher. It wasn't about color to her family as much as it was about prestige. She was expected to find and marry a rich Jewish professional as far as her father was concerned.

As he sat at the table and waited, Kevin seethed. Twice he almost got up and left before she returned, but then he realized he couldn't. When he had been cut from the NBA after his drug test, he reacted instantly and left without even looking for an alternative solution. He moved to New York without giving it much thought. And most recently he had broken up with Alicia because he acted before he considered all sides of the story. This time, as angry as he was, he was determined to hear Denise's explanation before he made any decisions. If he wanted to be treated like a man, he knew he needed to get his rash behavior under control and act like a man.

He contemplated his relationship with Denise and wondered if Mama wasn't right about her after all. Kevin really liked Denise. Over the past six months she had introduced him to things he'd never dreamed of. He had seen how the upper class lived and was happy to be included in Denise's free spending habits. But for whatever reason, he never made a true connection with her like he did with Alicia. Maybe it was the interracial thing, or maybe it was the fact that he was still in love with Alicia. Whatever it was, Kevin knew that as long as Denise made excuses about why he should not meet her parents, he would not be able to give her his heart.

"Hello, Mr. Brown." A voice came from behind as he sat immersed in his thoughts.

Kevin turned to see Alicia standing behind his chair. She was as gorgeous as ever, wearing a sleek gray pants suit.

"Alicia, what are you doing here?" He tried to conceal the smile that was creeping across his face. He was even happier to see her than he would have imagined.

"I was headed upstairs to a retirement party, when I spotted you sitting here. If you've got a minute, I'd like to talk to you. That is, if you don't mind?"

"No, I don't mind. The truth is we should have had a talk a long time ago." He pulled out the chair next to his, then glanced toward the bathroom as she sat down. "But are you sure we should be together with that order of protection and all?" He couldn't resist the slight jab after he had been so hurt by her legal action against him.

"First of all, I want to apologize for that. At the time, I didn't know what Michael had done." She rested her hands on the table and leaned toward him.

"So you know what Michael told me is what set me off, huh?" He was glad to finally hear that the boy was indeed lying.

"Yes. I figured Tyrone would have told you by now about how I found out. Your friend really saved me from Trevor that day."

"He did tell me about it, but it's good to hear from you that you understand now what was wrong with me."

"I do understand, but there's something else I don't understand."

"What's that?"

"Why did it matter to you anyway? That girl you're dating told me you'd been with her all along anyway." An accusatory look came across Alicia's face. She was still more angry and hurt than she thought. "You know, Kevin, that hurt more than anything else. Probably because even then I was still in love with you."

"What are you talking about?"

"Look, Kevin. It's over between us now, so there's no need to play games. Why not just tell me the truth?"

"Alicia, I do have a girlfriend, but I wasn't going with Denise until after you and I had broken up. In fact, I didn't even try to meet anyone else until you had me served with an order of protection. I kind of took that as a hint you wanted me to get lost."

He didn't appreciate what she had just accused him of. He was willing to acknowledge that he had acted too quickly when he broke up with her. He hadn't waited for all the facts. But one thing he had been through it all was faithful, and he resented that she was implying differently.

"Look, Kevin. You can tell me whatever you want. It doesn't matter now. But I know for a fact that you were with her while you and I were dating. How else could she have been eight months pregnant when she came to my apartment?"

She was becoming angry at the memory of her own embarrassment the day Denise's private detective had gone to the apartment, posing as Kevin's girlfriend.

"Eight months pregnant? What the hell are you talking about?"

Before Alicia could explain, Denise was standing beside the table, her expression a mixture of confusion and suspicion. She had overheard Kevin's last exclamation but hadn't yet figured out the context.

"Uh, Kevin, honey," Denise said as calmly as she could, "why don't you introduce me to your friend?"

Kevin turned to her and smiled at her perfectly flat stomach. There was no way Alicia knew what she was talking about if she thought his girlfriend was eight months pregnant. At the same time, he was suddenly nervous about introducing the women. After all, it is never comfortable introducing your ex to your current, and even more so when they happen to be of different races.

"Alicia, I'd like you to meet my eight-month-pregnant girlfriend, Denise," he said sarcastically.

At the same moment that Kevin was saying Alicia's name, Denise was remembering where she had seen that face before. The file from her private detectives had contained photographs of Alicia. Denise was surprised at herself for not remembering that sooner. Usually she was good with such details. Then again, she was still reeling from the meeting with her father. Now she knew what the eight-month-pregnant comment was about. For a split second she worried about her next move, then realized she was the only one at the table who knew the whole truth. It would be easy for her to play dumb and lie her way through this one. She decided to sit back and let Alicia make a fool out of herself.

"That's not Denise. Denise is black!" Alicia said indignantly. "Your girlfriend Denise was at my apartment, and she was a pregnant black woman."

"I'm not trying to be funny, Alicia, but she's the only Denise I've gone out with since the sixth grade. And as you can see, she's not black." Kevin wondered if too many beatings from Trevor had made this woman lose her mind.

"I don't know what's going on, Kevin, but a pregnant black woman claiming to be Denise came by my apartment with birthday presents for Michael." Alicia was beginning to get an attitude. "Now, you can play games with me all you want. But that woman looked Michael in the eye and told him the presents were from his uncle Kevin, and that you couldn't wait to play Legends of the Boxing Ring II with him. How would she know you and Michael had played that game together if she didn't somehow know you?"

Kevin hesitated while he thought for a second. He had told Michael he would buy Legends of the Boxing Ring II for his birthday the day he and Alicia had broken up. In fact, he had almost sent the game a few days before his birthday. He had been in the toy store with Denise and explained why he wanted to buy the game for Michael. She advised him not to send it, telling him it might be construed as a violation of the order of protection. He had heeded her advice reluctantly.

Now, as some of the pieces started coming together, Kevin was still confused but becoming suspicious of Denise. He looked at his girlfriend and wondered if she was really capable of such a scheme. Then he remembered how boldly she had lied to her father in front of him and figured she just might be capable of anything. He just couldn't understand who the pregnant black woman was and how she could figure into such a mess.

The look on Kevin's face as he stared at Denise was troublesome. She could tell that the wheels were turning in his mind as the three of them sat silently. He was trying to put the pieces together, and she knew it was only a matter of time before he figured out the connection with the video game.

She had gone one step too far when she advised the private investigator that bringing that specific video game would make the story more believable. Denise didn't know now what to do to stop Kevin from making that final connection and perhaps accusing her right in front of Alicia. She broke the heavy silence at the table.

"Excuse me, Kevin. As your attorney, I have to remind you that Alicia does have an order of protection against you."

Denise tried to smile at Alicia, but her jealousy had taken over, and she couldn't bring herself to look Alicia in the eye. She felt her position of power slipping away quickly. Kevin's response confirmed her fear.

"You know, Denise, the last time you advised me about the order of protection, we were in the toy store talking about that video game." Kevin turned his entire body to face her in a confrontational posture.

"What are you trying to say?" Denise asked helplessly, wishing she could scratch Alicia's eyes out.

"I'm trying to say that you're the only person I ever mentioned that game to. Did you or did you not have something to do with the woman who showed up at Alicia's door?"

Alicia turned to face Denise, eager to hear her response to Kevin's question. It was too much for Denise to see the look of superiority that came across Alicia's face as the lies were being revealed.

"Kevin! I can't believe you are asking me this. Do you really think I would lie to you?"

"Do I? I just watched you lie to your father's face not less than fifteen minutes ago. Why would I expect you to be any different with me?"

"Because I love you, Kevin."

"Well, if you love me, Denise, then tell me the truth, because I'm starting to wonder if you're capable of that." Kevin folded his arms and waited for a response.

Denise's bottom lip trembled, but she held back the tears. She gave Alicia an angry look, as if the whole episode were her fault. Her anger exploded into an angry tirade directed at Alicia.

"This is all your fault, you know! Why can't you just stay with Trevor? After all those gifts he got you, I'd think a woman like you would want to stick around! Why don't you leave me and Kevin alone?"

"What did you say?" Alicia demanded. "How did you know anything about gifts from Trevor?"

"What gifts?" Kevin asked, again in the dark.

Denise could no longer control herself. At this point she knew she had very little left to lose. She exposed the rest of her scheme.

"Fine! I sent the gifts, and I sent someone over there to pretend to be me. What did you expect me to do? Kevin is supposed to be my man, and he still calls out your name in his sleep. I would stop at nothing to keep you out of his life, Alicia," she sobbed. "I hate you."

Alicia ignored Denise's final words. The only thought resounding in her head was that Kevin still cared for her. After all their misunderstandings, she saw a glimmer of hope that the two of them could reconcile.

"Kevin, is that true? Do you really still dream about me?"

She reached across the table to touch his hand. Kevin pulled his hand away, and the tension was obvious in his entire body.

"Yes, Alicia, I do still love you, but—"

"Kevin!" Denise shrieked. "I can't believe you're doing this to me after all I've done for you. I bought you furniture, I took you on trips. Things she never could have given you. How could you throw away what we have?"

"What we have?" he asked in amazement. "We have nothing, Denise. Relationships are built on trust, and we don't have that. You can't buy my trust, and you sure as hell haven't earned it." He stood up abruptly and declared, "It's over."

Denise collapsed into a chair, racked with sobs. A waiter rushed to the table as Kevin stormed away with Alicia hurrying to catch him.

"Kevin, wait!" Alicia called as he walked out the door.

He stopped on the sidewalk and faced her. "What is it now, Alicia?"

"Did you mean that in there? Do you really still love me?"

"Yeah, I do, but right now I can't talk to you. You were willing to give Trevor as many chances as it took, but I made one mistake and you were ready to have me locked up."

"I'm sorry, Kevin. I'm so sorry. We really have some things to work out."

"Yeah, we probably do. But let me ask you this. Have you worked everything out with Trevor?"

Alicia hung her head as she remembered her son's father, who was waiting at her apartment. They had been back together since Trevor had started going to AA meetings. It tore her apart inside to think that she had let this man back in her life, especially since he had started drinking again. She told herself she was doing it so that Michael would have a father figure, but in her heart she knew that Trevor should not be that man. Her son struggled daily with the love that was tainted with fear.

"Alicia, what's your answer? Are you still with Trevor?" Kevin repeated.

She nodded silently to give him his answer. He shook his head, turned his back, and raised his arm to hail a cab.

"Well, I guess there's nothing more to say then, is there?" Kevin said sadly as he stepped into the waiting cab.

Once home, Kevin collapsed angrily in his living room and stared at the blank television screen. He could barely focus after the events of the afternoon. All he kept thinking about was how his mother had been right all along about Denise's true intentions. At that moment he missed his mama terribly. He knew it was time to call her and apologize. Anxiously he picked up the phone and dialed her number. There was regret in his voice when he spoke to her.

"Mama? It's me. You know, your long-lost fool?"

"Kevin. I knew you would call sooner or later, baby." Mama's words felt as comforting as a hug.

"Yeah, I just wish I'd called sooner. I'm so sorry, Mama."

"It's aw'ight baby. We all make mistakes sometimes. You're a grown man now. It just took me a while to realize it."

"I don't feel like a grown man, Mama. I broke up with Denise this afternoon. She wasn't the woman I thought she was."

"Oh, I'm sorry, Kevin. You aw'ight, baby?"

"Yeah, I'm okay. I just feel a little foolish, and I want you to know how sorry I am about the way I talked to you."

"I know, baby. Let's just put that behind us, all right?"

"Sure, Mama. Well, I'm gonna go. I need some time to sort all of this out. But I'll be sure to call you again tomorrow, so you can tell me all about what's going on down there. Okay?" Kevin was exhausted from the emotionally charged day.

"Okay, Kevin. I'll talk to you tomorrow, baby."

"Oh, Mama. I played basketball today."

"Really, Kevin?" Mama was surprised.

"Yeah, I was in the park, workin' out, and some guys asked me to play."

"Well, son, how'd you do?"

"I was rusty, but I played pretty good." Kevin laughed.

"Well, son, I'm glad you enjoyed yourself." She was excited for her son.

"I did, Mama."

"I love you, son." Mama felt she could talk to her son for hours after their reconciliation, but she could hear in his voice how tired he truly was.

"Bye, Mama. I love you too." He hung up the phone and released a huge sigh of relief. At least there was one part of his life he could always believe in.

33

TYRONE AND SYLVIA AND MAURICE

Tyrone carefully led Sylvia into the lobby of the Empire State Building. She was blindfolded. He planned their romantic encounter to be a total surprise. Earlier, he had made arrangements with his friend Manny, who worked as a security guard at the building. His friend was waiting for them by the guard's desk in the lobby and smiled when he saw them approaching. Tyrone put his finger to his lips to warn his friend not to speak.

"Tyrone, baby, where in the world are we?" The suspense was making Sylvia crazy.

"Just a while longer, hon, and you'll know. Wait here for one second."

"You mean you're going to leave me standing here with this blindfold on, all by myself?"

"Don't worry, babe. This is gonna take only a sec. I'll be right back, okay?"

He walked away before she could protest. She stood impatiently while Tyrone pulled his friend around a corner, where Sylvia wouldn't hear them speaking.

"Tyrone. What's happenin', papi?" the security guard asked.

"Nothin' much, Manny, what's up with you?" He gave his Puerto Rican friend a hug.

Manny glanced over at Sylvia standing by the elevator then did a little mock bump and grind.

"So you wanna get a little penthouse action, huh?"

"Yeah, I think she'd like that." Tyrone smiled.

"What woman wouldn't? That damn penthouse is what got Maria to marry me."

Tyrone reached into his pocket and handed Manny fifty dollars. "How long do I have?"

"Hour and a half, papi. Enjoy."

The elevator took nearly five minutes to reach the observation deck of the Empire State Building. Sylvia could tell she was on an elevator, but she had no idea where she was, especially since Tyrone's gentle kisses had been distracting her through the whole ride.

"Ohhh! Tyrone, you're driving me crazy. Now, how about taking this blindfold off me so I can relax and enjoy this?"

"It's almost time, Sylvia. I promised you something you've never done before, and this is it." He wrapped his arms around her and held her close.

"Tyrone, all this mystery is very exciting, but I don't know how much longer I can stand the suspense. Where are you taking me? I feel like I'm riding in a plane."

"Trust me, you're going to like this." He kissed her as the elevator doors opened. He held her hand to guide her out and stopped to take in the breathtaking view of New York City that only the Empire State Building could offer.

"Earth to Tyrone. Are you there, baby?" Sylvia asked as she almost walked into a wall.

"I'm right here, baby."

He straightened her blindfold and slowly guided her to the railing in front of the observation deck window. Placing his hands over both of hers, he guided her hands to the railing.

"Hold on to this," he whispered. "I'll be right back."

She did as he asked, waiting patiently while he took the candles, wine, and long-stemmed roses out of the duffel bag he had been carrying. He laid out a blanket on the floor, lit the candles, and set up the wineglasses. Returning to the railing, he removed Sylvia's blindfold and turned her around to admire the sparkling lights of Manhattan. She was breathless, and when she finally spoke, he was standing before her with the roses in his arms. Overwhelmed with emotion, she took the flowers and placed them near her face, inhaling their romantic fragrance. She placed them beside her on the floor and embraced Tyrone passionately. Neither spoke for quite some time.

When they finally separated, Tyrone took her hand and led her to the blanket. She smiled as he popped the cork and poured a glass of wine for each of them. Handing her a glass, he raised his in a toasting gesture.

"Here's to us, Sylvia. I might not be able to buy you all the fancy things you're accustomed to, but I can give you my heart."

"Tyrone, you've given me more than money could ever buy. You've given me back the self-esteem I lost so long ago. I could never repay you for what you have brought to my life." Her eyes glistened with tears.

Setting his wineglass down, Tyrone reached for Sylvia and pulled her closer. There was one more part to his design for the evening, so he sat up and faced Sylvia, looking into her eyes. He unhooked a gold chain from around his neck and held it in front of her.

"What's this?" She touched the chain to feel the key that was dangling from it.

"Sylvia, I know you're married, but this is my way of saying that it's all about you. I'm not big with words, so I'm just gonna give it to you straight. I love you. This is the key to my place. You can come and go as you please. As far as I'm concerned, your name's on the lease. I love you, baby. I hope you love me too." He embraced her tightly.

"Oh, Tyrone, I do love you. God knows I do." She kissed him passionately, inviting him to make love to her.

Maurice pulled his Mercedes out of the parking lot of Foxwoods Casino in Connecticut. Annoyed at the young woman next to him, he purposely drove around the sharp winding roads leading to the highway at a high rate of speed, hoping to scare her. Sharon, a petite nineteen-year-old, gripped the seat tightly as he drove down the dark, narrow road.

"You're not mad at me, are you, Maurice?" She closed her eyes as he barely kept the car under control going around a curve.

"Mad? Why would I be mad?"

"Because I didn't want to have sex with you on the first date."

"No, I can understand that," he lied. "Although I will admit I was a little upset when you wouldn't go down on me. I mean, that's not really sex."

"Well, it's sex to me. But you never know, maybe next time." She patted his leg to give him encouragement.

Trust me, there won't be a next time, he thought as a deer entered the roadway.

"Oh, my God, Maurice, look out!" She closed her eyes.

He maneuvered the expensive sports car like a professional race car driver, avoiding the deer by ten feet easily.

Make me waste my money and time, will you? he thought, snickering to himself as she opened her eyes.

"What was that?"

"Looked like a bear."

"A bear! Look, Maurice, you need to find a highway and get me back to New York. I don't wanna be out here in the woods with no bears and shit."

"Relax. I have my gun in the trunk."

"What good is it gonna do you in the trunk? Pull this car over and get the damn gun."

Maurice pulled the car over to the side of the road, then pulled the trunk-release switch.

"If you want the gun so badly, go get it. It's in my toolbox. You can't miss it."

"I'm not going out there!" she said with attitude.

"That's fine with me, but I'm not driving until somebody closes my trunk, and it was your idea to get the gun." He pulled the lever to recline his chair, then looked over at her and smiled devilishly before closing his eyes.

Sharon couldn't believe his arrogance. He was so nice during their entire date. That is, until she made it clear that they were not going to have sex.

"You know, Maurice, you're a real asshole." She opened her door and walked around to the trunk, finding the toolbox. "This damn thing is locked!" she yelled.

Maurice rolled down his window. "Just shut the trunk and bring it up here. I have the key in my glove compartment."

Grinning, Maurice brought his seat to an upright position as he watched Sharon in his rearview mirror. When she closed the trunk, he laughed hard, beeping the horn as he put his foot on the accelerator.

Sharon dropped the toolbox in disbelief and ran after the car. "You son of a bitch, Maurice! Stop playing fucking games!"

He stopped the car about a hundred feet away from her. Sharon breathed a sigh of relief when she saw the car stop.

"This fucking guy is crazy," she grumbled, turning around to pick up the toolbox.

Maurice was laughing so hard, he was in tears. He stepped out of his car and screamed.

"Hurry up, Sharon! I think I hear something in the woods!"

Terrified, she fell and broke the heel of her shoe trying to get to the car. Getting up quickly, she never looked back as she ran, still lugging the heavy toolbox.

Maurice, still laughing, bent over and picked up a rock. He threw it into the woods so that it ruffled the leaves.

"Oh, my God, Sharon! Did you hear that? It's a bear! Run, sweetheart! Run!" He got back in the car.

"Ohhh, shit!" she screamed, falling down again, facefirst in the dirt. Struggling back up, Sharon left the toolbox this time as she limped closer to the car.

Maurice buckled his seat belt and stuck his head out the window.

"Hey, Sharon, next time a guy takes you out and shows you a good time, you might want to make sure he gets laid!" He sped away, kicking up dirt and gravel in her face.

As he drove onto the highway, Maurice slammed his hand against the dashboard.

Damn, that was a fucking waste of time. And I lost a brand new toolbox!

He thought about his wife, hoping she would be awake when he got home. Not that it mattered. He would wake her. It was time she started to perform her some of her wifely duties. Since his VD scare, he had not had intercourse, and oral sex just wasn't doing it anymore. He sped home to find some satisfaction.

Sylvia pulled into her Jamaica Estates home, exhausted. The excitement and passion from her night with Tyrone at the top of Manhattan had sapped all her energy. And then he had insisted on a quickie at his apartment before they said their good-byes.

She passed Maurice's car in the driveway. "Shit," she mumbled, "I thought he was going to be home late tonight." She pulled her car into the garage.

Things had become very tense in the Johnson household in the past few months. Maurice had recently become upset every time Sylvia refused his sexual advances. The tables had turned, and Maurice was practically begging in the last few days. Sylvia, on the other hand, was finding him more and more repulsive every day. With Tyrone she was experiencing the warmth and security of unconditional love for the first time in her life. Her husband had become nothing more than an inconvenience. She had no interest in being in the same room with him, let alone being intimate.

Entering the house through the garage door, she walked past Maurice's study and breathed a sigh of relief when she saw the light coming from under the door. She tiptoed up the stairs to her bedroom and quickly removed her clothes in the dark. Fingering the key to Tyrone's apartment around her neck, she fantasized about running away with him to some island paradise where she could watch him paint and walk to the market with a straw basket.

Oh, God, Bernard was right, she thought as she unhooked her bra. *I'm going to have to divorce Maurice.*

"Where have you been?" Maurice said deeply, scaring her as he turned on the light. He had been sitting in the chair next to the bed for over an hour, waiting for her to come home. In the meantime he had drunk half a bottle of brandy.

"I said, where the hell have you been?" He slammed his hand on the night table.

"I had a club meeting," she answered nonchalantly.

"Oh, you did," he slurred smugly. "Well, how come Vivian and Jen didn't know about this club meeting? Matter of fact, Jen said you were over her house until five minutes before I called there."

"Well, ah, I was at her house. But then I had to go to, ahh . . . to a club committee meeting. You know, I didn't remember I was supposed to be there until I was halfway home."

She tried to laugh to diffuse his mood. He gave her a look that let her know he didn't believe a word she had told him.

"Why are you asking me all these questions about my whereabouts anyway? You're starting to make me think you don't trust me, Maurice. That's not good in a marriage. Maybe I should keep a closer watch of your whereabouts, as much as you disappear for days at a time." She hoped he would leave her alone if she put some of the blame on him.

"Hey, look, Sylvia, don't get all bent out of shape. I was just worried about you. That's all." Maurice's attempts at sounding sweet were so unnatural. "Doesn't a husband have the right to be worried about his wife?"

He stood up and walked over to her, wrapping his arms around her. His hands wandered down her back, and he was surprised but pleased to discover she was wearing a G-string, so her buttocks were exposed. He began to gently massage her.

"Have you been working out?" He smiled, breathing down her neck.

"Yes," she answered, thinking, *for the past six months, mother-fucker. Thanks for finally noticing.*

"You know, Sylvia. I've been waiting the past hour to make love to you." He kissed her neck romantically. "How about it?"

Sylvia contemplated agreeing just so he would leave her alone for a few days but decided against it when she realized how tired she was from her earlier escapades with Tyrone.

"That would be nice, Maurice, but I'm really tired. How about a rain check?" She faked a yawn.

"Rain check? I don't want a rain check. I want some sex!" He became agitated and grabbed her shoulders tightly. "What the fuck do I have to do to get laid around here anyway?"

Sylvia stared at him as if he'd lost his mind.

"I'm getting sick of your bullshit excuses, Sylvia. You're gonna gimme some and you're gonna gimme some tonight!"

"Maurice, I'm tired and I'm going to go to sleep," she responded flatly, and pushed him away, walking into the bathroom.

"Come back here, Sylvia, I'm talking to you! Come back here!"

He followed her to the bathroom, but she shut the door in his face. Ready to explode, he reached for the doorknob but heard the lock click.

"Open this door, Sylvia. Open this door now!" His face was burning red as he banged on the bathroom door. "Goddammit, I'm your husband. You can't deny me sex. It's your fucking duty!"

He was furious now as he stomped around the room, knocking over pictures and lamps. Sylvia cowered in the bathroom, wishing she had an escape. She had no idea what he was capable of in this state.

"If you don't open that fucking door right now, I swear to God I'm gonna break it down!"

He waited ten seconds, then ran toward the door, slamming his foot into it so hard that Sylvia heard the wood splitting. The frame had cracked, and he was able to open the door with one more shove. He marched over to Sylvia, who was standing across the room.

"What the fuck is your problem?" She tried to act as though she weren't as terrified as she really was. "That's a six-hundred-dollar door!"

"I'll tell you what my problem is," he shouted, grabbing her by the neck and lifting her off the ground. "My wife ain't giving me no pussy! What's it been now, Sylvia, four months since you let me get some? Well, tonight's the night, baby, whether you like it or not!"

She begged him to let her go as he dragged her by the neck into the bedroom.

Please, God, don't let him kill me, she prayed as she struggled to get air into her lungs. Maurice threw her on the bed, smiling as she gasped for air.

"Think you want to give me some now?" He frantically unbuckled his pants and dropped them around his ankles.

"Maurice, why are you doing this? Don't you understand this is rape?" she cried as she tried to crawl to the other side of the bed.

"You can't rape your wife," he said, stepping out of his pants. "Now shut the fuck up!"

"Please, Maurice, don't do this! Please! Ahhhhhh!"

He grabbed her leg and flipped her over on her stomach.

"Sylvia, do you know the only thing I've never tried in bed? Anal sex! I always wanted to try anal sex. But I never got around to asking you to do it."

Sylvia began to kick and fight even harder when she heard him say that. For a few seconds she was able to keep him at bay with her feet, until he slapped her hard.

Oh, God, please don't let him violate me like this. Please! she sobbed. He seemed to get more excited by her struggling.

Turning over on her back, she tried to smile through her tears as she told him in a trembling voice, "Okay, Maurice, listen, baby. I'm going to give you some right now. I swear it's going to be the best you ever had."

She desperately scrambled to get her panties off, opening her legs wide so that they could have intercourse. Maurice stood there, smiling almost psychotically. He was as excited as he'd ever been in the past. For some reason the violence-and-sex combination excited him in a way he had never experienced. He could feel his penis throb as Sylvia's fear escalated.

"Too late, baby. I don't want that anymore." He laughed, smacking her again as he grabbed her hair. "Turn over, bitch!"

"Nooo! Oh, God! Somebody help me! Please, Maurice, don't do this!"

He threw her onto her stomach, pinning her face hard to the mattress with his body weight. Enjoying her screams, he bit her shoulder hard as he positioned himself to violate her rectum.

She screamed as his teeth broke her skin. Reaching for the night table, she managed to get her fingers around the base of his reading lamp. Swinging it backward with all her might, she hit him squarely on the head.

"You fucking bitch!" He jumped up and grabbed his head with both hands to see if he was bleeding. Sylvia dragged herself off the bed and ran out of the room.

Downstairs she scrambled through a closet to find an overcoat to cover her exposed body, screaming as she heard him coming down the stairs. Throwing on her mink coat, she snatched her purse and keys and ran out the front door.

"What the fuck do I do now?" she cried, remembering that she had parked her car in the garage.

Maurice reached the door, still bleeding.

"Sylvia, come back, honey! I'm sorry. I didn't know what the hell I was doing."

He ran toward her, naked, as she opened his car and got in. She locked the doors just as he arrived. He watched as his terrified wife backed his car out of the driveway.

"Come on, Sylvia, I was just playing with you! It was just a little fun," he shouted after her. Looking down the road, he spotted one of his neighbors walking a dog and ran back into the house, slamming the door behind him.

Fingering the key around her neck, Sylvia sobbed as she drove to Tyrone's apartment. She knew she would never spend another night in that house with Maurice.

Sylvia was still shaking uncontrollably as she searched for a parking space on Tyrone's block. The tears had finally stopped, and she had become angry.

That son of a bitch was about to rape me, she thought incredulously, lighting a cigarette. *I can't believe this is happening to me.*

She sat in her parked car, finishing her cigarette, until she calmed down and decided exactly what she would do. Tyrone had given her the key only hours earlier, and here she was, preparing to use it under such horrible circumstances. But her only other choice was to go to a hotel, and she couldn't bear the thought of being alone after the ordeal she had just endured.

She entered Tyrone's building and slowly made her way to his apartment. Before taking the key from around her neck, she took a deep breath. Once she went in and explained everything to Tyrone, she knew there was no turning back. She opened the door and quietly called his name.

In the darkened room she heard him stirring as he awoke and switched on the lamp by his bed. He focused his eyes and looked stunned when he saw Sylvia standing in his doorway in her fur. Still too groggy to be sure, he thought she looked like she was shivering.

"A little warm for a mink coat, isn't it, baby?"

He walked across the room to hold her. He felt her body trembling as she burst into tears. Leading her to the bed, he helped her sit down. When he tried to help her take off the coat, she grabbed it and wrapped it more tightly around her.

"What is it, Sylvia? What happened, baby?" He held her tightly and rocked her.

"M-m-m-my husband . . . tried to rape me." She burst into tears again. Tyrone held her tight, and between her sobs Sylvia recounted the attack.

"What?" Tyrone shouted, standing up. "That's it, you're staying with me from now on."

Sylvia nodded her head sadly in agreement. "Tyrone? There's something else I need to tell you. Something I should have told you a long time ago."

"You can tell me anything, Syl. I love you." Tyrone sat back down and rubbed her back to calm her trembling body.

"I don't know how to tell you this." She was no longer worried about Maurice but about her relationship with Tyrone.

"Don't worry, just say it."

"My husband is Maurice Johnson."

"Maurice Johnson? As in my boss?" Tyrone stared at her in shock.

"Yes." Sylvia lowered her head.

"Damn, that guy's got a file on me two inches thick. You sure know how to complicate things, don't you?" He smiled at her. "It's okay."

"You're not mad that I didn't tell you sooner?"

"Mad? If I really cared about who your husband was, I would have asked you a long time ago." He looked into her eyes. "All I need to know is, do you still love him?"

"No, Tyrone, I don't love him. I love you. I love you so much." She kissed him.

He held her all night, soothing her each time her tears started again. They told each other repeatedly how much they loved one another, and Tyrone knew that he would never let her go back to her home.

"Sylvia," he whispered as he saw the first signs of daybreak through his window. She rolled over to face him. "Sylvia, where do we go from here, baby?"

"Divorce court." She wrapped her arms around him, and they fell asleep peacefully.

34

KEVIN AND ALICIA

Kevin reached his apartment building, winded from the effort. He had parked his car several blocks away and crept through a few backyards so that he would not be visible on the street. In the two weeks since he had broken up with Denise, she had literally been stalking him. Nearly every night she had been waiting in her car in front of his house when he came home. He had tried to avoid speaking to her, but one night she sat outside and blew her horn until he agreed to come out and talk to her. The conversation was mostly repetitive, with Denise pleading with him for another chance to prove herself and Kevin refusing. Finally she drove off in anger but vowed to be back to change his mind.

Since that night Kevin had been staying at Antoine's place, sneaking back only occasionally for clothes. The harassment had gotten to such a point that he hated going back to the apartment, even just to get his clothes. When school closed for Easter vacation in a few weeks, he planned to visit Mama for a week, hoping that by the time he returned to New York, Denise would have given up on her little crusade to win him back.

In spite of the inconvenience the arrangement with Antoine had worked out well, since Antoine spent most nights at Keisha's apartment. Kevin's only complaint was that his bookish friend didn't have cable television. This wasn't really a problem, but tonight Kevin wanted to see the big fight on Pay-Per-View. Normally he would have just called Tyrone and asked to watch the fight at his place, but with Tyrone moving Sylvia in, that was no longer an option. So he had snuck through the neighborhood to get back to his own place to watch the fight.

As he reached his door, he was grateful once again that his entrance was on the side. He didn't even bother to peek around the corner of the house to look for Denise's car. As he quickly closed the door behind him, he turned to see that his answering machine message light was blinking furiously. Fifteen messages. This woman was not letting up.

He pressed the erase button without bothering to listen to one message. In the past week he had received a minimum of twenty calls a day from her so he was certain he knew what these would say.

During the preliminary fights Kevin heard a car horn blaring outside and froze, cursing under his breath. He was certain it was Denise and walked to the window, expecting to see her white BMW in front of the building. Fortunately it was just a cab waiting for one of his neighbors. He breathed a sigh of relief and returned to watching the fight. After a while he fell asleep and missed most of the main event fight. He didn't wake again until the phone startled him at midnight.

"Hello," he answered, still half asleep. He bolted upright when he came to his senses and realized what a mistake he had made by picking up the phone.

"Kevin, honey, please don't hang up," Denise pleaded. "All I want is ten minutes of your time. I promise, after that I'll leave you alone."

Kevin didn't answer her right away. Instead, he walked over to his window and glanced out. Spotting Denise's car across the street from his building, he felt as if he were ready to explode.

"Denise, I can see your car parked outside. Why don't you just go home?"

"Kevin, unless you want me to start blowing my horn, you'll come out here." Denise's tone was dead serious.

Angered by her threat, he dropped his phone and stormed out of his apartment. He walked across the street to her car and glared at her as she rolled down the window.

"Hi, handsome." She smiled as if nothing were wrong.

"This is getting really stupid and really old, Denise. Why can't you leave me alone? Can't you see I don't want you?" He raised his hands in exasperation.

"I didn't come over here to fight, Kevin. I came over here to talk." Suddenly her tone became quite threatening. "Don't paint me into a corner, because you won't like what you see."

"What the hell is that supposed to mean?"

"Do you really think I'm going to let you go so that you can be with Alicia, or some other bitch? What are you, fucking crazy? If you're not going to be with me, you're not going to be with anybody."

Her threat actually made him take a step back. His expression let her know that her message was being heard loud and clear.

"You're threatening me?"

"You're damn right I'm threatening you. If you can't see we're meant to be together, then I'm going to make you see it. And if you think I'm a pain in the ass now, I get much worse."

Kevin looked at her with pure hatred for the first time. Clenching his fists, it took everything inside of him to turn around and walk toward his house instead of slapping the taste out of her mouth.

"Don't you walk away from me, Kevin! Don't you dare walk away from me! I made you the man you are today!" she screamed after him, getting out of her car.

"You have got to be kidding." He turned to face her, standing in the middle of the street. "What are you, my mama?"

"I might as well be! Look at you! Everything about you has Denise written all over it." She gave him a superior smile as she pointed at what he was wearing. "That sweat suit, those sneakers, that diamond earring. I bought all of it. Not to mention all that furniture in your house. You were living out of boxes before you met me, and you think you don't need me?"

"You know what, Denise, you can have all this shit back." He took off both shoes and threw them at her car. "I swear to God, you can have all this shit. Just leave me the fuck alone!" He took the earring out of his lobe and stepped out of the sweat suit so that he was standing in the middle of the street in a pair of boxers and his socks.

"Ahh, that's much better, now I don't feel like some cheap gigolo. I'll make sure to call a mover so you can get your damn furniture back tomorrow." He suddenly felt very free.

"So, do you want me to take your sister's life back too?" she asked him viciously. Kevin flinched from the sting of such a cold remark, and she was glad to see she had reached him. She continued to try to inflict pain.

"That's right, it was I who saved your sister when you and your mama couldn't do it, remember? I would think you'd at least be grateful for that."

Kevin lowered his head, unable to look Denise in the eye. She was right, she did help save his sister's life, and he did owe her his gratitude.

Suddenly her tone softened. "And I'd do it again, Kevin, because I love you."

"But, Denise, I don't love you," Kevin pleaded with her to understand.

"You don't mean that, Kevin," she told him with certainty. "And even if you do, I'll tell everyone you raped me before I let you be with someone else."

He gasped at her as the impact of her threat hit him.

"I mean it, Kevin. I've got enough panties with your sperm in them to make a convincing case, and we've had our share of public arguments." She got back into her car and offered him one final threat.

"Just so we understand each other, Kevin. I may love you, but I'll visit you behind bars before I'll let you be with someone else. I'll be talking to you real soon." She blew him a kiss as she sped away in her BMW.

Kevin picked up his clothes and walked back into his apartment. He was worried about the threat of rape charges. There was no guarantee she could even do it, or make any charges stick, but the prospect of it was frightening. A wealthy white woman still received the benefit of the doubt over a young black man, for the most part, in this country. As he sat in his living room, contemplating the possibility of Denise acting on her threat, his phone rang. It jolted him.

He grabbed the phone angrily. "What is it now, Denise? More threats?"

"Unc-uncle Kevin? I need your help." Kevin heard a child's voice through the sobs but couldn't make out who it was.

"Michael? Is that you, Michael?"

Kevin was surprised to hear from the boy. They hadn't seen each other since the breakup, and Michael had never called him on the phone. Some residual feelings of anger at Michael still lingered, so Kevin assumed the boy once again did not have the best intentions. He figured the boy was probably having a disagreement with his mother and needed someone to bail him out.

"I need your help, Uncle Kevin." The boy was crying as he spoke and sounded genuinely scared. Kevin began to wonder if maybe he wasn't crying wolf this time.

"Just relax, Michael. Try to stop crying. What's going on, little man? And what's all that noise I hear?" Kevin knew that his voice was calming the boy, because the sobs on the other end diminished slightly.

"My daddy's beating my mommy up. She's locked in the bathroom. Daddy said he's gonna kill her. He already hit her with a baseball bat."

Kevin could hear the commotion in the background. It sounded as if Trevor was trying to break everything in the apartment, shouting every obscenity in the book as he did it.

Immediately Kevin assumed Trevor was drunk. He wasn't sure if this was something he should get involved in. After all, Alicia was the one who had let Trevor back into her life, so in some respects Kevin thought this was her own fault. He considered just telling Michael to call the police, and staying out of it himself. But even as he thought this, he realized it was time to grow up and put his own hurt feelings aside. This woman was the victim of violence. In his heart he knew no woman deserved that, even if it was a woman who had broken his own heart. He still loved Alicia after all that had happened. He became enraged at the image of her on the receiving end of Trevor's baseball bat. Anger rose in him as his protective instincts took over. He knew he had to help her.

"Please, Uncle Kevin, you're the only one I know who is strong enough to beat up my daddy," Michael begged.

"I'll be there in a few minutes, Michael. Just go make sure the door is unlocked so that I can get in. Then get yourself right back in your room and put a chair under the doorknob. Do you understand?"

"Yes, Uncle Kevin. Just hurry, please! My mommy really needs you."

Kevin hung up the phone and raced to his car.

At Alicia's apartment Trevor was in a psychotic rage as he tore through the living room, smashing everything in sight. The bat that Michael had mentioned to Kevin was actually a plastic wiffle ball bat, but with Trevor's powerful swing, it was still enough to inflict damage. He'd been on this rampage ever since Alicia told him that they were through and asked him to return the key to her apartment. He'd been drunk, and the request sent him into violent rage.

For the few weeks prior, Trevor had sensed something was wrong with their relationship. Especially when Alicia had refused to make love to him and told him that she knew he had not sent the gifts he had taken credit for. The only thing Trevor could think of was that whoever had sent the gifts was now back in her life. He had repeatedly accused her of cheating on him, and although she denied it, her request for her key was all the proof he thought he needed. Without another word he had walked calmly into Michael's room, found the bat, and came out swinging. Alicia was knocked to the ground with the first blow.

"Bitch! Do I look like a fool to you?" he screamed, swinging again but missing her.

Alicia was certain she would be dead if the bat were made of wood. She scurried away from Trevor, screaming for Michael to get help. Images flashed through her head of beatings Trevor had inflicted on her in the past.

God, why the hell did I ever let him back in my life, she thought as he swung the bat, just missing her as she scrambled into the bathroom and locked the door.

"You really think I'm stupid, don't you? You've been trying to avoid me for two weeks! And now all of a sudden you want your key back?" Trevor tried his best to break down the door but to no avail. "Who is he? Tell me who you've been fucking, or I swear I'll smash everything in this damn apartment!" Trevor began swinging the bat wildly but stopped when he heard Michael come out of his bedroom and scream.

"Leave my mommy alone, Daddy! You're nothing but a big bully! I hate you! I hate you!" Michael picked up an ashtray and threw it at his father.

"I'm sick of you, ya little pain in the ass. You gonna learn to respect me." Trevor's eyes got small, and he threw the bat down to remove his belt. He chased Michael until he got close enough, then swung the belt. It landed with a smack on Michael's back, and he let out a howl.

"Mommy! Mommy!" Michael screamed as his father hit him again and again.

"Stop it, Trevor!" Alicia screamed, racing out of the bathroom.

"Why, you ready for your ass whuppin' now?" Trevor took a few steps toward her.

"No, but I'm ready to give one out, you fucking bastard." Alicia took a deep breath as she moved into karate stance.

"What the fuck you doin'?" Trevor laughed. "You been watching *Buffy the Vampire Slayer* again?" Trevor tightened his grip around his belt and walked forward.

I hope this shit works, Alicia thought as she waited for Trevor to come within striking range. When he did, she let out a loud "hi-ya!" as her foot traveled quickly into Trevor's stomach and knocked the wind out of him. Instinctively she followed the kick with a flurry of karate blows around Trevor's head, finishing him off with a swift kick between the legs. He dropped to the floor like a piece of lead.

Oh, my God! It worked, it really worked! She wanted to jump in the air with her fists raised but swooped the trembling Michael into her arms instead.

Kevin pulled his new car in front of Alicia's building exactly seven minutes after he had hung up the phone with Michael. It wasn't the Ford Expedition he had wanted but, rather, a 1997 Honda Civic. Still, he was proud of it, especially since he paid for it himself, without the help of Denise.

As he pulled up, he noticed several police cars in front of the building. He jumped out of his car and ran to the building. As he went down the hall, he stared angrily at a badly beaten man in handcuffs being escorted by two police officers.

Oh, no, Kevin thought when he recognized Trevor from pictures he'd seen. *If he looks like that, what does she look like?*

Kevin ran to Alicia's apartment expecting the worst.

"Uncle Kevin! Uncle Kevin!" Michael ran across the room, flying into Kevin's arms. The boy was still shaking. Kevin's eyes widened as he peered across the living room that looked like a battle zone.

"Where's your mom?"

"Right there." Michael pointed with a trembling hand. Alicia was walking out of her bedroom, followed by a female police officer.

"You okay?" Kevin was relieved that she didn't look too seriously hurt.

"My hand's a little sore but I'm okay. What are you doing here?" It was evident from her voice that Alicia was glad to see him.

"Michael called me. He said you needed help, but judging from the looks of Trevor outside, he was the one who needed it. What the heck happened?"

"My mommy beat the shit out of my daddy." Michael said, burying his head in Kevin's shoulder. Both officers laughed.

"Michael, what did I tell you about that word?" Alicia looked at the two officers. "I'm sorry about his language."

"It's all right. It's not like he lied," the male officer said.

"Ms. Meyers"—the female officer approached—"I think we have everything we need, for now anyway. Once you get together a list of the broken items, we'll see what we can do about getting you some restitution."

"Thank you, officer." She walked them to the door, then turned to her son. "Michael, this has been a very long night for both of us, and I think you need to get some rest. Come on and I'll help you get ready for bed."

"Can't I stay up and talk to Uncle Kevin a little longer?" Kevin let

Michael down. He could tell by Alicia's voice that she was emotionally drained.

"No, it's time for bed, kiddo," Kevin told the boy. "Now, go ahead in your room and your mom will be in there in a minute."

Kevin gave Michael a high-five and said good night. He watched the boy walk into his room and then turned to ask Alicia, "Hey, I know it's none of my business, but you wanna tell me what's going on around here?"

"I stood up for myself, Kevin. For the first time in my life I stood up for myself. And you know what? It felt good."

Alicia looked like she was about to cry, so Kevin walked over and wrapped his arms around her. Alicia felt as if she could hold on to him forever. She had stood on her own tonight, and now it felt good to have a little support.

"Mommy! Mommy!" Michael called.

"Let me go check on him." Alicia reluctantly let go of Kevin. "I still need to talk to him about everything that's happened tonight."

"Take your time. I'm not going anywhere." Kevin bent over to start cleaning up the mess.

Several hours passed before Alicia was able to calm Michael enough for the child to fall asleep. Kevin checked in on them several times, but for the most part he waited in the living room, cleaning up, while Alicia comforted her son as only a mother could. When she finally left Michael's room and closed the door, Kevin stood and reached out for her hand. He helped her get settled on the couch.

"Kevin, I really can't thank you enough for coming here. There's not many brothers who would do that after the way I treated you." She hugged him tightly.

"Most brothers don't feel the way I do about you, Alicia. You're very special to me."

"I can see that now." They shared a peaceful silence before Alicia changed the subject. "Michael is really terrified that Trevor might come back. I just know he's going to have nightmares all night."

"You know, Alicia, he might not be so wrong. There's no telling if Trevor is gonna make bail." Kevin knew the words were frightening, but he wanted her to be prepared. "No offense, but he might have killed you if that was a real bat."

"I know."

"Look, why don't I stay, spend the night on your couch in case he does try to come back?"

"I'd like that." The relief was evident in her voice. She had been un-sure if she could ask Kevin to stay but knew she would feel much safer with him there.

They stayed up for another hour, though neither of them had much to say. Just being together was healing enough for the moment. After a while Alicia headed for her bedroom, hoping she would be able to fall asleep. Kevin stayed on the couch with a small blanket to cover him.

A few hours before dawn Alicia came back into the living room and stood beside the couch.

"Kevin," she whispered, "are you awake?"

"Mmm-hmm." He rolled over and squinted his eyes to see her in the dark. "Are you okay?"

"I still can't sleep. And I keep thinking about you out here on this uncomfortable couch."

"I'm fine, Alicia."

"Do you want to come stay in my bed with me?"

Kevin sat up, a little surprised.

"I want us to get back together, Kevin. I'm not saying it has to be today. The truth is, I need a little time to get myself together."

"I could probably use a little more time myself," he replied. She held his hand as he stood up. Gently he put his arms around her.

"Come to bed, Kevin. I just need you to hold me."

"Are you sure about this?" he asked.

"After all the mistakes I've made, I know I'm right about this. This is where you belong."

Under the covers with his arms surrounding Alicia, Kevin felt some-thing he never had with Denise. He felt the warmth of love. They both had things to work out on their own, and it was going to take time be-fore he and Alicia could repair their damaged relationship. He'd prob-ably have to go to counseling with her, but it was all going to be worth the wait.

35

TYRONE, SYLVIA, AND MAURICE

Sylvia stomped up the stairs to the Alternative High School for Boys with the intention of confronting her husband. She had come to inform Maurice that she was divorcing his sorry ass, the sooner the better. Checking her watch, she was happy to see that it was only 12:30 P.M. She knew this was Tyrone's lunch hour, and he would not be at the front desk until after his workout. She wanted to do this on her own. Entering the building, she walked down to the office and smiled at Mrs. Rogers, the school secretary.

"Hi, Mrs. Rogers, how are you?"

"I am blessed, Mrs. Johnson, how are you?"

"I'm going to be great in about fifteen minutes. Is my husband in?"

"Yes, he's been expecting you ever since you called." She knew it wasn't her place to ask what Sylvia's last comment meant.

Maurice was sitting on the corner of his desk, looking at a file, when Sylvia walked in.

"Sylvia, I'm so glad you came. I've really missed you." He tried to hug her.

"Don't put your hands on me." She pushed him away and sat down in a chair in front of his desk.

"Look, I know you're still upset about last week. But I just want to apologize. I had no cause to treat you like that." He tried to sound sincere.

"You were going to fucking rape me! Do you really think your apology is going to make me forget about that? Fuck you, Maurice."

"Sylvia, it was the alcohol that made me act that way. Just come home with me, please. I'll do whatever it takes to make our marriage work. I'll go to therapy, a marriage counselor, whatever you want me to do. I just want you to come home, sweetheart. I need you."

It was so unlike Maurice to beg, but he was desperate to have his wife back.

"Look, we need to get away, be a family again. How about you, Jasmine and me go away for two weeks in Paris? Come on. You love Paris this time of year."

He walked around his desk, opening a drawer, and handed her three tickets. Sylvia glanced at the tickets, then up at Maurice. She was amazed to see genuine tears glistening in his eyes.

"Sylvia, I've done a lot of stupid shit over the years. But since you've been gone, I realize that I really need you, baby." They both turned when they heard a knock on the door.

"Mrs. Rogers said you wanted to see me, Dr. Johnson?" Tyrone stuck his head in the door. He did a double take when he realized it was Sylvia sitting in the office.

"Yes, Mr. Jefferson, come on in and have a seat." Maurice wiped his eyes and smiled as Tyrone walked in. "This will take only a second, Sylvia."

Tyrone's nervousness was apparent as he walked slowly into the room and took a seat next to Sylvia. A few days before, Sylvia had dropped the bombshell that Maurice was her husband. Now Tyrone was afraid that in her mood of revelations, she might have told Maurice about their affair.

"You know my wife, don't you, Mr. Jefferson?" Maurice was back to his old self, smiling devilishly as he leaned back in his chair.

"No, I haven't had the pleasure," he answered as perspiration began to form on his forehead. "Nice to meet you, Mrs. Johnson," he said stiffly.

"Oh, sure you have, Mr. Jefferson." He looked over at Sylvia. "Haven't you two met before?"

"No, I'd remember someone as handsome as him." She gave Tyrone a look of reassurance to make him relax.

"You know, Sylvia, three weeks ago Mr. Jefferson filed a stolen badge report. Didn't you, Mr. Jefferson?"

"Yes, sir, Dr. Johnson. I'm still trying to find that badge."

Maurice reached into his shirt pocket and pulled out a badge, tossing it to Tyrone.

"Is this your badge? I found it a couple of days ago."

Tyrone looked at the serial numbers and smiled. "Yes, sir, this is mine. You don't know how happy I am you found it. They were going to take three hundred dollars out of my next check to replace it." His relief was short-lived.

"Let me tell you how I found it. You two will get a real kick out of this. My wife here's been gone from the house for about two weeks, and she's got my car." He smiled wickedly at her. "So now I'm forced to drive her car. Well, the other day I get in real fast and sit down. Out of nowhere, I get this sharp pain in my ass."

"Isn't that ironic?" Sylvia laughed out loud. "You've been a pain in my ass all my life."

"I reach down in between the seats and I find your badge, Mr. Jefferson. Any idea how it got there?" Maurice's eyes went back and forth from Sylvia to Tyrone. The two of them were in shock. "So how long have you two been fucking?"

"Probably about the same amount of time you've been fucking those girls from 1-900-BLACK-LUV," Sylvia retorted.

Maurice was shocked that she knew about the date line. "Listen, Sylvia, my argument is not with you. It's with Mr. Tyrone Jefferson over here."

"Oh, your argument is with me all right, because he's not the one divorcing you, I am." She smirked.

"Divorce? You can't be serious."

Maurice was visibly shaken by her last words. He had always believed in her unconditional love. He never thought things between them would get to the point of divorce.

"Oh, yes, I can. My lawyers plan on serving you with papers this afternoon."

"This is all your fault, Jefferson." Maurice stood and pointed his finger in Tyrone's face. "And from this day forward I can promise you a life of fucking hell. Get the fuck out my office. You're fired."

"Don't you fire me, Maurice. I don't give a fuck how mad you are. Transfer me, suspend me, but don't you fire me. I've got two little girls whose mothers depend on the money I send them."

"If you're so worried about your kids, tell my wife you're never going to see her again. Tell her that she needs to go home to her husband and work things out. Otherwise, I promise you will never work security in the state of New York again."

"Fuck you, Maurice! He doesn't need you or this shitty-ass job. Tyrone's an artist. He'll make it with or without your job. Besides, you don't have the power to fire him."

Tyrone thought about it. "You know what, Maurice? Sylvia's right. You have no legitimate reason to ask the board to fire me. Fuck you!" He embraced Sylvia.

"You think I'm going to let you get away with this, Jefferson?" Maurice snapped a pencil in his hands. "That's my wife we're talking about." He slammed his hand on the desk, frightening Sylvia.

Tyrone grabbed Maurice by the tie, pulling him sharply down against his desk. "Not only do I think I'm going to get away with it, I already have. And don't think I forgot you tried to rape her." He let go of the tie when Sylvia tapped him on the shoulder.

"Forget him, he's not worth the effort," she whispered.

Maurice stood up and straightened his clothes. "So this is what it's come to, huh, Sylvia? You'd rather be with some scumbag security guard from the projects than with me?"

"Yeah, that about sums it up." She hugged Tyrone.

"All right, then. I want your shit out of my house by the end of the week."

"Your house?" She took a deep breath to calm herself. "You know what, Maurice, I'll gladly take my stuff out of that house. It's got nothing but bad memories in it anyway."

"Oh, and I'm not letting you have any of my money either."

"Your money? Ha! Daddy left that money to me." Sylvia sat calmly in her chair and checked her manicure. "Besides, my lawyer told me to take all the money out of the bank before I came over here. I hope you have lunch money, because all our joint accounts are closed."

"You bitch!"

Maurice tried to jump across his desk but was met by Tyrone, who shoved him back.

"Don't even think about it or I'll break your pretty ass in half."

"You two think you're really cute, don't you? Well, don't worry. I've got enough cash squirreled away until my lawyers can get the money you've taken." Maurice slammed his fist on his desk, then pointed his finger at Tyrone. "But you, Jefferson, you're finished around here."

There was a knock at the door and Miles, head of school security, walked in without waiting for an answer.

"Miles, just the man I wanted to see. Can you escort Mr. Jefferson off the premises? Once I talk to the superintendent, he won't be working with us."

"You don't have to talk to anybody. I quit." Tyrone kissed Sylvia just to piss Maurice off as he walked out the door.

Miles could feel the tension in the room as he watched Tyrone walk out of the office with his arm around Maurice's wife. He had no idea what had just happened, but he had other business to attend to. He stood in front of Maurice's desk and stared at the man.

"What is it, Miles?"

"Dr. Johnson, I think we have a bigger problem than Jefferson."

"Not another fight?"

"No, sir, it's the police, and they wanna speak to you." Miles went to the door and gestured for the two plainclothes policemen to enter.

"Are you Maurice Johnson?" the taller of the cops asked.

"Yes." Maurice nodded.

"Do you own a 1999 Mercedes license plate 451-LHJ?"

"Yes, why?" Maurice felt a little chill.

"We'll ask the questions Mr. Johnson," the shorter cop told him.

"Do you know this girl?" The taller officer handed Maurice a Polaroid.

Not this shit again, Maurice thought. He'd left the woman asleep in his cabin in Vermont over the weekend.

"Yes, officer, I know her. Her name is Valerie Gordon. We went out this weekend."

"Well, Mr. Johnson, Ms. Gordon says you raped her."

Maurice laughed. "Does taking your clothes off and straddling a man till you have a climax constitute rape? 'Cause that's what happened, officer."

"Well, sir, that's not the version Miss Gordon reported to us, so you'll have to come answer some questions."

"Look, this can all be cleared up very easily," Maurice said confidently. "I have a videotape of our lovemaking on which I'm sure you will clearly see it was consensual."

"You've got to be kidding." The officer smiled at his partner. "And just where is this tape, sir?"

"It's in the safe in my home. I can take you there to get it right now if you'd like."

"That won't be necessary, Mr. Johnson. But just to make sure I'm getting this right. You are admitting to having sex with Miss Gordon?"

"Yes, I did have sex with her, but it was consensual."

"Mr. Johnson, would you place your hands behind your head?"

"What? Why?" Maurice pulled his hands away from the officer.
"You're under arrest for the rape of Valerie Gordon."

"I didn't rape her! I told you it was consensual. Look at the tape."

"Valerie Gordon couldn't consent, Mr. Johnson. She's only sixteen, and that makes you a statutory rapist among other things."

"She told me she was twenty-one!" Maurice cried.

"Next time maybe you'll ask for ID. If there is a next time." The tall officer chuckled.

Maurice was in shock as the officers cuffed him and read him his rights. He was led out of the school in handcuffs for the entire student body and faculty to view. And if that wasn't embarrassing enough, Tyrone and Sylvia were standing at the school exit when the police brought him out of the building.

The next day Sylvia pulled her car into an illegal parking space and ran up the stairs to Tyrone's apartment. She dropped her key three times before getting it in the door, and she was bubbling with excitement as she finally turned the knob. She'd just left the post office, where she received a very important certified letter.

"Tyrone!" she screamed, bursting into the studio apartment. Tyrone was sitting at his easel, painting a picture of his two daughters, and immediately jumped out of his chair.

"What? What is it?" he asked, concerned. "Somebody bothering you outside?"

"No," she said breathlessly as she raced toward him, "but I've got the answer to all your dreams right here in my hand." She waved the manila envelope in the air.

"What are you talkin' about, Syl?" She reached into the envelope and pulled out a smaller one, addressed to Tyrone. She handed it to him with a huge grin.

Tyrone ripped the envelope open quickly and pulled out a letter.

Dear Mr. Jefferson,

It was a pleasure speaking to your agent, Sylvia Johnson. She has been a good friend for years and, I must say, a very tough negotiator. As you know, we had preliminary talks at Bernard's memorial before "Children of Color" was destroyed. Now that I've had the opportunity to see your portfolio, I would like to offer you an exclusive contract to handle your work. Enclosed *you will find a check for $100,000 as an advance. Ms. Johnson will be express-mailed the remaining contracts within the next few days.*

I look forward to having you as part of the Walter Black family of artists.

Sincerely,
Walter Black, Jr.

"Is this what I think it is?" Tyrone's eyes were wide with wonder. Sylvia nodded, waving the check for him to see.

Tears began to roll down Tyrone's face. He stood speechless with the woman he loved, staring at the picture he'd been painting of his daughters. Sylvia wrapped her arms around him, grateful that all the pieces were finally falling into place for her man.

36

ANTOINE AND KEISHA

Antoine sat in his living room, staring at an unopened envelope from the Washington, D.C., school district. Impressed by the recent effort Tyrone made to further his art career, Antoine had decided to take a step up the education ladder and try for an administrative position. He had sent his résumé to over a dozen districts that had advertised openings for school principals. In the last two weeks he had received five envelopes similar to the one he was holding in his hands, and he was afraid this would be another nicely worded rejection. When he just couldn't stand the suspense any longer, he tore open the envelope and read the letter inside.

Dear Mr. Smith,

Thank you very much for interviewing with the greater Washington, D.C., school district. After long consideration, we would like to offer you the position of principal of our new high school for literature and mathematics. As you probably know, the board was impressed with your curriculum ideas and strategies for increasing S.A.T. test scores, evidenced by your success in increasing the scores in your present school.

We understand that a decision of this magnitude takes time, so we don't expect an answer right away. But please understand that the district would like to have someone in place by the end of this school year. I look forward to hearing your answer within the next few weeks.

Sincerely,
John Diamond
Superintendent of the
Washington D.C. Schools

"Yes! Yes!" Antoine jumped in the air, shouting. He headed for the door and ran down the stairs to Keisha's apartment. Opening her door with his key, he danced his way into her apartment.

"Keisha, honey, where are you?"

"In the kitchen, Antoine."

Antoine ran into the kitchen and found her cooking dinner. He wrapped his arms around her waist, kissing her gently.

"Dinner will be ready in about twenty minutes." She closed her eyes and enjoyed his soft kisses against her neck. "Antoine, hon, you'd better stop or I'm gonna burn this chicken."

"Let it burn. I'm taking you out to dinner tonight anyway." He placed kisses all over her neck and shoulders.

"What's gotten into you?" Keisha turned off the stove and faced him.

"I was just offered a job as principal of a high school!"

"Oh, Antoine, I'm so proud of you." She kissed him excitedly. "I guess that means if I'm bad, I'm gonna have to go to the principal's office."

"Yeah, I'm going to have to come up with a real special punishment for a bad seed like you."

"So what borough are you going to be in, sweetheart?" she asked as she led him into the bedroom.

"I'm not. I'm probably going to have to move to D.C. at the end of the school year," he replied, unbuckling his pants.

"What?" she barked, snapping her head toward Antoine as her skirt hit the ground.

"I'm moving to D.C. You knew I applied to a school district in D.C. I thought you'd be happy for me."

"You said D.C. was a last resort! There's over a hundred high schools in New York City alone. What about the schools in Long Island you applied to?"

"The city schools wouldn't give me fair shake without a recommendation from Maurice, and the Long Island schools all hire from within."

"Well, maybe that was true when you sent out your applications, but what about now? Maurice is in jail. They should be givin' you his job anyway."

"What am I supposed to do, Keisha? Wait around to see if they would consider me for that job? Opportunities like the one in D.C. don't come around every day. I can't just pass it up because of what *might* happen."

"Antoine, you can't move to D.C." She had stopped undressing by this point in the conversation.

"What do you mean, I can't? Look, Keisha, you're my girlfriend, not my mother. Don't you ever tell me what I can or cannot do," he said angrily. "I don't tell you what to do with your beauty shop. Don't tell me what to do with my career."

"What the fuck is that supposed to mean? I been bustin' my ass, trying to conform to what you think a good woman should be, ever since we started going out. Then you give me shit because I want you here with me and your fucking baby? Fuck you, Antoine!"

Behind all the attitude she was throwing, Keisha was close to tears.

"You must think you're talking to one of those girls in your shop. Don't you dare use that kind of language with me." He hesitated, then grabbed her shoulders. The true gist of her statement finally sunk in. *"Baby!* Oh, shit! Don't tell me you're pregnant."

She nodded, looking down at the floor.

"When the hell were you going to tell me? On the way to the delivery room? Jesus Christ! This can't be happening."

"I just found out this morning when I went to the doctor. Why the fuck you trippin' anyway? You're gonna be a great father."

"Maybe I don't want to be a father. You ever think about that? God! How the hell did this happen anyway?"

"How the fuck you think it happened? You stuck your dick in me."

"You did this on purpose, didn't you?" he accused.

"No, I didn't do it on purpose! But I'm not ashamed of it. I'm thirty-five years old, Antoine. How many more chances am I gonna get to have a baby?"

"Damn! Why couldn't you have waited till we were married?" He was in a state of panic.

"Because you never asked me to marry you. You've been layin' up with me for over four months and I haven't even heard you say, 'I love you' once. So why the fuck would I think you're going to marry me?"

Her words struck Antoine deeply. There was no way he could deny that they were true. In the time they had been together, she had told him she loved him on several occasions, but he just could not bring himself to say it to her.

"You know how I feel about you, Keisha. I just don't want a baby right now. This whole thing's just going to fuck up my life."

She gasped, devastated that he could think their child would ruin his life. It made her furious that he was being so selfish.

"If you were so damned worried about me getting pregnant, how come you never used a condom or even asked me about birth control?"

"Birth control's a woman's job, not a man's," he argued, pounding his fist against the wall.

"Oh, my God! I know you don't believe that, do you? How can one man be so smart and so stupid at the same time?"

"I don't know what I believe. I'm not even sure if this baby is mine." He regretted the comment as soon as he said it.

Keisha, enraged, began to sob as she grabbed a heavy book from a shelf and threw it at him.

"Motherfucker, if you don't wanna be this baby's daddy, you don't have to be. But don't you ever accuse me of being a slut. Now get the fuck out my apartment!" she screeched.

He thought about apologizing for his last comment, but Keisha gave him no time as she continued her tirade.

"You oughta be happy I can have your baby. That's more than I can say about the last bitch you fucked with!" She grabbed her crotch as if she were a man.

Antoine was too distraught to even ask her what the gesture was supposed to mean. He put on his clothes and walked out of her apartment back to his own. He was numb. He never expected to conceive a child out of wedlock. The truth was, Keisha was right. He had been stupid.

In his apartment he slumped on the couch. He wondered how he could have had sex with her for months and not ever talked to her about birth control. He was not ready to be a father, and now he was feeling trapped because of his own stupid mistake. He picked up the phone and dialed Kevin's number.

"Hello," Kevin answered, breathing hard.

"Hey, Kev, this Antoine. You got a minute? I really need to talk."

"I'm kinda busy, Antoine. Can I call you back in about a half hour?" He was still breathing hard, and Antoine wondered if Kevin had gotten back with Denise when he heard a female voice in the background calling "Hang up the phone, loverman. I want some more."

"Okay, just make sure you call me back. Keisha's pregnant," he blurted out. The words had shocked Antoine with their directness, and they must have floored Kevin. There was silence on Kevin's end of the call.

"Kevin, did you hear me?"

"Sorry about that. I had to go to another room to get some privacy. Did you say Keisha's pregnant?"

"Yeah, she is. And I don't know what I'm going to do. Think you can sneak out and have a drink? I really need to talk things out."

"No problem, Antoine. You know I'm here for you, bro. But you should talk to Tyrone, not me."

"Don't get me wrong, Kevin. Tyrone's my best friend next to you, but you said it best yourself. We're like the devil and the angel. We never see eye to eye on anything."

"Look, Antoine, Tyrone's matured a lot since he's been with Sylvia. Plus, I don't know anything about kids. You guys keep forgettin' I'm only twenty-three. He's been in your position two times, and you've seen what kind of father he is. Look, he's gonna be at the school until nine. Miles is letting him clean out his locker. Why don't you run on over there and talk to him?"

Antoine had long forgotten how young Kevin was. He had taken for granted that his friend was older because of the maturity with which he carried himself. But young or not, he was right. Tyrone had more experience than both of them when it came to dealing with pregnancy and children. Antoine just hoped his friend could put aside the jokes for once, because he knew he would not be in a humorous mood.

"You're right, Kevin. I'm going to catch a cab over to the school right now."

Antoine walked down to the cabstand next to Benny's Bar, at the corner of his block. He asked the dispatcher for a cab, then stepped outside to wait.

"Antoine, what's up, my man?" Benny the bartender was standing in the doorway of his bar and had spotted Antoine on the sidewalk.

"Hi, Benny, how you doin'?" Antoine walked over to shake his hand.

"Good, real good. I heard you and Keisha hooked up. Now, that's what I call a woman. You better watch out. A girl like that will get you into trouble." He winked.

"You don't know the half of it," Antoine replied sadly, but the sentiment went unnoticed by Benny.

"Ay, whatever happened to that stripper, uh, I mean makeup woman, you used to go with?"

"Man, we'd probably be planning our wedding now if she had quit her job at the Men's Club, but I really don't want to talk about it right now."

"No problem, man." Benny said good-bye and walked back into his bar.

Antoine's cab pulled up to the sidewalk, and he climbed in the backseat.

"Where to, boss man?" the cabdriver asked in a heavy foreign accent.

Antoine hesitated for a second. He had intended to go straight to the school to seek Tyrone's advice about the baby, but now he knew he had something else to work out first. He could not begin to make decisions about his impending fatherhood until he was certain that there was no chance for him and Shawna to be together.

"Six fifty-four Highland Avenue in Jamaica. I'm going to see an old friend."

37

ANTOINE AND SHAWNA

During the ride to Shawna's apartment, Antoine changed his mind about fifty times and almost told the driver to turn around and bring him home. But he knew that if he didn't face the situation then, it would come back to bite him later. And even though he wasn't quite sure how he felt about Keisha, he knew he at least owed her a true explanation of his feelings. So he continued his cab ride to Shawna's in the hope that he would be able to sort out his confused feelings.

As the cab arrived in front of Shawna's apartment, Antoine paid the driver, his hands shaking nervously as he handed over the money. The cabdriver smiled gratefully when he told him to keep the change. In his anxious state he didn't notice that he had handed the man a twenty-dollar bill for an eight-dollar ride. He stepped out of the cab and walked slowly up the pathway, each step full of fear and anticipation.

"Who is it?" Shawna asked when she heard his knock.

"It's Antoine, Shawna. Can I come in?"

Shawna couldn't believe he was standing outside her door. A million thoughts ran through her mind at once. She missed him deeply and was overjoyed that he was there to see her. He had been her first real boyfriend and she could not deny the love she still felt for him. But her happiness was tainted, because she knew that if she acted on her love and reconciled with him, Keisha would surely tell her secret to exact some revenge. As she looked through the peephole, her defenses melted with the sight of that baby face that she loved so much. There was no way she could ask him to leave without talking to him.

"To hell with Keisha," she thought. "I'll figure that out later."

"Just a minute, Antoine." She straightened out her tight-fitting dress and took a deep breath, praying silently that he and Keisha had broken up.

Unconsciously she arched her back slightly, so the first thing he noticed when the door opened were her much-enhanced breasts.

"Hi, Antoine, it's good to see you. What brings you over to this side of town?" she asked as casually as she could.

For a second he was speechless. He couldn't believe how beautiful she looked with her face recently made up and her hair in braids. And as much as he tried not to stare, his eyes were drawn immediately to her shapely new breasts.

Shawna blushed. There was no doubt about what he was looking at.

"Like the new addition?" she asked proudly, doing a quick model turn right there in the doorway.

Her boldness embarrassed Antoine, and he tried to take his eyes off her chest and look her in the eye. Almost involuntarily they traveled straight back down to her new curves. Shawna adored all the attention and could have stood there to let him stare all day, but she spotted her nosy landlord peering at them from his garden. So she invited Antoine inside.

Nervously he stepped into her apartment and walked straight to the love seat in her tastefully decorated living room. The colors were muted pastels, the paintings that hung on the walls were mostly still lifes. As he looked around the room, he happily noticed that his pictures were still hung throughout. It felt good to know she still thought about him.

"So, what brings you over here?" Shawna asked. There were three other chairs in the room, but she sat down next to him on the love seat, their thighs touching.

"I was just in the neighborhood and thought I'd stop by. It's been a long time." He paused and looked directly in her eye. "I wanted to make sure we were still friends."

"Well, you can't be my friend, Antoine."

"Why?"

"Because all my friends give me a hug when they come over."

She smiled flirtatiously, opening up her arms. He hugged her tightly, and the tension left his body. She was so soft, he didn't want to ever let go.

"I missed you, Shawna. I really missed you."

"Not as much as I missed you." She broke their embrace and looked at him seriously. "But what's up, Antoine? I know you well enough to realize that you just don't pop up on anyone."

"Yeah, you do know me pretty well, don't you?" He took his glasses off and wiped them with his handkerchief. "I need to ask you a question."

"Ask me anything you want." She was nervous.

He was silent for a few seconds. He was afraid to speak for fear she would tell him she no longer felt the same way about him. Glancing down at her hand, he saw the engagement ring he had given her. It was still on her left ring finger, and the sight of it gave him the confidence to ask her where they stood.

He touched her hand, then the ring. "Shawna, do you still love me?"

In an instant Shawna knew she wanted to scream yes at the top of her lungs. But the image of Keisha stopped her. She knew that starting over with Antoine left her very vulnerable to being exposed, and she wasn't sure if she was ready to deal with that. Somehow she needed to be sure that her rival was no longer a threat.

"Well, that all depends," she said hesitantly. "Is it true that you're dating Keisha?"

Antoine's face dropped. He could not imagine how she could have known about him and Keisha. Maybe she was just guessing, but he didn't want to risk lying about it. Things were such a mess, he had nothing to lose at this point.

"Well, yeah, we've been seeing each other."

"Oh, you've just been seeing each other, huh? I never did understand what you could see in that hussy."

"Wait a minute, Shawna." Antoine was upset with Keisha, but he couldn't let Shawna disrespect her. "I don't expect you to understand why I would be with her. You two obviously had your differences, but she and I found that we have more in common than I thought. What was I supposed to do? Be alone for the rest of my life?"

"The rest of your life? What are you saying, Antoine? Do you love her? I need to know if you love her." Shawna was so afraid of what he might say, her hands were trembling.

Antoine exhaled loudly, wiped his face with his handkerchief, and stood. This was very difficult, and he had to put a physical distance between them. He paced across the room.

"I don't know if I'm in love with her." He lowered his head in shame. "Some days I wake up and think she's everything I ever needed. Other days I wake up wishing it was you lying next to me." He stopped walking and looked straight in her eye. "God, Shawna, I don't know. I might be in love with her. That's part of the reason I'm here."

"I don't understand."

"Before I can have anything with Keisha, I have to be sure that we're over. That you don't love me and you don't want me." He walked over and took her hand. "I might not be sure if I love Keisha. But I'm positive I love you."

Shawna closed her eyes and took a deep breath. She was surprised when she felt Antoine's lips pressed warmly against hers.

Oh, my God, Antoine, you don't know what you're doing, she thought as she accepted his tongue into her mouth. When she finally broke the kiss, she stared into his eyes for almost a minute without speaking. There didn't seem to be a road she could take that wouldn't be paved with sorrow. If she took Antoine back into her life, she would have to live in constant fear of her secret being revealed to him by Keisha. But if she told him it was over, she would mourn his loss for a long, long time.

"Antoine, why did you come here? If only you knew how complicated you've just made things." She pulled her hand out of his grasp and stood. "I still love you, Antoine, more than anything in the world. I just don't think you can accept me for who I am."

"Shawna, I love you. And if I really love you, I have to accept you for who you are. But you're right. I still don't know if I can deal with the thought of you being naked around other men." Antoine folded his arms to make sure his point hit home.

"How many times do I have to tell you? I'm not a stripper, I'm a makeup artist."

All the anger and hurt she had felt during the end of their relationship came rushing back stronger than she imagined it could.

"Maybe we don't need to be together if you can't even trust me!" she shouted as she rushed into her bedroom. After all the time she had spent missing him, the strain of having Antoine with her again and all its uncertainty was more than she could bear. Her bedroom was the only place she could escape to think for a few minutes.

Antoine waited quietly in the living room for her to return. He wanted to chase after her but decided he better give her some time to cool off. It was a confusing moment for both of them, and he could understand the emotional roller coaster she must be on just then. After all, he did just show up on her doorstep after nearly five months and expect her to pour out her heart.

Finally she returned from the bedroom carrying a large photo album. She stood in front of Antoine, holding the book. He waited for her to say something or put the book down, but she didn't. He decided she must be waiting for him to speak first.

"What's this for?"

"This is the story of my life. It's a scrapbook I've kept since I was about ten years old."

She flipped through the pages until she reached one near the back of the book. As she examined the page, a smile came to her face. Antoine was glad to see it replace the sadness in her eyes and was eager to see what had made her happy again.

"What's that, Shawna?"

"These are the certificates I won two weeks ago. Want to guess what they were for?" she asked sarcastically.

Before he could answer, she walked over to a shelf and picked up a trophy. She laid the photo album on the shelf in the space where the trophy had been and brought the award to Antoine.

"You might not think this is much," she told him defiantly, "but it means something to me. And it proves I was telling you the truth about the Men's Club all along." She handed it to him.

"For Shawna Dean, nineteen ninety-eight exotic makeup artist of the year," Antoine read out loud as a look of regret came across his face.

"Oh, my God, you really are a makeup artist." He placed the trophy on the coffee table. "I don't know what to say."

"There is nothing to say. You should have trusted me, Antoine." Tears rolled down her face.

"Oh, my God!" she said as she felt the tears. "Look at my mascara running all over my face." She rushed out of the room again.

Antoine sat alone again, feeling the weight of his mistake. If he had been more trusting in the first place, he and Shawna would never have broken up, and he would not be in the mess he was in with Keisha. Instead, he had listened to the suspicions of people like Benny and Tyrone and allowed their doubts to become his own. Now Shawna was crying in her bedroom, and he didn't know what he could do to change things.

He wandered around and looked at the snapshots of the two of them that were still displayed on bookshelves and side tables throughout the room. He looked at each of them fondly as he recalled how happy they had once been. Picking up the trophy from the coffee table, he read the inscription once more and walked sadly over to the shelf to replace it. He lifted the photo album and replaced the award.

Settling on the love seat, he flipped through the album to learn more about the woman he loved and thought he had lost for good. The further he got in the book, the more obvious it became to him that this album that supposedly represented Shawna's life was full of photos not of her but of some young man. Antoine assumed from the resemblance that he must be Shawna's brother. It wasn't until he came to the more recent photos that he began to find pictures of Shawna.

"I didn't say you could look at that!" Shawna practically shrieked as she ran panic-stricken out of the bedroom. She snatched the book away from him violently and ignored the look of confusion on his face.

"Sorry, Antoine, I'm not ready to share this book with you yet," she told him as she wrapped her arms tightly around the cover.

"I'm sorry. I wasn't trying to pry, Shawna."

"I know, Antoine. It's just that this album holds all the secrets to my life." She was still clutching the book tightly. "And I don't think I can share them with anyone yet."

"That's fine by me," he answered nonchalantly, although his mind was racing, trying to imagine what kind of secrets she could be so protective over. To start with, he wanted to know who was the young man in all the early photos, hoping his identity would shed some light. He tried to make his question sound as innocent as possible.

"But why didn't you tell me you had a brother?"

"What brother? I don't have a brother."

In Shawna's nervousness, her mind did not make the simple connection between Antoine's question and the pictures of her pre-hormone-injection days. She hadn't looked at the early photos of herself for quite some time because she couldn't stand the way she looked before she had her Adam's apple shaved down. As it dawned on her exactly what Antoine was referring to, she was relieved that the doorbell rang before she answered him.

"Oh, that must be Roberta. I'm supposed to do her face for a date tonight."

She walked over to the door and looked through the peephole. Relieved to see that it was indeed Roberta, she opened the door slowly, trying to think of an excuse to get rid of her before she said the wrong thing in front of Antoine.

Please, don't let her run her big mouth, Shawna prayed, hoping that her friend would notice the expression on her face that was meant as a warning to be careful about what she said.

"You sure took your time," Roberta barked, walking past her into the living room. "Oh, I'm sorry. I didn't realize you had company," she said as she caught sight of Antoine.

"No, that's quite all right, Roberta. I was just about to leave."

"Antoine, why don't you stay and watch me do Roberta's makeup? Then you'll understand why my job is needed at the club."

She was right. Made up, Roberta's looks were barely passable, but as she stood in Shawna's living room now with no makeup on, she was downright ugly.

Shawna had asked him to stay because she had an ulterior motive. She had decided fifteen minutes before, while she was brooding in her bedroom, that she was going to give him more oral pleasure than he had ever had. When she discovered him with her book, she had been coming out to seduce him. Her mind was made up. She had convinced herself that after he felt the magic skill of her mouth, he wouldn't care *who* she was. Roberta's knock on the door had only delayed her plans as far as she was concerned. Once she finished the woman's paint job, she was going to give Antoine a royal treatment that he would never forget.

"I don't know, Shawna. Maybe I'll just go over to Benny's and have a drink. I really need to think."

"Please, Antoine. You can have a drink here. I really want you to stay so we can finish our discussion later. Maybe I can clear up some of your questions."

He looked at his watch. It was after nine, and he knew the school would be locked up, so he couldn't go talk to Tyrone. The thought of going to Benny's was suddenly not so appealing, since he realized that Keisha might be there. He figured that staying there would be the lesser of two evils.

"Sure, why not? I'd love to see what you do." He sighed as he got up and walked over to the small bar Shawna had set up. He poured himself a strong drink. While his back was turned, Shawna hid the photo album, hoping he would forget about it, at least until she had him hooked.

Shawna sat Roberta in a chair in the living room and Antoine was impressed as he watched her slowly transform her friend into a rather decent-looking woman. When Shawna finished, Roberta stood up and ran to the mirror in the bathroom.

"Oh, girl, you outdid yourself," she exclaimed as she walked out of the bathroom.

"I didn't do anything. I keep telling you I'm just bringing out the beauty that's there," Shawna lied to spare her friend's feelings.

"Oh, my God," Roberta said. "Look at the time. I gotta go." She hugged her friend, then looked at Antoine. "It was nice seeing you again, Antoine. I told Shawna you were the kind of guy that would love her for who she is and not what she was."

"Well, I know you have to go, girl," Shawna interrupted loudly as she shoved Roberta to the door. "Antoine and I have so much to talk about." She didn't wait for Roberta to respond before she shut the door in her face.

"What was that all about? What did she mean, love you for who you are and not what you were?"

Shawna walked over to the love seat and sat down beside Antoine. She literally had a thousand different thoughts running through her head. Each one of them was more confusing than the next. After a long while, during which Antoine kept shifting uncomfortably in his seat, she decided it was time to lay all her cards on the table.

"I have something to tell you, but first I want a kiss," she told him in barely a whisper.

Antoine looked at her affectionately. He was afraid that she was going to tell him that she was a prostitute or that she had cancer. What he was about to hear would change the way he looked at women for the rest of his life.

He leaned forward to kiss her and was pulled in tightly by Shawna's urgent grip. She kissed him as passionately as she could, exploring his mouth with her tongue until Antoine broke the kiss, gasping for breath. Shawna knew this could possibly be their last kiss, and she wanted to remember it forever.

"Wow, that was some kiss!" He was still gasping for air. "Now, what did you have to tell me?"

Shawna stood up and began to pace slowly in front of him. She wanted to tell him the truth, because she knew he was going to find out soon enough. Her charade would not last forever, and she was finally admitting it to herself, though she had known it all along. Even if by some miracle she could prevent Keisha from giving up the information, someone like Roberta would eventually slip up. Shawna wanted him to hear it from her first. When she finally gathered her courage, she spoke rapidly.

"That wasn't my brother you saw in my album." This was one of the most painful moments in Shawna's life, but she knew there was no turning back now.

Antoine watched her for a few minutes. Slowly the reality of the situation was seeping into his consciousness. Before he asked his question, he had an inkling of what the answer would be, and he was terrified.

"Well, who is it, then?"

"It's me," Shawna said so quietly that he could not hear.

"What did you say?" He stood up, struggling to hear her words.

"It was me in those pictures, Antoine." She moved away from him slightly.

"That's not even funny, Shawna. That would mean you're a man."

He looked at her beautiful new breasts and around at the feminine living room. It was nearly impossible to fathom that this person he had fallen in love with was really a man.

Shawna was silent, trembling.

"Shawna, why would you play with me like this?" He started to become agitated. "Just tell me who's in the picture."

She began to cry and repeated her words. "It's me. But I'm going to have an operation soon to become a complete woman."

There were no words for the rage that overtook Antoine. What come out of his mouth sounded more like a roar as he threw anything that was within his reach. Framed photos flew across the room and shattered against the wall. Books landed in every corner after he ripped the pages out. In a frenzy he pounded his fists against the wall until there was a gaping hole in the Sheetrock. Then he turned his fury on Shawna.

She tried to escape his reach but did not move fast enough as he lunged at her over the love seat. He grabbed her hair and yanked her head around as he screamed obscenities at the top of his lungs.

"You motherfucker! Tell me this is some kind of sick fucking joke! Tell me you're not a man! Tell me you are not a man!"

The words flew out faster than a locomotive, and his fists flew just as fast, pounding Shawna about her face and head. She fell to the floor and curled up in the fetal position.

Shawna screamed for help, praying her landlord was still outside and would hear. Fear gripped her as she imagined the end of her life. There was good reason for her to worry when Antoine grabbed a brass candlestick holder from a nearby table. He raised it high above her head, trembling, a crazed look in his eyes.

"Tell me you're not a fucking man, or I swear I'm going to fucking kill you!" he screamed. Suddenly he was startled out of his violent trance by a rapid knock at the door.

"What the hell's going on in there?" Shawna's landlord demanded.

Antoine dropped the weapon, which landed with a thud very near Shawna's head.

"You are so fucking lucky someone was here to stop me, because I swear to God, you were five seconds away from being dead," he hissed as he turned to leave. Shawna did not budge from her defensive posture on the floor.

Throwing the door open, Antoine came face-to-face with her landlord. Without a word he shoved his way past him and stormed out of the building. The landlord rushed to Shawna's side and slowly helped her up from the floor. He helped her limp to a seat and grabbed the phone.

"What are you doing?" she asked painfully through her swollen lips.

"Calling the police. What else would you expect me to do about that animal?"

"Please don't do that," she begged, and he looked at her incredulously.

"What are you talking about? He could have killed you!"

"I know, I know," she answered sadly. "But it's much more complicated than you know."

Mr. Good couldn't imagine anyone having a valid reason for doing the damage that he saw to his apartment and to Shawna's face. But he had learned long ago to stay out of his tenants' business. He placed the phone back on the receiver and went to the kitchen to get ice for Shawna's face.

38

ANTOINE, TYRONE, AND KEVIN

It was almost midnight when Antoine finally stumbled to the block he lived on. He had walked home from Shawna's. It had taken two hours, all of which he spent deep in thought. For at least the first two miles it was all he could do to control his rage and not go back and finish the job. But as he walked farther, he realized that would not solve the problem he was left with. Even if Shawna were dead and gone, he knew he would never trust any woman as blindly as he had trusted her. And much, much worse, he now had doubts about his own sexuality.

He worried that perhaps there were obvious signs about Shawna's true identity that any perfectly straight man should have recognized. His mind wandered back over the length of their relationship, and of course he was able to come up with things he felt he never should have missed.

She was awfully tall for a woman, with those big damn hands. Why didn't I know what she really meant when she kept talking about her operation? No breast operation costs so much that you need to take a second job. And no woman nowadays is so uptight about giving some up unless she's got something to hide. He shuddered at his own ignorance about what he now thought were obvious details.

A wave of nausea hit him as he realized that less than two hours before he had had his tongue inside Shawna's mouth. He silently thanked God that things had never gotten further. As difficult as it was to remain celibate during that time, he was now extremely grateful. If much more had happened, he would be in need of some serious psychiatric help. Stopping suddenly, he doubled over and threw up on the sidewalk for the fourth time. The first time was right in front of Shawna's building.

As he approached his own neighborhood, Antoine stopped in front of Benny's Bar, his hand on the door. All he wanted to do was end all the painful thoughts and self-doubt that were swirling around in his head. He knew that Benny could mix a few strong drinks that would take care of that. Opening the door slowly, he glanced around at the bar's patrons. Benny saw him at the door and waved to him. Antoine returned the wave with a weak smile but knew he couldn't go in there. He was in no mood for pleasantries, even if Benny was his favorite bartender and somewhat of a friend. He closed the door and trudged toward his own building.

He planned to open a bottle of rum and drink himself into oblivion. The irony of the situation hit him as he remembered the last time he had gotten dangerously drunk in his apartment. Then, he had been drunk because he had lost Shawna. Now he wanted to get drunk to lose any memory of her. His head pounded with an intensity he had never felt.

Passing Keisha's apartment, he paused momentarily. A thought crossed his mind. At least with Keisha he had proof that she was indeed a woman. Maybe he could go to her and apologize, then give her some good loving the way only a real man can. He laughed wryly and imagined pounding his chest like Tarzan, a true he-man.

Although some good sex might have dispelled his own fears just then, he knew he wouldn't be getting any from Keisha that night. After all he had said to her during their fight earlier, she wouldn't be giving anything up without another round of verbal abuse. Antoine knew he couldn't put himself in that situation. He didn't want to risk letting Keisha get a rise out of him because all his rage at Shawna was still pretty close to the surface. It could resurface at any time, and Keisha didn't deserve any of the pain he still wished he could inflict on Shawna.

"Yo, Antoine, what's up?" Tyrone's voice startled him. He and Kevin were sitting on Kevin's car, parked at the curb in front of Antoine's building.

"What's up, guys?" he answered sadly. "I didn't even see you standing there."

"I can see that." Kevin walked over to his friend and spoke gently. "What happened to you, man? Tyrone and I waited at the school till ten o'clock for you. I was worried about you. You okay?" He could see that Antoine was not in good shape.

"Sorry, guys," he replied, unable to look his friends in the eye. "Right now I feel like less than a man."

"You're not the only one to feel like that after you got your girl pregnant, Antoine," Tyrone told him. He had made a promise to himself that he would refrain from his usual jokes tonight. He knew how it felt to be worried about a pregnant girlfriend. Jokes were not what Antoine would need from his friends.

Tyrone placed his arm around Antoine's shoulder sympathetically. "I couldn't even look in the mirror when my girl got pregnant with my first daughter."

Antoine looked up at his friends. He had shared most, if not all, of his personal life with the two of them in the past year. Now he was at a crossroads. Should he tell them that Shawna was a man? Would they understand and be supportive, or would they laugh and ridicule him? He was desperate for someone he could talk to about the depth of the situation, but something stopped him from telling his best friends. Recalling their night in the Men's Club, he remembered that Tyrone had seemed to be enjoying Antoine's trouble. Tyrone seemed to think it was funny that Antoine's girl might work in a place like that, and he kept egging Uncle Billy on to tell more about the most raunchy aspects of the club. Antoine was afraid that if he shared his latest dilemma, Tyrone might find a way to twist that into a joke also. He wasn't ready to take that chance yet, so he decided to keep Shawna's secret to himself.

"Look, why don't we go upstairs? I don't want to see Keisha right now," Antoine suggested. The three of them walked up the stairs to Antoine's apartment and sat down in the living room.

"So, your girl's pregnant, huh?" Tyrone stated this more than asked, ending a five-minute silence.

"Yeah."

"Does she want to keep the baby?"

"Yeah, at least that's what she told me." Antoine lowered his head in shame.

"What about you, Antoine? What do you wanna do?" Tyrone asked as he searched his pockets for a cigarette.

"If you had asked me that a couple of hours ago, I would have told you the last thing I want is a baby. But I've had some time to think things through." Antoine looked over at the picture of Keisha. "Real men take care of their responsibilities, don't they?" He looked at Tyrone, then at Kevin. They both nodded their agreement.

Tyrone was especially proud of Antoine at this moment, because he felt a man's greatest responsibility was to his children. It had taken him years to earn the trust of his daughters' mothers after his initial desertion. After he made the decision to truly devote himself to his girls, their mothers eventually praised him for his fathering ability, even though neither woman was able to make a relationship with him work. Tyrone knew it was pretty rare for a single woman to speak as highly about the baby's father as these two spoke to their daughters about him. He also knew that the next best thing for a child, if the parents couldn't stay together, was for the parents to be respectful to each other. For Antoine to say he was ready to accept the responsibility of fathering was a first step in the right direction.

"I'm a real man, right?" Antoine asked, his mind on things totally different from Tyrone's. He was still concerned about his sexuality. "I mean, you wouldn't think I was gay or anything, would you?"

"Of course you're not gay. We *are* discussing the fact that your girlfriend is pregnant, aren't we?" Kevin gave Antoine a confused look. "What the hell are you talking about anyway?"

"That's right, Keisha's my girlfriend. One hundred percent woman, wouldn't you say, fellas?" He smiled, ignoring Kevin's question. "You always said you liked her body, didn't you, Tyrone?"

Before Tyrone could answer, Antoine was babbling again.

"What did you guys think about Shawna?"

"She was all right. I really didn't get to know her that well." Kevin wondered why Antoine was acting so strangely paranoid.

"Would you have gone out with her if you met her first?" Antoine continued to interrogate the men.

"I don't know, Antoine, that's your ex-girl. I never looked at her that way." Kevin wrinkled his brow in confusion as he answered.

"What way? You didn't think she was attractive? Or you didn't think she was a woman?"

"Hold on a minute, Kevin." Tyrone stopped his friend from answering. He was worried about the bizarre way Antoine was acting. "Antoine, are you okay? You're acting a little strange, man."

Usually, of the three of them, Antoine was the most rational and the most logical. He wasn't prone to ranting the way he was then. This behavior was way out of character for his friend, who usually made so much sense.

"What's going on, Antoine? And don't bullshit me," Kevin demanded.

"Look, I've got a problem and I really want to talk to you guys about it." Antoine cupped both hands around his face and sighed. "It's just that it's so embarrassing." He suddenly felt sick again as another image of him and Shawna kissing flashed across his mind.

"Look, man, you don't have to be embarrassed around us. We're your brothers. We're not going to laugh at you." Kevin gave Tyrone a dirty look. "Right, Tyrone?"

"Listen, Antoine, I know I joke around a lot, but I also know when to be serious. I know tonight is not the night to be joking you. Believe it or not, I can be sensitive once in a while too." Tyrone smiled kindly. He wished there were some way he could help his friend out of the obvious pain he was in.

The thought of telling his friends he had been intimate with a man for the better part of a year made Antoine feel nauseated. But the thought of living with the knowledge alone made him feel worse. His friends' kind words had made him feel that he could trust them with his horrible secret. Finally he got his stomach under control and wiped away his tears.

"I don't even know how to tell you guys this—" He was still trying to get the words out.

"Hey, brother, just say what's on your mind," Tyrone replied gently, trying to help. He went to stand beside his friend as a show of moral support in this obviously difficult time.

"I think I might be gay." He couldn't look them in the eye.

Both Kevin and Tyrone were stunned into silence. Kevin was so shocked that he unconsciously took a few steps backward.

"Look, Antoine, I'm not into that gay shit. So if this is a joke, it ain't funny," Kevin told him seriously.

Instinctively he knew Antoine would not be the one to play a joke as deep as this, but he wished his friend would say he was only kidding. For all of his promises of support for Antoine, he wasn't sure he could handle this.

"I said I think I might be gay. I'm just a little confused about a few things and was hoping you two might help me figure it out." Antoine's words were defensive. He could hear the homophobia in every one of Kevin's words and wished he had kept his mouth shut.

"What would make you think you were gay? I mean, you like women. Don't you?" Kevin asked, searching for any way to help his friend conclude he was straight. He was worried that he wouldn't be able to maintain this friendship if he thought Antoine was really gay. "And what do you mean by 'figure it out'?" he continued. "I'm tellin' you, Antoine. I'm not into that gay shit."

"Sit down, Kevin," Tyrone demanded, suddenly taking charge of the situation. He was appalled at Kevin's sudden lack of support.

"Antoine is supposed to be our best friend, our brother, and you're treating him like piece of shit. You should be ashamed of yourself, man." Kevin sat down without a word.

"Now, what the hell would make you think you were gay? You're about as gay as I am." Tyrone turned his attention toward Antoine.

"Would you say being in a relationship with a man for the better part of a year would classify you as gay, or at least bisexual?"

"Yes, I would, but are you telling us you've been having a relationship with a man that we didn't know about?" Tyrone was totally confused. "How'd you have time between Shawna and Keisha?"

"I didn't. That's just it. I just found out tonight that Shawna's a fucking man!" Antoine shouted. A rush of relief swept over him as the words finally came out. He looked at his friends for a response, but they just stared at him in shocked silence.

"Now, that's some deep shit," Tyrone finally said, not quite sure what else he could say after a revelation like that.

"He didn't say what I think he said, did he?" Kevin asked Tyrone in a monotone. His eyes never left Antoine's face.

"I said Shawna's a man," Antoine repeated. The words came easier the second time, as if he were lifting an enormous chain from around his whole being. "Can you believe it? I was dating a chick with a dick and didn't even know it."

Both Kevin and Tyrone sat silently as Antoine began to recount the events as they had unfolded at Shawna's apartment. Kevin felt shame for the conclusions he had jumped to just minutes earlier when his friend had first mentioned the word "gay." After Antoine had been given a chance to explain his fears about his own sexuality, Kevin knew without a doubt that the fears were unfounded. His friend was not gay.

Hearing his story, Kevin could understand how Antoine would temporarily lose his mind. He was glad his friend had not actually acted on his murderous thoughts, but he could understand the rush to violence. And he could understand the paranoia Antoine was experiencing. Both Kevin and Tyrone knew they would have to rally around their friend to help him through this very emotional time.

"Like I said before, that's deep." Tyrone broke the silence. He lit a cigarette and took a long drag before he continued. "She sure had me fooled. Usually when I meet a tall chick, I check for an Adam's apple.

But she was pretty good, 'cause the few times I've been around her, I never spotted the slightest bulge in her neck."

"No, Tyrone, there were some signs," Kevin interjected. "We just never looked for them. I remember when I was dating Alicia she used to always say that there was something strange about Shawna. And what about at the Men's Club? Remember what that Amed guy said to Billy? 'I didn't know you were into her type, Big Daddy.' The signs were there. We just never really looked for them."

"I can't believe I was such a fool. Her hands were bigger than mine. I should have guessed right away!" Antoine cried.

"I don't know what to say, Antoine, except I feel for you, man. If it was me, I would have broken every bone in her goddamn body." Kevin looked at his friend sympathetically. "Damn, if it was me who was dating a man, I would have taken this information to my grave."

"Hold on a minute, Antoine." Tyrone stood up and walked over to his friend, taking a drag on his cigarette before crushing it in a nearby ashtray. "First of all, you're not gay. In order for you to be gay, or even bisexual, you would have to have known that she was a man and accepted the relationship for what it was. Second, if I had met her first, I would have tried to hook up with her. So you're not gay. We're all stupid."

"He's right, Antoine. We all thought she was a woman." Kevin patted his friend on the back. "Look, I'm sorry about the way I jumped on you when you said you thought you were gay. I let you down when you needed my support. Maybe I'm not always as mature as I think I am."

"That's all right. I'm not as mature as I think I am either." Antoine stood up and stretched, walking over to the picture of Keisha on his table. "All I can do is think about myself while poor Keisha's downstairs worried about if she's going to raise a baby by herself. Serves me right for finding out about Shawna. I was an asshole for even going over there when I knew Keisha needed me."

"Yeah, you were," Tyrone replied with brutal honesty. "That woman loves you, Antoine. But you never gave her a real shot because inside you wanted to be with Shawna."

"I gave her a chance—"

"Who you fooling, Antoine? Yourself maybe, 'cause you're not foolin' me." Tyrone reached into his wallet and took out a picture of his girls. "You fucked up, Antoine, just like I fucked up when I got my daughters' mothers pregnant. Now it's time to make up for that mistake and be a good father."

"Tyrone, I'm not even sure if I'm in love with Keisha."

"You don't have to be in love with her to be a father. You just have to be a man. Go downstairs and talk to her, man. Tell her exactly how you feel. Then work on your problems. If you two don't stay together, then, so be it. Just take care of your child. I promise it'll be worth your while."

"Thanks, man." Antoine wrapped his arm around Tyrone in a hug. "I needed to hear that. I'm just glad I heard it from you."

"No problem, brother. Listen, I have to get back to Sylvia. She's getting the rest of her things out of her house. It'll be just my luck Maurice will make bail while she's in the house by herself. Who knows what else he's crazy enough to do."

"I better get back too. Alicia's probably getting worried," Kevin added, looking at his watch.

"Alicia?" Tyrone gave Kevin a strange look, then smiled. "Talk about a blast from the past. When'd you hook up with her?"

"About a month ago. I was waiting to see if everything was gonna work out before telling y'all."

"Well, is it?" Tyrone asked.

"Better than I coulda ever imagined."

"What about that order of protection?"

"She had it rescinded."

"Well, I hope she finally gave you some?" Tyrone looked skeptical.

"A gentlemen never tells." Kevin smiled from ear to ear. Tyrone shook his head, laughing as he walked down the steps to Kevin's car.

"I hope you know what you're doin', Kev. I like Alicia, but you know what happened last time," Antoine cautioned.

"I know, Antoine, but things are different this time. Alicia's changed a lot." Kevin patted Antoine on the back. "And so have I." He followed Tyrone down the steps.

"Listen, guys, I really appreciate what you've done for me tonight. Every man should have friends like you," Antoine told them.

Antoine watched his friends leave and looked up at the star-filled night sky, saying a small prayer of thanks for his friends. After how they supported him tonight, he knew he could not ask for better men by his side. With the newfound strength that their conversation had given him, he resolved to face Keisha. He knew it wouldn't be easy, but he was willing to deal with her anger at his betrayal. He was willing to be a man and take care of his responsibilities.

He walked down the block, heading for an all-night deli. As he entered the shop, he smiled at the Korean man behind the register and went straight to the assortment of flower arrangements near the back. He picked out a small bunch of lilies, Keisha's favorite flower, then headed back toward Keisha's apartment. He was unsure of what was about to take place. It was entirely possible that she would still be too angry to even let him in the door. He hoped that she would invite him in though, because he felt confident that they could work things out to do right by this child. He knocked timidly, holding the flowers in front of him.

"Who is it?"

"It's me, Antoine."

"Why didn't you use your key?" Keisha opened the door with major attitude.

"I was afraid you might not want to see me. But I brought a peace offering. I thought you might like these." He raised the flowers to her and smiled humbly. Keisha tried to hold back a smile as she grabbed the flowers from him.

"This doesn't change anything, ya know. I'm still gonna have this baby whether you like it or not."

She turned to walk away but left the door open, and Antoine took it as a sign to enter. He followed her into the living room and sat next to her on the couch.

"I know nothing's changed, sweetheart. I guess you just caught me off guard earlier. The last thing I was expecting was for you to tell me that you're pregnant. But I'm here now, and I'm always going to be here." He kissed her.

"Oh, Antoine, I just want us to be happy. I love you so much and I want you to be happy that I'm carrying your baby."

She was so happy about his change of heart that she could no longer keep the attitude she had been trying to use to punish him. She threw her arms around him.

"I'm happy too, but I'm not going to lie. I'm a little confused about us." He gave her a little squeeze, then looked into her eyes. "Keisha, I love that you're a beautiful, bright woman. But I'm just not sure if I'm in love with you." He braced himself for a smack, but it never came.

"I understand," she said, looking up at him sadly. "You need more time. I know I can't force you to love me. Just promise me you'll be around when the baby needs you."

"I'm going to do the best I can, Keisha."

They sat silently for a while, both trying to collect their thoughts.

"Oh, Antoine," Keisha finally told him with very little emotion. "Shawna called. She said you broke your watch during the fight at her place. She's going to have it repaired and mail it to you." Her expression never changed, and he couldn't tell if she was upset that he had been over there.

"She also said to tell you she was sorry." She still wasn't giving away anything with her facial expression.

"I don't need her to apologize. If you knew what she was apologizing for, you'd flip."

"I do know. I've known for quite some time," she answered gently.

"Wh-why didn't you tell me?" He stuttered in shock. He couldn't believe that she had known such monumental information and chose to keep it a secret. She was supposed to love him.

"Did you really want to know, Antoine?" She hesitated, giving him time to think about his answer. When he didn't respond, she continued.

"Look, Antoine. I know you've always cared about Shawna more than you cared about me. Don't you think I had every reason to want to destroy her chances of ever being with you again? Telling you this secret would have been the best way for me to get rid of my competition, wouldn't you agree?"

"You're right, I suppose."

Antoine hung his head shamefully. He realized it must have hurt Keisha deeply to learn that he had gone to Shawna's apartment on the same day he learned of her pregnancy. Yet here she was, telling him how she had considered his feelings before her own in this whole mess.

"Keisha, I've been so selfish lately. I'm finally starting to see that the whole time I've been with you, I've been thinking about my own needs. I was so wrong, and I'm so sorry."

Keisha hugged him tightly. His words were comforting to her after all the pain she had felt that day.

"Antoine, I've been through a lot for you. I went through a lot to get with you, and I've worked really hard to be who I thought you wanted me to be."

"I know, Keisha. You have gone way beyond what I deserve for the selfishness I've shown you. It's time I start behaving like an adult."

"Yeah. Maybe you could take a few lessons from me," she said playfully, lessening the tension between them.

"Maybe you're right," he said, laughing in reply. "So, can we start over, Keisha? I will make every effort to give you the best that I have from now on."

"I want that for me, and for this baby of ours," she told him as she placed her hands on her stomach.

"For both of you." He smiled, placing his hands on top of hers.

For several minutes neither spoke. They held each other tightly as each reflected on the day's events. Both knew that they had a long, difficult journey ahead of them. But if they could make it through the challenges that lay ahead, each had faith that they would do what was best for them and their child.

Suddenly a thought came to Keisha, and she pulled away from Antoine. She looked him directly in the face. Her question was not exactly accusing, but there was fear in her voice.

"What about that job in D.C.? Are you still taking it?" She was afraid he would once again put his career desires first and leave her alone in New York.

Antoine breathed a loud sigh before he answered.

"Earlier today I never would have thought I would say this. But I'm going to call them and tell them I can't take the job. I have more important things to take care of here right now." Antoine wasn't happy about having to make this decision, but he felt good knowing he was doing the right thing.

"Oh, Antoine!" Keisha threw her arms around him. "I am so proud that my baby will have a father like you. And you know what they say, what goes around comes around."

"What do you mean?"

"You're doing the noble thing for your child. That unselfish decision can only bring you good. I bet there's still a job waiting for you somewhere here in New York."

"I hope you're right, Keisha." He sighed again, holding her. He felt ready to face whatever formidable tasks were in store.

39

TYRONE AND SYLVIA

Kevin and Tyrone got into Kevin's car and buckled their seat belts. Neither of them said a word until the car was a block from Antoine's apartment. Each was silently trying to digest the story their friend had just told them.

"Well, what do you make of that?" Kevin finally asked as he pulled up to a stop sign.

Tyrone stared into space.

"Tyrone, did you hear me?" he asked after receiving no response.

"Yeah, I heard you. I was just thinking about what I would have done in Antoine's situation." He shook his head in disbelief. "I'll be honest with you, Kev. A year or two ago I would've gone to the first crack house I could find. I'd be sucking on the glass pipe, tryin' to forget all about my girl bein' a man. And when I spent up all my money, I'd be scheming to get some more."

"Damn, you were really hooked on that shit, weren't you?" Kevin knew he would also have a nearly impossible time in Antoine's situation, but he was amazed at Tyrone's solution.

"Kevin, there was a time I would have sold my soul to the devil for another hit," he admitted. "Who am I fooling? I would have sold your soul to the devil, too, if you let me."

"Yeah, that stuff's pretty bad. My cousin Chip sold all my mama's silver for twenty dollars once, just to get some crack," Kevin recalled.

"Let me tell you somethin' about crack. It's the most dangerous drug man has ever made. Not so much because it destroys individuals, but because it destroys families." Tyrone looked out the window at the housing project they were passing. "Crack will make you steal from your mama, your daddy. Hell, I'm embarrassed to say it, but I stole my daughter Donna's mother's food stamps when I was smoking."

"Get the fuck outta here!"

"Kevin, I'm not gonna lie. I was so far down the food chain, once I thought about selling my body for crack." Tyrone hung his head in shame and embarrassment.

"What stopped you?"

"I swear to God, Kevin, if you tell anyone about this, I'll kill you." Tyrone looked at Kevin seriously. "That includes Alicia. I know how easy it is to share secrets with your woman."

"Listen, Ty. This seems to be the day for revealing secrets. But you can trust I'm not gonna tell anyone. So, what stopped you?"

"No one stopped me. I stood in the street for about three hours one night, tryin' to get someone to pull over. But I was looking so bad and so skinny back then that as soon as any cars pulled up, they'd speed off, probably afraid that I had AIDS or somethin'." The memory of that chapter of his life made Tyrone shiver.

"So, if some guy had pulled over, you woulda done somethin' with him?" Kevin looked over at his friend with the same homophobic look he had given Antoine earlier.

"Look, Kevin, I hope you don't mind, but I'd rather talk about something else." Tyrone could see that his friend might not be mature enough for this type of conversation. Kevin was a good friend, but he had already proven once that day that he was not totally removed from his conservative upbringing. Tyrone decided to end the conversation before things got silly.

"Sure, man, I'm sorry. I can see where that could be painful to talk about." They both became silent as Kevin tried to concentrate on the road. "Ty, can I ask you somethin'?"

"Yeah, sure, man. As long as it's not about crack or getting high."

"Are you really goin' to move to California?"

"I'd like to, but I don't know if I can." Tyrone bit his bottom lip, and his expression changed to one of unhappiness. He was torn between his desire to start a new life and the knowledge that he couldn't just go.

"Why not? You always said you wanted to get the hell out of New York. Here's your big chance."

"Don't you think I know that?" Tyrone rolled down the window and lit a cigarette. "There is nothing I'd like better than to pack up everything and move Sylvia to the West Coast." He exhaled the smoke wistfully, daydreaming about the art career he could embark on in

California. "But I got responsibilities here. You keep forgetting about my two daughters. My girls need their father, and I need them."

"Damn! First Antoine can't move to D.C. because Keisha's pregnant, then you can't move to California because you're afraid of being separated from your kids. I'm beginning to think kids're more trouble than they're worth."

"I'd do anything for my girls, Kevin. I'd never just leave them. I made that mistake once before."

Both men were silent for a while as they drove to Sylvia's house.

"I'm thinking about movin' back to Virginia when the school year ends," Kevin announced to break the silence.

"Why? You just hooked back up with Alicia. I thought you said things were goin' good."

"They are. If I go back home, I'm takin' her with me."

"And she's going for that?"

"It was her idea. She can't stand New York anymore. It's got nothing but bad memories for her."

"She sounds like Sylvia." Tyrone threw the cigarette out the window. "Sounds like you two already made up your minds?"

"Not entirely, but we're getting there. We've spent a lot of time talkin' about it."

"Well, whatever you do, I'm happy for ya."

"Of that, my brother, I had no doubt." Kevin smiled.

"Go down to the corner and take a right," Tyrone told Kevin as he maneuvered down the elegant streets of Jamaica Estates. Unlike most other parts of Queens, this area was full of large stately homes on wide, tree-lined streets.

"Damn, I never knew they had houses like this in Queens." Kevin was amazed at the beauty of the well-kept homes.

"Neither did I until I met Sylvia, but this is nothin'. You should see the houses her friends live in out on Long Island. Now, that's living!"

Tyrone directed Kevin to Sylvia's house, a large five-bedroom brick Tudor with ivy growing over the front of the house. There was a large moving van in front of the house and five very beefy movers carrying boxes from the house to the truck. Kevin pulled the car in behind the moving van and Tyrone stepped out.

"Hey, man, thanks for the ride," Tyrone said as he opened the car door. "I'll see you at work tomorrow." He paused and then laughed. "Damn, I keep forgetting I don't work there anymore."

"You won't forget after you cash that hundred-thousand-dollar check." Kevin laughed, reminding his friend of his good fortune. "Tyrone, I love you, brother. Don't be a stranger just 'cause we don't work together anymore."

"Don't worry, bro. Other than my moms, you and Antoine are the only family I got." Tyrone waved good-bye as Kevin backed out of the driveway. Looking over his shoulder, he saw Sylvia walking out of the house toward him.

"What's wrong, sweetheart?" she asked, wrapping her arms around him.

"Nothing, I just realized how lucky I am to have two friends like Kevin and Antoine."

Tyrone put down the two suitcases he was carrying and smiled as he stepped out of Los Angeles International Airport. He put on a pair of dark sunglasses when he felt the bright sunshine on his face. Closely behind him followed Sylvia, holding the hands of his two young daughters. Both girls were excited to be in California after their long plane ride. Another woman walked behind them, carrying the girls' luggage.

The woman was Lynn, the mother of Tyrone's younger daughter. Although she and Tyrone had not been a couple for over eight years, they were able to come to an amicable agreement that allowed Tyrone to move to California without losing contact with his daughter Kim.

After Kim was born, Lynn, who was only eighteen at the time, took various minimum wage jobs to support herself and her infant. She had always known she had the potential to obtain a college degree. But after Tyrone deserted her, she was alone. Her life was reduced to work and child care, and she spent many lonely nights resenting Tyrone for leaving her alone with such a huge responsibility.

It was not until Tyrone returned and joined her in parenting Kim that she was able to be less bitter. Over the years the two had been able to develop a friendship that enabled them to give Kim all the love she needed to be a happy, well-adjusted little girl. When Tyrone wished to leave New York, he approached Lynn with a plan that would benefit all of them.

Sylvia and Tyrone would move out to California, and Kim would live with them. Lynn would also move to the West Coast and get her own place, close to her daughter. Out of his hundred-thousand-dollar advance, Tyrone had given ten thousand dollars to Lynn so she could find an apartment and begin paying college tuition. Lynn was ecstatic to finally be getting the chance to pursue a higher education. She would study for a degree in hotel and restaurant management, an interest that had developed over the years she worked in fast food restaurants. They had agreed that after Lynn finished her schooling, she and Tyrone would reconsider the arrangement to work out some sort of joint custody.

Kim was overjoyed to be moving. She liked Sylvia and was proud to tell her friends at school that she would be living with her daddy out where all the movie stars live. But the happiest detail for her was that she would actually get to live with her half sister, Donna.

Donna's mother, Bettie, had been approached with a similar arrangement but declined. She had a fiancé in New York and had no interest in leaving the state. At first she told Tyrone he would have to be satisfied with visitation for a few weeks during every summer vacation. Tyrone didn't argue with her, but after a few days he returned to her with another idea.

Like Lynn, Bettie had shouldered the responsibility of raising her child alone for a long time. It had not been easy. In her immaturity she falsely believed that all she needed to rescue her was the right man. A string of bad relationships left her in even worse financial straits, feeling totally degraded. She finally met Maury, a New Jersey car dealer, who showed her the love and respect she needed. They had great plans for their future and had expected to include Donna in them.

When Tyrone approached Bettie the second time, he talked to her about how he understood the difficulties she had endured. He accepted responsibility for some of it and apologized again for not growing up soon enough. But he explained to her that he was now settled in his life and wanted her to have the same chance at satisfaction that he had been given. He begged her to consider sending Donna to California just for a year so that she and her fiancé could begin their life together. It would give Bettie the time she had never had to concentrate only on herself.

Bettie wouldn't give him an answer immediately but discussed the issue very seriously with both her fiancé and her eleven-year-old daughter. The decision was not an easy one for any of them. Donna wanted to stay with her mother because they had been together for so long, she couldn't imagine living apart. But she was, after all, still a child, and very enticed by the idea of a pool in her backyard and her younger sister under the same roof. After much heartbreaking discussion they decided that Donna would try it for a year, visiting New York during each of her school vacations.

Now the group was happily standing outside the airport terminal, watching a driver pile their luggage into the trunk of a limousine. As soon as they had claimed their bags, Tyrone was prepared to hail a cab to take them all to the hotel where he had reserved two adjoining rooms. To their surprise, a chauffeur stood near the baggage carousel with a sign that announced he was waiting for the Jefferson party from New York.

As they climbed into the luxurious limo, the girls immediately opened the miniature refrigerator and pulled out two sodas. Tyrone stretched his legs out and smiled.

"We're going to the Los Angeles Hilton," he told the driver.

They planned to stay there for a week or two until they could find a house. Lynn had already rented an apartment, so after dinner Tyrone would put her in a cab and send her to her new home.

"I'm sorry, sir," the driver told him, "but Mr. Black has asked me to bring you to him before you go to the hotel. He has some details he'd like to work out with you."

Tyrone gave Sylvia a quizzical look, but she just winked at him. She had overseen most of the contracts for Tyrone's employment with Walter Black. For the most part, he just signed whatever she put in front of him. Now he had no idea what other details Walter could need to discuss with him. He smiled nervously at Sylvia, then leaned back on the headrest, closed his eyes, and enjoyed the first limo ride he would take in Los Angeles.

Tyrone fell asleep during their ride to the beautiful Hollywood Hills section of Los Angeles and had to be awakened by Sylvia when the limousine pulled into the driveway of a large white stucco house. The house, a beautiful contemporary that was landscaped with colorful flowers, shrubs, and fruit trees, was situated on top of a hill overlooking the city.

"Man, look at this view." Tyrone whistled as he stepped out of the limo. "That Walter Black sure knows how to live." Sylvia just smiled at him.

"Mr. Black will see you inside the house."

The chauffeur walked around to the trunk. He opened it and removed the suitcases, which he took over and placed next to the entrance.

"Hold on, man," Tyrone told the chauffeur. "You might as well leave that in the trunk if we're going to the hotel."

"Just following Mr. Black's instructions, sir."

"Well, my dear, I guess it's time I meet the mysterious Mr. Walter Black. So far he's been full of surprises, wouldn't you say?" Tyrone squeezed Sylvia's hand. She placed her head on his shoulder as they happily walked to the front door.

Walter Black, a tall, well-groomed man, opened the door and gave his guests the smile that had won him so many loyal patrons over the years. He reached out his large, powerful hand to shake Tyrone's, then welcomed the group into the house.

Inside the foyer, sunlight poured in from the skylights in the cathedral ceilings. The girls gasped at the size of the entryway and the spacious living room to the left. This part of the house alone was bigger than any apartment either girl had ever lived in. They raced into the living room, where there was a white grand piano, without waiting for an invitation.

Tyrone was about to reprimand them, but Walter Black stopped him with his hearty laugh. The adults stood in the foyer and engaged in small talk about the flight and the beautiful scenery they had enjoyed on their drive to the home. The girls, meanwhile, tested every overstuffed seat in the living room, then continued their exploration into the kitchen. After a few minutes they raced back to their father, bursting with news.

"Daddy, Daddy, Daddy!" shouted Donna. "You have to come see this kitchen. Everything is just sparkling, and it's so big, there are *two* refrigerators! Can you believe it?"

Everyone laughed as Kim continued the narrative where her sister had left off.

"If we lived in a house like this, we could use one whole refrigerator just for ice cream," she fantasized. "Are we going to live in a house like this, Daddy?"

"Well, girls," Sylvia answered for Tyrone, "as a matter of fact, we are going to live in this house. Your rooms are right up those stairs." She pointed, and both girls tore up the staircase, squealing with delight.

Tyrone's jaw was hanging open as he looked at Sylvia, trying to understand what had just happened.

"What are you talking about, Syl? I know Walter gave me a generous advance, but don't you think we should start smaller than this?"

"Tyrone, darling," she said sweetly. "You seem to forget that we're a team now, and you're not the only one with money, you know. I have had my eye on this house for years, ever since I first started visiting Los Angeles. When I started negotiating your contract with Walter he let me know that this place was available."

"Are you sure we can afford this?" He was unable to believe any of this was truly happening.

"I guess you really *don't* know what she's worth, do you?" Walter laughed. "Besides, I expect that with the art studio I had built in the back for you, you're going to be one productive artist for Walter Black Enterprises. Money is not going to be a concern for you, I'd say."

"Uh, art studio?" Tyrone stammered.

"Sylvia, you saw the plans. Why don't you take him back there and show him? I'm going to head back to the office and let you all get settled," Walter told them. "I'll see you in my office tomorrow morning to introduce you to my staff, Tyrone."

"Mr. Black, I can't thank you enough for everything. I look forward to a long, prosperous relationship with your company," Tyrone told him as the men shook hands.

After Walter had gone, Lynn headed upstairs to check on the girls. Tyrone whooped and hollered, then ran through every room in the house. In each room he would look at Sylvia with a child's awe in his eyes. Ending his run back in the foyer, he grabbed Sylvia and swung her around in an ecstatic embrace.

"I can't even believe I'm here, Syl. I can't believe *we're* here! I owe this all to you," he told her exuberantly.

"Oh, Tyrone." She kissed him. "I love you. I love you so much."

Antoine sat behind the large desk in the office that once belonged to Maurice Johnson. After being arrested for statutory rape, Maurice had been fired and the school board scrambled to put an interim principal in place until interviews could be conducted. Antoine's reputation was stellar, and it was well known that it was his leadership ability that had turned the English Department into the highest performing group in the school. His contributions had been noted in his record many times, and since he was well respected among the faculty and staff of the school, the board decided he was the natural choice to fill the spot. Of course, they informed him that he would need to apply officially and go through the same interview process as all other candidates if in fact he were interested in becoming the school's next principal.

As he sat behind the desk, he was attempting to fill out part of the application, but his mind wandered. He thought about his friend Tyrone and wondered how his new fairy-tale life was unfolding in California. He picked up the phone and dialed the first few digits before he realized it was only five-thirty in the morning in L.A. Placing the phone back on the receiver, he smiled.

Life was really taking off for him and his friend. Antoine had a strong feeling about the possibilities of getting the principalship. This would be the ideal situation for him, since he was now dedicated to staying in New York to help Keisha raise their child. Their relationship had been strengthening every day, and he no longer doubted his potential to be a father. After the two had gone to Keisha's first sonogram appointment, Antoine saw his baby's heart beating on the monitor, and suddenly he knew what his purpose in life would be. That same night he had taken her to dinner and said the words "I love you" for the first time.

Antoine's mind then settled on thoughts of Kevin. With the recent good fortune that he and Tyrone had found, he wished his friend could find the same kind of happiness. Kevin might still have been immature in some ways, but Antoine knew his friend had a big heart and deserved some satisfaction in his life. He vowed to do whatever he could to help his friend find his way to happiness.

40

MAURICE

Maurice was terrified as he stared at the cold gray cement walls of the central booking jail. He'd been waiting three days to be arraigned, but because he was arrested on a Friday afternoon he had to wait until Monday to see the judge.

What the hell am I doing here? he asked himself. He stepped on the foot of the huge white corrections officer when the heavy steel doors slammed behind him.

"What's wrong with you—Johnson?" the officer screamed, looking down at his clipboard to find Maurice's name before pushing him away. "You really must not wanna see the judge."

"I'm sorry, officer. I promise it won't happen again."

"See that it doesn't."

Officer Kirkland gestured to the rest of the inmates waiting for arraignment to follow him. Kirkland was one of those men who needed his job to make him feel important. Outside of work he was a nobody. Inside he wielded his status as a corrections officer as if it made him president of the United States.

The group followed Kirkland down the long corridor for what seemed like forever before they reached another steel gate. Kirkland shouted to the officer in the security booth.

"I've got twelve going to see the judge!"

"No problem," the officer shouted, opening the gate.

Kirkland proceeded with the group down the corridor toward the courthouse. Before they reached their destination, he barked his final orders to them.

"Listen up, 'cause I'm only gonna say this once. When I call your name, I want you to follow me into the courtroom and stand in front of the judge. I don't want any of you to say a word unless the judge or your lawyer speaks to you. Got it?" Everyone nodded. "Now go in there and have a seat till you're called." Kirkland pointed to a ten-by-ten cage, and the inmates walked in. They sat on the floor, since there were no available seats. After an hour on the cold floor Maurice heard someone announce his name.

"Johnson!"

"Yes?" He sprung to his feet.

"Time to see the judge." Kirkland opened the gate, and Maurice followed him through a door into the courtroom.

He was relieved when his lawyer, Greg Thomas, joined him in front of the judge.

"You okay, Maurice?" Greg whispered as the judge reviewed some paperwork.

"Yes," Maurice lied as he felt his stomach begin to ache.

"Get yourself together. If we're lucky, you may be home tonight." Greg turned his attention to the judge.

Maurice tried his best to straighten himself out. He was still wearing the same suit he had on when he was arrested, minus the tie and belt the corrections officers had taken. It was dirty, but he looked more presentable than most of the other defendants he had been confined with.

"Your honor, the next case is Johnson versus the People of New York, second degree rape and endangering the welfare of a minor," the clerk said loudly.

"Well, Mr. Abraham, what do we have here?" the judge asked the district attorney.

"Your honor, we've got a high school principal having sex with a sixteen-year-old. The evidence is pretty overwhelming. Not only does the defendant admit to having sex with the victim, he videotaped it." The D.A. picked up the tape. "The people are asking for one million dollars bail."

"Well, Mr. Thomas, do you have anything to say for your client?" The judge addressed Maurice's lawyer.

"I'd like to enter a motion to dismiss, your honor." He handed both the judge and the D.A. his motions.

"What's this all about, Mr. Thomas?" the judge asked.

"Jurisdiction, your honor. The alleged crimes never took place in the state of New York. They all occurred in Vermont, where the age of consent is sixteen."

"Is this true, Mr. Abraham?"

"One minute, please, your honor." The D.A. turned and whispered to the arresting officers, who were standing behind him. When he turned back to the judge, he looked disgusted. "I'm afraid that is true, your honor."

The judge looked down at the motion in front of him and frowned.

"You know, Mr. Johnson, men like you sicken me. We put you in charge of our children, and you take advantage of them." The judge removed his glasses to rub his eyes.

Maurice nudged Greg Thomas. "She told me she was twenty-one," he whispered. Greg raised his hand to silence Maurice so that the judge could continue.

"Mr. Johnson, I have a sixteen-year-old daughter, so you have no idea how much it pains me to do this. The motion to dismiss is granted, case dismissed. Mr. Thomas, I suggest you get your client some help." The judge banged his gavel with finality.

Maurice was shocked. "Did he say case dismissed?"

"Yes, he did," Greg answered, turning to the table behind them for his briefcase. The two men walked to the back of the courtroom and out the doors.

Outside the courtroom Maurice turned to Greg. "Thanks, Greg. This is another fine mess you've gotten me out of."

"You heard the judge, Maurice. You need to get some help." There was no warmth in Greg's voice.

"Come on, Greg," Maurice insisted arrogantly, "I told you the little whore said she was twenty-one. If you had seen her first, you woulda jumped on her too."

"You just don't get it, do you? I don't care what she looked like, Maurice. The bottom line is that girl is only sixteen. Whether you're free or not, can't you see that's wrong?"

"What am I supposed to do, ask everyone I screw for proper identification?"

"How about screwing people your own age? Maurice, you have a twenty-year-old daughter. What would you do if a forty-five-year-old man took advantage of her?" Maurice stood silently, staring at his friend and lawyer. "I thought that might get your attention." Greg walked back in the courtroom, leaving Maurice to consider what he'd just said.

"You're Maurice Johnson, aren't you?" A very pretty brown-skinned woman approached him.

"Yeah, why?" Maurice was still thinking about Greg's last comment and really didn't appreciate the woman's intrusion.

Smack! The woman slapped him hard enough for everyone in the courthouse lobby to hear. The blow had surprised him enough that he almost fell over.

"I'm Valerie Gordon's mother, you son of a bitch! How dare you violate my daughter?" She tried to swing again, but a teenage girl held her back.

"Come on, Ma," the girl pleaded.

A small crowd gather around and Maurice was still trying to steady himself from her blow.

"Let go of me, Valerie!" the girl's mother commanded.

Maurice took a good look at the girl when he realized she was the one he had left in Vermont and spent three days in jail for. She didn't look twenty-one now. She looked sixteen in her jeans and sweatshirt, but Maurice knew it was her, minus the sexy clothes and makeup. She'd worn a weave over the weekend, but now her hair was in cornrows, and she really did look like a child. *What the hell did I do?* he thought, for the first time feeling some true remorse.

"You think you gonna get away with rapin' my baby and leavin' her up in Vermont? Well, I'm here to tell you when my husband comes home on leave from the army next month, your ass belongs to us!" Maurice was about to offer a sincere apology, but she swung, landing another loud smack against his face. Two sheriff's deputies stopped her before she could land another blow.

"Let her go, officers. It wasn't her fault, it was mine," Maurice said through clenched teeth.

"Okay. But you get out of here," one officer told him. Maurice nodded and walked toward the courthouse exit. In all his escapades he had never thought enough about the women he mistreated to care that they were someone's daughters, someone's sisters. But Greg's words reminded him that if the same situation were reversed and it was his Jasmine who was left in Vermont, his heart would be broken. Greg's words weighed heavy on his conscience, and Valerie's mother's slap burned on his face.

Maurice made sure he was the last one in, to give himself time to try to calm his nerves. As he entered the room and glanced around at the people waiting behind the Plexiglas partitions, he spotted the woman he had been so eager to see. He walked slowly to the partition and sat in front of her.

Three weeks before, Maurice had been arrested for statutory rape and endangering the welfare of a minor. Now, although he was a free man, things could not be worse for him. His wife left him for a school security guard and cleaned out his bank accounts. He lost his job even though he won the case against him. The New York City Board of Education did not care whether Maurice was in New York or Vermont. The fact that he had sex with a minor, especially one who was enrolled in their school system, was more than enough grounds for his dismissal.

Now, at the suggestion of his psychiatrist, he was sitting in front of the one person he believed could answer some questions and help him make some changes in his life. He picked up the phone nervously.

"Hi, Diane." He smiled. He had not seen the woman since junior high school, and she was more beautiful than ever.

Diane was fifty-eight years old with a dark complexion that was smooth as silk. Her long black hair was streaked with gray and put up in a bun, and her dress was a prison-issue orange that brought out the red tints in her skin. She was a stunning woman, and the years had been very kind.

"Do I know you?" she asked in a seductive Haitian accent.

"Come on, Diane, it's me, Maurice." He stared at her in amazement. Almost thirty years had gone by, and she still had the same affect on him.

"Maurice? Maurice who?"

"Maurice Johnson, from Bobby Kennedy Junior High School? You took me to Chicago and Indiana, remember?" He could see by her expression that she still had no idea who he was. "Reese. You use to call me Reese."

She looked at him strangely, then her eyes opened wide.

"Oh, my cute little Reese with the red suspenders."

"Yes, that's me." He sighed, happy that she finally recognized him.

"You're Reese Johnson?" She took a long, hard look at him.

"Yes, Diane. I'm Reese Johnson. Everyone calls me Maurice now." He smiled at her, turning his head to the right so that she could see his best side.

"Damn, you got old!" She frowned.

The insult was like a slap in the face, but Maurice tried to keep his emotions under control.

"Yes, Diane, I've gotten a little older. I guess we all have."

"So how'd you find me anyway?" she asked, taking a long drag on her cigarette.

"They've got something on the Internet called findanyone.com. It cost five hundred bucks, but it was worth it."

"So, I guess you think you're pretty smart, huh, finding me in jail and all." She never gave him a chance to answer. "So, Mr. Smarty Pants, what brings you all the way up here to see me? Looking to testify against me for what I did to you in the past?"

"No, Diane, I would never testify against you. Besides, the statute of limitations passed a long time ago."

"So, what do you want, then?"

"Some answers. There hasn't been a day gone by that I haven't thought about you and what you might be doing."

"I thought about you too, Reese. You were different from the others." She took another drag on her cigarette as she pictured him in his youth. "It was more than sex for you, wasn't it?"

"Much more, Diane." He swallowed hard, trying to continue without shedding a tear. "I was in love with you. I would have done anything for you. I just never understood why you left me in that motel room."

He couldn't hold back the tears any longer. Diane looked at him with pity as she touched the glass. Her explanation was absurd, but in her warped mind she found it reasonable.

"It was your beard, Reese. One day I woke up and noticed you were getting facial hair. It was the most disgusting thing I had ever seen. I honestly became repulsed by the fact that you were getting older." She looked at him and cringed. Any hint of sympathy had completely vanished. "And you're even more repulsive now that you're older. It's making me sick just thinking that I used to sleep with your old ass." She spit on the ground in disgust.

Maurice sat in stunned silence for a long time. Diane smoked her cigarette, seemingly unconcerned. Maurice couldn't believe what he was hearing. She had been the love of his life. He would have gone through hell and high water for the woman, and now he was learning she had dumped him because he had hit puberty. It was more than he could fathom. As he struggled to regain his composure, he couldn't help but think his entire life had been a lie.

So much of who he had become was based on how Diane had treated him. He really believed that she was in love with him when he was a young, impressionable student. Her sudden, cruel rejection at that campsite had shaped his character from that day forth. His terrible relationship with his parents, his failed marriage, his abuse of so many young women, could all somehow be traced back to that event. And now it was finally dawning on him that Diane was just a very sick woman. And if that were true, then he was beginning to realize his own life had been somewhat insane.

"Did you ever think what you did to me might ruin my life?"

"Do I look like I give a shit?" She let out some more smoke.

Finally he knew there was nothing more he could say to this woman. He stood up without another word and turned to walk away. Diane was incensed that he would leave so abruptly.

"Where the fuck are you going?" she shouted through the glass. "You didn't even leave me any cigarette money." She stood up and knocked on the glass to get his attention, determined to have the last word.

Maurice spun around to face her. He wanted to ignore her, but some sick fascination made him curious to know what else she had to say. He sat back down and picked up the phone.

"What?" he asked flatly.

"I just wanted to know, before you leave. Do you have any sons?" She began to laugh maniacally.

"You are one sick bitch. I can't believe I ever cared about you," he shouted as he slammed down the phone. Getting up from his chair, he took one last glance at her before the guards buzzed him out of the visiting room.

41

KEVIN

Kevin kissed Alicia tenderly as they stood at the door to her apartment. He didn't want to leave her but knew he had to get home and ready for work. Plus Alicia had made a steadfast rule that Kevin had to be out of the house before Michael woke up. She loved Kevin and one day hoped to marry him, but until that day she was going to do her best to set an example for Michael.

"Did I tell you I love you today?" Kevin kissed her.

"The way you made love to me last night told me everything I needed to know. But, yes, you did tell me you loved me." She smiled. So did he.

"I'll see you after work," he said tenderly.

"Okay." She kissed him again. "Kevin?"

"Yeah, babe?"

"I love you."

"I love you too."

They said good-bye once more, then Alicia closed her door. He heard the dead bolt lock into place. Kevin walked down the hallway and was horrified by what he saw when he opened the front door. His Honda was still parked by the curb, but long, jagged scratches stretched from the front to the back. The words *I'm an asshole* were etched into the car in at least twenty different locations. Kevin's eyes went wide with rage as he ran to the car to inspect the damage, his fists clenched angrily.

I'm gonna kill that son of bitch, Trevor, he thought. Trevor was the only one he could think of who would do this.

When he reached the car though, he found a newspaper clipping that identified the true identity of the vandal. The headline on the clipping read MAN ACCUSED OF RAPE SWEARS IT WAS A SETUP. Kevin's mind immediately registered alarm when he realized it was Denise who had done this to his car. He slumped against the hood, real fear overtaking him. The amount of damage she had done must have taken her half the night to accomplish. And in such a busy neighborhood, she must have gone to great lengths to finish it without being noticed. If she was capable of this, she was capable of making false accusations, he was sure of that.

"My God, she's really gonna do it. She's really gonna accuse me of rape," he muttered in disbelief.

His first thought was to tear the clipping to shreds, but his instincts told him it might benefit him later if he saved it. Angrily he got into his car and sped home. Now he felt even more urgency to get to work. If Denise was actually planning on going to the police, Kevin knew he needed to talk to some people who could later vouch for him. He wanted to see Antoine and Miles, the head of school security, as quickly as possible.

By the time he got home and showered, his nerves were a complete wreck. In the shower he had contemplated several times calling in sick, thinking he could never make it through a day in this nervous state. He even thought about returning to Alicia's apartment, but his terrified feeling that Denise would really go through with her plan convinced him to get to work to talk to Antoine.

He walked to his car full of trepidation, searching the neighborhood suspiciously with every step he took. His heart stopped momentarily as two white men drove by his building very slowly in a black Ford Taurus. Kevin had seen the same cars used by undercover detectives and was positive these men were there investigating charges against him.

He rushed to his car, hanging his head to conceal his face. He put the car in gear and sped past them as they stepped out the car. They stood beside their car, bewildered, as they watched him pass. Kevin didn't hear what they said but could tell that one of them was speaking about him as he pointed to the Honda. The other man nodded in agreement, and from his rearview mirror Kevin saw them get back into their car.

He raced all the way to work, checking his mirror at every turn to be sure the black Taurus wasn't following him. As soon as he arrived at work, he headed for the security office and asked Miles to come with him to the principal's office to assist with a problem.

The men arrived at the office, and Kevin gave Antoine and Miles the particulars of the bind he was in. Before the first bell the three of them discussed the seriousness of the situation and Kevin's possible options. After his experience with the black sedan, each of them fully expected that he would have to deal with the police in the near future. Miles, who had been a New York City police officer for fifteen years, recommended that he make a journal to account for his whereabouts over the weeks since his breakup with Denise. Kevin would need to remember where and with whom he had been on certain days. He needed to be prepared for whatever the police asked him. Antoine arranged for coverage for several of Kevin's gym classes so that he would have time to get his documentation straight.

An hour later he was still sitting in the faculty lounge, compiling the journal, when Antoine and Miles came in, followed by the two white men.

"Kevin," Antoine told him, "these men are here to talk to you. I think it would be in your best interest to do so."

Antoine's voice sounded very official, and Kevin momentarily felt betrayed. Then he realized that his friend was only doing his job. If in fact these men were police, he couldn't reasonably expect his friend to conceal his presence in the school building. He took a deep breath and prepared to defend himself against the false charges he was sure these men were about to inform him of.

The two men sat at the table across from Kevin. Miles and Antoine stood silently in the doorway, and Kevin tried not to make eye contact with anyone.

"Mr. Brown," the first man began, "my name is Byrant Marx, and this is Fred Harmon. We have something we'd like to talk to you about."

Kevin nodded seriously but offered no words in reply.

"I work for your agent, Mr. Hirschfield, and Mr. Harmon here is the coach of the Italian basketball team, the Allegro."

"Basketball? You mean that Italian team that keeps calling my mother?"

Kevin was totally confused. He had been mentally preparing for arrest, and now these men were there to talk to him about basketball. He turned to Antoine, who was standing in the doorway with a huge grin on his face.

"Mr. Brown," said the coach, "our team was very close to winning the European Championship last season. We're very interested in your talents, because we believe that with you at point guard we could win the championship."

"I really appreciate that, but basketball just isn't for me anymore," Kevin repeated automatically as he had a hundred times before to his mother. "I haven't even played organized ball since the Hornets cut me almost two years ago."

"We're willing to hire a personal trainer to get you in shape for the season. And I'll be honest—you look like you're still in tremendous shape."

Kevin smiled at the compliment. After all of his lunchtime sessions in the weight room with Antoine and Tyrone, he was without question in the best shape of his life.

"Can you honestly tell me you haven't thought about basketball?" Coach Harmon asked with a smile. He had been coaching for over twenty years, and the one thing he knew about star athletes was that they always thought about the glory days.

"I took a look at the films of you in the NCAA Division II Championship game. I was impressed. I've got a seven-foot-two center who would work perfectly with your style, Kevin. I'm asking you to come play for me."

"I wish I could, Coach Harmon, but I have a new relationship starting and we're moving to Virginia to be closer to my mother. And my mother really needs me. There is no way I'm leaving the country now." Kevin lowered his head after Antoine caught his eye and frowned at his answer. "I'm really sorry, especially since you're right, I do want to play basketball again. But now's not the right time for me."

"Mr. Brown, I totally understand what you're going through. But before you can take care of others, you have to take care of yourself."

Kevin laughed. "You sound like my mother."

Marx scribbled something on a piece of paper and passed it, folded, across the table to him. "This is the amount the Allegro are willing to pay you to play basketball for them. I think for this kind of money your mother and new girlfriend might be willing to move to Europe. What do you think?"

Kevin unfolded the paper and read it. *One million dollars per year for two years with a $300,000 signing bonus.* He refolded the paper and stared at Marx. His mind was spinning. He never dreamed they would offer him so much money. He couldn't calculate the number of years it would take him as a teacher to earn that kind of money. With this kind of money he could pay off the hospital and get them off Mama's back.

After so many months and years of denying his love for the game, with this offer in front of him Kevin had to finally be honest with himself. He did still love the game and he did still want to achieve his dream of a professional basketball career. A wave of hope washed over him as he recognized how close he could be to reaching that goal. These men were here offering him everything he had ever hoped for.

"Is this offer serious?"

"I have the contracts for you to sign in my briefcase, as well as a cashier's check. Minus my agency fee, of course." Marx reached for his bag.

"Kevin," the coach told him, "we understand the problems you had with the NBA, but if you're willing to take a drug test, we'd love to have you."

Kevin looked over at Antoine. As much as he wanted to sign the papers, he needed some reassurance from his friend that it was the right thing to do. Antoine tried to act as professionally as he could, smiling as he discreetly nodded his approval to Kevin.

Kevin was relieved that they had been so open about the issue of his failed drug test and that they showed faith enough to give him a second chance at his dream. He easily agreed to another test, certain they would find nothing, since he had vowed to never make that mistake again. For another half hour the men worked out the particulars of the deal. Kevin would be allowed to finish the school year as a teacher, then fly directly to Rome to be evaluated by the team's physicians. Provided the drug test results were negative, he would return to the States to get his affairs in order, then return to Italy in October for the start of their training camp. Mr. Marx and Mr. Harmon agreed that they could give Kevin a week to discuss their offer with Alicia and his mother. After that time they would meet again to finalize the contracts.

After the meeting ended, all involved exchanged handshakes, and Miles escorted the two men out of the building. Antoine and Kevin stayed in the faculty lounge, and an awkward silence surrounded them as Antoine settled into a chair across from Kevin.

"I guess both of my best friends are leaving me, huh?" he asked sadly.

"Yeah, it looks that way. I wish I could say something that would make it easier. I can't believe how much things have changed in just a year."

"Looks like the Three Musketeers are going their own separate ways," Antoine mused. "The amazing thing is that we all had things change for the better."

"Who you tellin'?" Kevin laughed as he marveled at how far each of them had come in one short year. "You're interim principal. Probably gonna be principal. Tyrone's starting a career as a professional artist. And me, all of a sudden I'm gonna be a pro basketball player, even if it is for a European team."

"Well, I guess our ladies could have picked worse, wouldn't you say? Take the rest of the day off, Kevin, and go see Alicia. You can afford it now." He patted his friend on the back and returned to his duties as interim principal.

Kevin watched Antoine walk out of the lounge, then looked down at the paper on which the offer was written. A wide smile spread across his face, and he leaned back in his chair. His life was almost perfect now. He had Alicia's love, and now it looked like he wouldn't have to worry about Mama's financial problems. Now, if he could just figure out what to do about Denise.

42

DENISE

Denise paced back and forth as she stared out the window of her plush office. In the three months since she and Kevin had split, she had lost almost fifteen pounds. When they had first met, she had the figure and grace of a supermodel. Now she looked more like a drug-abusing child of the sixties. Her clothes were two sizes too big and hung on her gaunt frame. Her hair and makeup had not been done in days, making the dark circles under her eyes even more prominent.

Since the night she had seen Kevin's car in front of Alicia's apartment, her mental health had been in a vicious downward spiral. It started when she took out her key and repeatedly scratched vulgarities into Kevin's car. The job had taken her hours, and every time a car passed or someone walked by, she knew she was in danger of being caught. She didn't care. Her only concern was sending Kevin a message.

For days she obsessed about the fact that he had been to Alicia's. In Denise's warped mind Alicia was the only thing preventing them from getting back together. She repeatedly made calls to his apartment and actually spent a twenty-four-hour period parked in front of Alicia's building with a knife when Kevin wasn't answering his bell. When Kevin never showed, she was bold enough to pound on Alicia's door in the middle of the night. A neighbor finally told her that Alicia and Michael had moved with the help of a nice young man. The neighbor never said Kevin's name, but in her heart Denise knew it was he who had helped them move, and she was enraged.

Meanwhile, she was still trying to function as a lawyer for the firm. She had continued to take on cases, although her success rate had slumped to nearly zero since the breakup. Her father started to worry about her performance at work but never asked her what was the cause. All he did was offer her time off to get herself together, which Denise refused. The final straw happened during a malpractice case over which a black woman judge presided. The case was not going very well for Denise, who was unprepared, and the judge had made many rulings against her. After the judge overruled several of her objections, Denise lost it in the courtroom. Jumping over a table and diving toward the judge's bench, she screamed nearly incoherently, "I'm sick of you black bitches ruining my life!"

She was immediately escorted from the courtroom and held in contempt of court. Her license was suspended pending disciplinary hearings by the bar association. For over a month she stayed at home, waiting for the bar's decision, staring at the walls and refusing to eat. She had assigned her private detectives to search for Kevin and was waiting impatiently to receive word from them. They were having trouble finding him since the academic year had ended and he no longer taught at the high school. Finally they were able to confirm that he had flown to Europe and was about to embark on a European basketball career.

Upon hearing the news Denise was ecstatic. She decided that no matter what happened with her law license, she was going to take a year off from work and move to Italy. That way, with Alicia in the States, she could rekindle her relationship with Kevin. She thought a baby was probably the best way to keep Alicia at bay, so she threw away her birth control pills. She had even gone so far as to buy airline tickets, but the detectives advised her to wait in the States until they could get more definite information about Kevin's schedule and location. Reluctantly Denise waited, but when she could no longer stand hanging around her house, she returned to her office.

The employees in her office knew immediately from her appearance and demeanor that she was no longer in her right mind, but since she was the boss's daughter, they kept their opinions to themselves. It wasn't too difficult for them to steer clear of her since she stayed locked up inside her office all day, refusing to speak to anyone but her secretary. Alone at her desk, she would sit for hours, plotting her next move. At one point she even contemplated murdering Alicia if it became necessary. This was what she was doing when her secretary came in to announce the arrival of the private detectives.

"Mr. Nunn and Mrs. Jones are here to see you."

"Thank God! They're almost an hour late. Well, what the hell are you waiting for? Let them in," Denise commanded.

Momentarily Lisa Jones stepped into the office, dressed in sharp size-six business attire. She looked fabulous for someone who had recently had a baby. Smiling at Denise politely, she had to work hard to conceal her shock at Denise's appearance. The woman was downright frightening. Lisa looked at her partner, Dominic, and could tell he was thinking the same thing.

"Okay, do you finally have some information for me?" Denise blurted out before they could even be seated.

"Well, he stayed in Italy until mid-July, but he's been back in the States almost six weeks, Ms. Shwartz," Dominic reported. "The reason it took us so long to find him after his return from Italy is that he didn't come straight back to New York."

"I should have figured that. Lemme guess, he went to visit his dear old mama in Virginia?" Her voice was dripping with sarcasm.

Dominic nodded. "He spent most of the summer with her."

"Well, at least he's away from that bitch Alicia."

Dominic and Lisa exchanged a glance. They knew each other well enough that they could communicate with hardly a word. They were both wondering if they should share the rest of the information they had uncovered pertaining to Kevin and Alicia. But before either could speak, Denise started firing questions at them at a frenzied pace. She was desperate for information.

"Okay, when is he scheduled to go back to Europe? I want to make sure my plane and hotel reservations coincide with his arrival." She smiled for the first time in days. "Oh, make sure you find out where he's going to be living. And, Lisa, I want tickets to all his games, home and away. Kevin's gonna need a familiar face cheering him on, don't you think?"

"Ms. Shwartz, there's someth—"

"I'm sorry for cutting you off, Lisa, but I need to know. When is Kevin coming back to New York?" The thought of him back in the city made her feel better. There was no doubt she was an addict, and Kevin was her drug.

"He's already back," Dominic stated flatly, beginning to tire of Denise's relentless questions. "He rented a van two days ago and began picking up relatives on his drive up from Virginia."

"What the hell's going on? Are they having some type of family reunion or something?"

"This is going to be a little hard for you," Dominic started to say slowly. There had been a wild look in Denise's eyes since the moment they stepped in her office. He knew she could snap at any moment, and he did not want to be the one giving her the information that would cause it.

Lisa sensed her partner's discomfort and thought it would be easier on Denise if she heard it from another woman. She rose from her chair, walked around to where Denise was sitting, and placed a hand gently on her shoulder.

"He's getting married, Denise. He and Alicia are getting married in less than a week."

"*NOOOOO!!!!!!*" Denise screamed. She dropped her head down on the desk and sobbed hysterically.

It took a while for Lisa and Dominic to calm her. When they finally did, her hysteria turned to rage, and all she wanted was revenge.

"I want you to help me set him up for rape," she demanded, glaring at the two of them. "I want him behind bars, so that he hurts the way I hurt."

Both Dominic and Lisa were silent, neither of them moving. The room was so quiet, it was as if no one were even breathing. Finally Lisa stood, shaking her head slowly from side to side.

"I've done some pretty crappy things since I became a private detective, Denise. Most of them while I was working for you. But I refuse to take part in any scheme that will send an innocent man to jail." She picked up her bag and stormed out the door, followed closely by Dominic.

"That's okay," Denise screamed at the door as they shut it. "I don't need your help. I'll do it myself!"

43

THE REUNION

Kevin, Tyrone, and Antoine stumbled into Benny's Bar on the eve of Kevin's wedding. Tonight they were reflecting on their friendship, which had started when they were merely acquaintances in a school, their one common interest a desire to work out in the school weight room. Now they were together to celebrate the marriage of Kevin and the successes of all three of them.

They were considerably drunk, having enjoyed that time-tested male ritual, the bachelor party. Tyrone's uncle Billy had hosted the party, so needless to say, there were more than enough naked women for everyone's viewing pleasure. But when things started to get a little out of hand, they left. Tyrone, who missed his friends after almost three months in L.A., suggested they go to Benny's, where they could have a drink and catch up on old times.

Benny greeted the three men warmly. Over the past year he had grown quite fond of the trio. He felt almost like a proud papa, his boys returning home after making their way in the world.

"Benny, let me have two beers for my friends and a brandy for me," Antoine said as they settled at the bar. "Matter of fact, pour one for yourself. Kevin's getting married tomorrow, and you ought to celebrate too." He patted Kevin's back proudly.

"Well, if that's the case"—Benny laughed happily—"the first round's on me, gentlemen." He handed them each a drink, then addressed Kevin. "Congratulations, young brother. You are about to embark on quite a journey. Stick with it. It's worth it."

"Thanks, Benny." Kevin smiled.

He had heard enough negative press about marriage from the men at his bachelor party. Now he was grateful for Benny's encouraging words. He loved Alicia with all his heart but needed to hear reassurance that they were doing the right thing. After all, they had been together for only a few months since their reconciliation. He could honestly say that those months had been idyllic. Alicia and Michael had accompanied him to Italy, where he proposed to her. Then they spent the rest of the summer with him in Virginia, getting to know Mama and Kevin's sisters. They had all been overjoyed when Kevin announced the engagement. Kevin and Alicia had grown to love each other even more, and their bond had deepened to the point that neither could imagine life without the other. There were times, though, when he worried they were marrying too soon. Maybe, he thought, they wouldn't be walking down the aisle so quickly if he were staying in the country. But the fact was that he was leaving, and he couldn't imagine going without her. Positive advice like Benny's just reminded him again that in his heart he knew this was the right thing for them and for Michael.

"Damn, it's good to see you guys." Tyrone held up his glass for a toast. "To my brothers and my friends. May the bonds of friendship keep us close, no matter where we are."

"Hear, hear!" Kevin and Antoine chimed in unison.

"So, Antoine, what's this I hear? I'm seated next to the new principal of the Alternative High School for Boys?" He patted Antoine on the back proudly. "Hey, if I'd known you were going to be principal, I might have stuck around."

"Yeah, the superintendent just informed me yesterday that the chancellor approved my appointment." Antoine tried to appear modest, but a proud smile soon spread across his round face.

"Those boys have a good chance of making it with you as principal, Antoine. I'm proud of you." Tyrone smiled.

"I appreciate that, Tyrone. But what do you think about this guy over here?" He gestured toward Kevin. "He's already made two Italian commercials."

"It's no big deal," Kevin said humbly. "The team's just promoting me as the next step toward a European championship. They shot the commercials as soon as they got the results of my drug test. But what about you, Ty? How are things in sunny California?"

"Things couldn't be better, my friend. I was really worried about all of us becoming an instant family, but it's working better than I ever expected."

"Well, you have to remember, Sylvia is already a mother."

"Yeah, but it's different when they're somebody else's children.

Sylvia is just starting a new life, without that bastard Maurice. She could go off and lead the single life she never enjoyed, but she chose to stay and help me raise my girls."

"You're right about that," Antoine said. "She certainly is beautiful and classy enough to have her choice of men."

"I know that. Sometimes I can't believe that she chose me. But when it comes down to it, we both have something to offer each other. Whatever it is, it works," Tyrone said with a satisfied grin.

"Amen to that," Kevin offered, holding up his glass for another toast.

"I'm actually thinking about going down the aisle myself sometime soon," Tyrone said.

Kevin and Antoine looked at each other with a knowing smile. Their friend, who had fancied himself the biggest dog of the three, was talking about settling with one woman. Tyrone had always said that marriage was a trap. It was ironic how a good relationship could change even the biggest of players.

"What about you, Antoine? Got any plans to make Keisha an honest woman?" Tyrone asked.

"I'll be honest with you guys. I haven't given it much thought. Things have been going so well between us, I'm afraid to change anything. After all that happened with Shawna, I just want to take things slowly until my head is together."

"I can respect that," Tyrone said.

"Thanks. But the good news is I'm totally into this fatherhood thing. After seeing the sonogram we decided to name the baby Antoine, Jr. I just don't think marriage is the right step for us yet."

"Hey, if it works for you, that's great. But who knows? We might be here again in a year or two toasting your wedding." Kevin raised his glass. "Here's to three guys that are no longer lookin' for love." They tapped their glasses and exchanged congratulations until Tyrone's announcement interrupted their festivities.

"Yo, Kev, I don't mean to be a party pooper, but look who just strolled through the door."

"Aw, shit." Kevin lowered his head when he saw Denise walk into the bar. "How the hell did she find me here?"

"She really doesn't give up, does she?" Antoine asked in amazement.

"No, she doesn't," Kevin said angrily.

"Damn, what happened to her, Kev? She used to be beautiful. Now she's lookin' like a crack head." Tyrone couldn't believe how sick she looked.

"I don't care what she looks like. She's ain't my problem no more." Kevin sipped his drink and refused to look in her direction.

"Duck down, Kev. Maybe she won't see you." Tyrone told him.

"It's not gonna work, Tyrone. She knows what you and I look like." Antoine took a sip of his brandy. "Sit up, Kevin. You're getting married tomorrow. You don't have to hide from her."

Kevin raised his head and reached for his beer. He finished his drink in one gulp. "Where is she, Antoine?"

"Over at the bar."

"Not anymore. Benny just pointed her in our direction." Tyrone watched Kevin's whole demeanor change as Denise approached. "Stay calm, Kev, she's not worth it. Just try to ignore her."

"Easy for you to say, Ty. She ain't been stalking you."

"Kevin!" Denise's voice was dripping with attitude.

"Denise, well isn't this is a coincidence?" Kevin said sarcastically. "What are you doing here?"

"I've been looking for you all night." Denise replied sharply. "Now I can talk some sense into you."

"I don't have anything to say to you, Denise. Especially after what you did to my car."

"That's nothing compared to what I'm gonna do if you don't come outside and talk to me," she demanded.

"What the hell do you want from me Denise?" Kevin slammed his hand on the table.

"I want you to call off this stupid wedding." She placed her hands on her hips.

"How'd you know about the wedding?" Kevin turned his head to glare at her suspiciously.

"Haven't you figured it out yet? I know everything about you *and* your friends." She looked at Antoine and Tyrone. "Hey, Tyrone, does Walter Black know about your little crack problem?"

"Yeah, he knows I'm in recovery," Tyrone smirked, shaking his head at her threat. "Speaking of recovery, looks like you been hittin' the old pipe yourself, huh?"

Antoine busted out laughing.

"You think that's funny, don't you, Antoine?" She pointed a finger at him. "You never did like me, did you?"

"No Denise, I can't say I ever did," Antoine took another sip of his brandy.

"Yeah, well you better talk some sense into your friend, or I might just call the chancellor and let him know you're having a baby outta wedlock," she threatened. "He might not think that's such a good example for the kids." Antoine's face was expressionless.

"I don't like people threatening me, Denise," he said through clenched jaws.

"So talk to your friend, or I just might have to follow through on my threats." Denise smiled at him wickedly, then turned to Kevin.

"Ya know, you are really crazy, Denise," Kevin stared into his empty glass.

"Am I crazy, Kevin? If I am, you made me this way. You and that bitch Alicia."

Kevin still had not looked up from his glass, and it angered her. She grabbed a beer bottle from a nearby table and threw it to the ground.

"Look at me, damn it!" She'd finally gotten his attention, and he turned to face her. "I want you to call off this crazy wedding," she pleaded.

"Kevin why don't you go outside and talk to her? She's creating a little scene here," Antoine advised. The entire bar was focused on them now, and Benny was headed their way. "We'll be here if you need us."

Kevin stood up and headed for the door. The second he was out the door he spun around with clenched fists. "Always gotta have it your way, don't you Denise?"

"I was perfectly willing to honor and obey. Just like that bitch you're gonna marry tomorrow."

"Yeah, well if she's a bitch, what the hell does that make you?"

"The woman who's gonna make your life miserable if you don't call off this wedding."

"Look, what do you want from me?"

"I want you to call off this ridiculous wedding. You don't wanna marry her. You're still in love with me," Denise stated with certainty.

"You are so wrong. I don't love you. I pity you."

"Pity! Why the hell do you pity me?"

"Look at you. Tyrone was right! You look like a crackhead." Kevin spun her around so she could see her reflection in the window of the bar. "You used to be so beautiful, Denise. What happened to you?"

Denise couldn't bear to look at her own reflection. "You did this to me!" She turned and began to pound her fists against his chest.

Kevin grabbed her by both wrists. "Denise, you need to let go. I don't love you. Where'd you get that idea anyway? I never once told you I loved you. I'm gonna marry Alicia tomorrow because it's her I love. And no one is gonna stop me." He let go of her wrists and she got right up in his face.

"You think so? Well if you don't call off this wedding, you're going to jail for rape tomorrow." Denise reached into her pocket. "See this? This is the key to your apartment. You probably didn't even know I had a copy made, did you? I've planted enough evidence in your apartment to have you put away for ten years."

"It won't work, Denise," Kevin said confidently.

"Why won't it? I'm a lawyer, and I think I know enough to get an innocent man put away."

"You really are pathetic, Denise." Kevin laughed. "Turn around and look."

Denise turned to see several people from the bar standing around the entrance to Benny's. They had come out hoping to witness a good fight, and in her frenzy Denise hadn't even noticed their presence. Now they had all been witness to her threats of what she thought was a perfect set-up. She had made Kevin's apartment look like a struggle had taken place, left her fingerprints all over, and even dropped a pair of torn panties near the bed. A public confrontation was to be the final part of her plan. She would confront him at the bar and then later tell the police that the fight had continued at his apartment, where he raped her. But she hadn't planned to lose her composure and threaten him in front of these people. She sobbed hysterically when she realized how completely her plan had failed.

"You can't get away, Kevin! I will get what I want!" she insisted through her tears.

"No, Denise. For once in your life, you can't have everything you want," Kevin told her as Antoine and Tyrone came to his side. "I'm sure you have enough of a legal mind left to know that I'm the one with the evidence now. If you ever come near me *or* Alicia again, I'd say I have enough to get your privileged ass locked up, wouldn't you?" Kevin and his friends headed back to the bar without another word.

Benny approached Denise on the sidewalk and told her as gently as possible that she would have to leave the premises. She never stopped sobbing as he helped her to her car.

"You all right miss?" Benny asked with concern.

"Do I look like I'm all right," Denise wiped her face and her mascara ran across her face.

"No you look like you could use somebody to talk to." Benny handed her his handkerchief.

"Well, where the hell am I going to find someone to talk to at this time of night?"

"I'm available." He said pointing to himself.

"Really?" she was surprised.

"Yeah, there's a twenty-four-hour diner down the street. We can get some coffee. That is, if you'd like to."

Denise stopped her sobbing and looked up at Benny. He was old enough to be her father, but his smooth, dark skin reminded her of the man that one psychiatrist had said caused her attraction to black men. She wondered if Benny had the same kind, gentle heart that her childhood chauffeur had.

"We can get some coffee and talk," she told him almost in a whisper.

"Okay, that's sounds good. Just let me tell the other bartender to lock up for me." Benny was back in a flash, and he climbed into the passenger seat of Denise's car. Glancing at the young blonde in the seat beside him he thought, *This just might be my lucky day.*

Inside Benny's, Kevin, Antoine, and Tyrone sat down with a few more drinks. None of them mentioned Denise. It was as if the whole incident outside had never happened. Each of them was more interested in sharing this time with his friends on the night before Kevin's marriage. As they reminisced, the men recognized their good fortune. Each was thankful for the bond they had forged and the support each had given and received. They knew theirs was a friendship with great value, one that each of them planned to hold onto like a precious treasure for the rest of their lives.

First Baptist Church of Jamaica was standing room only as over three hundred of Kevin's and Alicia's friends and relatives crowded into the church to watch them exchange their vows. Tyrone and Antoine stood next to Kevin, dressed in traditional black tuxedos. He had asked both of his friends to be his best men. Alicia had six women, including her own sister and both of Kevin's, assisting as her bridesmaids. Their sophisticated, burgundy-colored dresses complemented her straight, fitted gown, made from the finest silk. Michael carried the rings down the aisle, dressed in a miniature version of the tuxedo that Kevin wore. Simple white bows and a single lily decorated the entrance to each pew, as a symbol of the peace the couple had found with each other. And Mama sat in the front pew, her eyes glistening with tears of joy.

Minister Thompson delivered a few opening remarks about the spiritual gift of love that the two were privileged to have found together. This was greeted with a chorus of "amen" from various members of the congregation. Then the minister began the traditional ceremony that would end in the exchange of vows and their first kiss as man and wife.

Kevin and Alicia stood nervously before the minister, holding hands. They were both so happy to be where they were and eager to start their life together. The minister addressed the congregation with that phrase that has been heard at countless weddings before.

"If anyone here knows any reason why these two should not be joined together in holy matrimony, speak now, or forever hold your peace."

There was the customary silence after the minister's request, during which Kevin actually had a vision of Denise busting through the church doors to state her objections. He squeezed Alicia's hand tightly during the moment of silence as the minister waited for anyone to speak. Kevin breathed a sigh of relief when the minister continued the ceremony uninterrupted. The rest of the service was picture perfect.

The minister offered up thanks and praise for the joyful union of these two young souls and then pronounced them man and wife. Joyful applause filled the church when Kevin and Alicia exchanged their first wedded kiss. Michael rushed between them, and they swooped him up in their arms.

The guests followed behind Kevin and Alicia as they walked back down the aisle. They burst out of the church doors into the warm September sunshine, prepared for whatever their future held.

Epilogue

Maurice sat in the comfortable leather recliner in the office of Doctor Jerome Stanley. He had been visiting the psychiatrist's office for the past ten months, and Doctor Stanley was amazed at the speedy progress this patient had made. When he left the prison after his visit with Diane, Maurice had finally made the honest choice to change his life. He had hidden nothing of his past and his behavior from the doctor, and didn't even balk when the doctor suggested he go for an AIDS test.

As terrifying as the prospect was, Maurice had the test done. He thought for sure that as some sort of poetic justice for all of the women he had abused, God would strike him down with the horrible disease. When his results came back negative, he felt he had been given a second chance and vowed to learn from his mistakes.

When Sylvia contacted him about their pending divorce, he signed the papers without any battle. He was finally giving her back the life that he had taken away so many years before. In return, she was actually very fair in the financial settlement, leaving him with the money he had earned over the years and only keeping her family inheritance. Maurice had even been able to salvage his relationship with his daughter, Jasmine, who now lived in the city.

As they wrapped up another session, Dr. Stanley complimented Maurice on his accomplishments over the course of their work together.

"You know, Maurice, I have to admit, when you first came in to see me you were a real son of a bitch. I had some serious doubts about whether or not I could help you."

"I know, Doctor Stanley. Believe me, I know. But I can't tell you how much better I feel. Things are really starting to stabilize for me. I've even started going to church regularly."

"That's encouraging news. The next time you come in, I'd like to hear more about this wonderful woman you've been seeing."

"She really is special. And I know I'm getting better. In the six months I've been with her I haven't even thought about another woman!" Both men laughed, for they knew this was a true milestone for Maurice.

When Maurice made it back home, he put his key in the door, whistling. He was happy, genuinely happy. Life was starting to feel right for him. And he had a good woman by his side. He smiled, as he smelled the fabulous scent of spices wafting from underneath the door. His new friend was in his beach house in Sag Harbor preparing a special dinner for him. As part of his therapy, Maurice had agreed to abstain from sex until he and the doctor mutually agreed that he was ready. His girlfriend had amazingly understood, telling him she thought most people rushed into sex too soon, anyway. He felt as if this woman had been sent to him as some sort of redemption, and he was incredibly grateful. He knew he had a long road to recovery, but planned on having her by his side the whole way.

As he opened the door, he stuck his head in and called out softly to the woman he knew he was falling in love with.

"Shawna? I'm home."